Seeking Mansfield

First Edition
First Printing, 2017

Book design by Christopher Loke
Cover design by Christopher Loke
Cover images by Christian Gertenbach/Unsplash; Alexandria/Pixabay

Flux, an imprint of North Star Editions, Inc.

Library of Congress Cataloging-in-Publication Data (Pending)

978-1-63583-002-6

Flux
North Star Editions, Inc.
2297 Waters Drive
Mendota Heights, MN 55120
www.fluxnow.com

Printed in the United States of America

For Mom

Seeking Mansfield

KATE WATSON

flux ®

Mendota Heights, Minnesota

CHAPTER ONE

~𝓕~

Finley Price was a fool.

She stared at her computer screen with a dry mouth, absent-mindedly rubbing one of the small, circular scars branded into her right shoulder. The words "Mansfield Theater Youth Application" mocked her in bold font, as if they knew she didn't deserve the spot. As if they knew how ridiculous she was even to apply.

Yet here she was, her free hand hovering over the mouse. Like a fool. Surely, it wouldn't hurt to just answer another question. It's not as if she had to submit the application.

So answer something, already. But a highlighter smudge on her computer desk caught her eye. She scrubbed it, trying to get the streak of orange out. Hmm. It was stubborn. She frowned, swiping her thumb across her tongue and trying again.

Success!

She leaned back in her chair and stretched. She started to yawn and her jaw cracked. She winced and sat upright.

How could you apply for this? she asked herself, hearing Nora's voice in her head. *Is this how you repay the Bertrams for taking you in? By neglecting everything you owe them to chase some childish little dream? Have you forgotten how they saved you?*

Finley massaged her jaw just below her ear. *No,* she thought. *No, I haven't forgotten.*

She was about to close her laptop when Oliver's signature knock at her door interrupted her. She exhaled and rolled her chair away from her desk. "Come in."

The door opened, and her godparents' son entered wearing a Pac-Man t-shirt, the stretch around each sleeve showcasing the fact that he'd recently started lifting weights. Oliver's light brown hair was messier than usual. She couldn't help but smile as he walked in.

"Hey, Fin. I just wanted to—wait, is that your Mansfield application?" He crossed the room, squinting at her screen. "You still haven't completed it?"

"It's not due till the end of May," she said as Oliver dropped to his knees beside her. He smelled like deodorant and . . . was that cologne? Whatever it was, it smelled nice. Manlier than he normally went for, but nice. "I still have weeks to get it in."

"You mean you have weeks to psych yourself out and convince yourself you don't deserve it." He nudged her with his shoulder. "Right?"

A grumble escaped her throat. She pushed off the desk so that she spun in the computer chair, her eyes catching on framed posters and antique movie cameras and the countless playbills lining her bookshelf. When she'd made a full circle, Oliver grabbed her armrest, stopping her. She frowned. "I still haven't asked your parents, and I don't know if your mom will be able to spare me, anyway. It's so time-consuming. I shouldn't think—"

"Of yourself, for a change? Of your future? Fin, my mom would be the first person to tell you to do it."

She shook her head. He couldn't understand what it was like to owe a debt like she owed to his parents. "She's been so sick lately, Ollie. She relies on me."

The muscles in Oliver's jaw tensed, a clear indicator of his annoyance. "Then she relies on you too much. And don't argue," he said before she could protest. He leaned down to type over her, his arm bumping her vintage film reel lampshade. "Here, let's just take this one blank question at a time. 'Your grade in the fall.' Really? S-e-n-i-o-r. One down. 'Ethnicity.' There's no button for half-Brazilian, half-Irish. So, should I type in Brazil-ish?"

She pushed his arm. "Ha-ha."

"Okay, 'The parts of professional theater you are most curious to learn about.' Ooh, this is tough. Why don't they have a 'nothing' option, or an 'I know more about all of this than you' option? I guess we'll have to settle on . . ."

He clicked on "directing," "production," and "play analysis and criticism."

"How do you know those are the ones I want?"

His eyebrows arched above his sky blue eyes. "Could it be because I've seen six-point-four million plays and movies with you in the last two years?"

"Maybe," she said, smiling. She was nine months younger than Oliver, so they'd always been friendly growing up. They'd only grown closer since she'd moved in with his family.

"Exactly. I know these things, Fin."

As Oliver kept going through the application, Finley pulled her legs up under her chin. She picked at the frayed hem of her too-long jeans and watched him. He was so casual, so self-assured.

"Finally, an answer you've completed already. 'Why do you think it's important for high school students to experience theater?'" She watched his face light up as he read her answer.

Her heart stopped. He was reading her answer.

"Stop!" she said, trying to grab the laptop from him.

He sprang to his feet, holding the laptop overhead. He stared straight up and continued reading, even as she jumped to grab it from him. "Stop, Fin. This is good stuff! 'Theater allows us to experience a lifetime worth of emotions from a life we have never actually lived. Through *Antigone*, we feel a fierce loyalty to family that transcends reason and self-preservation. Through *Camelot,* we suffer the heartache of a star-crossed love we have never—' Hey, I was reading that!"

Finley climbed onto her swivel chair and grabbed the laptop from him, snapping it closed. "You can't just read my essays, you turd. They're private!"

Oliver grinned and helped her down from the chair before dropping onto her bed. "They're good, Fin. Really good. You're a lock."

She flushed. "I'm not, either. It's the most competitive program in Chicago." Her wavy black hair cascaded in front of her face as she sat cross-legged on the chair. "But it would be amazing. The chance to put on a production with some of the best actors in the business? To be mentored by Tony Award-winning directors?" She sighed.

"Are you going to mention your dad?" he asked. She shook her head. "Don't you think they'll figure it out, Finley *Price*? If the name isn't enough, try to remember you're the chick version of him."

She stared at a movie poster of her dad that hung above her bed. He looked so handsome and vibrant, with his deep, kind eyes. She'd give anything to be half the person he had been. "I am not," she said. "Besides, he was going by Peres when he performed there. I doubt they'll make the connection."

"Pedeez." He copied her pronunciation. "It sucks that your dad had to change his last name for Hollywood."

Her smile faded. "If all he'd lost to Hollywood was his name, he'd have gotten off easy."

Oliver's face fell. He leaned forward, his elbows on his knees, and grabbed her hand. "I'm sorry. I didn't mean to—"

She shook her head and tried to keep her hands from trembling. "It's okay. Besides, I don't know who pressured him to change his name more, Hollywood or my mom. She liked exotic, not ethnic." She let go of Oliver's hand and adjusted the sleeve on her right arm. She hated talking about her mom. Hated thinking about the person she'd become. Hated remembering what she'd done . . .

Finley shivered. She looked down at Oliver's clasped hands. He'd been picking at his cuticles again.

"You know," she said, "if you can't leave your hangnails alone, you're never going to achieve your dream of becoming a hand model."

His eyes popped and he covered his mouth with both hands in horror. "No!"

She laughed, then squinted. "Hold still. You have an eyelash right under your eye. Right here." She gestured to her own face as if it were a mirror.

He wiped at his face. "Did I get it?" She shook her head. He wiped again. "Now?" He picked at his cheek.

She giggled. "Are you even trying? I think you pushed it *into* your eye."

"Get it."

"I'm not going to get it."

"Fin, come on, you have to get it before it scratches my cornea and I go blind."

"Blind? Be serious."

He started to stand. "Okay, if you really want my impending sightlessness on your hands—"

She pulled his arm and he sat back down on the bed. "Okay, okay. Just stay still." She breathed in slowly and drew closer to his face. He widened his eyes, but instead of looking up, he looked right at her. When she touched his face, she was surprised by how warm he was. "It's clinging to your bottom lashes. Don't blink. Okay . . . steady . . . got it."

She leaned back from him and held the eyelash in front of his mouth. Then she noticed his face. He looked . . . dazed.

"Ollie, are you okay?"

* * *

~O~

Oliver blinked.

"Ollie, are you okay?" Finley repeated.

His eyes flew down to the delicate finger in front of his face, an eyelash resting on it.

"Oh, yeah, I'm fine," he lied.

Her wrinkled brow smoothed. *Of course she believes you,* he thought. *She trusts you.*

"Okay, then make a wish."

He looked at the twenty-seven freckles dotting her naturally tan face, then stared into her big, dark eyes. He was about to blow on the eyelash when a knock sounded at the door. He leaned back, and Finley's hand fell. Before she could say anything, the door flew open and in waltzed his younger sister, Juliette, her boyfriend Raleigh lumbering behind her.

Juliette was a sophomore, yet in the last year she'd easily become one of the most popular girls in school. With how much time she spent making her hair the right shade of blonde and her face the right shade of tan, it was easy to forget how brilliant and calculating she was—calculating enough to spread a series of rumors over spring break that made Raleigh break up with his long-term girlfriend just after school started up again. As captain of the baseball team, Raleigh Rushworth already had plenty going for him. But his dad was also a senator, making Raleigh not only one of the richest kids in their already rich school, but also the most famous. So when Juliette sat next to him on the first day back from break in his one and only AP class (US Government), well, naturally, she got her man.

Too bad he was a mouth-breathing clown.

"Wow, cool room. Kind of freaky clean though, don't you

think?" Raleigh gaped as he glanced over the vintage Broadway and Hollywood posters to look at the more current ones, including the ones of Finley's dad. "Man, you have a serious thing for that Gabriel Price dude, don't you? My mom was obsessed with him, too. She made me watch a documentary about him after he died, you know? Um . . . what was it called?"

Juliette smirked. *"From Golden Globes to Deep Space Probes: The Gabriel Price Story."*

Oliver clenched his jaw, wanting to strangle his sister. Or better yet, get her grounded for life. Oliver's dad was protective of Finley, more protective than affectionate, really. He claimed it was because he and Mr. Price had been best friends almost from their first day at the University of Chicago. Boys from opposite parts of the world, brought together by the luck of the freshman roommate system. But Oliver knew that wasn't it, not completely. He was pretty sure it was guilt. Guilt for what a horrible wife and mother Mrs. Price turned out to be. After all, when Oliver's parents had started dating, they'd introduced Finley's parents to each other. But Mr. Price was supposed to fall for a different roommate: Aunt Nora, not Mrs. Price.

If Mr. Price and Aunt Nora had gotten together, Finley would be his cousin . . .

He shuddered. *There's a cold shower when I need one.*

Raleigh snapped his fingers, pulling Oliver from his thoughts. "That's the movie! How'd you know, Jules?"

Juliette shrugged. She was the only person who wanted to keep Finley's dad's identity a secret as much as Finley did. While Finley didn't want people treating her differently because of it, Juliette didn't want her being popular because of it.

Fortunately, Finley wasn't paying attention to Juliette. She cast Oliver a disbelieving glance, then gestured toward Raleigh. The guy was still talking.

"I mean, I haven't even heard of most of these. *Raising Arizona.*

Best in Show. Rear Window," Raleigh was saying. "Oh, that last one's Alfred Hitchcock, huh? That's cool."

Oliver watched Finley, her face an open book. He knew exactly what was going through her mind. She longed to give a sarcastic retort, but by the way her arm was crossed over her body, rubbing her right shoulder, he knew she felt too vulnerable. It probably didn't help that, at six-foot-five, Raleigh was nearly a foot and a half taller than she was.

"Do you, uh, like Alfred Hitchcock?" she asked.

Raleigh snorted. "I like his name. *Hitchcock.* That's awesome."

Oliver caught Finley's *"Did that just happen?"* look while Juliette told Raleigh to grow up.

"You must really love movies," Raleigh told Finley.

"It . . . it's complicated."

Raleigh didn't hear her. "Juliette, why can't you have posters of fat old guys like the Godfather in *your* room instead of guys like Harlan Crawford?"

Juliette rolled her eyes. "We aren't getting into this again, Raleigh. Besides, Harlan Crawford was in two of those Gabriel Price movies that Fin has on her wall."

"Yeah, as a little kid, not shirtless with, I don't know, melted butter on his abs."

Finley looked at Oliver and mouthed, *"Melted butter!"* Oliver stifled a laugh.

"Whatever, Raleigh," Juliette said. She turned to Oliver, who still couldn't hide his smirk. She narrowed her eyes and scratched her face with her middle finger. "Listen, dork, I just came up to get you because Aunt Nora's downstairs. She has some announcement for Dad about the firm or something. So come. You, too, Fin."

As Juliette and Raleigh left the room, Finley leaned into Oliver. "Do you think Raleigh knows that 'the Godfather' isn't Marlon Brando's actual name?"

Oliver laughed and stood. Knowing he shouldn't, he held out a hand to pull her up. His stomach flipped as she took it. "Of course not. But more important, do you think Marlon Brando used butter on his abs?" he asked.

"Skinny Brando or Fat Brando?"

He pretended to consider this. "Both."

"Of course," she said, laughing again as she started for the door. Then she stopped and turned to face him, her smile gone and her rich, dark chocolate eyes pleading. "Promise not to leave me alone with Nora?"

"I promise. But remember, she can't make you feel small if you don't let her."

"She can't if you're around," she said, squeezing his hand. She turned and exited the room.

Her words stopped him. Her spark had dimmed with Juliette and Raleigh's intrusion. His aunt's presence would surely extinguish what remained. He hated how fragile she was with them. She was so much stronger than she knew. He felt proud that he brought that side out in her. That he had earned her trust, not by protecting her, but by encouraging her, by challenging her. And he had almost risked all the trust he'd earned over the years with that stupid eyelash.

CHAPTER TWO

~𝓕~

Finley followed a bickering Raleigh and Juliette downstairs. She almost wished they'd go be blond and obnoxious somewhere else. But Nora was waiting, and Finley planned to use the couple as human shields until the woman was gone.

When they reached the second floor, Finley caught a whiff of the older woman's perfume. Her breath hitched. She wished she could feel pity for Nora, since her husband had passed away and Mrs. Bertram and her family were all Nora had left. They at least shared that isolation in common, considering Finley had only her brother Liam, and he was in college. But she remembered too many of Nora's snide, passive-aggressive remarks, too many cruel comparisons to her mother to feel anything but apprehension. She steeled herself as she followed Juliette and Raleigh into the expansive library.

Nora was sitting in a leather wingback chair, her lips pursed as she read something on her phone. In a gorgeous designer suit and tall heels meant to intimidate, she looked ready for court, as usual. She rose to greet them.

"Juliette—Raleigh, how nice to see you! How are your parents?" she asked, shaking his hand. Finley slipped behind them and crossed to a bookshelf across the room, praying Nora wouldn't notice her.

"Good," Raleigh said.

Juliette swatted Raleigh and bounced up to her aunt, who hugged her. "They're great, Aunt Nora. Senator Rushworth has been talking to me about my Model UN summit. He's already giving me pointers."

Nora smiled, making her look prettier and, well, nicer than usual. They continued their conversation, talking about how Juliette was enjoying her sophomore year, how Raleigh's baseball season was going, and his dad's work.

"Well, how exciting for you both," Nora said. "I've been meaning to talk to the senator for ages, but with how busy our schedules are, we haven't been able to connect. Raleigh, do give your parents my best, won't you?" Raleigh nodded, and he and Juliette sat on a dark leather couch.

Nora turned to Oliver, who had just walked in, and asked him about his volunteering. Finley rubbed her shoulder and watched their exchange. Nora smiled, asking questions, complimenting her nephew. It was rare, but at times like this, Finley could almost see why her dad had dated Nora in college before falling for her roommate, Finley's mom. And she could almost see the resemblance between Nora and her sister Mariah. The difference was that when Finley's godmother looked at her, she kept smiling.

"Well, I'm not surprised that you're doing so well in all your activities. Just be sure to keep your grades up," Nora was saying to Oliver. "I can hardly believe you'll start college in the fall."

Finley ran a finger down the spine of one of Uncle Thomas's beautiful first edition books when Nora's tone shifted.

Here it comes.

"And Finley," Nora said with a hint of sharpness. Finley turned to face Nora, catching Oliver's encouraging smile from just beyond the woman. "I understand you have a new computer. And I've never seen you wear that sweater. Aren't you fortunate to have such generous godparents?"

Finley looked at her feet, bare except for her Havaianas. The flip-flops, a gift from her brother, were the only new things she had on, and yet Nora made it sound as if she was draped in Chanel on the Bertrams' dime. Finley tucked her exposed feet beneath her wide-leg jeans, hand-me-downs from Juliette. Like the laptop. "Yes, Nora."

Just then, her godfather entered the room in a pinstripe suit that matched his salt-and-pepper hair. "Now, Nora, Finley knows how lucky she is. It was like pulling teeth just to convince her to accept Juliette's old laptop. This girl's too modest," he said, putting a hand on Finley's shoulder. She flinched, and Uncle Thomas dropped his hand.

She wanted to kick herself, especially with Nora flashing her a little sneer. *This Hallmark Moment brought to you by Post-Traumatic Stress Disorder.*

Uncle Thomas cleared his throat. "Anyway, Nora, what's the news?"

Nora spun on her Jimmy Choos to face him. "I just heard from Aaron's nephew clerking with the Illinois Supreme Court. They're going to hear your case."

"What?" Uncle Thomas's eyes popped. "Nora, you know what this means?"

She grinned. "You have a hell of a lot of work to do?"

"I have a hell of a lot of work to do!" He beamed, already striding from the library. "Let's go tell Mariah."

Over the fading rap of Nora's stilettos, Raleigh asked Juliette, "What was that about?"

"Some human rights case of Daddy's."

Oliver frowned. "Have some compassion, Jules. Juana deserves justice."

"Why? What happened?" Raleigh asked.

"She was a pregnant, undocumented immigrant stopped for rolling through a stop sign a couple of years ago," Oliver said. "She told the officer she was going into labor. Instead of believing her, he said she was resisting arrest, threw her in his squad car, and denied her access to a hospital. She ended up delivering in a holding cell, handcuffed to the bench, and the ambulance didn't make it until after she delivered." Oliver paused. "Fin, I don't remember the rest. Will you tell him?"

Finley turned from the bookshelf. "Me?"

Oliver leaned against a table. "Yeah, remind me what happened after she delivered."

She gave him a mutinous glare. He was always doing stuff like this, asking her questions he knew the answer to just to force her to talk. If he weren't her second favorite person in the world—after Liam, of course—she'd hate him for it. Instead, she just wanted to pinch him.

She cleared her throat and looked at Oliver, not Raleigh. "The, uh, cord was wrapped around the baby's neck and he wasn't getting enough oxygen. They were rushed to the hospital, and the doctors did all sorts of tests on the baby. It turned out that he had brain damage from the lack of oxygen." Finley's voice caught. She glanced at Raleigh.

He was on his phone, like Juliette next to him. "Yes!" Raleigh mumbled. "Take that, zombie."

Finley looked back at Oliver, who just shook his head.

Moments later, Uncle Thomas and Nora reentered the room. "Grab your things, kids. I'm taking you to Gino's to celebrate," Uncle Thomas said.

They all stood, but Nora gestured to Finley without looking at her. "Finley, I need to go back to the office to draft a memo about Thomas's case. Why don't you stay with Mariah in case she needs anything." It wasn't a question.

Finley nodded. Of all the things Nora could demand of her, at least she'd picked the one thing Finley wanted to do. "Of course, Nora."

"Come on, Aunt Nora," Oliver said. "Dad, Finley can come, right?"

"It's okay, Ollie. I don't mind," Finley said before Uncle Thomas was put on the spot. "In fact, I insist. I couldn't forgive myself if your mom needed something and I wasn't here to help."

"But Fin—"

"Oliver, it's settled," Uncle Thomas said. "Thank you for helping, Finley. We'll bring you back a pepperoni pizza with extra jalapeños. Now come on, kids, let's go."

The look Oliver gave her was a mix of anger and apology. As gratified as she was by his concern, though, she felt more comfortable staying. Aunt Mariah needed her, liked her, even. Sure, Uncle Thomas knew her favorite pizza and occasionally put his hand on her shoulder, but it was for the memory of her dad more than it was the reality of Finley. And Juliette—well, the girl hadn't murdered her in her sleep, at least.

Soon the celebration party had left, and Finley was downstairs in the kitchen making her godmother a sandwich. She could have heated something that the cook had left, but Finley needed Aunt Mariah to know how grateful she was for her. That she would do anything for her. Besides, with its gleaming stainless steel appliances and white cabinets, the kitchen felt out of place in the otherwise classic, elegant home. Finley knew the feeling.

"Sweetie," Aunt Mariah said, shuffling into the room in her dressing gown, "you know you don't need to make me a meal." She looked tired, even with her makeup and dark blonde hair done for a change.

Finley darted around the kitchen island to help her onto a stool, but her aunt waved her off. "Oh, Finley. I have fibromyalgia. I'm not a . . . oh, I don't know, a Fabergé egg."

Finley laughed, but she still eased her godmother down. "Great. Now I want scrambled eggs instead of a turkey sandwich," she teased. "Thanks a lot, Aunt Mariah."

"If it's made from Fabergé eggs, I do, too," Aunt Mariah said, laughing. Then she winced. "Sweetie, I know you've been waiting to see *The Snow Queen* with me, but this flare-up just won't die down. Why don't you and Ollie go see it without me, and when I'm feeling better, we'll go to something else?"

Aunt Mariah's chronic pain kept her from leaving the house for most outings, let alone for luxuries like plays or even pedicures. Yet, that pain hadn't stopped her from being by Finley's hospital bed two years ago. When Finley was laid up with a broken jaw and a side of trauma—courtesy of her mother—her godmother stayed by her for two days straight, holding her hand, watching TV with her and Liam, and texting her oldest son, Tate, to bring them chocolate shakes at all hours of the night. She drove Finley and Liam home from the hospital herself the day they moved in with the Bertrams. Finley had loved her ever since.

"No, I can wait," Finley said, slicing Havarti cheese. "If we miss it this year, we'll see it next year when Cadillac Theater puts it on again." She smiled at her aunt. She'd wait for a decade's worth of flare-ups to pass if it meant getting to see it with Aunt Mariah. "You just take it easy."

She put the finishing touches on her aunt's sandwich and slid it across the counter. "Thank you, dear." Aunt Mariah smiled before adjusting herself carefully. "Oh, and I meant to ask you a favor. Meghan Grant loaned me that book last month, and I simply can't make myself get interested in werewolves. Could you return it to her along with an excuse about, oh, how about you tell her that reading is giving me headaches?"

"And if she offers to give you the audiobook?"

"She wouldn't do that, would she? You know what? Better to tell her I thought it was interesting, and let her read between the lines. Do you mind?"

Finley chuckled. "Not at all, Aunt Mariah."

After finding the book in question, Finley walked into the grand foyer, where she pulled a jacket from the coat closet before opening the door and stepping out into the cool spring air.

She was down the Bertrams' stairs and up the Grants' in a matter of seconds. She rang the doorbell and waited outside of the neighbors' stately brownstone, standing on the edges of her sandaled feet. Ten seconds went by. Twenty. She tried the doorbell again, and this time, she heard voices.

"You have to stop doing everything he says. He's just using us, like he always does!" a girl's muffled voice said.

"This isn't like last time," a boy was saying. Their voices were getting closer. "It's not like he's asking me to date some vapid costar or get a bunch of speeding tickets. He's worried I'll get cut from the play."

"Like they're going to cut you from the play," the girl was saying, just as the door opened. "You're Harlan Crawford."

Harlan Crawford.

Harland Crawford—in all his dimpled glory—and his also-famous sister, Emma, were standing two feet from Finley.

She fell speechless.

"Can I help you?" Harlan asked, his light green eyes just as piercing as they were on Juliette's posters. "Do you work for my aunt, or something?"

Finley blinked.

"Excuse my little brother," the boy's beautiful, smiling sister said. Her curled chestnut hair was pulled back into a low, wide ponytail, but a single, neon pink braid framed her face. She was nearly the same height as Harlan, who was short for a boy, even with his tall, beachy brown hair. Of course, they were both taller than Finley. "Were you looking for Mrs. Grant? She and our uncle are at dinner, but can we leave them a message, or . . . ?"

"Um," Finley said. She looked down at the book clenched in her hands and realized she was still wearing that ridiculous apron. She wanted to slink back home and curl up beneath her bed.

Then Harlan huffed. "Look at her, Emma. She probably doesn't even speak English. *¿Tú hablas inglés?*" he asked, belaboring the words. Condescension oozed from his tone, snapping Finley from her daze.

"Yes, and Portuguese," she answered coolly. Then she looked at Emma. "I'm Finley Price. I live next door with the Bertrams. My aunt asked me to return this book to, well, to your aunt." She dropped it in Emma's hands. "Could you thank her for Mariah Bertram?"

Emma hissed at Harlan and stepped in front of him. "You have to forgive my baby brother. He left his manners in Hollywood and, well, I clearly got all the class in the family." She took the book, then reached out a long, thin hand with a silver knuckle ring on her index finger. "Emma Crawford. It's a pleasure to meet you."

Harlan edged his sister out of the way and leaned toward Finley in the doorway. His grin was unapologetic. Predatory. "Yes, it's a pleasure."

Finley backed up at his nearness. Something about his smile made her want to run, to shrink down and not be seen. And yet . . .

"So, it was Emma and . . . I'm sorry, I didn't get your name," she said with a mix of nerves and spite.

His eyebrows jumped, and a small leer played on his face. He looked her over. "What rock have you been living under?"

"Excuse me?"

"I'm Harlan Crawford."

Finley shook his hand. "Nice to meet you. Are you new to the area?"

An incredulous Harlan looked at Emma, then back at Finley. But still, he smiled. Slyly. "Yes. You see, I'm an actor . . ."

"Wait, weren't you in that talking dog movie?"

Harlan's expression turned dark, and Finley fought the urge to snort. Emma grabbed her brother's arm and started pulling him back from the door. "Thanks, Finley. We'll make sure our aunt gets the message. See you around."

Emma closed the door, leaving Finley laughing and trembling.

When she returned to the house, Aunt Mariah had finished her sandwich.

"Did Meghan ask how I liked the book?"

Finley wiped off the counter, her hand still shaking. "She wasn't home. Her niece and nephew are visiting, though."

"Oh, that's nice."

Harlan's grin flashed in Finley's mind. *Hardly.*

CHAPTER THREE

~*F*~

When the Bertrams heard that Harlan and Emma Crawford were staying next door, a fervor overtook the home. Yes, they were wealthy and brushed up against the upper crust of Chicago society. But Hollywood society was a different matter altogether, particularly as they'd known Finley's dad before he got famous and her mom before she'd become Ms. Illinois. The Crawfords represented all the glitz and glamour that her dad had tried to shield his family from; the Bertrams didn't know better than to be drawn in.

While Uncle Thomas and Aunt Mariah wanted to send over a welcome basket, Nora wanted to invite them all over for dinner, along with Senator and Mrs. Rushworth, of course. Oliver had taken to looking out the windows for a glimpse of either of the Crawfords, and Finley thought he'd even made an effort with his hair.

Juliette bought a new wardrobe, got a facial and manicure, and had her stylist "reimagine" her whole look. Which, Finley thought, was almost exactly like her old look, but with more makeup and a lot more bounce, in both her hair and her bra. And, in typical Juliette fashion, she'd found an in with the Crawfords before they'd even unpacked their bags. She told her family all about it when she joined them in the breakfast nook on Saturday morning.

"I ran into Harlan outside the other night," Juliette said, as if she'd really just bumped into him rather than stalking him like prey.

Finley had gotten home from work at the same time that Harlan's driver had pulled into their street that night, no doubt returning the boy from some sordid outing. Juliette had shoved past Finley without even a hello just as Harlan had stepped out of the car.

What a coincidence.

"Harley was so sweet," Juliette continued. "And so genuine, you know? Anyway, I invited them all to come to the street fair with us today. He said yes." She flipped her hair into Finley's face.

"You should have mentioned it before now, Jules," Oliver said, on Finley's other side.

"That would have been nice," his dad agreed, "but their company is welcome all the same. That was very thoughtful of you, Juliette."

Juliette smiled prettily. "Thank you, Daddy. I was just trying to act the way you and Mom have always taught me."

"Laying it on thicker than the butter on Brando's abs," Oliver murmured on Finley's other side.

She hid her smile behind her hair.

A few hours later, Finley waited on the sidewalk with Oliver and Raleigh while Juliette and her dad knocked on the Grants' door. Oliver shifted from side to side.

"What's going on with you?" Finley asked before gasping dramatically. "Why, Oliver Bertram, are you *starstruck?*"

"What? No," he said, though his fidgeting told a different story. "It's not like I've never met someone famous before."

"Who is that?" Raleigh asked.

Finley opened her eyes wide at Oliver.

He gestured to Raleigh. "Uh, your dad, for starters."

"Yeah," Finley said, hoping Raleigh believed them. "It's not like the Crawfords are a bigger deal than he is."

Raleigh puffed his chest out like a peacock. "You know, you're right."

The door to the Grants' home opened, and Mr. and Mrs. Grant came out with their niece and nephew, who were decked out in typical star camouflage—trendy hats, scarves, and big sunglasses. Before the door closed, two hulking bodyguards followed them out. So much for discretion.

The group came down the stairs, and Juliette made introductions. She placed her hand on Harlan's shoulder.

"Harley, Emma, this is my dad, Thomas Bertram, my brother, Oliver—"

Raleigh bumped Oliver and Finley out of the way, his arm extended. "I'm Juliette's boyfriend, Raleigh. Raleigh *Rushworth,*" he said meaningfully, shaking their hands with his meaty paw.

Emma and Harlan met each other's eyes. "Oh. Wow," Emma said, the corners of her mouth twitching. Oliver groaned quietly beside Finley.

"Yeah, wow. It's just . . . what an honor to meet you," Harlan said, looking up at the far bigger boy.

Raleigh gave him a kingly smile.

Juliette looked as if she wanted to shrink Raleigh to ant size and squash him underfoot. "Sorry," she told the Crawfords. "Raleigh's father is a senator—"

"Jules, they know. Duh," Raleigh said.

"Of course," Emma said, somehow sounding gracious and teasing at the same time. "Raleigh, it's good to meet you." Then she peeked past Raleigh right to Finley. "Hey, it's Finley, right? Good to see you again. And this is . . . Oliver, was it?"

Finley didn't have to nod; Oliver answered for her. "Yeah, um, good to meet you. I forgot you met Fin already."

The group started walking, and Emma stayed with Oliver and, by extension, Finley.

The beautiful girl's smile was effortless. "I'm not surprised. I'm not actually sure she knows who we are beyond our relation to our aunt and uncle."

Oliver's eyebrows practically reached the sky. He gave Fin a curious glance before turning back to Emma. "Um . . ."

"Unless . . . were you messing with my brother?" Emma asked, narrowing her eyes at Finley.

Finley sank into the ground. "Guilty."

To her surprise, Emma laughed. "Ooh, I think I'm going to like you, Finley." She looked at Oliver. "And you, too. If you're lucky."

Oliver tripped. Emma laughed again and pulled him along. With a small frown, Finley followed.

The air was filled with the savory smells of salt and meat as they neared the bustling fair. Booths lined the crowded streets, selling everything from imported cheeses and wines to hipster t-shirts featuring bacon mustaches. Finley had somehow been pushed into the middle of their large group, with Oliver and Emma to one side, and Harlan, Juliette, and Raleigh to her other. Uncle Thomas was just ahead with the Grants outside of a little tavern, where they were getting a couple of large charcuterie plates for everyone to share. The group stopped and waited for the adults.

"This is all so delightfully quaint," Emma said, gesturing grandly around them. A fellow festival-goer bumped into her arm.

Quaint? Finley held back a smirk. *It's an artisan food festival, not a quilt convention.*

"Yeah, it's pretty cool," Oliver said, snacking on a cheese plate, utterly oblivious to Emma's implication. "But you should see the annual art fair. It's amazing."

"Is that what you want to be when you grow up? An artist?" Emma put her hand on Oliver's arm.

"Not unless stick figure art is making a comeback," Ollie joked, his cheeks looking hot despite the cool afternoon.

"Will you join the family business, then, and go to law school one day? Put the system on trial?" She teased and smiled at him easily, like they were old friends.

"My brother Tate is following that path, like my dad did. Everyone figures I will, too."

"Why do I get the feeling that isn't what you want to do? What does your heart of hearts yearn for, Oliver Bertram?"

"I don't know. Isn't that what college is for? Figuring yourself out? Maybe I want to study philosophy or archaeology." He cleared his throat. "Or social work."

Emma's laugh tinkled. "Social work! I can see that now. You laboring in obscurity while your dad and older brother make headlines fighting evil and injustice. You couldn't be content with that." Her hazel eyes fixed on him, and suddenly her playful mood was gone. "Could you?"

"The world needs people who care about other people. I could be content with that." Oliver looked down at his plate, and Finley glanced away before he caught her eavesdropping.

On the other side of her, Juliette's eyes were glued to Harlan's, while Raleigh just smiled and towered over everyone.

"Is this a typical weekend for you?" Harlan was asking Juliette. "Your boyfriend accompanying you on cute little outings with your family?"

Instead of rolling her eyes, Juliette batted them. "And why do you want to know?"

"Didn't you know? I'm an observer of the human condition. I'm trying to understand how the life of a typical Chicago teenager differs from that of a Manhattan one."

How he managed to make such inane comments sound suggestive was beyond Finley. But not beyond Juliette, evidently. She arched an eyebrow at Harlan.

"If you want typical, I'm not your girl."

Before Harlan could respond, Raleigh grabbed Juliette's arm and pointed to a booth selling turkey legs. "Check it out—that turkey leg is as big as your head! Let's go get one, Jules!"

Juliette's face went hard. "Raleigh, why don't you go get it and come back? It's rude for me to leave our guests."

Raleigh frowned and looked at Finley. "Fine. Then do you want to come, Fin?"

The entire group turned to Raleigh. Fin caught Oliver trying hard not to laugh. He poked her side, and she had to push his hand off with her elbow while staring dumfounded at Raleigh.

Fortunately, Juliette spared her answering. "Did you seriously just ask another girl to go with you to get food?"

"Finley's nice to me. What's the big deal?"

Finley watched Harlan's gaze go from amused to calculating. "Yes, why would you mind your cousin and boyfriend getting a turkey leg together? Or is that code for something?"

Juliette spun on him, managing to look both beautiful and slightly terrifying. "First, she's not my cousin. Our dads were just roommates at U of C."

Just roommates, Finley thought. *Wow.*

"And second," Juliette continued, turning sultry, "what guy in his right mind would ever cheat on me?"

"No one, I'm sure," Harlan said.

"Good. Then we agree that you're coming with me," Raleigh said, pulling Juliette along just in time for the Grants and Uncle Thomas to return with plates of the most delectably fragrant meats.

The group muscled through the crowds to find an empty table on the patio of one of the restaurants taking part in the festival. A few moments later, Raleigh and Juliette joined them. Juliette was able to squeeze in beside Harlan, but at his size, there was no way Raleigh would fit. He stood over Juliette, smiling and eating his turkey leg.

"So, Harlan and Emma," Uncle Thomas said, "your aunt tells me you're performing in Harvey Weinstein's final production at the Vows Theater. What an honor."

Finley started. "You are?"

"Are you familiar with the Vows Theater?" Harlan asked.

"Of course!" Juliette smiled, a pretty, petty thing. "She works there, don't you, Fin?"

"Does she?" Harlan asked, looking at Juliette.

Uncle Thomas smiled. "She's been working there for nearly a year now. We're very proud of how hardworking Finley is."

Finley blushed, and her cheeks only got redder when Juliette opened her mouth again.

"Yes, Finley's the hardest working janitor in the city."

It was such a thoughtless, ignorant comment. Finley hated how much it stung. Juliette had said it so quietly that no one else had heard. No one but Harlan.

The boy snorted. Finley wished the ground would swallow her whole.

Unaware, Uncle Thomas prompted Harlan to continue.

Harlan leaned back. "Well, I've recently decided I'd like to take up theater, and Mr. Weinstein would like to convert Vows Theater into a nightclub. The timing is . . . kismet. Mr. Weinstein's arranged a star-studded cast to put on a two-week limited engagement leading up to the closing of the theater and the opening of the club. To give the theater closure, we'll perform the same play that Vows opened with seventy years ago."

"A Midsummer Night's Dream," Finley mumbled as Harlan said it out loud. He didn't hear her.

He rattled off a series of Hollywood A-listers who would costar with him. "I'm playing Lysander, Emma will play Helena, and a few people from Broadway you've never heard of are filling in the other roles."

Leave it to the guy on the cover of Teen Beat *to assume no one would know the names of Broadway stars,* Finley thought.

"Helena?" Oliver said to Emma. "Your brother's going to be given a spell to fall in love with you for half the play?" At Emma's look of surprise, he nudged Finley. "I have a really good theater teacher."

Emma smiled at Finley. She looked as if she was going to say something, but Harlan was still talking.

"Now, I know what you're thinking. Chicago's not exactly known for theater; why not stay in New York and just do Broadway, regardless of Mr. Weinstein? Well, as it turns out—and I promise, this surprised me more than anyone—I'm a sucker for family." Harlan gestured to his aunt and uncle, who laughed.

Finley wanted it to be a throwaway line; he was that big of a dink. But the way he looked at his aunt when he spoke . . . it was the first honest thing he'd said all day.

"There's also the matter of our parents' uber-messy divorce," Emma said, clouding only briefly. "You'll see it on TMZ soon, if you haven't already. This gave us a nice excuse to get out of their crosshairs."

Mrs. Grant smiled across the table. "But most important, you love your poor, childless aunt and uncle." Mrs. Grant looked at the rest of the table before looking back at her niece and nephew. "This was my last chance to spend time with them before Emma leaves for university in France in the fall and before Harlan shoots his next blockbuster." Her smile was sincere and loving in a way that made Finley's heart ache.

"Right," Harlan said, returning her smile. "There's always that."

"Well, we're glad to have you as neighbors. Mansfield Square has gotten a little too old for the kids' liking," Uncle Thomas said.

"I've wondered why our block is called 'Mansfield Square.' Was the original owner named Mansfield?" Mrs. Grant asked.

"No, the founder of Mansfield Theater lived here in the 1920s and ran rehearsals out of his home while the theater was being built. He was the only famous resident of our little row—until now, of course," he said, gesturing to Harlan and Emma. "And the name stuck."

Mr. Grant asked Uncle Thomas something else, but Finley had

stopped listening. She stared at the slices of meat and cubes of cheese still on her plate.

"Chicago *is* known for theater, you know," she muttered to Oliver. Unfortunately, it was Harlan who responded.

"Excuse me?" Harlan said. "Did you say something?"

The table seemed to go quiet. Finley gritted her teeth. "I was just saying that Chicago *is* known for theater."

Harlan looked around the table and then returned to her, a half-smile on his face. "Is it? Well, far be it from *me* to know. I just wish someone had told New York."

Everyone else laughed. Everyone except Oliver. He nodded almost imperceptibly, as if to say, *Go on.* She stared at her plate and opened her mouth. "Chicago is the birthplace of improv and slam poetry. David Mamet got his start in Chicago. *Spamalot* and *Grease* both premiered here, along with Tennessee Williams's last play. Five different Chicago theaters have won Tony Awards. Peter Boyle, John Belushi, Bill Murray, John Malkovich, Stephen Colbert, and Tina Fey, among others, all got their start in Chicago. Believe me, New York knows," she said, breathless. She hadn't dared inhale during her diatribe for fear she'd stop.

She *should* have stopped, because everyone was staring at her. Even Uncle Thomas's eyes were wide, making her wish she could disappear beneath her hair. Or the table.

Beside her, Harlan laughed. "I stand corrected. Forgive me, *Miss Price*," he said, with the barest trace of sarcasm. "I didn't realize I was speaking to an enthusiast."

"I think the word you're looking for is 'aficionado,'" Uncle Thomas chuckled. "It's nice that you kids already have so much in common. It's too bad Tate and Liam can't be here."

"Who's Liam?" Emma asked.

"Our godson, and Finley's older brother. He's Notre Dame's leading forward in soccer," Uncle Thomas said proudly.

Mrs. Grant asked Raleigh about his future plans, which Juliette answered for him, but Finley tuned it out. She felt so stupid, putting herself on the spot like that. She should have just swallowed her tongue. What had made her so reckless, so bold? Harlan's smirk, no doubt.

"Great job," Oliver whispered in her ear. Finley looked up to see him smiling at her. Over his shoulder, Emma was studying him. Then she smiled at Finley and leaned in, too.

"Totally. Way to put my brother in his place."

Finley shook her head. "That's not what I was trying to do. I didn't want him to feel bad, but—"

"He was being a bully and he deserved it. I'm glad I'm not the only one who notices," Emma said. Oliver smiled.

There was a lull in the conversation as Mr. Grant asked if anyone wanted seconds. When everyone declined, Raleigh cleared his throat loudly from above them.

"You know, in sixth grade, I played Rooster in *Annie*."

CHAPTER FOUR

~ℱ~

The sun was just direct enough and the wind just absent enough to make the Bertrams' roof-deck tolerable in the chill April air. Weather permitting, the deck was Finley and Oliver's favorite homework spot. Unfortunately, since the street fair last weekend, Emma Crawford had become a fixture in their lives, including during homework time.

Which was just super.

"When will you be finished?" Emma asked Oliver, her long legs slung over her chair. Finley couldn't understand how the girl, wearing high cutoff shorts and a tie-dyed tank top, wasn't freezing.

Oliver looked over his math paper. "I don't know, maybe twenty minutes?"

"You know, I'm really good at math. I could always fill in a few of these for you."

"Um, I don't think that—"

She laughed. "You're blushing! Isn't he blushing, Finley? I think he thinks I was serious." She raised a perfectly manicured eyebrow.

Finley frowned and tried to see Oliver's reaction from the corner of her eye. Emma was right. He was blushing.

Oliver's papers rustled. "Anyway, if I could only find the answer key . . ."

A paper fell to the deck. Finley scooped it up and held it out to him, adopting an English accent. "Oh, you mean *this* answer key?"

Oliver scrunched up his face. "Why do I know that line?"

"Not telling." A smile tugged up one corner of Finley's mouth.

"Do you want a hint, Ollie?" another voice said from behind them. Harlan's voice.

Finley's gaze shot to the door, where Harlan, Juliette, and Raleigh were standing. How long had they been there? Long enough, obviously.

"I'm sorry, Miss Price, was I interrupting something?" Harlan asked.

She turned back to her homework.

"Yeah, give me the hint," Oliver said. Finley could feel Oliver's eyes on her, but she didn't meet them. The last thing she wanted to do was encourage Harlan.

Harlan and the others walked toward the table. "Stop me when you have it. The movie's from 1987, based on a book. It's one of the most quoted movies of all time. The director helped popularize mockumentaries in the mid-eighties."

"Aw, look at that, Fin," Juliette said, bumping Harlan with her hip. "You're not the only movie-obsessed freak in the neighborhood anymore." How could the girl both insult and flirt in a single breath? She was wearing little more than Emma, though she already had goose bumps covering her arms. It was April. In Chicago. Did these girls hate themselves? "Fin's like that guy from that Tom Cruise movie . . . you know . . ."

"*Rain Man,*" Harlan said.

"Exactly."

"So what movie are you guys talking about?" Raleigh asked Oliver.

"*The Princess Bride,*" Oliver said. "I can't believe I missed it!"

"I love that movie!" Juliette said.

"Everyone does," Harlan said. "Though I don't like it quite as much as Christopher Guest's other work."

"Who?" Raleigh asked.

"The six-fingered man," Oliver said, glancing at Finley before looking at Harlan. "So Harlan, what's your favorite of his movies?" he asked. It was exactly what she wondered.

"Hmm. *Waiting for Guffman*, maybe. Or *Best in Show*."

Finley closed her eyes. Could this get any worse?

"Wait," Raleigh drawled. "Fin, isn't that one of the posters you have in your room? Fin's a huge movie buff."

And worse it was.

"Really?" Harlan asked. "That surprises me."

Finley leaned closer to her homework, praying for Harlan to get bored, for them to drop the subject, for Raleigh to shut off his stream of consciousness for once in his life before revealing anything more . . . like all the posters of the one person she didn't want Harlan thinking about . . .

It was too much to hope for. "Oh, yeah," Raleigh continued. "She even has a poster from that movie y—"

"Raleigh, don't you have a big tournament coming up this weekend?" Oliver interrupted.

Finley shot him a grateful glance through her hair. He returned it as her panic subsided. Meanwhile, Raleigh told them all about his upcoming game. And Harlan grabbed a chair and sat next to his sister. In her periphery, Finley could tell he was still looking at her. He was probably upset that she'd pretended not to know who he was.

At least he didn't know who she was.

Raleigh was pouting at Juliette, who was on her phone. "It's a big deal, Juliette. You have to come to my game."

"It's just the semifinals, Raleigh. It's not like it's the state championship."

"Juliette!"

"OMG, calm down. I was just teasing."

"That's not what you said at lunch."

"Get over it. I said I'll come."

Finley felt eyes on her and turned her head to Oliver's table. But they weren't Oliver's eyes, they were Emma's. The girl flashed her a quick half-smile that said, *I know, right?* Finley surprised herself by returning it.

"Maybe we could all come. I love baseball," Emma said.

"Right, Ems is a huge fan," her brother jumped in. "Huge. We'd love to come. Next Saturday night?"

Raleigh puffed up his chest, as if being a giant wasn't intimidating enough. "Yeah. Guess I'll see you there."

"Yeah," Harlan said. "And probably, you know, here for the next couple of hours."

Raleigh's face grew red. Juliette pulled a book from her bag. "Come on, Raleigh, let's finish studying while the sun is still out. Oh, and Fin, I forgot to tell you. Liam just talked to my dad. He's coming home after spring semester ends."

Finley sat up. Juliette couldn't have led with this? "He is? I haven't heard from that dork in days, and last he mentioned, he was going to Mexico after the semester to try out for a pro team. Ollie, can I use your phone to check email?"

Oliver handed it to her. Liam never texted her because her old flip phone was so unreliable, always dropping calls and missing texts. Instead, they emailed each other almost daily. She navigated to her email and found one unread message from Liam.

"Wait," Emma said, looking horrified. "You don't have a cell phone?"

"Not a smartphone," Finley said, not looking up from the screen.

"Emma," Juliette said, "it's not like she has a budding social life. She has a janitorial job and is in two clubs—drama and Oliver's humanitarian club—and that's only because Daddy mandates a minimum of two clubs for the sake of college applications."

Emma didn't answer Juliette. Instead, she turned to Oliver.

"Still, it's a safety risk, if not a social one. What if she gets lost and needs a map?"

"I don't know. I guess Finley's always with us, and . . ."

"Oliver, she can't even check her email without you. She needs a real phone. In fact . . ." Emma trailed off as she dug around in her bag. She pulled out an iPhone in a case that featured Chuck Norris riding a bear over a rainbow. She held it out to Finley. "Here, take it."

Finley finished reading the email and gave Oliver back his phone. "No, Emma, I really don't need one. I can call and text. I don't need anything fancy."

"This is hardly fancy. It's an old phone. All I use it for now is extra storage for pictures and apps. And you can't convince me that you're content without access to social media and email. How do you win arguments? Keep current with boys or extracurriculars?"

Oliver jumped up. "Crap, thanks for the reminder." He shoved his books in his bag and ran for the stairs. "See you guys later."

Emma frowned. "Where is he going?"

Juliette shrugged, but Emma wasn't looking at her. She was looking at Finley.

"He volunteers with a crisis line one night a week," Finley said.

Emma tapped a finger on her cheek. Finley took advantage of the distraction and pushed the phone back toward the girl. "It's really nice of you, but I can't take it. The only reason I haven't bought a better one is because I don't want to use my paycheck for something I don't need, and I'm saving up for college. But if I ever find the need, I'll buy one."

"Suit yourself. But I hope you'll just let me know rather than waste money on something I have a bunch more of in my room."

Finley nodded. "Thanks, Emma." She put her head back down and, mercifully, finished her homework in peace.

* * *

~O~

Oliver wiped his brow and cranked the volume on his iPod. As the music roared in his ears, he upped the speed on the treadmill. His AP Psychology notes were on the stand in front of him, but his eyes kept sliding off the page.

In two minutes, Finley would be coming in to run.

He shook his head. He shouldn't be thinking like this. He shouldn't be thinking about how good she looked in her little shorts and baggy *Doctor Who* t-shirt. He shouldn't be so glad that the shirt used to be his.

No, he should think about Emma. Gorgeous, smart, teasing Emma, who had a way of trailing a finger down his arm that set his whole body on fire.

Perfect.

The door to the exercise room opened. To his surprise, in walked his older brother, Tate. Oliver pulled his earbuds out.

"Hey, man, what are you doing home?" he asked, out of breath. "Freshman dorms don't have enough going on?"

"Dad asked me to come in to the office with him today so he can show me some paperwork on Juana's case. Thought I'd get in a run this morning before heading to his office."

Oliver's eyebrows flew skyward. He dropped the speed to a jog. "At 7:00 a.m. on a Saturday? You look like crap. Have you even been to bed yet, or were you out playing poker with Yates all night?"

"'A fool and his money are soon parted,' bro. And Yates is very, very foolish." Tate grinned, running a hand through his slick blond hair. "I still keep a pair of gym clothes in my car so it looks like I just returned from a run if Dad sees me coming home late. Early. Whatever. Worked in high school."

"Yeah, but not so well when there's a rainstorm." As if on a crack of thunder shook the house.

Tate winked. "Good thing I'm a lucky, lucky boy. Dad wasn't around to see me stroll in from last night, and I came out eight hundred bucks richer."

He sat on the weight bench just as the door opened, and Finley walked in. Her hair was pulled back in a high ponytail, wisps falling around her face. The *Doctor Who* shirt engulfed her, but not so much that Oliver couldn't check out her legs. He snapped his eyes up.

Tate caught his eye, looking impressed.

Oliver ignored him.

"Hi, Tate," Finley said with a yawn, getting on the treadmill beside Oliver.

"Well, hey there, Fin." Tate stood up. "You've grown since Christmas, haven't you? You must be five-foot-nothing by now."

Finley smiled indulgently. Tate—handsome, muscular, charming Tate—was one of the few people she felt comfortable with. He'd always teased and flattered her so outrageously that Fin had quickly learned not to take him seriously, which meant he didn't threaten her. Even so, Oliver was glad she didn't know what Tate was thinking. *You jagweed.*

"Five-foot and a half-inch, sucka," she said as she started running. "When do you and your dad and Nora leave for Springfield?"

"Next week. But Aunt Nora isn't coming. She's staying back to cover things at the firm."

Finley stumbled but resumed her pace. "Oh." She raised the incline. "Are you excited?"

"That Aunt Nora will be here torturing your cute little butt instead of badgering me about my potential? Yes." He laughed. "Only joking, Fin. Sure. It'll look great on my law school applications one day." Tate yawned and threw his long arms out in a lazy stretch. "All right, kids, good workout. I'll catch you later."

When Tate left, Oliver picked up his pace. "Speaking of applications, how's yours coming along?"

Finley's brow creased. "It's not."

"Fin, don't make me send it off for you."

"You wouldn't!"

"I should. If I don't see proof that you've sent it at least a week before it's due, I can't guarantee I won't submit it for you."

Her eyes flew to his, her ponytail bouncing. "Ollie, please. You can't."

Inexplicably, Oliver felt annoyed. No, not just annoyed. Upset. Why couldn't she see herself? See how brilliant and capable and beautiful she was. "You know, Emma's right about you. You need something that's all your own."

"Is this about some smartphone? You know I don't care."

"It's not just that. It's everything! You need your own interests and things. Hell, you need your own clothes."

"They're not all hand-me-downs. Don't try to pretend I didn't win this shirt fair and square." She smiled, panting.

"I'm still protesting that, but that's not the point." He huffed. "You deserve more than a secondhand life."

She narrowed her eyes. "Have you and Emma been talking or something?"

"Emma? No, why?"

"She was getting on me again about that yesterday."

"When did you and Emma see each other yesterday?"

"I saw her at Vows last night when I was cleaning the bathroom, of all places. She told me that it was ridiculous that I was cleaning toilets when I should be free to grow up. As if having a paying job is somehow beneath me. She was on me to join more clubs. Buy my own clothes. Get a phone."

Huh, he thought. He knew Finley didn't appreciate people's judgments about her job, but the girl was incapable of thinking of herself. He hadn't realized Emma was so perceptive, or—and he knew this was judgmental of him—that she could care about someone else when there was nothing in it for her. He liked being surprised. "I'm glad she did it. I'm glad you and Emma are friends."

"I doubt she considers me a friend."

He punched the STOP button. "Come on, Fin. Do you really think so little of yourself?"

She looked taken aback. "No, I just I think she's doing it for your benefit more than mine."

"My benefit? What do you mean?"

"Isn't it obvious? She likes you."

Oliver's face grew hotter. He dropped his head and leaned down into a deep stretch. "Emma Crawford does not like me."

"She's flirted with you every day for two weeks. She hangs out with you while you're doing homework, and believe me, I know how boring that is."

He shook his still ducked head and stretched a hamstring. "No way."

Finley paused, during which time she upped her pace. "So. You don't like her, then?"

"This whole conversation is moot. And your way of distracting me from the Mansfield application." He took a long drink from his water bottle. "Send it, Fin," he said, and crossed to the door.

He peeked back as he left the room. Finley was frowning. And she looked too good in his stupid shirt.

* * *

~F~

Later that afternoon, Finley was running down the stairs when she heard voices from the bottom of the staircase. She slowed when she heard her name.

". . . just grabbing Fin, Juliette, and Ollie. We're going to Raleigh's baseball game," Emma was saying.

"Unfortunately, Finley's already worked three nights this week, and my sister can't spare her again," Nora said. To Emma. Because Emma was here to hang out.

Finley's chest burned with humiliation. Why had Emma brought her into this? Couldn't the girl content herself with Oliver and Juliette? Steps padded from behind her, and Finley turned around to see Oliver coming down the stairs. *Just great.* She couldn't meet his eyes.

"Mrs. Bertram must have changed her mind from earlier." Emma's voice bounced up the stairwell. "She said she was feeling well today and wanted Finley to go." Oliver walked down a few more stairs and stopped on Finley's step, listening.

During the pause that followed, Finley felt Oliver's eyes on her.

Emma continued. "Well, hopefully I can find some other way to keep Raleigh from getting suspicious of my brother and Juliette. I thought Finley's presence would keep him from thinking the rest of us were on a double date to his game." A sigh echoed up to them. "I suppose it's inevitable that he'll feel threatened by my brother. No one around here needs Senator Rushworth for anything, do they?" Emma's laugh was pure, unaffected innocence, and Finley had a moment to appreciate just what talented actors the Crawfords were. Oliver looked impressed, too.

"I can stay with Mariah tonight, in which case Finley won't be needed after all," Nora said. "Enjoy the game."

Finley gaped. "Did that really just happen?"

Oliver grinned and resumed his descent. "I think it did."

They ran into Emma when they reached the last flight of stairs.

"I was just coming to find you. Are you guys ready?" Emma's ever-changing stripe was a deep red today, and it curled around her face as the rest of her hair cascaded in perfect, fat waves down to her shoulder blades. She looked like a punk rock Audrey Hepburn, with black cigarette pants stopping just above spiky platform ankle boots.

"That was awesome, Emma," Oliver said.

She put her hand on the rail. "Sorry?"

"We heard you with my aunt. That was really cool of you."

"Oh, it was nothing," she said, looking at Finley. "It's ridiculous for you not to come."

Finley didn't know what to say. Other than Oliver, no one had ever stood up for her like that. She found it hard to speak. Especially to Emma. "Well, thanks. For, you know, caring," she told the other girl. She paused, wishing she hadn't overheard anything. Wishing she wasn't now indebted to this beautiful, confident girl. Wishing Ollie didn't know. "I'll go get Juliette."

"I'll come with you," Emma said. "Ollie, do you want to get my brother and meet us outside in ten?"

Oliver agreed, and soon Finley found herself walking back upstairs with Emma. "Thanks again," she told her. "That was unexpected."

Emma looked at her sideways. "You're pretty down on yourself, aren't you?"

"No, I'm just . . ." How could she put this? "I never want to take for granted how good the Bertrams are to me."

"What do you mean?"

In that moment, she wished Emma was a bit more like Harlan: oblivious to anyone but herself. Finley rubbed her right shoulder. "My dad died a few years ago, and my mom . . . wasn't able to take care of Liam and me. Liam was already eighteen, so he'd have been okay on his own. But if it weren't for the Bertrams, I'd be in foster care right now."

Emma's eyes widened. "How did your dad die, if you don't mind me asking?"

Finley did mind, but it would be rude not to answer after the girl went out of her way to stand up for her. She swallowed. "Car accident. He was on his way to work when a drunk driver hit him. He died on impact."

"That's just wrong." They took several steps in silence and reached the third floor, where Juliette's room stood in between her brothers' rooms. "What did he do for a living?"

Fortunately, Finley was spared answering. Juliette opened her door as they approached. She was texting someone. "Two secs. I'm almost ready," she said without looking up. She was wearing new everything: boots, jeans, accessories. Juliette popped back through her room, which looked like an Abercrombie & Fitch had exploded in it, and disappeared into her bathroom in a cloud of perfume and hairspray. At least she'd thought to take down the posters of Harlan.

"So, your dad? What did he do for work?"

Finley grimaced and looked away. Emma really was nothing like her brother. "He was an actor."

Emma cocked her head. Then her eyes went wide. "Oh, Fin. Your dad was Gabriel Price, wasn't he? I can't believe I missed the connection. You look just like him. I mean, your eyes alone . . ."

"Please don't. And don't tell your brother, okay?"

"My brother? Why not?"

"I just don't want it to be an issue. Please?"

"Sure, of course. But you should know that my brother loved your dad. Like, worshipped him. He was a really great person."

Finley nodded. "I . . . I'm going to go downstairs, okay? See you in a bit."

She flew down the stairs and dropped onto a step near the bottom. She didn't break down, no matter how badly she wanted to. She just breathed. Breathed and missed him. Missed the way he'd never made her feel forgotten or overlooked. Missed how he'd video chat with her twice a day while filming on location. Missed how he always told her he was coming home a day later than he was so he could surprise her at school or with a tickle attack in the middle of the night after catching a red-eye home. Missed how he'd hold her for what felt like hours when she had a bad dream or a tough day. Missed never feeling like an intruder. Missed never feeling indebted to anyone for "saving her." Missed the sense of pure, unconditional belonging he always made her feel.

She just missed him.

Several minutes later, she heard the other girls heading down. With a sniff, she ran downstairs, grabbed her coat from the foyer closet, and stepped outside where Oliver and Harlan were talking. Dressed in identical black shirts and jeans, Harlan's bodyguards flanked him. Finley barely managed to keep her eyes from rolling.

"Hey, are the others behind you?" Oliver asked, studying her face.

"Yeah. They should be out in a minute."

"Well, you came just in time to settle a debate about *The Godfather: Part II*. Better than the original, or not?"

"Unh-unh. You're not going to trick me into getting into this with you. I'd rather debate *Home Alone* versus *Home Alone 2*."

Oliver and Harlan laughed.

The door opened, and Emma and Juliette walked out. When Juliette saw Harlan, she lit up and stowed her phone. She crossed directly to him, and they climbed into Harlan's black SUV, bodyguards in tow. The school was only a quarter mile away, but Emma looped an arm in Oliver's and another in Finley's and pulled them along with her into the vehicle.

When they reached the baseball field, the game was just getting started. Raleigh waved at Juliette from the pitcher's mound. They sat a few rows from the top of the bleachers, but even in disguise, Harlan and Emma got waylaid by fans and their families for autographs. Emma ducked away from him, but Harlan grinned and gave hugs and posed for cameras, his bodyguards always hovering nearby.

One of Juliette's classmates grabbed Harlan's phone and punched her number into it, and Juliette sprang up. She floated down the bleachers and joined Harlan. The girl, obviously not willing to commit Juliette-induced social suicide, scurried away. Through the first inning, Juliette was by Harlan's side with every autograph.

"Is it always like this?" Oliver asked Emma.

"You have no idea," Emma said. Then she made a pained face. "Sorry, Fin, of course you must know as well as anyone."

The ping of a ball turned their heads. The left fielder ran hard and slid, catching the pop fly. From the mound, Raleigh looked relieved.

Finley's words came out in a rush. "It's fine, Emma. Let's just act like nothing's different, okay? Because nothing is." She didn't care how desperate she sounded. Harlan and Juliette were slowly coming up the bleachers.

"Speaking of acting," Oliver said to Emma, "how are rehearsals going?"

She scrunched her face. "Exhausting. I'd forgotten just how many late nights are involved, and I've only been rehearsing for a couple of weeks. Nothing like being a last-minute publicity replacement."

"When's opening night?"

"Three weeks."

"How awkward is it playing your brother's love interest?" Oliver asked.

"Not bad, considering Helena loves Demetrius, not Lysander. It's actually pretty funny. Honestly, the actor playing Demetrius is making it more awkward than acting with my brother could ever be."

"Why?" Finley asked.

"He gives me the creeps. He takes the scenes too far and doesn't exactly cut when the director says cut."

"That's not right," Oliver said, frowning. "You should say something to the director."

Emma just shrugged. "It's only a few more weeks. I'd rather not make a fuss. But . . ." she peered at Oliver, then looked away. Artfully. "No, never mind."

"What?" he asked. She shook her head. "Come on," he urged. "What is it?"

She paused. "I was just thinking how nice it would be to rehearse with someone who wasn't one more squeeze away from a restraining order. But you're so busy—"

Well done, Finley thought. *Just the right desperation in the eyes, the right hesitation in the voice.*

Oliver blinked. "You want me to help you rehearse?"

"I know, it's silly. I just don't have any friends here, and—"

Yeah, because who would want to be friends with the famous Emma Crawford?

"You'd be better off rehearsing with Fin," Oliver said, pulling Finley from her snarky thoughts.

"What?" Finley stammered. "No, I don't think she would." *Because she doesn't need either of us.*

Emma shook her head. "Forget I asked. I didn't want to make this into a big thing." But Finley caught her flash of angst—the perfect touch to contradict her words and soften Oliver's heart.

Oliver exchanged glances with Finley, and her heart softened, too. "Maybe we could both help," he said. "Fin knows more about acting than anyone."

Emma bit her lip. "You guys would really help me?"

Oliver smiled while Finley internalized a sigh. "Yeah. We'll help," he said.

Like you planned all along, she thought, knowing she was being unfair to Emma. The girl had been nothing but nice to her, for heaven's sake. So why did she rub Finley the wrong way?

By the top of the sixth inning, Raleigh still had a no-hitter, and the game was interesting enough that even Juliette was watching. They were crushing the other team 9–0, meaning their perfect record was safe, yet the bleachers were still full. Everyone wanted to see if Raleigh could pull it off.

Harlan had gone to grab them all snacks at the bottom of the fourth but had evidently been ambushed by fans. Friends and fans had rotated through to say hi to one or all of them, including a guy from Finley's drama club that Oliver teased her about afterward. But not even Emma—poor, famous, friendless Emma—had more visitors than Juliette.

"Raleigh is killing it!"

"You are so lucky. Raleigh Rushworth is hot!"

"He'll be drafted for sure!"

"I heard a scout from the Cubs is here. Is that true?"

"You must be some kind of good luck charm."

When she wasn't addressing Raleigh's fan club, Juliette was fielding their texts. The more compliments Raleigh got, the more Juliette seemed to remember that they were, in fact, dating. By the time Harlan returned with drinks and Red Vines, Juliette barely noticed him.

"Mm, thanks," was all she said when he handed her a Diet Coke, returning to her texts with a smile.

The crowd oohed in unison, and Juliette looked up as the umpire yelled, "Strike two." After two strikeouts, an error, and a walk, there were runners on first and second, but Raleigh still held his no-hitter. He threw again—a ball—and Finley found herself holding her breath. The batter had a full count. Raleigh wiped his sweaty face with his sleeve.

"I didn't take you for a baseball fan," Harlan said in a low voice to Juliette.

Finley's eyes flickered to the bench below. She watched Juliette incline her head slightly. "I'm a fan of my boyfriend."

Raleigh wound up, and the ball shot like a bullet. The batter made contact hard and the ball soared into deep right field. The crowd moaned and cursed and shouted at the ball to go foul.

"Get out!" Juliette cried, waving the air. "Out, out!"

The ball hooked to the right, high over first base. The right fielder darted past the foul line, gunning toward the fence. He leapt into the air, glove outstretched. The ball fell into his glove.

"Out!"

The crowd erupted. Another inning was over and Raleigh's no-hitter was intact.

Finley watched Harlan whisper into Juliette's ear, but she blew him off. She jumped up and ran over to the dugout fence, waving and squealing at a beaming Raleigh. Harlan scowled. He texted someone, then turned around to his sister.

"I'm leaving. I'll catch you at home," he told her. He gave Oliver a nod, ignored Finley, and started down the bleachers.

Emma jumped up. "Wait, Harley." She turned back to them. "Thanks for offering to help. Are you guys okay walking back?"

"Of course," Oliver said.

"Okay, I'll see you later." Emma smiled and started to follow her brother when she stopped. She turned back around and kissed Oliver's cheek. Then she ran down the bleachers without looking back.

Several of their classmates wolf-whistled and heckled Oliver. His cheeks were ablaze. "I don't know what that was about," he told Finley.

But Finley knew all too well. The whole night had been perfectly orchestrated to lead up to this moment. She just wished she knew why it bothered her.

CHAPTER FIVE

~O~

A week later, Oliver knocked on the glass door to the study, opening it when his father waved him in.

Papers, files, and pictures were strewn all over the spacious room. Wearing his University of Chicago Law sweater, his dad blinked at the wall clock and pushed away from his mahogany desk. "Ollie, what are you doing up still?"

Oliver sat on one of the leather seats opposite his dad, clutching papers in one hand. With the other, he gestured to his flannel pajama bottoms. "I'm on my way to bed, but I wanted to ask you something before you leave tomorrow. It's about Finley. She'd kill me for talking to you about this."

His dad's brow wrinkled. "I understand, son. What is it? Is she in some kind of trouble at school?" He shook his head. "She had three Bs on her last report card. I should have hired her a tutor, shouldn't I? How bad is it?"

Oliver waved his hand. Leave it to his dad to worry about school over anything else. "No, it's nothing like that. She's doing fine in school." His dad looked relieved. "Dad, I don't know how else to say this. She needs a life."

"A life? I think we've given her a very nice life here."

"That's not what I mean. She needs a life outside of our house. Half the keys on her old flip phone don't work. She's friendly with people at school, but do you know she's never hung out with any of them? She's only in clubs because you insisted. Otherwise, she's either picking up trash at Vows or helping Mom after school. She's never even been to a school dance, Dad."

His dad frowned. "Finley has always had a keen sense of her obligation to this family. What would you like me to do about it?"

Oliver lifted the papers he was holding and handed them to his father. Finley would hate it if she knew he was doing this behind her back, but he couldn't risk her fading into nothing. "This is her application for the Mansfield Theater Youth Program. It's due in a few weeks. She has to have her guardian's permission to apply, and I'm worried she's not going to ask you about it."

"So you want me to just sign it and send it in?"

"No, I want you to sign it in case she doesn't ask you on her own. If she does, just pretend this never happened. But if she doesn't, I'm planning to send it in for her."

"You really think it's appropriate to go behind her back like this?"

Oliver frowned. Of course it wasn't appropriate. But what else was he supposed to do? He couldn't just let her miss out on the chance of a lifetime. "She'll get over it. But she'll need to know that you and Mom support her. Otherwise, she'll just decline it."

His dad rubbed his eyes. "I don't like this for a lot of reasons, Oliver, one of them being that I don't know if we should expose Finley to that life."

"She's already been exposed, Dad. A thousand times over. This is what she wants to do."

"If she wants to do it badly enough, she'll come to me herself. Besides, encouraging that life means encouraging that lifestyle. I'm familiar with the Mansfield program. The youth council puts on productions with real actors. I'm not sure it's the right thing, given her family history."

Oliver jumped to his feet. "Fine. You know what? Be like Aunt

Nora. Just keep crushing Finley's spirit in the hope that she'll be nothing like her worthless mother, and let's see how that works out."

"Sit down," his dad snapped. "Don't you dare take that tone with me. No one is more invested in Finley's happiness than I am." He took a deep breath, and the red slowly drained from his face. "If you think this will contribute to that happiness, then I'll support her." He grabbed the papers and signed them, then put them in a desk drawer. "But don't send them in; you're better than that, Oliver. You need to give her every opportunity to ask me herself. I know you love her, but you can't control her. That's not fair to her."

Oliver hated how true his dad's words *should* ring. He couldn't meet his eyes. "You're right, Dad. Thanks."

"Is there anything else?"

He spoke quickly. "I think you should hire Mom a full-time nurse. Mom has always resisted the idea of a nurse because she thought it would keep her from fighting. But it isn't working. She's not getting any better, and Finley thinks she owes it to Mom to pick up the slack. We both know Aunt Nora agrees, which only makes it worse for Fin. If Mom has a nurse, though, it could make Aunt Nora feel better about Finley's other pursuits."

He was surprised to hear his dad snort. "Son, if I could figure out a way to make Nora feel good about anything, I'd have done it years ago. I think you're right about the nurse, though. This flare-up has lasted too long for your mom to be so stubborn," he said with a fond, if concerned, smile. "I'll talk to your mom and call someone first thing tomorrow."

Oliver smiled and looked at the documents surrounding his dad. "How's prep going?"

"As well as it can. It's nice having Tate around. And just think, when you graduate law school in a handful of years, the Bertrams will take over the firm." His dad's face broke into a tired grin. "Nora won't know what hit her."

A lump formed in Oliver's throat. He half-smiled. "Yeah, well, uh, good luck with prep, Dad. And thanks for the help with Finley."

His dad was already rolling his chair back to his desk. "See you in the morning, son. Get some rest."

CHAPTER SIX

~*F*~

In the early morning, rough hands and the stench of alcohol shook Finley awake. She gasped. Her heart hammered, and she threw herself back against the headboard. She curled herself into a tight ball, trying to protect her head and face. This couldn't be happening. What had she done this time? The hands clutched her shoulders. She wanted to cry, to scream out, but her throat closed before she could speak, before she could beg her mom not to—

"Fin, take it easy. It's just me," a voice said. A male voice. "Fin, come on. It's Tate." A hand touched her shoulder more gently. She risked a glance under her arm.

It really was Tate.

Just Tate.

She dropped her arms and legs, trembling from the sudden spike of fear. She tried to shake off the panic electrifying her nerves, but she couldn't. Worse still, she couldn't keep tears from filling her eyes.

"Man, I thought you were past that crap with your mom," Tate said, his hand still on her shoulder and his words slurring.

She didn't answer him. She pulled her shirt over her nose to keep from smelling him as tears spilled down her cheeks. Tate fell to the other end of the bed, his face in the covers. He was wearing his jeans and sport coat from last night.

"Wh-what's going on? Are you okay?" She glanced at the clock. Almost 5:00 a.m. What time had she gotten home from work? It felt like her head had just hit the pillow. "I thought you guys weren't leaving till seven. Is Uncle Thomas—"

Tate grabbed his head and moaned. "Stop with the questions, already. I need your help."

Her eyes felt sandy and her head light, but she nodded, suppressing a shiver. Being so close to that vile stench was almost more than she could handle. "What is it?"

Tate propped himself up on his elbows. His eyes were bloodshot, his face was peaked, and he looked moments away from passing out. "Pack."

Two hours later, Finley was just jumping out of the shower, scrambling to throw on some clothes. Packing for Tate had been harder than expected, considering half of his belongings were still in his car. But she'd finally put everything together and gotten Tate sober enough and showered enough that his dad wouldn't suspect anything but a headache. But now she was about to miss saying good-bye to them if she couldn't find her . . . jeans! She slid into them, left her hair wet, and darted from her room and down the stairs.

The family, including Nora, were all waiting in the foyer when Finley jumped the last few stairs. "How nice of you to join us," Nora muttered. "I hope your beauty rest was worth almost missing this."

Finley's brow creased and a knot formed in her stomach. If Nora had any idea what she'd been doing all morning, would she be any nicer? Probably not. She'd say Finley owed it to the Bertrams to help even more.

Forget her, she thought, trying to convince herself.

Uncle Thomas and Tate were walking down the line of family, hugging them and imparting advice. They wouldn't argue their case in front of the Illinois Supreme Court for a few weeks, but with preparation, interviews with media outlets, and meetings with lobbyists, they planned to travel between Springfield and DC for the better part of May. Finley found herself sadder than she'd expected as she snuck in between Juliette and Oliver. Juliette, on the other hand, looked far too excited for someone who wouldn't see her dad or brother for nearly a month.

"I'm so proud of you, Daddy. You, too, Tate. It's so admirable of you to fight for that poor woman—"

"What was her name, again?" Oliver asked his sister.

Juliette ignored him. "It makes me proud to be able to go to school and tell everyone just what my dad is doing."

Uncle Thomas smiled and put a hand on his daughter's cheek. "Thank you, sweetie." He leaned down to hug her. "Now, I want you to mind your mother and older brother while I'm gone. And with all those AP classes, you need to keep up with your studies." Juliette nodded enthusiastically. "Oh, and I don't want you leaving this house for a party or a dance or anything without Finley by your side."

Wait, what?

Juliette's eyes became saucers. Still, Finley's eclipsed them.

"What?" Juliette demanded. "Daddy! We . . . we aren't even in the same circles! She's not in my grade or any of my clubs at school, and we don't—"

"I don't want to hear it, Juliette."

He turned to Finley. Through her shock, she could barely hear his words. Why was he doing this? Didn't he realize that being stuck to Juliette for the next month was the last thing either of them could want? Had she upset him somehow? "Finley, I don't expect you to join all of Juliette's clubs, of course. I just want you to feel free to be the intelligent, beautiful sixteen-year-old I know and love. Now give me a hug."

He slowly put his arms around her, giving her time to prepare, she knew. After a pause, Finley hugged him back. She couldn't remember him ever hugging her before. The sensation was less unpleasant than she'd feared. Nice. Maybe even a bit wonderful. "Live a little, Finley," he whispered. "Your aunt will be just fine."

When they parted, Finley's eyes were wet and her nose was tingling. She gave him a small smile, which he returned. Then he moved down the line to talk to Nora about firm business.

Tate looked meaningfully at Nora. "Good luck with that," he told Finley before giving her a quick kiss on the cheek. Her eyes followed him past Nora, who was shaking her head at her.

* * *

Later that day, Finley ran into the kitchen after school, with Oliver behind her. She dropped her bag on the island and grabbed a Mountain Dew and a granola bar.

"Fin, come on. We have to get over there," Oliver said.

"I know. I'm sorry. I'm just feeling so faint. I didn't have a chance to eat lunch because the players were putting up signs across campus, and I forgot to eat breakfast—"

Oliver set down his bag and stepped in front of her. "Eat." He opened a granola bar and shoved one end in her mouth. "And I know you didn't forget breakfast. Why on earth did you help Tate pack? He had all week to do it, and you worked last night! You probably got, what, four hours of asleep?"

Her mouth full, Finley shrugged. "He needed me. You know I don't mind helping."

Oliver grabbed her another granola bar and pushed her toward the front entrance. "Not when it's Tate," he said, not quite under his breath.

She snorted and let him push her. "Or when it's Emma, obviously."

His voice brightened. "That's true."

The walk to Old Town took less than fifteen minutes. She had taken this walk hundreds of times, but she never tired of it. She knew every crack in the sidewalk, every silver maple and green ash along the way. She slowed as they walked past St. Michael's Church, a beautiful, old brick building that had somehow survived the Great Chicago Fire of 1871. She admired it for as long as she could, until Oliver dragged her onward.

"Every time," he chuckled.

Soon, they reached Vows. She paused at the glass door of the three-story Baroque theater, while Oliver grabbed the door for her. Her heart fluttered with anticipation. She loved the first step into a theater. The lights, the fanfare, the smells. No matter how many times she stepped inside one, it always took her back to being a little kid and seeing plays with her dad. It's why she'd taken a job cleaning the place. Everything about the theater reminded her of him. He'd been famous on Broadway long before he became Hollywood's leading man and before a string of bad movies and worse investments made him an A-list footnote starring in a cable sci-fi series.

They entered the gold and maroon lobby, and Finley held her breath. A moment later, she heard a cough.

She covered her face with her arm. "I should have warned you about the paint fumes and the dust from all the drilling, huh?"

Oliver kept coughing. "You're trying to punish me for the crack about Tate, aren't you?"

She pushed him down the hall, feeling muscles on his back that she didn't remember. She kept her hands on him a little longer than necessary. "Whatever you have to tell yourself. Just keep walking, pal."

They crossed the ornate lobby, dodging ladders, tool belts, and men installing neon and strobe lights. Emma had told them rehearsals would be in the ballroom rather than the main theater, as a state-of-the-art sound system was being installed there. They wound around the lobby until they reached the ballroom. The heavy doors were propped open, and Emma was sitting cross-legged on the floor, her script on her lap, muttering to herself. Her head flew up when she saw them.

"You came!"

"Of course we came," Oliver said. Emma jumped to her feet and ran to them. She hugged Oliver and pulled him to the stage.

Finley bit her lip, hesitating. She already felt out of place. Emma set Oliver up on the stage, talking and flirting. *What am I even doing here?* Finley wondered. After a minute, Emma came bouncing down for her.

"Thank you so, so much," she said as she ushered Finley up beside Oliver. She positioned them with a critical eye, then stepped back.

"Okay, so I'm having a hard time envisioning this scene. My love interest, Demetrius, has just had a spell cast on him so he finally falls in love with me, Helena. He proclaims his love for me and I don't believe him. So I just want to get a feel for what sort of contact they would have. Is he fawning all over me, grabbing my hand? Anyway, I need you guys to help me block this." She handed them scripts. "Ollie, start here, waking up."

His eyebrows arched. "Like, get up from the floor?"

Her smile dripped sauciness. "Do you have a problem with me seeing you wake up, Mr. Bertram?"

His face went red and he dropped to the floor. Emma laughed. "So, Fin, will you play me? Helena? I want to see the placement, the movements, everything. I need to get this down before our actual rehearsal tonight."

Finley's heart dropped into her stomach. Then lower. "You can't be serious. You can't want me to act."

"Of course not. I just want you to help me block it. Sorry, theater term. I mean, I want you to help me see where I should stand, how far apart Demetrius and I should be, that kind of thing. You don't have to act, just read the words."

Finley's pulse trebled and her ears went hot. She knew what blocking was. And she also knew that blocking was the director's job.

There was something more at play here. There had to be. She looked down at Oliver, who simply smiled and waited. "I'd rather not—"

"Yes, please, Emma. Spare the girl the pain," Harlan's voice interrupted from the back of the ballroom. Finley's discomfort spiked. He was so presumptuous, so patronizing, with that little smirk.

That infuriating little smirk.

She stood straighter, holding Emma's gaze. "Just the one scene, then?"

"Yes, please!"

Harlan sat in a chair near the front of the room, sneering. Still on the stage floor, Oliver started the scene. "'O Helena, goddess, nymph, perfect, divine!'" he said, rubbing his eyes, then standing up as he continued the scene. With the scripts in one hand, he grabbed Finley's hand with his other. His eyes were glued to the script, but that didn't keep him from overacting. "'Thy lips, those kissing cherries, tempting grow! / That pure congealèd white, high Taurus' snow / Fann'd with the eastern wind, turns to a crow / When thou hold'st up thy hand.'" He dropped the scripts and brought her hand toward his mouth. "'O, let me kiss / This princess of pure white, this seal of bliss!'" His lips touched her hand.

Finley's ears felt as if they were going up in flames. Her hand tingled where he'd kissed it. Still, Harlan's smirk drove her onward. "'O spite! O hell! I see you all are bent / To set against me for your merriment. / If you were civil, and knew courtesy / You would not do me thus much injury.'"

The more she spoke, the more she lost herself in the words. She knew a pain more intense than Helena could ever imagine, and she channeled it now. A longing to be loved, to be seen, to *matter* filled her. She layered that emotion with Helena's bitter certainty that it was all a cruel joke. She was alone. No one cared. Looking at Oliver and Harlan in turn, those emotions were far too easy to conjure up.

As she reached the end of her lines, she let her eyes well with tears and stared down Harlan, injecting a hint of venom into her words. "'None of noble sort / Would so offend a virgin, and extort / A poor soul's patience, all to make you sport.'"

To her surprise, Harlan jumped from his chair and marched up to the stage, addressing Oliver. "'You are unkind, Demetrius; be not so; / For you love Hermia: this you know I know.'" He stood between Oliver and Finley, reaching for Finley's hand. She tugged it from his grasp. "'And here, with all good will, with all my heart / In Hermia's love I yield you up my part; / And yours of Helena to me bequeath / Whom I do love'"—Harlan's thumb grazed Finley's cheek like a whisper, causing her breath to catch—"'and will do till my death.'"

Dang, he was good.

Emma sputtered. "You guys, that was amazing!" Oliver chuckled. "Okay, Oliver, you were embarrassing. But Finley," she paused. Finley looked at Emma's boots. She dreaded what was coming next. "You were incredible. There was so much passion in your words! Your body showed the truth in every phrase. And to call up tears on cue?" She glanced skyward, clasping her hands. *"Magnifique.* You should seriously consider acting."

Finley clutched her right shoulder and glanced around the room. She wanted this to stop. There were too many eyes on her.

"Sister, I believe you're forgetting the star performance?" Harlan held out his hands expectantly.

"No, I mentioned Finley," Emma said.

"Pfft. You wouldn't know acting if it—"

"All right, enough." Emma shoved her brother. "Let's try the scene again from the top. But now that you're here, Harley, Oliver can help me, and Finley can run lines with you."

So this was the plan all along. To get her and Oliver here, then relegate Finley to the sidelines so Emma could have license to flirt and be fawned over by Oliver.

Not a chance. Acting opposite Oliver was one thing, but acting opposite Harlan Crawford? Watching him demand her love, all so Oliver could demand Emma's? A sick feeling settled in her stomach.

"No, I can't," Finley said, stepping off the stage. Emma started to protest. "My shift starts in a few minutes. I can't, okay?" She speed-walked to the back of the room, almost tripping over cords and chairs, despite the protests behind her. Once in the hallway, she slid down a gilded wall and put her head on her knees. The sounds of laughter reached her from the ballroom.

What was she thinking, watching them? Was she just supposed to help another girl win over her best friend? Was she supposed to watch Oliver fall for this gorgeous, funny, clever girl while Harlan teased and taunted her?

No, thank you. It was one thing to help the Bertrams. She would do anything for them. Unless it included helping one of them hook up with a Crawford.

"What are you doing on the floor? Picking gum off of it or something?" Finley looked up to see Juliette standing over her, all long legs and blonde hair and sparkly lip gloss.

"No," Finley said. "I just have a headache."

"Oh, that's good," Juliette said, looking around. *That's the concern I've come to know and love,* Finley thought. "Where are the others?"

"In the ballroom. And, uh, Harlan's in there, too."

Juliette smoothed her hair. "Oh?"

"How was Raleigh's tournament? Did they win?"

Juliette was already walking in the direction Finley had pointed. "Nope."

Fifteen minutes later, Finley was in her custodial uniform, even though her shift didn't start for an hour. The oversized, worn gray shirt was almost comforting. It reminded her of her place. She told herself that as she slipped back into the ballroom and hid behind an enormous pillar.

Juliette was reading lines with Harlan while Oliver and Emma rehearsed together. Emma looked beautiful and confident in her role, but she had a tendency to close herself off at tense moments. Meanwhile, Harlan already had the rhythm of his character down, but little mistakes others made tended to throw him off. He struggled to stay out of his own head. It was a common problem with actors moving from the screen to the stage. Film offered so many takes, so much on-the-spot guidance. But theater had to be organic. Harlan's acting, while strong, felt clearly rehearsed.

Still, both couples looked natural together. Comfortable. Juliette was surprisingly watchable, especially when compared with Oliver, who was truly awful. But he was having fun, grabbing Emma's hand, begging on his knees, worshipping at her feet. Emma scorned him, acting as hurt as Helena deserved. When they finished the scene, she broke down laughing and fell into Oliver's arms.

Finley felt a pang in her heart as she watched them, but it was only a matter of time. Emma was stunning, witty, and confident in all the ways Finley wasn't. Oliver would be a fool not to fall for her.

She kept watching until she thought she saw Oliver looking around the room for her. She snuck out and returned to the hall, where she put in her earbuds and started vacuuming.

* * *

When Finley finished her shift at ten o'clock—an hour after rehearsals typically ended—Oliver and Juliette were waiting for her, finishing their homework in the hall. On the short cab ride home, they told her all about the actual rehearsals, which Harlan had somehow managed to let them stay for.

Oliver seemed so energized as he told Finley one story after the next. She smiled and laughed along with him, but every movement drained her more. Emma was responsible for this happiness. Not Finley.

It felt fitting that Nora was waiting for them when they got home. She wore a pair of wicked heels, but the expression on her face made it clear that her shoes had failed her in court today. "Where have you been?" she demanded as Finley walked through the door. When Juliette and Oliver appeared a moment later, she toned down the menace.

Finley looked at the others. "Um, working?"

"Before that. Where were you after school?"

Oliver spoke up. "Aunt Nora, we all went to Vows to help the Crawfords rehearse, and then they invited Juliette and me to stay for their actual rehearsal with the rest of the cast."

Nora's smile looked strained. "Juliette, Oliver, that was kind of you to allow Finley to tag along. I hope Harlan and Emma didn't mind."

Juliette laughed, breezing by Nora and kissing her cheek. "I doubt they even noticed she was there, Aunt Nora. It's not like scrubbing toilets was going to bother them."

Oliver shook his head. "Nice, Jules." To Nora, he said, "Emma and I both invited her along before rehearsal. She was actually a huge help. She had some feedback that I think will make a big difference for them. Emma was pretty thrilled about it."

"Was she?" Nora said, turning her back to Oliver so only Finley could see the disbelief in her eyes. "Well, how very *lucky* for them that you were there. I'm sure your thoughts were *invaluable*."

"They really were," Oliver said. It was a testament to Nora's subtlety that even Oliver didn't catch the sarcasm in Nora's words.

Finley sure did.

"Kids, is that you?" Aunt Mariah said from the kitchen before Nora could say anything else. In yoga pants and a sweatshirt, Aunt Mariah moved with more energy than she had for weeks. Months, even. "Oh, and Finley! I was so surprised that you weren't home when I came downstairs earlier. I told Nora, I can't remember the last time you weren't here right after school." Aunt Mariah's smile reached her eyes while Nora's held a fierce indictment.

"Mom, you look great. How are you feeling?" Oliver said,

squeezing Finley's shoulder when he passed her to hug his mom. Maybe he *had* noticed Nora's tone.

"Yeah, Mom, I haven't seen you up this late since Christmas," Juliette said.

"I don't think I've felt this good since Christmas," Aunt Mariah said with a smile and a hug. "Now who wants hot cocoa? I know it's late, but I've been craving it all night." She and Oliver and Juliette went into the kitchen, pulling up stools around the island. Finley hesitated.

"I'm glad to see you could follow Juliette and Oliver around this afternoon instead of helping Mariah when she needed you," Nora said, as if she were sincerely happy instead of boiling with sarcasm. "Your ingratitude shocks me," she whispered. "How you can eat their food, sleep under their roof, accept their generosity, and then repay them by shirking what you owe them? It's appalling."

She shrank beneath the woman's gaze. "I thought the new nurse—"

"No, you didn't think, *period*. That's the problem with you. Thomas gave strict instructions that Oliver and Juliette include you. They're *stuck* with you. But Mariah needs you, and you don't even care. I'd hoped, under the Bertrams' influence, you'd become better than your mother," she said. "I can see I was wrong."

With that, Nora walked into the kitchen and pleasantly wished the others good night.

Finley just stood in the foyer. If she'd been slapped, punched, even shot, she couldn't have felt more shocked. The injustice, the viciousness of the comment brought tears to her eyes. She was nothing like her mother. *Nothing*. The thought made her feel sick.

Disgusted.

Worthless.

"Hey, Fin?" Oliver said, stepping out of the kitchen. "You joining us?" She looked away. He didn't need to see her crying.

"I'm going to call it a night," she choked out. "Say good night to your mom for me, okay?"

She started for the stairs when Oliver tugged on her hand and pulled her back toward him.

"Fin, are you okay?" He drew her face around to his. "What happened?"

"Nothing. It was nothing." She tried one more time to walk away, but Oliver held fast to her hand.

"Hey, you know you can tell me anything. What's really going on?" he insisted.

She was half tempted to tell him, to admit that she was upset because of the unimaginable things Nora had just said to her. But the idea of someone else knowing—of *Oliver* knowing—what Nora had said filled her with a shame so visceral, it coated her organs and stopped her throat.

Because what she couldn't admit to Oliver, what she could barely admit to herself, was that Nora wasn't wrong. No, Finley was nothing like her mother, but she *was* ungrateful. She resented Juliette's pettiness. She wished she didn't have to work so tirelessly to prove herself to her godparents. She longed to be accepted and respected for who she was rather than for what she did. Yet she owed them everything. How dare she wish for more? She craved their love when she should have been trying to prove hers.

So no. She couldn't tell Oliver what was going on. That burden was hers alone.

"I'm just tired." She forced out the words, trying to keep her voice from quivering. "It's been a long day. You know how it is."

"No, I don't." He grabbed her shoulders, like he wanted her to pay attention. "You work yourself to the bone, trying to prove your worth to everyone when you can't even see it yourself. Why can't you just . . . why can't you see it already?"

She sighed. Even if she told him, he'd never be able to understand. "You don't—"

"No, listen to me," he said, and he sounded angry now. "*You matter.* You need to understand that. I *need* you to understand that."

He was so adamant, and she wanted so badly to believe him. "I know," she said.

"No, you're just saying that to get me to stop talking. Don't deny it."

She looked at her feet.

Oliver growled and pulled her into a hug. She felt him shake his head against the top of hers. "Finley Price," he said, huffing out a breath of frustration against her hair.

He wasn't letting go, and somehow, she knew he wasn't going to until she hugged him back. She reached her arms around him, sinking into the hug, letting herself revel in the warmth of his faith in her. When she felt his hand stroke her hair, his touch was so tender, she could have cried all over again. He pulled back slightly to peer into her eyes, and this time, she didn't hide from his gaze. She peered back.

"You matter to everyone." He placed his hands on either side of her face. "To me. Do you understand?"

She held his wrists, her eyes misting. "Ollie—"

"Fin," he said. Then again, like an echo. "Fin."

The pressure of his hands softened on her cheeks, as if she had suddenly become breakable. The way his fingertips barely touched her sent a wave of electricity down her body. He looked as if he was going to say something more, and she fixed her gaze on his lips, waiting. Had he always had that freckle on his lip? How had she never noticed it before? Her eyes returned to his for a second that stretched into an eternity. She was having a hard time remembering why she was sad. Because she couldn't be sad, not with Oliver. She could never be sad with Oliver. Especially not now, with his thumb stroking her cheek, with his breath tickling her face, with his—

"Ollie, get in here!" Juliette called. They flew apart. "You know I can't make hot cocoa for crap."

Oliver turned toward the kitchen to respond to his sister.

Finley ran for the stairs.

CHAPTER SEVEN

~*O*~

The next few weeks were a blur of preparing for finals, hanging out with the Crawfords during rehearsal breaks, and trying to forget that damn near-kiss. Near miss. Whatever.

Oliver still couldn't believe he'd tried to kiss Finley. Something had happened just before that moment to make her so upset, so vulnerable. And what had he done? Tried to take advantage of her. He felt disgusted with himself just for thinking of it.

Fortunately, Finley had done the kind thing by ignoring it. Of course she had. She was probably embarrassed for him, judging by how fast she'd run when Juliette had interrupted them. It was strange how he could feel mortified and relieved and disappointed at the same time. If she hadn't run . . . if he'd actually kissed her . . . He couldn't think like that. It was confusing and wrong, and he couldn't think like that.

She'd done the kind thing, and now he needed to do the right thing and back off. That's why he'd decided to see where things could go with Emma. The girl was gorgeous and funny and unpredictable, and she'd made it clear she liked him. With Finley's rejection still stinging, Emma's interest was like balm on his festering wound. Even with how busy they were, Emma managed to make him feel as if he mattered, texting him throughout the day, dropping off snacks for him when he was studying, asking him to help her run lines. And the way she always touched him, bumping her leg against his, letting her fingers trail down his arm when they were talking . . .

Emma Crawford liked him. Emma *freaking* Crawford.

Now that she was planning to stay in Chicago through the summer, he was even more excited about the play coming to an end. It would finish its run right after finals, making it feel oddly symbolic—it marked the end of high school and the beginning of everything that came after. He *needed* after. If it couldn't be with Finley, he'd be lucky for it to be with Emma.

"It's a good thing the play starts Saturday. I don't know how much more of this I can handle," Emma told him when he met her at the theater after school. They were hanging out in an already renovated room a little way from the ballroom, where formal rehearsals were held. At Emma's insistence, Finley was there before her cleaning shift started. Whenever Fin took a break from her homework, Emma picked her brain, asking her acting questions and even wanting feedback on her director's notes. It was funny how Finley could be in her element in those moments and then look out of place as soon as she returned to her homework. Like now.

But Emma couldn't be making her uncomfortable—she was beyond nice to Fin. Just last week, Emma had admitted to Oliver that Fin was her new pet project: she was determined to bring her out of her shell. He liked that side of Emma. He liked a lot of sides of Emma.

"Are you excited about the play?" Finley was asking Emma, looking up from her homework only briefly.

"Oh, who can muster the energy for excitement?" Emma groaned. "There's a reason I'm taking a break from acting, and it's not just for *la Sorbonne*. It makes messes out of people. Just look at how awful my dad is, and he's just our agent. I'm glad Harlan sees through all of this. I'd worry if he didn't."

·Oliver thought he heard a sound from Finley, but she didn't say anything.

"So why did you sign on for the play?" Oliver asked.

"When the lead broke her ankle, our dad tried to tell us Weinstein wanted a change in the cast, but there's no way that's true. He requested Harley personally." She made a face. "I think the real reason my dad brokered the deal is so he could double his fee and then use the money on drugs and divorce papers."

"That's awful," Oliver said. "Why do you guys put up with it?"

"I'm doing it for Harley and he's doing it for our dad." Finley tried to hide her disgust, but it must have shown on her face, because Emma said," "Don't judge him like that. What teenage boy doesn't crave his dad's approval?"

Finley dropped her head, a frown on her face. "Maybe you're right." She returned to her laptop when her frown deepened. "You have to be kidding," she said under her breath.

"Huh? What's wrong?" Emma asked.

"Chen just emailed me the drama club minutes, and they voted me president for next year!"

"And why is that a bad thing?" Emma asked.

"Because I missed the meeting today, and I didn't put my name in for president, and Rosa was the director this year, and it's not fair to her—"

"But they obviously voted you in for a reason," Emma said. She glanced at Oliver. "What am I missing?"

He half-smiled. Noticing Harlan standing at the door on his phone, he gave him a nod. "Fin doesn't believe in stepping on toes. She was the stage manager for the spring production, but someone ended up finding some acting and production notes she'd been keeping, and everyone ended up deferring to those notes over Rosa's, including Rosa. So Fin's worried Rosa will think she was going behind her back."

Finley was already on her phone, standing in a corner of the room. "Rosa? Hey, I'm really sorry. I don't know what happened—"

Harlan stowed his phone and stared at Finley's back. "Is she serious?"

"What do you mean?" Oliver asked.

"This," he pointed to her pacing. "Something good happened to her and she's upset?"

"By the way it happened, sure. On top of that, it puts undue attention on her. If you haven't noticed yet, that's definitely not her style."

"I've noticed," Harlan said, still studying Finley. "Or maybe I haven't. She makes herself hard to notice, doesn't she? She's too pretty to be so inconspicuous."

"I've never found her hard to notice," Emma said. "And not just because she's pretty."

Oliver smiled at her.

Finley was sitting cross-legged on the floor now, her hair covering her face. Harlan turned away from her. "Ems, you just like anything Ollie likes."

Oliver's chest warmed at Emma's wink. "True."

Finley's call ended and she returned to the group. "Well, it looks like Rosa put my name on the ballot, so I'm not getting out of this anytime soon."

"It'll look good on your application," Oliver said.

"What application?" Emma asked.

"To colleges next year," Finley answered, before Oliver could say what he really meant: the Mansfield Theater Youth Program. "And with that, I need to get to work." She packed her things into her bag.

"I'm heading downstairs. I'll walk with you," Harlan said.

Finley's eyes shifted around the room. "With me?"

"Well, since Rosa isn't here . . ." Harlan said with a smile oozing with charm that Fin was sure to hate. Oliver smiled to himself as the awkward pair left the room.

* * *

Far too early Saturday morning, Oliver and Finley were grabbing snacks for their volunteer project when a distraught Emma came over.

"Are you sure you have to go?" Emma asked him in the kitchen, her hair piled adorably atop her head. She was wearing pajama bottoms and a tank top, despite the brisk morning. She looked, well, hot. But desperate, too. "It's just, I could really use the help."

"Help?" Oliver asked, tossing Finley a bottled water across the kitchen. When she caught it, he raised his eyebrows to her. "Nice."

"Yes, help," Emma said. "I need distraction, you guys. Or maybe I need to run lines again. I don't know. But I could really use you." She set her big, hazel eyes directly on Oliver, and he thought she might cry. He glanced down at her hands, where she was fidgeting with her cuticles. He'd never seen her look so vulnerable. He hated this.

"Ems, I'm sorry. I'm the president of Make a Difference, and this is a big event. But we'll be home by one, two at the latest. I can, I mean, *we* can come over then," he said, feeling his cheeks burn. Why did Finley have to be here right now? Why did Emma have to look so pleading and beautiful and fluster him like this?

"I have to be at the theater by two. Could you maybe ditch out early? Only like an hour! Please?" she asked.

Oliver hesitated. "I don't know, Ems. What kind of message would that send?"

She grabbed his arm. "The kind that says you *care* about people in need! Please, Ollie. Please." Then she glanced at Finley. "You too, Fin."

"I'm sorry, Emma," Finley said. "I'm committed to be there until one. But I can stop by when I'm done, if you want."

Oliver watched Emma's face crumple. "It's okay, guys. I shouldn't make you choose between volunteering and helping a friend. I'm just nervous. There's a lot riding on this play, and tonight, especially. I'm just taking out my nerves for Harlan on you guys."

"Nerves for Harlan? What do you mean?" Oliver asked.

Emma put a hand to her mouth. "Nothing. Sorry. I shouldn't have said anything. Have fun volunteering. I'll see you later." She rushed out of the kitchen. Oliver glanced at Finley, who had a funny expression on her face. Then he darted after Emma.

"Emma," he said. "Ems!" She turned around at the door, tears in her eyes.

"I'm sorry, Ollie," she said, covering her face. Oliver put a hand on her bare shoulder, the feeling of her skin doing funny things to his stomach.

"What's going on? Why are you so concerned about Harlan?"

She sniffed. "You can't tell him I told you, okay? Our dad said the word around Hollywood right now is that this is a make-or-break moment for him. If the play doesn't do well, no one will sign him on to do theater again, and it'll probably hurt his movie career, too. I mean, who wants to sign the guy who butchers Shakespeare? I . . . I just don't want to screw it up for him."

"Emma," he said, holding her shoulders to look at her, gorgeous in spite of the tears. "You're going to be amazing. I've seen you rehearse dozens of times now, and you're flawless every time. Harlan has nothing to worry about. Neither of you do."

She took a deep breath, then hiccupped and leaned her head against his arm. She put a hand on his forearm, running her manicured fingernails over his skin. His whole body erupted in goose bumps. "Do you really think so?" she asked.

"I know so," he said, his voice suddenly hoarse. He removed his hands from her shoulders, but she grabbed onto them before they dropped. Her fingers laced through his, and he worried his voice would be an octave higher when he next spoke. He cleared his throat. His pulse quickened. "How about this: I'll leave at eleven, grab some falafels on the way home, and meet you at your place, okay? Four hours building bookshelves will be plenty."

Her face lit up. "Really? You'd do that for me?" She threw her arms around him, hugging him tightly. When he let go, she grabbed his face. "Thank you," she whispered. Then she brought her lips to his, kissing him softly, quickly. Just long enough to make his own lips part in response, his body go all tingly, and his heart rate reach approximately forty-seven thousand beats per minute.

Then she released him.

With a smile, Emma grabbed the door and ran outside into the cold.

Dazed, Oliver turned toward the kitchen, praying that Finley hadn't seen any of that. She was nowhere in sight.

He drew a deep breath, then exhaled in a mixture of relief and regret. "Fin!" he called after another moment. "You ready?"

He heard the sound of a bag zipping, and Finley appeared in the hallway, smiling. "Yep. Everything okay with Emma?"

He fought the urge to sigh. "Yeah. She's just worried about screwing this up for Harlan. I guess their dad is putting a lot of pressure on him to make this a success, or there won't be any more theater gigs coming his way. Maybe not even movie roles, either."

Finley frowned. "That doesn't sound likely. I can see him not getting his pick of theater roles, maybe, but movies?" She shook her head. "I don't know." Oliver grabbed their coats and they stepped outside.

"I don't, either, but Emma seems convinced of it. Listen, how would you feel about leaving the event at eleven to see Emma and Harlan before they go to the theater?"

Finley put an arm through her black jacket, covering her bright orange volunteer shirt. "I don't think I should. I'm signed up to man one of the tables from noon till one."

He smacked his forehead. "Ah, right. With me."

"Yeah, but that's fine." She jumped over a puddle on the sidewalk. "If you need to help Emma, I can handle the table by myself."

"Are you sure? I feel awful backing out on you. And the rest of the club," he added.

She kept her eyes on the uneven ground. "Sure. Just wish Emma luck for me."

He wished it were disappointment keeping her eyes down instead of cracks in the cement. "Fin, are you sure you'll be okay without me? I can tell Emma I'll meet her after we're done."

Finley cocked her head to the side, her cheeks already flushed from the pace. "Ollie, are you worried about me?" She smiled. "I'll be fine."

Oliver smiled back, but inside, his stomach was roiling. Emma had kissed him, and as much as he'd liked it, all he really wanted was for Finley to be upset that he was going to ditch her to spend time with another girl. He wanted her to be jealous. Which was a total douche move. He shouldn't toy with her like that. And he shouldn't take advantage of their friendship, of the fact that he'd been her protector—no, her *empowerer*—for the past two years. No matter how badly he wanted to.

Besides, Finley obviously didn't see him like that. How many times did he have to test these waters before he got it through his head that he couldn't swim? He'd already tried to kiss her! Tried and failed. Crashed and burned. *She doesn't like you,* he told himself. *She probably sees you as a brother. Suck it up. Move on.*

Like on to Emma. Emma freaking Crawford, who was so confident and exciting and painfully hot. He could like Emma.

He just had to give Finley up first.

CHAPTER EIGHT

~ℱ~

That evening, Finley sat in Aunt Mariah's lush lemon and gray sitting room while she painted her aunt's toenails, a biweekly tradition of theirs.

"So, Chen was volunteering today, too?" Aunt Mariah asked. "Isn't he the boy Ollie was teasing you about? The one from your drama club?"

Finley shook her head. "I know what you're trying to say, but he doesn't like me."

"He conveniently signed up to help M.A.D. today—a club you just so happen to be in, dear. He likes you." Her aunt pursed her lips. "Now, are you sure I can wear this light a pink on my toes? I think I'm too pale."

Finley looked up from the towel covering the antique coffee table as she finished the topcoat. For as well as her aunt had been recently, she still looked frail. Her blonde hair was a bit too wispy, her beautiful face a bit too gaunt. Finley smiled at her. "It looks great, Aunt Mariah. Very classy."

Her aunt nodded and picked up a silver tray covered in nail polish. "And what color will you be wearing tonight?"

"Oh, you don't need to—"

"You protest every time, dear, yet I can't remember the last time you didn't have your toenails done," she said with an arch expression. Finley grinned. "Now, I think you should try this red, but I know you'd never allow it. So how about teal?"

Juliette walked through the door as Aunt Mariah was shaking the nail polish. "Oh, fabulous," she said, dropping onto the love seat next to Finley. "I could use a pedicure." She picked up several colors, settling on the red Aunt Mariah had just put back down. Juliette handed it to Finley. "Here."

"Sure," Finley said, grabbing the polish.

"Juliette, I was just about to paint Finley's toenails," Aunt Mariah said.

"Like Fin cares about that stuff, Mom." Juliette put her foot on Finley's knee.

Finley's chest burned and she bit back a snarky comment, instead saying, "It's fine, Aunt Mariah."

"I know it's fine," her aunt said, snapping her fingers. "Now give me your foot." Finley's heart swelled. She smiled and put her foot on the table, so the three of them were sitting in a triangle.

"So, Juliette, how was dinner with Raleigh?" Aunt Mariah asked.

Juliette answered while she played on her phone, reclining on the couch. "We went out to eat with his parents at that super chic new restaurant, 40th Floor, and it was *so* yummy. The coach of the White Sox was there with his wife, and he stopped by to shake hands with the senator. He even talked to Raleigh. It was a-ma-zing."

"That's great—"

Juliette sat up, yanking out her foot so fast that Finley painted a stripe of nail polish on her own jeans. "OMG, you won't believe it! Brooke 'Nose-Job' Newsome is at the play tonight and she's been live-tweeting it. Check this," she said, angling the phone for everyone to see.

OMG. @HarlanCrawford is so HAWT!!!! #futureboyfriend

I could watch @HarlanCrawford read a biology textbook.

@EmmaCrawford on stage. Beautiful! NEED HER DRESS FOR #PROM

OMGEEEEE!!!! Harley given love potion, is flirting with own sister. CANNOT STOP LAUGHING!!!! #amidsummernightsdream

You go, Helena!!! @EmmaCrawford tell those men where it's at!!! #amidsummernightsdream

@HarlanCrawford is best Lysander evah!!!! #TheCourse-OfTrueLoveNeverDidRunSmooth #amidsummernightsdream #futureboyfriend #onetruelove

"Okay, and now it's just a bunch of blurry pictures with hashtags about how she and Harley are meant for each other. Rein it in there, Nose Job."

Finley wanted to make her stop. Wanted to grab the phone from her hands and scour the feed. Because she saw a tweet Juliette had missed.

@OllieBertram in the house supporting my girl @EmmaCrawford #lovethem #cutecouple

She felt sick. Finley hadn't even thought to wonder where Oliver was tonight. Now she wished she didn't know.

"Juliette, try to be nice. I'm sure she's a lovely girl," Aunt Mariah said, patting Finley's foot. Finley dropped it and brought the other one up for her aunt.

Juliette was still seething at her phone, but she gave her mom a fake apology and returned her foot to Finley's lap. "Of course, Mom. At least the play is going well. It just sucks that we can't see it till the last night. We're like the Crawfords' closest friends in Chicago. We should get to go at least one more night!"

"The show has been sold out for months, dear. No doubt tickets are at a premium, even for the stars. I think it's very nice of Harlan and Emma to have thought about how much more fun you'd have on closing night, getting to go to the club opening after. It's a historic moment, all of this happening on the same night. Don't you agree, Finley?"

Finley nodded, unable to look up. Oliver was out with Emma. They were a couple. It was done. She didn't need to think about whatever it was that almost happened between them a couple of weeks ago. She didn't need to worry about what it meant or wonder if she'd misinterpreted Oliver's intentions when he'd leaned in. She didn't need to process anything or decide anything.

It was done.

She tried to ignore the burning feeling in her stomach and swiped a wet Q-tip along the tops of Juliette's toes, removing smeared toenail polish. "There, Juliette. You're all set."

Juliette looked down from her phone and wiggled her glossy toes. "You could have a real future in a nail salon, Fin. Doesn't she give the best pedicures, Mom?" She didn't wait for her mother's answer. "Anyway, I'm going upstairs to read *real* reviews that aren't from an obsessed stalker before I go to bed. Love you." She kissed her mom's head and left without saying a word to Finley.

Nothing out of the ordinary.

* * *

Over the next two weeks, Finley saw little of Juliette and even less of Oliver. If not for finals and the fact that he was now dating Emma, Finley would almost have thought he was avoiding her. Sure, nothing was official, but even Juliette and Aunt Mariah talked about it at home as a done deal. At dinner when they teased him, Finley thought she saw a hint of something like doubt in Oliver's eyes. But Emma would win him over.

In fact, if Finley didn't know better, she'd think Emma was trying to win *her* over.

Since opening night, Emma had made a point of stopping by the house in the morning before school, even when Oliver was already gone. And even though tomorrow was closing night and Emma was busier than ever, the girl had insisted that Finley come over to her house today after her last final.

As Finley walked out of the school for the last time that school year, she realized she'd been too hesitant at Emma's invitation; the girl was waiting for her, bodyguards and all.

"Oh, hey, Emma," Finley said, gripping her bag closer.

"Hey, Fin!" Emma's trademark stripe had been dyed a honey brown for the play, along with the rest of her hair. But her prissy-punk look was otherwise intact, along with her Jackie O sunglasses and big scarf. "I'm so glad you're coming over. I need some serious girl time."

"Yeah, thanks for inviting me," Finley said. "Did . . . did you come to walk me home?"

"No, Harley and I were coming back from the theater. Come on," she said, leading Finley to a black SUV.

"What? Harley? Is he going to be there?"

Emma gave her a confused look. "We're driving home together. But yes, he lives there, remember?"

Finley flushed. "Oh, right. Yeah."

Emma towed Finley past crowds of students laughing, talking, and making plans for the summer. She waved at onlookers, posed for pictures, and thanked well-wishers who halted their twenty-yard walk to the SUV. Yet even though the spotlight was on Emma, Finley couldn't help but notice the looks she was getting from people. In fact, she heard someone ask: "Who's that with Emma Crawford?" She hoped they never got an answer.

When they finally made it to the car, Harlan greeted them from the backseat. "Miss Price," he said, smiling wide enough to show dimples.

"Hey." She tried to wait for Emma to get into the vehicle, but the girl was still waving at fans.

"Are you planning to join us, or were you just desperate to say hi to me?"

"Emma invited me—"

His smile widened. Or sharpened, maybe. "I know, I know. Will you please come in? I won't bite."

One of the bodyguards ushered Finley in, and Emma behind her. The burly man closed the door, got into the passenger seat, and the other bodyguard started the car. Finley tried to shrink herself into the leather seat to keep from touching Harlan.

"We haven't seen you lately. Where have you been hiding?" he asked.

"I haven't been hiding. You've been in a play."

"Oh, is that right?" His voice was too teasing and familiar. "So why haven't you been stopping by before rehearsal? Did you decide we'd had all the help we could get?"

Eyes anywhere but on him, she said, "What help could I give either of you?"

"You mean apart from all the advice you've given me the last few weeks? *And* the tips you gave Ollie to pass on?" Emma said, swatting Finley's hand. "Oh, I know you didn't ask him to pass them on, but he couldn't help it. Anyway, you were right about how I was closing my body off when I was uncomfortable with physical contact. And that idea to think about everything that could go wrong on stage as Helena was just genius. It's such a relief to be ready with her reactions in case anything goes wrong."

"That came from you?" Harlan asked. "But that was brilliant. *I* hadn't even considered that."

Finley shook her head. "They weren't secrets. Your director and costars would have told you all that."

Emma looked at her over her sunglasses. "They hadn't told us yet. You really helped, Fin. One of my reviews specifically mentioned how 'strong, yet achingly vulnerable' my Helena is. You know your stuff."

Finley stared out the windshield. *Please, stop talking.* The last thing she wanted was Harlan finding out who her dad was. She couldn't handle seeing his reaction if he realized. Worse, she couldn't handle the thought of him acting differently because of it, not being a jerk to her simply because of her dad. That fakeness was the reason she wanted nothing to do with Hollywood. Ever. And Harlan Crawford was the young face of Fake Hollywood.

Harlan and Emma were talking around her now. She felt a moment of gratitude to Emma for not pushing it, a moment that quickly passed when she remembered the girl had been the one to start the conversation in the first place.

When they reached Mansfield Square, Finley followed them through the garage into the house. The Grants' home wasn't quite as big or quite as grand as the Bertrams', but it was still beautiful. Whereas the Bertams' home was all subdued with classic antiques, the Grants' felt new, but with eclectic pieces that felt both retro and modern all at once. Harlan and Emma's movie posters lined the staircases at least up to the third floor, where the girls left Harlan to go into Emma's bedroom.

Emma's room surprised Finley. Instead of being bold, like Emma, it had a sophisticated, quiet, Paris-themed look. An old-fashioned clock sat next to an Eiffel Tower on an eggshell blue dresser. On the wall hung a large black-and-white picture of a younger Emma and Harlan in front of the Louvre with their parents. Finley recognized them from the tabloids. The picture could only have been five or six years old, yet the parents bore little resemblance to the ones on TMZ. They looked happy and in love.

"It's weird how people can change, isn't it?" Emma said.

Finley whirled around. "I'm sorry. I didn't mean to pry."

"I invited you over, Fin. You're hardly prying." Emma stood next to her and studied the picture. "Isn't it just bizarre how they could go from being good parents to being total crap? Dad had already produced a lot of big movies at this point, so it's not like fame was sprung on them—like they won the lottery or something. But they started growing apart. Rather than get a divorce or just keep their little affairs secret, they had to air everything to the world. It's like they just stopped caring about anything except trying to humiliate each other. And us."

Finley frowned. She thought she understood something of Emma's pain. "I'm sorry, Emma. I can't imagine how hard it must have been to find out that your parents were cheating—"

"I wouldn't have minded the affairs so much if they'd kept them to themselves. Everyone has skeletons. Smart people just keep them buried instead of dragging them out in front of the media and the whole world. It's humiliating." Bitterness filled her voice. "Can you see why I'm going to college on another continent?"

Finley flashed Emma a tight smile, but inside, she tried not to be horrified. Her parents were cheating on each other repeatedly, and the only thing Emma cared about was being humiliated by it all? Finley mentally shook herself. She couldn't compare their ordeals. If this was how Emma responded, who was Finley to judge? And yet, deep down, she *was* judging. After everything with her mom, humiliation had never even occurred to her. *No*, she thought, *it was just trumped by sorrow*. It had taken a back burner to the shame she felt at never being enough for her mom. It had been eclipsed by fear.

"Anyway, let's move on from our childhood trauma, shall we? I was hoping you could help me pick out a dress for tomorrow night at the club."

Finley laughed, stopping when she saw Emma's reaction. "Wait, are you being serious? You want me to give you fashion advice?"

"Not advice, silly. I have four dresses that I can't decide between. I was hoping you'd tell me," she paused, "which one you think Ollie would like best."

Finley went cold. "Oh, um, I don't know if I'd be the right person for that job. Maybe Juliette—"

"Don't be absurd. You're Ollie's closest friend in the world. No one knows him better than you. Certainly not Juliette." The way she said Juliette's name told her exactly what Emma thought about Oliver's sister. And it wasn't flattering.

Finley felt stuck. If she kept pushing the issue, it would just belabor things and make them even more awkward. Besides, Emma was trying to be nice, trying to be a friend, no matter the agenda. Oliver would want her to be nice in return. She smiled through the ache in her heart. "Okay, sure. What do you have?"

Emma's closet was enormous. She had more clothes than she could wear in months. She pulled out four garment bags and laid them on her bed.

"Now for the dress behind door number one!"

She tried on all four dresses, and in the end they agreed on an ivory one-shoulder, A-line dress that ended a few inches above the knee. With a thick gold belt at the waist, the Grecian dress made her look every inch the modern Helena. She was stunning.

Finley's throat tightened. "It's perfect. Ollie will love it."

Emma's smile dazzled. "Do you really think so?"

Finley nodded, wanting more than ever to leave. Emma seemed to really like Oliver. Seeing her excitement over him firsthand—without him even being there—was torture.

"Okay," Emma said, slinking out of the dress and throwing on yoga pants and a sweatshirt. "Your turn."

"Sorry?"

"Let's go to your place. I want to see what you're wearing to-morrow night."

There was no point in arguing. Both girls knew Oliver was picking up Tate from the airport, so Emma couldn't have a hidden plan for Oliver to find her.

Did she really just want to be Finley's friend?

Finley rose to her feet. "All right, let's go."

Emma called to her brother as they walked downstairs. "Harley, I'm heading to Fin's. Come get me on your way to the theater!"

"Okay, but you have twenty minutes!" he yelled back.

"Stop yelling and just text each other like normal kids, already!" Mrs. Grant said, appearing at the bottom of the stairs with a smile on her face. "So, what did you decide?"

"The flowy Grecian dress."

"I knew that was the one. You'll look beautiful, sweetie. Like always."

Emma gave her aunt a kiss on the cheek, and she and Finley headed next door and up the three flights to Finley's room.

Finley pushed the door open with a stab of self-consciousness. Her room was nothing like Emma's. It was a shrine to a Hollywood she no longer believed in but couldn't let go of.

She wrapped an arm around herself, squeezing her right shoulder, and watched Emma's reaction. The girl stopped at the entry and looked all around, taking in the framed posters, the film reel lamp shades, the velvet theater curtain turned window curtain, the collection of old movie cameras. "This. Is. Awesome."

A smile came unbidden to Finley's face. "Really? You think so?"

"Um, yes. Are you kidding? Where did you find all this stuff? It's incredible!"

"A bunch of it was my dad's. Uncle Thomas took it out of storage for me when I moved in. My mom didn't—" She stopped herself. She'd never talked about her mom before.

Emma leaned down to inspect the film reel lamp shade. "Your mom didn't what?"

Didn't know about Dad's storage shed, or else she would have sold everything in it to buy oxy and alcohol. Instead, she said, "She didn't care about it. Liam has a bunch of stuff, too."

"Well, it's the coolest. You have killer taste." She strode over to Finley's closet and threw it open. "Wait, is this it?" She glanced behind her, looking around the room, then back at the sparse closet. "You're kidding, right? This is it?"

Finley felt too embarrassed to answer.

Emma rifled through the hangers. "Ugh. Too long. Too brown. Wait, this is really cute—oh, no, is that mustard? Juliette gave you a dress with a stain on it? And you kept it? Let me guess: you felt guilty throwing it away. Or maybe you thought you could put a funky brooch over it, which isn't the worst idea." She kept searching until she pulled out an empire waist lace dress in cornflower blue. "Ooh, this is pretty, and it looks small enough to fit you. Did Juliette wear it to a formal a couple of years ago or something?"

Finley snorted. "No, this is the one she took with her as a backup in case someone spilled punch on the other dress."

"Better than mustard," Emma said. "Anyway, it's perfect. Try it on."

Of course it was sleeveless.

"Oh, no. I'd rather not wear that one."

"What, is it haunted? Stop being so ridiculous. It's cute, and the color will be great on you." She thrust it into Finley's hands and pointed her toward the en suite bathroom. "Just humor me."

Finley's heart beat wildly in her chest as she went into her bathroom. She looked at herself in the mirror, looking small and pitiful and afraid. She shook her head, trying to psych herself up. *It's just a dress. Emma probably won't even notice.* She disrobed and slid into the dress, fumbling with the zipper at the back. She managed to pull it two-thirds of the way up, but even zipped, it still wouldn't have mattered. Panic flared in her chest.

"Fin? What's taking you so long in there? I have to leave in like five minutes."

Finley inhaled slowly. "Nothing. The zipper's just stuck." She heard rustling outside the door. Then it opened. Horror rooted her in place as Emma walked in.

"Here, let me."

Finley whipped around so that her right shoulder was angled away from Emma. She made a quick curtsy. "Ta-dah! See? It's fine. It's perfect," she said, trying to rush Emma from the bathroom.

But Emma's gaze was fixed on the mirror, which gave her a clear view of Finley's scarred shoulder. A clear view of three deep, hideous cigarette burns, courtesy of Finley's mother.

Emma's eyes widened. "Oh, Fin. I had no idea."

Finley shook her head, trying not to cry. "It's fine. Please don't. Don't talk about it, okay? It's fine. It's not a big deal."

Emma stepped forward and put a hand gently on Finley's shoulder. "I'm sorry," she whispered.

Tears spilled from Finley's eyes. She didn't know what she hated worse: Emma seeing her secret shame, or Emma being so upset by it. "It's okay, all right? I'm just going to change out of this. I'll wear something else."

Something in Emma seemed to snap. She looked up at Finley. "No, you won't. Wait here."

She ran back into the bedroom and returned moments later, handing Finley a champagne shrug. "Throw this on over it."

Finley hesitated, then put it on. It looked good. Great, actually. Emma smiled. "See? You'll look gorgeous."

A rush of gratitude overwhelmed her. "Thanks," she whispered. The other girl smiled in the mirror. "You're welcome."

Finley changed back into her jeans and t-shirt. When she went back into her room, Emma was staring at a poster of Finley's dad. She turned around with a sniff. "Harley just texted me. He's downstairs, so I have to run. I'll see you tomorrow?"

Finley nodded. And when Emma gave her a hug before leaving the room, she didn't even mind.

CHAPTER NINE

~O~

Oliver and Juliette knocked at Finley's door. "You decent in there?" Juliette asked.

Feet padded across the soft carpet, and the door opened to show Finley.

Oliver's breath caught. She stood barefoot in a blue dress that looked as if it was made for her, hugging curves that she normally tried to hide and stopping at her knees. He fought the urge to look at her legs. Her skin glowed against the blue dress, and her hair hung down in soft waves over her shoulders.

She was stunning.

"Glad to see someone's getting use out of that old thing," Juliette said. "But please tell me that's not what you're doing with your hair."

Finley stood on the edge of one foot, grabbing her hair. "Oh, I—"

Juliette pushed her into her bathroom. "No offense, but I can't be seen with you looking like this. Only a homeless person would wear her hair down with this outfit."

The door to the bathroom was ajar, and the reflection showed Juliette pulling Finley's long black waves into a loose side ponytail, leaving out some wisps here and there. Then Juliette rummaged through her own clutch and took out a tube of lipstick, deciding that the shade Finley had chosen was "horrific." Finally, she ushered

Finley back out of the bathroom, made her change her heels, and pointed her in Oliver's direction.

"What do you think?"

Oliver blinked, and his brain wrestled with his mouth to make words. Truthfully, he'd liked her look a little better before Juliette's interference. But still.

Still.

"Um, yeah. She looks . . ." *Beautiful. Perfect,* he thought. "Great."

"That's an overstatement, but she's not embarrassing, at least. Let's go," Juliette said.

The girls walked down the stairs in front of him. Finley complimented Juliette on her sequin dress, and Juliette asked her about Emma's outfit. It was all quickly lost on Oliver. He'd been avoiding Finley for days, weeks, to focus on Emma. And the truth was he liked Emma a lot. He'd hoped his feelings for her would help diminish his feelings for Finley, but obviously they hadn't. Not completely. Not yet.

At the bottom of the stairs, they met Tate and Raleigh, who like Oliver were in slacks and sport coats. Tate's eyes widened in Finley's direction, making Oliver glower.

"Dude, how hot does Juliette look?" Raleigh said.

Tate and Oliver turned to him. "You know she's our sister, right?" Tate said. Oliver heard Finley turn a snort into a cough.

"Oh, right," Raleigh said.

Tate grabbed Finley's arm before Oliver could even debate if he should or not. "I, however, have no problem admitting how good Fin looks," Tate said, earning an eye roll from Finley. "Damn, girl." He took her arm and led her down the hall, through the kitchen and dining room to the back door. They stepped into the garage. "Fin, if I didn't know better, I'd think you *hadn't* been pining away for me these last few weeks. You should be emaciated with grief, but instead, I see curves. You heartless beast." Finley laughed and hit him in the shoulder with one of Juliette's old clutches.

Oliver unlocked the car doors, gritting his teeth so hard they ached. "Dude."

Tate grabbed the keys from him and grinned, escorting Finley to the passenger seat. On the way back around to the driver's seat, Tate said, "Just because you're too smitten with Emma to recognize the hotness of our girl here, doesn't mean the rest of us are." Tate held the driver's door open and climbed in.

"Enough," Finley said, laughing from the passenger seat.

It infuriated Oliver to see how Tate could get away with flirting like this. Fin never took him seriously, so he could just say anything he wanted, cross every line. Yet Oliver couldn't even give her a compliment without feeling like a creepy perv-bag.

"Yeah," Oliver echoed as he slid into the backseat. "Enough."

Soon, they were at the theater, where Oliver struggled not to find Finley's enchantment with the spectacle adorable. Tate pointed out ridiculous outfits and people with food in their teeth or slacks stuck in their socks to make her laugh. A guy from school came over to talk to Finley about how the theater would transform into the club after only a thirty-minute post-performance intermission (an obvious excuse for the dude to chat her up if ever there was one).

And Oliver just stood by her, mute.

These conversations should have belonged to him. He should have been the one joking with Finley, the one sharing facts and trivia and anticipation. But now he avoided looking at her even when she was trying to catch his eye. He couldn't stand not to be near her, but he couldn't—he wouldn't—get too close. No matter how confused or hurt she looked.

It was torture.

Finally, mercifully, it was time to take their seats. They walked down to the tenth row in the center of the orchestra section, the best seats in the house, Finley had said on the drive over. Raleigh and Juliette filed in first, then Tate and Finley followed, leaving Oliver for last. To sit right next to Fin for two and a half hours.

Tate kept talking to her, fortunately, and flirting with her, unfortunately. At least Oliver was spared having to talk. But just as the lights flickered their warning that the play was about to start, Finley leaned over to him. "Are you okay?" she whispered.

The pit of his stomach felt heavy. After a moment's hesitation, he looked at her. Her eyes were huge, her cherub lips pursed in concern. She was heartbreakingly vulnerable. His façade cracked, and he smiled. "Yeah, I'm just nervous for the Crawfords. They've had a couple of rough reviews this last week, and they need tonight to be perfect."

Finley nodded, biting her lip. "I thought I'd done something to upset you."

"Never. How could you possibly upset me?"

"I don't know."

"No, I've just been busy with finals and . . . supporting Emma. I couldn't be upset with you."

She nodded, playing with the program on her lap, before whispering, "Well, she's really lucky to have you. I'm happy for you guys."

And there it was. Finley was happy he was dating another girl. She didn't like him. It was over. It had to be over.

The lights dimmed. The curtain opened. And out came the players.

Harlan appeared as Lysander with his beloved Hermia, and they plotted to run away from her arranged marriage to Demetrius. Shortly after, Emma entered as Helena. She hung on Demetrius, pleading in vain for him to return her love.

Harlan was incredible. His Lysander charmed and engaged. Quickly, the audience was ready to run away with him, too. Yet Emma's role was the more soulful. She lamented her unrequited love for Demetrius with a conviction so real, Oliver shifted in his seat. He hung on her words, ever more aware of the object of his unrequited affection sitting next to him.

"'And as he errs, doting on Hermia's eyes,'" Emma bemoaned

about her Demetrius, "'So I, admiring of his qualities. / Things base and vile, holding no quantity, / Love can transpose to form and dignity. / Love looks not with the eyes, but with the mind; / And therefore is wing'd Cupid painted blind.'"

Emma's eyes seemed to find Oliver, though he knew that was impossible. He moved subtly farther from Finley. *Things base and vile*, he thought. Like his feelings for Finley? Someone he had watched over and supported for years? He couldn't help but risk a glance at her. She looked uncomfortable, too. Only two months ago, he would have asked why.

But not now.

He sat stark upright and focused on Emma. The lovers had all fled to the woods, where the Fairy King instructed his minion, Puck, to give Demetrius a love potion to fall in love with Helena. Puck, however, mistook Lysander for Demetrius. When Harlan awoke in love with his sister, the audience erupted with laughter. Harlan grabbed his sister's hand, pressed it to his chest, and groveled at her feet.

"'The will of man is by his reason sway'd; / And reason says you are the worthier maid. / Things growing are not ripe until their season; / So I, being young, till now ripe not to reason.'" His earnestness caused still more roars of laughter.

Meanwhile, Emma shook and kicked him off at every turn. Convinced that Harlan's Lysander was mocking her unreciprocated love for Demetrius, she ran from him, saying, "'I thought you lord of more true gentleness. / O, that a lady of one man refus'd / Should of another therefore be abus'd!'"

Oliver glanced around the theater and took in the faces in the audience. The Crawfords had bewitched them. He smiled.

At intermission, Oliver was able to avoid Finley and her graver-than-expected look by catching up with a few people he knew from school. He laughed off their comments about him and Emma.

He purposefully took his seat at the last possible moment, sitting down right as the lights dimmed.

The second half brought the lovers' story to a head, with Lysander and Demetrius, still under their love spells, coming to blows over Helena's love. Harlan and his foe were fighting over his sister, trading insults and verbal jabs. And then the worst happened.

Harlan tripped.

He crashed to the floor, and for a split second, Oliver could swear that the entire audience was holding their breath. Beside him, Finley gasped. But Harlan rose to his feet and dusted himself off, scowling at Demetrius, saying, "You dare to fell me? Curse you, knave. If I have fallen, it is as love's slave." And he continued the scene as if the Bard had planned it all along.

It was masterful.

Puck soon remedied his mistake, and the lovers woke in the forest as if from a dream, with Demetrius in love with Helena and Lysander and Hermia reunited. At last, Puck addressed the theater: "'If we shadows have offended . . .'" he began, but Oliver stopped paying attention. He turned his head ever so slightly to see Finley, her eyes brimming, reciting the words along with Puck. He saw Tate's hand reach out for Finley's and give it a small squeeze, and he remembered something.

Her father had played Puck on Navy Pier almost exactly five years ago, the week of Finley's birthday. Liam had told him about it. Their family always made birthdays a huge deal, but her dad's filming schedule for *Supernova* had kept him from being there for the actual day. So when Finley's class took a field trip to see an amateur performance, her father called in a favor and came out playing Puck. When Finley saw her dad, Liam had said, she giggled until she cried.

Tate had remembered. *Tate.* For a moment, Oliver's will faltered. She shouldn't have to rely on his flaky brother; she should be able to rely on him. After all, Oliver was her best friend. She probably wanted to talk to him about it. *Needed* to talk to him. Surely, it wouldn't hurt—

He stopped himself.

No. He couldn't go there. He couldn't let himself fall back into being her main confidant when it meant falling for her, too. He had to back off; it was for her own good. It was for *his* sanity.

Puck's speech was over, and the cheering started. Oliver stood, clapping and whistling along with the rest of his party. Flowers were handed to the bowing players. The applause for each member of the cast was resounding. But the applause for Harlan was deafening.

He had stolen the show. And judging by the audience's reaction, his career in theater was guaranteed for life.

The cast returned backstage and the audience was quickly ushered out so the magic of converting the room into a dance floor could happen. On the way out of the theater, Finley, who was walking in front of him, glanced back. This theater was being changed into something else. He knew that was akin to sacrilege in her mind.

But he didn't ask her about it.

A text from Emma told him to gather everyone by the backstage entrance in thirty minutes so they could get their VIP passes for the club. Oliver relayed the information and told them he'd meet them there. He hung back, watching Tate flirt with Finley and Juliette fight with Raleigh, and counted down the minutes from thirty.

CHAPTER TEN

~*F*~

The gold wallpaper on the third floor of Vows felt different on Finley's fingertips than the wallpaper on the first two floors. She couldn't remember if it was newer or older. She wouldn't go back downstairs to check until she had to, and by then, she'd probably be too tired to care.

She walked by laughing groups and couples making out against walls. She poked her head into rooms with house music, Top 40, and even local bands. Everywhere she went, there were three constants: people, loud music, and alcohol. So much alcohol.

That's what made this wing of the barely lit third floor such a gem: it was empty. After nearly three hours on the verge of panic, she could finally breathe, deeply and slowly, relishing air that was free of the cloying stench of alcohol and bad memories.

When she'd first stepped into the main ballroom hours earlier, the sights and smells had assaulted her. Someone nearby had dropped a wine glass, and it shattered on the floor, taking Finley with it. She was back in the old apartment, hiding beneath the rickety kitchen table. Her mother was throwing glasses on the floor near Finley to punish her for saying she missed her dad. The glass exploded all around her, and she tucked her limbs inside one of Liam's jerseys to escape the worst of it. Liam had grabbed his mom's arm, and the pair had knocked into the chandelier, which cast manic, menacing shadows all over the dingy dining room.

The ballroom's strobe lights had pushed Finley over the edge. She'd tried to escape to an employee break room, but she'd forgotten her badge, so she'd holed up in a bathroom instead. She'd stayed there until she felt strong enough to wander the halls. And wander and wander.

She glanced down at her cracked, old flip phone. It was 12:26 a.m. This night had been miserable, although the play had been anything but. She kept going over and over the performance in her mind. Harlan's recovery when he tripped had been nothing short of world-class, even if something about it had been off. She'd been coming back to it for hours. He'd managed to look angry right away—not surprised. How was he not surprised?

Maybe he really was that good an actor. Or maybe watching the play beside Oliver had clouded her mind too much.

Oliver. No matter what he tried to tell her, he was avoiding her. It sucked that he hadn't talked to her tonight. She'd wanted to talk to him about . . . everything. Just like normal. But especially her dad. She couldn't enter a theater without missing him. Tonight, along with the constant triggers of her mother's alcoholism, had been especially difficult. Yet Oliver had eyes for Emma and Emma only.

It hurt.

Thank heavens for Tate. He'd been her sole distraction, her only comfort in an evening practically designed to set off every repressed PTSD symptom she could imagine.

She was turning a corner when she heard a low giggle. She stopped at the sound of a familiar voice.

"Mmm, Harley."

Against her better judgment, she popped her head around the corner and saw Juliette pressing Harlan against a wall, her fingers in his hair. "You know I have a boyfriend."

In the dim hallway, she saw Harlan smile. Juliette was kissing his jaw. "*I* know you have a boyfriend. Do you?"

Finley pulled her head back around to her side of the hallway. "I could have a new one, if you wanted," Juliette said.

There were more kissing sounds. Finley closed her eyes and was about to head back down the hallway when Juliette's voice stopped her. "Did you hear me?" she asked Harlan through more and more kisses.

"Mmm?" Harlan mumbled.

"I said I could have a new boyfriend, if you wanted." Juliette's voice was clearer now.

"Come on. You like me, I like you. Let's just focus on this. Right now."

"Are you saying that you *don't* want to date me?"

"I'm just saying—"

"That you don't want me for a girlfriend."

"Jules, I don't want *anyone* for a girlfriend. That's not my thing."

Juliette's laugh was harsh. "I can't believe I was about to break up with my boyfriend for you."

Harlan snorted. "Don't break up with Raleigh for me. Break up with him because he's a joke."

"You are unbelievable! After weeks of chasing me, this is all you wanted? Someone to hook up with?"

"I wasn't doing all the chasing, babe."

"Don't you 'babe' me. Go to hell, Harley!" The sound of furious footsteps spurred Finley to action. She ran down the hallway, ducking into yet another bathroom just before being seen.

She threw herself onto a teal chair and stared at her feet. *Poor Juliette*, she thought. *Poor Raleigh.*

She stayed in the bathroom with her thoughts until 1:00 a.m., when her phone vibrated.

Fin, 911 dwnstrs. Tate

Finley sprang up, running from the bathroom and her hidden

third floor wing. Bass sounds boomed in her ears and echoed in her chest. The hallways were crammed with people, and she had to wind through them to get to the main ballroom. She stopped and steeled herself.

She isn't in there. You can do this.

Finley barged into the room, where a dance floor now occupied the space of the stage, and booths and tables had replaced the theater seats. Breathing through only her mouth, she ran through the dark upper balcony, the neon and strobe lights taunting her. People had to scream at each other to be heard, and it was everything she could do not to flinch, not to remember her mom's screams.

She shook her head and focused, scanning the room as best she could. She couldn't see Tate anywhere. But she saw Harlan and one of his costars in the middle of the floor, surrounded by people eager to dance with him, touch him. Finley's eyes skipped past him, her heart beating in time with the frantic music.

She didn't want to be here.

She hoped Tate was okay.

A staircase led from the upper balcony down to the dance floor, and she fled down it, bumping an entwined couple with her clutch.

"Hey!" a voice cried just loud enough to be heard over the DJ.

Finley stopped and looked back up the stairs. The couple was Juliette and Raleigh. Juliette looked intense, Raleigh flush with happiness as he wiped lipstick from his mouth. "What's up, Fin? Having fun?" he yelled.

Finley jumped two stairs up and yelled in Juliette's ear. "Have you seen Tate? I got an urgent text from him."

Juliette rolled her eyes, cupping her hand around Finley's ear and pointing with her free hand. "He's at the bar, of course."

Finley darted down the stairs. The dance floor was packed. She squeezed herself through sweaty bodies, desperate to get to Tate. If not for her fear that something was wrong, she would have collapsed into a ball on the floor. She felt so small, so boxed in. The smells and bodies were overpowering. The lights disoriented her, making her feel as if she was trapped in a nightmare. With every blink, she saw her mother's hateful face raging at her. She tried to stop blinking.

Finally, she pressed herself through to the bar. Tate sat next to a small, angry-looking young man, laughing.

Finley snaked through to him, grabbing his arm and yelling, "Are you okay?"

Tate's face lit up. "Fin, you exquisite creature, you!" he exclaimed, his eyes a little too wide, his smile a little too loose. He was still happy, which meant he was only buzzed. A truly drunk Tate was a truly self-destructive Tate. He put a hand up to the side of her face, his thumb rubbing light circles on her temple. She breathed through her mouth and let the sensation calm her racing heart. "Meet my newly poor friend, Yates," he said.

Yates barely looked at Finley, but she didn't care. She locked eyes with Tate. "Are you sure you're okay?"

Tate's brows knit together, and for a moment, the cloud covering his bright blue eyes seemed to pass. He leaned toward her, bringing his face so near that she could have tasted his breath if she weren't trying to avoid tasting or smelling anything at all. "You came running for me?" he asked.

"Of course I did," she said, realizing too late how overly earnest she sounded. But she was too relieved that he was okay to filter herself, and Tate didn't seem to mind. He tucked a strand of hair behind her ear, leaving a trail of tingles where his fingers brushed her skin. Then he put his free hand softly on the back of her neck, peering at her the whole time. His touch was so careful, his gaze so intimate. And it was all so far beyond his normal flirtation.

What was going on here?

Their breaths mingled between them, and Finley couldn't help but study each angle of Tate's handsome face, each strobe light reflecting from his eyes. And he was doing the same with her. After weeks of being overlooked and ignored by her best friend, it felt good to have someone just look at her. See her. When he leaned in farther, she didn't draw back, though she knew she should.

Tate held her gaze.

Finley held her breath.

Gently, slowly, he brought her face closer. Closer. Then he tilted her chin just far enough away that his lips brushed her ear instead of her lips. His breath danced across her neck, setting off a tremble that went up and down her body. "You could save a guy. You know that, Fin? You're incredible."

She closed her eyes, swimming in the feeling of his words, letting the chaos all around her fade away.

But a heartbeat later, an arm was on hers, pulling her from Tate, yanking her from the moment.

"Fin!" Oliver yelled over the music. "Just the girl I was looking for."

Finley blinked, and the room rushed into focus. She looked at a bleary-eyed Oliver, then back at Tate. He ran his thumb over her face one last time, but he was already shaking off his stupor . . . or shaking it back on. "I think someone needs saving," Tate said.

Oliver was grabbing her arm, trying to tug her away, but she tugged back. "You're sure you're fine, Tate?" she asked. "You said it was an emergency." She held up her phone as a reminder.

He gave an exaggerated nod and an easy smile, all traces of his earlier intensity gone. "Oh, that! It wasn't for me. It was for Oliver," he said, gesturing to his impatient brother. "He was asking for you." For an instant, Tate's smile became real again. Then he winked and turned back to his friend.

Finley spun around to Oliver, who was practically dragging her to a semicircle of couches twenty yards away. "I have to sit down," he moaned over the thumping bass as they pushed through the crowd. He was acting so odd, sick even, that she almost regretted not having run to him instantly. Almost.

Finally, they reached the couches, and Oliver fell to the cushions, pulling her down beside him. His head tipped back and he started laughing. No, giggling.

"What the hell, Finley?" he said, staring up at the ceiling. "You let Tate break all the rules, but when I try, you go running. It's not fair!"

She frowned. "What are you talking about? What rules? And are you okay? Tate said you've been calling for me."

"Oh, right, because you always come running for Tate," he said with a hint of taunting.

Her eyebrows shot up. She grabbed his head, bringing it to face her when a wave of nausea struck her. He reeked of alcohol. It was nothing like Tate's barely-there vodka breath; this drink was coming out of Oliver's pores in a flood of rotten citrus. Instantly, she went tense. Her breathing sped up. The walls of the club faded away, and the kitchen walls were closing in on her. Adrenaline coursed through her body. Her muscles grew tighter and tighter, coiling for a flight she knew she couldn't take.

She couldn't believe how betrayed she felt. "Have . . . have you been drinking?"

"Never, Fin," he slurred. "You know I don't drink."

His breath was poison. She gagged, then gagged again. She swallowed and covered her nose. She couldn't break down now. Not now. "Ollie, where's your drink? What did you order?"

He waved a hand. "Oh, I just told them to get me that fruity Brazilian drink. You know, the one you like so much."

"*Guaraná?*"

He snapped, dropping his head back onto the cushion. "That's the one! I couldn't remember the name, so Emma got it for me. But I gotta tell you, this one tasted weeeeird."

Finley threw a hand over her face, remembering too well the stench of her mother's drink of choice. She squeezed her eyes

shut, wanting to block everything out, but that only left room for
memories.

She was in her room now, scurrying beneath her bed and hud-
dling in the corner as her mom stumbled drunk into the darkness.
She was shivering and plugging her ears while her mom cursed her
husband and screamed that *this drink* was the only good thing to
come out of Brazil. Finley was praying for her mom to pass out before she started looking for her, before she got really, really mad . . .

No. She wasn't with her mom. She was in a theater on a couch
with Oliver. And Oliver would never hurt her, not knowingly.

"They gave you a *caipirinha,* Ollie!" she cried, tears burning
her eyes. "It's like extreme alcohol!"

Oliver sat up, laughing. "That explains the taste!" He fell forward
against her, and she caught him awkwardly. She slid under his arm
and plopped him back against the couch, but he didn't release her.
She slumped against his side. The pungent odor was so strong; it
was everything she could do not to run. As it was, her entire body
was trembling as she disentangled herself from him.

"Ugh, I feel funny, Finney." The beat from the speakers punc-
tuated his laugh. "I mean, I feel funly. Funly? I mean . . . Finley." He
sat up and tilted his head so it was resting against the side of hers.
She had to breathe through her mouth to keep from throwing up.

"Just take it easy, Ollie. You need water and sleep. And we have
to get you home!" she said in his ear.

"Funny that you're here taking care of me, isn't it? When it's
usually the other way around?" His nose was almost touching her
cheek. "Emma thinks you're like a sister to me. Better than the one
I have." He snorted. "Except you're closer to me than that. Maybe
too close." He grabbed her face, turning it so their foreheads were
together. His eyes fixed onto hers, and he looked ragged. Wretched.
"You were so sad and broken when you came to us, Fin, and it hurt
so much to see. All I wanted to do was fix you, you know? So I made

all these rules, and now I can't handle them anymore, and Tate doesn't follow them, and you let him, and I can't take how badly I want to break the rules, but it's not right! And . . . and . . . I just can't care about you like that anymore."

Finley tore herself from his grasp, the tears in her eyes finally spilling, burning a trail down her cheeks. "What? Why are you saying this, Ollie? What did I do?"

He shook his head and yelled. "Nothing! That's the whole problem! You've never done anything! But I'm there, all the same, watching over you. I say I want you to be strong, but all the while I'm waiting to swoop in, waiting for you to need me! I can't go on like this. You can't need me the same way anymore if I'm going to move on." He dropped his head. "I need you not to need me."

Finley wrapped her arms around herself, feeling more exposed than she'd ever felt in her life. She was fighting so hard to stay in the present, but the present was only giving her more pain. She couldn't take it anymore.

A sob ripped through her chest. She jumped to her feet and ran.

"Finley!" Oliver yelled from behind her.

She elbowed her way through the floor, jostled like a pinball, not bothering to wipe her tears. Her eyes flew around the club, desperate for a place to hide. Finally, she caught sight of the Crawfords' VIP section. She waved her pass and stumbled past the bouncer.

Once through, she crashed onto a couch and shoved her face into a pillow, trying not to fall apart. She was drowning in the smell of alcohol and her memories. Yet all that agony was overshadowed by what Oliver had said to her.

He needed her to stop needing him. He wanted to move on.

And she knew, although he hadn't said it, it was because of Emma Crawford.

She hated the girl with a foreign, fiery passion. Hated her stupid hair and her stupid long legs and her stupid lovely face. She hated that she'd begun to see the girl as a friend. A close friend. And she hated that, even now, she couldn't really hate her.

It's not like Emma knew that Finley was in love with Oliver.

"Miss Price? Is that you? Are you okay?"

Finley's head flew up; a form leaned over her. Harlan. She shrank into the couch. "Don't get any closer! If I smell any more alcohol, I'm going to pass out," she shouted.

He dropped onto the couch beside her and put his hand against her forehead. She recoiled from his touch.

"You're acting strange. Did you drink something? Are you sick?"

She scowled and wiped her tears. "Of course I didn't drink something. But I'm not kidding. You have to back up. I think I'm going to hyperventilate."

He looked puzzled. "I'm not drunk, you know. I haven't had a sip," he said, as close to her ear as she'd let him get.

"Oh, sure. Right," she yelled back. She put her hands over her mouth and tried to regulate her breathing.

"Why would I lie to you?"

"I don't know . . . to save face? I saw you out there, dancing like you had a feral animal in your pants."

"Feral animal? Really? I guess *'Dancing with the Stars'* isn't in my future, huh?" He smiled. "I don't drink, and I'm not drunk, Miss Price."

"I've seen pictures of you drunk at clubs, *Mr. Crawford.*"

"I'm flattered that you pay so much attention," he said loudly. "But I'm surprised you believe everything the media shows you. TMZ is hardly the bastion of ethical journalism."

Bastion? She studied his face, multicolored lights bouncing all over it. "You're really not drunk?"

"Smell my breath. Breathalyze me. Whatever. I swear to you, I don't drink."

She put her hands down. "Why lie?"

"Publicity. My dad's my agent, you know, and he tells me where to go and how to act to best promote whatever movie I'm in at the moment. If it's a rom-com, I need to be seen publicly with a serious girlfriend. You know, out at dinner, holding hands at basketball games. If it's an action movie, I need to get caught speeding or cliff-jumping or something reckless."

"So why don't you drink? If you really don't drink, that is?"

He wrapped his hands around the glass in front of him and held it up to her to smell. On closer inspection, Finley realized his rum and Coke was virgin. He put the glass down.

"My mentor was killed by a drunk driver a few years ago. I promised myself I'd never risk someone else's life for something so meaningless."

Finley bit her lip. "Your mentor?"

"He was the kindest, most talented actor I've ever worked with. He's the real reason I'm in Chicago right now instead of New York."

"What do you mean?" The unsteadiness in her voice had nothing to do with having to shout to be heard.

Harlan moved closer. "About five years ago, I did a talking dog movie, as you so kindly pointed out when we met. And it was terrible. I was lambasted in the press. I almost quit acting altogether. My mentor gave me some advice that's always stayed with me. He said, 'Harley, when you feel like they're taking your soul, disappear into something that will let you find it again.' For him it was theater. When all the crap started happening in New York with my family, the pressure for exclusives, for me to reveal all the dirt I know about my own parents . . . it became overwhelming. I thought I'd take a page from my mentor's book."

Finley stared at his glass, which Harlan now clutched like an anchor. "He sounds really special. Who . . . who was he?"

Harlan paused. After a few seconds of no response, she looked up at him. "Your dad."

She broke their gaze, shaking her head. "You knew? I can't believe Emma told you."

"Emma didn't tell me anything. I've suspected it for a while, what with your speaking Portuguese and borderline fanaticism for all things theater. I didn't want to bring it up if you didn't."

A group of girls approached the velvet cord. "You were amazing, Harlan!"

"We loved it!"

"We love *you!*"

The bouncer loomed over them, but Harlan waved him down. He walked up to the velvet cord. He took their Sharpies and signed their limbs and chests while the girls giggled and snapped pictures with their phones.

After a few minutes, he came back to the couch, sitting closer than before. Finley leaned toward him. "That was really nice of you."

"What, signing those girls?"

"No, I mean about my dad. Not making it a big thing."

Harlan tapped his glass. "He meant a lot to me, too. How do you know I didn't keep from talking about it because it was hard for me?"

Finley studied his face. "I don't. But I guess that wouldn't surprise me."

He grinned. "Do you always say what you're thinking?"

She frowned. "No, actually."

"Should I be flattered?"

"Definitely not."

He laughed. "You don't like me, do you?"

She hesitated. Her body may have been wired to run, but her mind was ready to fight. The urge to scream at someone was overwhelming. She'd never known such a feeling.

"Should I? You kissed Juliette when she had a boyfriend, and you walked away when she offered to break up with him. How could I like someone who treats people like they're disposable?"

To her surprise, Harlan grimaced. "I can't believe she told you.

In case you hadn't noticed, Juliette wasn't exactly unwilling. But I wasn't trying to break them up."

The ear-splitting music spurred her anger. "That's even worse! If you didn't want to be with her, then why did you do what you did?"

"Because it's all I've ever known! Can you imagine if everything you saw from a parent was a lie? If they were one person in front of the world and another behind closed doors?" Finley started trembling. "When I was little, I idolized my dad. He was so famous and charming. But it changed him. He started thinking he deserved everything. Including people. You can't know what it was like. It's everything I can do *not* to become him."

Finley balled her fists, barely containing a fury that terrified her. "You have *no idea* what you're talking about. You didn't have to act like your dad, you chose to because it was easy. And I bet you've done the easy thing your whole life. Sure, you took a step away from the spotlight to regroup, but that's still for your benefit, isn't it? In the real world, people have to work hard to become who they want to be. They have to sacrifice what's easy for what's right! You can only act the way your dad wants so many times before you start becoming that guy. And if you ask me, you're pretty freaking close."

"Whoa!" he yelled, grabbing Finley's hand to pull her down. When had she stood up? She jerked her hand from his, and he recoiled. "Hey, I'm sorry, okay?"

"I'm not the one you need to apologize to. Juliette is. Raleigh, too, for that matter. And probably hundreds of other Juliettes and Raleighs—"

"Okay, I get—"

Shouting and retching interrupted them. Finley and Harlan jumped back as the velvet cord and stands crashed to the ground. And at their feet, kneeling in a pool of vomit, was Oliver.

CHAPTER ELEVEN

~𝓕~

Harlan helped Finley round everyone up to leave while Emma cleaned up Oliver. Finley didn't have the heart to see him. Or the stomach. Juliette seemed to suffer from a similar malady; she didn't even come to the VIP section. She and Raleigh simply took a cab home.

Because Harlan was the only sober one of the group with a driver's license, he took the car keys from Tate. He had a valet bring the SUV around to the back of the theater to avoid any media attention. As grateful as Finley was for the help, she was confused. Harlan wasn't drunk, and any attention he garnered would have been favorable after such a superb performance. So what was he doing?

Harlan and Tate each took one of Oliver's arms and dragged him through the theater's back entrance to the black SUV. They shoved Oliver into the middle seat, and Harlan handed the valet a handful of bills. "Thanks for the help, man," Harlan said before slipping into the driver's seat. Emma and Tate sat on either side of Oliver in the back, so Finley climbed into the front.

Harlan put the SUV in drive and headed out of the alley into the still-busy streets. He looked both ways when stopping at a red light. He used his blinker. He didn't check his phone as text upon text came in.

Who was he?

"Why are you doing this?" she asked.

Harlan glanced over at her. "What do you mean?"

"Why are you taking us home? You didn't need to do this. You're missing your own party. You avoided the media, even though the publicity would be great. Why?"

Harlan cocked his head. "What do you mean, the publicity would be great?"

"Because your performance was outstanding. Your . . . recovery was stronger than could be expected from most seasoned stage actors. I'd be surprised if critics don't consider your line about falling as love's slave an addition worthy of Shakespeare."

"Why did you say that so funny? My *recovery?*"

"Because you staged it. I can understand why—like I said, it was masterfully done. But you shouldn't have done it. Your performance was impressive enough."

Harlan laughed, shaking his head. "You are the strangest creature."

"What do you mean?"

"You can't stand me, yet you have no problem calling me out and complimenting me at the same time? I don't understand you, Miss Price."

"Why do you call me that?"

Harlan had a smile in his voice. "I honestly don't know. It just suits you. Would you rather I call you Finley? Or Fin?" She shifted. Hearing her name on his lips felt odd. Intimate. "In answer to your original question, though, I'm helping because Oliver is my friend. Isn't that what friends do?" He turned onto their street.

Finley leaned toward him, checking the backseat to make sure none of them were listening. "But after everything with Juliette, why would you—"

"There's hardly an 'everything' with Juliette," he said quietly. "She was using me more than even you could argue I was using her. Juliette liked me because I'm an upgrade: more famous and less absurd than Raleigh. I'm sure she'll remember all the perks of dating him when she joins his family on vacation next week or when Raleigh gets drafted."

As much as she wanted to, she couldn't argue with him. She'd thought the exact same thing when Juliette had first flirted with Harlan. But that didn't excuse what he'd done; it just evened out the blame.

She settled back into her seat. Lights were on inside the house. Maybe Aunt Mariah was still up. Harlan pressed the garage door opener and they pulled in.

Emma and Tate pushed and pulled, respectively, to get Oliver out of the vehicle. He moaned, grabbing his head, while Tate recruited Harlan's help getting the nearly unconscious boy into the house. Finley grabbed the back door. And her heart dropped.

Uncle Thomas was standing in the doorway, his arms folded across his chest. Even in pajamas, he looked terrifying.

"What is the meaning of this?"

Finley wanted to shrivel inside of her dress and heels. Uncle Thomas's eyes passed over her and the Crawfords. He looked at Tate, his brows tied together in fury.

"Is your brother drunk?"

Tate smiled. "Welcome home, Dad. It's not a big—"

"He means," Harlan interrupted, "it's not what it looks like, sir. Oliver was given the wrong drink."

Finley snapped to her senses. She looked at Uncle Thomas, trying not to tremble. "That's right, Uncle Thomas," she added breathily. "He asked for a *Guaraná*—you know, that Brazilian soda? They didn't know what it was, so they gave him a *caipirinha*. I swear."

Uncle Thomas stared down his son. "And Tate, can you imagine why a bartender wouldn't have carded a teenage boy? On the club's opening night? Or did he maybe have help?"

"I'm afraid that's our fault, Mr. Bertram," Harlan said, gesturing to his sister. "Emma and I gave everyone VIP passes, and it appears that the bartender didn't card him because of that. I guess he was afraid of offending us."

Uncle Thomas's nostrils flared. He waved them into the house. He breathed in deeply through his nose as Finley passed him, smelling her. Her throat tightened. How could he even imagine she'd drink? Yet he did the same with each of them, lingering on Emma.

"Juliette took a cab—" Harlan began.

"She got home fifteen minutes ago," Uncle Thomas said. He took over for Harlan, dragging Oliver into the kitchen and depositing him on a chair. Emma set Oliver's jacket on the counter.

"We're really sorry that this happened, Mr. Bertram," Emma said. "If we had known . . . well, we're just really sorry."

Uncle Thomas nodded. "Thank you for seeing the kids home, Harlan. Emma."

"Of course," Harlan said, handing him the keys. Then he looked at Finley. "I'll see you soon," he said, with a smile only she could see, "Miss Price."

Finley's ears went hot. She nodded. Emma hugged her as she left. "Text me tomorrow as soon as you're up," she whispered. Finley's stomach lurched. Emma's breath smelled exactly like rotten citrus.

Finley stared at the girl's back as Uncle Thomas saw her and her brother out. When he returned, he looked like he could spit fire.

"I don't think I need to tell either of you how disappointed I am," he said to Finley and Tate, gesturing to a moaning Oliver. She stared at her feet to hide her tears. "Tate, help your brother upstairs. I expect to see all of you in my study tomorrow morning. Seven o'clock sharp. Enjoy what little sleep you can get."

* * *

Uncle Thomas's words proved correct. At five to seven the next morning, after almost no sleep, Finley stood outside his study. Oliver was already in there. His back was to her, but he looked shaky. She couldn't hear what they were saying, but she could tell from the occasional sharpness that Uncle Thomas was still angry.

Tate ambled down the stairs, yawning. When he reached her, he draped his arm over her shoulders casually, but flirtatiously. As always. She wondered how much he remembered about last night, not that it mattered. He could remember every smoldering look and it wouldn't change anything. It was one of the things she liked most about him. "Don't worry, Fin. The first few minutes are always the worst. But he softens up in the end, every time. Especially if you aced your finals."

She almost smiled. But then the French door opened, and Oliver came out. His puffy eyes were bloodshot, and the shower he'd clearly just taken wasn't enough to wash off the stench of alcohol. Oliver didn't meet her gaze. He just walked to the stairs gingerly.

Uncle Thomas stood at the door. "Finley, please come in," he said, his voice softer than she had expected. He closed the door before crossing the room to sit at his desk. "Oliver explained that you had nothing to do with what happened last night. In fact, he was quite insistent that anything anyone did wrong last night had nothing to do with you." Then he smiled. "If it wasn't Oliver, I'd almost wonder what you two were hiding."

She smiled weakly.

He paused and cleared his throat. "We don't talk about your mother very often, but I hope that last night wasn't as difficult for you as I fear it was. I'm . . . I'm proud of you, Finley. You've grown into a lovely young woman. And you're stronger than you think."

A rush of warmth filled her chest. *Am I?* she wondered. Her pulse tripled. *Prove it.*

"Uncle Thomas, I wanted to ask you something," she said, hardly believing her own voice. "I'd like your permission to apply to the Mansfield Theater Youth Program."

He beamed, pulled a form from his desk, and slid it to her. "I thought you'd never ask."

Through a small smile and blurry eyes, Finley glanced down. She blinked at Uncle Thomas's signature at the bottom of her consent form. How had he known? Was this really happening?

"Once you've mailed that in, how would you like to get your friend next door and go shopping? She needs a good influence in her life, and you need a new smartphone to call Vows Theater."

She pulled her eyes from the page. "Call Vows? Why?"

"You have a full few months planned already, what with your volunteering and summer theater group. I think you should quit your job and enjoy yourself for a change. You've earned it."

His smile was so kind, and she didn't know how to handle it. His approval made her heart go haywire. "I . . . I'll think about it. Thanks, Uncle Thomas."

He reached into his wallet and handed her a stack of bills. Her eyes widened. "And please, get yourself some new outfits while you're out. You've had enough hand-me-downs, Finley. It's time for something new."

CHAPTER TWELVE

~ℱ~

That afternoon, Finley stood on the edges of her flip-flops waiting for someone to answer the Grants' door. After what felt like an hour, she was just turning to leave when the door opened.

"Going somewhere, Miss Price?" Harlan asked behind her.

Finley closed her eyes, then turned around. "I didn't think anyone was home."

Harlan looked amused. "Well, you certainly waited long enough, didn't you? You must have been standing here, what, seven whole seconds?"

She clenched her jaw. "Is Emma home?"

"She is," he said. "Come in."

He led her inside, closing the door behind her. She suddenly felt caged. "Emma's just on the phone with the *Chicago Tribune* entertainment editor, but she should be done in a minute. In the meantime, would you like to continue your lecture on the subject of my faults?"

Finley looked him in the eyes. "Sorry."

"Don't be sorry," he said. "It was invigorating, having someone tell me how they actually feel about me." He still wore that same look of smug amusement. Like he was laughing at her.

"Listen," she said, "I wasn't lecturing you, but if I'm the only person who's ever pointed out this stuff, then you need more real friends in your life and fewer people on the payroll."

Harlan's eyes widened. At the same time, the door to the Kelly-green den opened, and out walked Emma.

"Fin, you minx! I thought you were going to text me this morning. What happened?"

Finley stepped around Harlan, gripping her purse. "That's actually why I'm here. My uncle gave me money to get a new cell phone. He thought maybe you'd like to go pick one out with me."

Emma fell against the wall, sighing. "Does that mean he doesn't hate me?"

"Why would he hate you?"

"Right, because you didn't notice I was tipsy last night."

Oh, I did. "Well, um, I guess he wasn't too upset. He actually sort of insisted I take you with me. He even gave me money for regular shopping, too."

Emma perked up. "Why didn't you start with that, silly? I'll grab my purse and be back in a mo. Harley, call for a cab, will you?" she asked as she darted up the stairs.

Finley braced a sigh. More time with Harlan.

He sent a text off, then looked up at Finley, his arms folded tight across his chest. "You know, I'm not the coldhearted bastard you think I am."

Finley shook her head. "I don't think that."

"Then what *do* you think about me?"

"Honestly?" she asked. He nodded. "Most of the time, I *don't* think about you." Harlan turned a deep shade of red. Finley shook her head again. "I just mean, I don't think about you any more than I'm sure you think about me."

His eyes squinted, but his face was still flushed. "Well, maybe that's the problem," he said. She gave him a flat look, but he continued. "No, it is. Like, maybe if we were paying more attention to each other, I could have at least gotten more acting tips from you."

"You didn't need any tips from me."

"Because of my 'impressive performance'?"

She rolled her eyes. Of course he'd throw her words back in her face.

The sound of feet in the stairwell signaled that Emma was coming back down, but Harlan was undeterred. "Listen, whether you want the compliment or not, I owe you for last night."

Emma jumped the last few steps to the main floor, interrupting them. "It's true, Fin," she said. "You saved his butt by telling us to prepare for the random stuff that could happen on stage. You're sort of a theatrical genius." She was already opening the door to the outside, where a black car was waiting. "Now, enough. Let's go. Bye, Harley. Fin, wave bye!"

She waved without looking back.

"Michigan Avenue and Oak Street, please," Emma instructed the driver as they slid into the backseat. Finley wasn't even annoyed that the girl was taking over. Bossiness was part of the Emma Crawford experience.

Emma turned toward her as soon as they were settled. "Now, tell me everything. Was Mr. Bertram super angry? Are you guys in trouble?"

"Yes and no. He was really disappointed in us. I don't know if Tate and Oliver got in trouble, but I don't think so."

"And you clearly didn't, or he wouldn't have handed you money and told you to go shopping."

Finley glanced up at the driver, feeling embarrassed. "No. I think he just wants me to get out more."

Emma linked her arm in Finley's and sat back against the seat. "I've been telling you that for like two, three months? I'm glad I'm not the only who sees what you need. And don't try to tell me that Oliver does, too. We both know he sees what he wants to see. He can't imagine a world where you don't rely on him. It's sweet, really. But it's hardly flattering. You're a capable, intelligent girl. You don't need him."

Finley couldn't answer, didn't know how to process whether Emma was right or not. The girl's words reminded her too forcefully of what Oliver had said last night: *I need you not to need me. Whether or not I need him, that ship has sailed.*

The cab pulled over in front of the Drake Hotel and Finley gave the driver a twenty. She joined Emma at the top of the famed Magnificent Mile, feeling utterly overwhelmed.

Emma grinned at the brick buildings and teeming streets. "Don't worry, Fin. You're in good hands."

* * *

~O~

Oliver sat on the floor of the Grants' family room playing video games with Harlan. It was relaxing, this mindless game. And he needed mindless. All day, he'd beaten himself up over what had happened the night before at the club. He couldn't remember everything; it was a blur of words, urgency, and Finley's face. But underneath all that was a layer of shame. He had a sneaking suspicion he'd blamed Finley for his conflicted feelings, and the thought of putting his guilt on her made him feel sick. He needed to talk to her. He *had* to apologize.

Harlan's car overtook his, and Oliver jammed a button, shooting a rocket at Harlan. He missed.

"Hey, so I wanted to ask you something," Harlan said over the sound of an explosion.

"Shoot," Oliver said.

"Emma mentioned your volunteer group is pretty busy this summer. What would you think about me volunteering with you guys?"

Cars whizzed by Oliver. "You want to volunteer with M.A.D.? Seriously?"

"Yeah, seriously," Harlan said. He sounded annoyed. "Why is that such a surprise?"

Oliver jerked his remote, narrowly avoiding a crash. "No, dude, it's not a surprise, it's awesome. I just assumed you were going back to New York now that the play is over."

Harlan's car was creeping up on him again, so Oliver released nails all over the track, popping Harlan's tires and causing him to collide with a unicorn. "I've been thinking of taking the summer off to spend time with Emma, actually. And this way, I can take plenty of time picking my next project."

"What does your dad think?"

"He's furious. All the more reason to do it."

"Well, I think it's a great idea, and not just because M.A.D. could use the help."

Harlan tilted his remote, dodged a grenade, and breezed through the finish line. "Cool. Thanks, bro."

Oliver finished three cars behind him just as they heard the front door slam.

"Looks like our girls are back," Harlan said, tossing his remote. "Should we go say hi?"

Oliver's stomach twisted, but it was time. He needed to be with his girlfriend and his best friend together. And he needed to apologize. He followed Harlan to the stairwell, where Emma's voice carried up to them.

"Fin, I love you, but I still want to strangle you. You didn't want the Hermes bag, even though it was so gorgeous I wanted to make out with it. But you hardly bought enough clothes to last a week. Why even bring me along?"

Oliver wrinkled his nose at Emma's tone. Was the girl actually mad? At Finley?

They reached the bottom of the stairs, and Emma grinned when she saw them. She bounced over to Oliver and threw her arms around him, kissing him playfully. She tasted like Dr. Pepper and fries, and he liked it more than he should with his best friend and Emma's brother in the room. When she let go, he swallowed and looked at Finley. "Did you have fun?"

She looked flushed. "Yeah, though I think Emma was two seconds from drop-kicking me."

Oliver shifted. If Emma was really that angry—

But Emma was smiling at Finley. And Finley was smiling back. "Girl, I was going to karate chop you in the tatas," Emma said, causing Finley to laugh and Harlan to grin. Emma leaned into Oliver. "Seriously, Ollie, Fin is the worst shopping partner in history. I've had bodyguards who care more about accessories than this girl does. Do you know she was thinking of getting a plan without unlimited texts? I didn't even know they made those! What is wrong with her?"

Finley scoffed, and Harlan jumped in, teasing Emma. Oliver watched his friends, his girlfriend. This would be okay . . . once he apologized to Finley. Which he needed to do now.

He was about to ask to talk to her when Emma ducked under his arm.

"Anyway," she said, "what are you doing here, Ollie?"

He pointed at Harlan, who excused himself to take a call.

"I was waiting for you. But get this, Harlan's going to volunteer with M.A.D."

"Cool. Takes the monkey off my back," Emma said.

Oliver smiled. "Oh, you talk a big game, Ems, but aren't you a big supporter of the Animal Welfare League? I know I've seen pictures of you at some of their events."

She swatted his chest. "Googling pictures of me now, are you?"

"So you don't want to volunteer, too?" Finley asked. "Come on, it's fun."

Emma laughed. "Sweetie, ask me to give money, and I will

donate anytime you want." Then, turning to Oliver, she squeezed his cheeks and said, "Oh, don't make that disappointed face." She kissed him. "And speaking of donating, Fin, I heard you're in charge of a clothes drive? I have some stuff to donate, if you want it." Finley nodded. "Cool. Ollie, grab Harlan when he's done and come up, too."

Emma grabbed Finley's hand, about to drag her upstairs when Oliver's guts about exploded.

"Actually, I need to talk to Fin real quick," he said before he could back down.

"Fine. Just send her up when you're done," she said, swatting his butt before running up the stairs to her bedroom.

He didn't know whose face was redder—his or Finley's. She clutched her shoulder. She was clutching her shoulder because he'd made her feel vulnerable and ashamed. This was his fault.

"What did you—" she said.

"I'm so sorry—" he said at the same time.

She dropped her head. "Sorry."

"No! Don't apologize. I need to apologize to *you*." He wanted to put a hand on her shoulder, but the thought of touching her after whatever he'd said last night made him feel even worse. "I can't believe I let myself get drunk last night—I can only imagine how much that must have upset you." His voice was thick with emotion. "And I . . . I don't even know half of what I said to you, but I know it was all wrong. Fin, you're my best friend, and I . . . care about you more than I can say. I never want that to change. Can you forgive me?"

Her mouth was pinched. "Just . . . just warn me if you're going to drink again, okay? I don't think I can be around it—"

"I'm not drinking again, Fin. Not for years. Maybe not ever." He clutched his head and stomach and pretended to puke.

Her smile was weak, but it was there. "I'm going to go upstairs."

"Okay. And seriously, I'm really sorry, Fin."

"Thanks, Ollie."

* * *

Twenty minutes later, Oliver and Harlan were up in Emma's room, where Finley was sorting shoes and clothes into bags. Three bags in all.

Oliver's eyes went wide. "That's a lot of clothes."

Emma danced over to him and kissed his cheek. "And I'm a lot of nice. Would you guys mind taking everything downstairs for Fin?"

"Sure," Harlan said.

Finley stifled a yawn. "Thanks. I'm going to head home. I don't think I can handle looking at any more clothes." She half-smiled at Emma. "And thanks again, Ems. I had fun today, Hermes bag aside." Emma laughed and rolled her eyes. Harlan followed Finley out to the hallway.

"I'll see you out," Harlan told her, turning back to wink at Emma.

When they left, Emma wrapped her arms around Oliver. "What was that about?" Oliver asked.

She kissed his jaw, and his skin tingled, radiating out to his whole body. "You mean my being so selfless and nice?" she mumbled in his ear.

It took him a long moment to pull his thoughts together. "Mmm. No, I mean Harley being nice to her. I thought they didn't get along."

"Oh, funniest thing! I guess they were talking last night in the VIP room for a while, and she was calling him on what a crappy person he can be. He's never had anyone talk to him like that—besides yours truly, of course—and I think he kind of liked it."

Oliver's head cleared and he backed away slightly. "What do you mean? Do you think he *likes* her? I don't know if that's a good idea."

Her arms still around his neck, Emma arched an eyebrow and pulled him closer. "I'm bored with this conversation." She leaned into him slowly, teasing him with her mouth. "I think it's time we moved on to something else. Don't you?"

His eyes closed as Emma's lips trailed across his neck and jaw, stopping just short of his mouth. He waited for a kiss, but instead, he felt her nose bump into his. He opened his eyes, tasting her breath, getting drunk on her smell. He wanted more. He stared at her lips and tried to gather his thoughts, but she was just so . . . hot. He cupped her face in his hands. "Yes. Move on. Let's. Now." He caught a glimpse of her lips turning upward just before his mouth landed on hers.

CHAPTER THIRTEEN

~*F*~

The next day, Finley felt different. As if the second act had just begun in a three-act play. Her talk with Oliver yesterday had been difficult. As much as she'd tried to process what he'd said when he was drunk, she couldn't figure it out. So instead of replaying it over and over in her head, she'd decided to accept his apology and move on. Just as he was doing. With Emma.

Stop it, she told herself. *We're past this, remember? Just focus on the fact that Liam's coming home and Harlan will be out of town all week doing interviews. It's a new day.*

It *was* a new day. Sure, Emma and Oliver were together now, but she liked Emma. Being around them as a couple was not, in fact, the worst thing that she could imagine, even if her insides knotted up whenever they kissed.

And she wasn't avoiding them by reading in the library instead of hanging out with them on the roof-deck. It just looked like rain. Really.

The call for dinner sounded throughout the house, as hollow as her lie. She closed her book and waited until she heard Oliver and Emma pass before heading down. She was just turning for the kitchen when the front door opened, and in came Juliette. She walked past Finley without looking at her.

Good to see you, too.

Finley followed her down the long hallway to the dining room, where everyone was already seated, including Nora and Emma. Uncle Thomas smiled at her while she sat down and the cook served dinner.

"I can't say how much I missed you all the last few weeks," he said. "I'm so happy to see each of you."

He grabbed his wife's hand and smiled around the table again before digging into his meal. Everyone began eating and talking. Juliette stewed in silence across from them.

Partway through dinner, Uncle Thomas was explaining how the arguments went. Nora peppered him with questions about the justices, and Aunt Mariah tutted when Uncle Thomas made a rude comment about one of their hairpieces.

"How was Juana through all of it, Uncle Thomas? How's her son?" Finley asked.

Uncle Thomas focused on Finley, his eyebrows uncharacteristically arched. "Thank you for asking, Finley. Juana was stronger than I could have hoped. Her son has been getting very good care. In fact, he's just taken his first steps."

She cleared her throat, wishing her heart wasn't pounding so much. She felt Nora's eyes burning into her. "You were both great on *60 Minutes*. No matter what the court decides, I'm sure public opinion is in your favor."

"Thank you, Finley," he said. "I hope so."

Nora's perfectly manicured red nails rapped her glass. "Thomas, I just hope you'll reconsider running for state attorney general—"

"I won't, Nora. You know I'm not interested in politics," Uncle Thomas said.

"You're being shortsighted, Thomas," Nora said. "The exposure would be incredible for business, and Rushworth already said he'd support—"

"Nora," Uncle Thomas said, a hint of chastisement in his voice, "I'm not interested."

Nora huffed, turning toward Juliette. "You've been quiet, dear. How was your day? Are you looking forward to going on vacation with Raleigh and his family?"

"Sure."

An awkward pause followed, and even Nora didn't seem to know how to respond.

"So, you guys are going to Costa Rica tomorrow, right?" Emma asked. "I'm so jealous. And I'm sure Harley will be disappointed he couldn't say good-bye to you two lovebirds."

Juliette's eyes flew to Emma's. "So . . . he's not coming back this week, then?"

"No," Emma said. "His interview schedule has him out of town until at least next week."

Juliette stared down at her plate.

Uncle Thomas set down his utensils. "Juliette, you don't have to go if you don't want to. The Rushworths would understand if we told them you wanted to spend time with me after I was gone for so long." He smiled at her.

"Not want to go?" Nora said. "That's absurd. Of course she wants to go, don't you, Juliette? They vacation with at least half a dozen of Chicago's most influential families."

Juliette's reluctance vanished. She pasted an excited grin on her face. "I'm fine, Daddy. Seriously, who wouldn't want three weeks in Costa Rica? It's going to be amazing!"

"Are you sure, sweetie?" Uncle Thomas asked.

"Positive."

"All right. Mariah, should we call the Rushworths to make sure Juliette has everything she needs?"

Aunt Mariah nodded, but Nora patted her sister's hand. "Why don't I call for you?" Nora asked. "You two must want to enjoy your time together now that Thomas is back."

The corner of Aunt Mariah's mouth rose. "Thank you, Nora. That would be helpful."

Nora put down her napkin. "I'll take care of it now. It was a lovely dinner, Mariah, Thomas."

They all said their good-byes to Nora, and moments later, Juliette asked to be excused so she could pack.

"I worry it'll be lonely for you both with Tate and Juliette gone," Aunt Mariah said to Oliver and Finley.

Finley smiled. "Not with Liam getting home this weekend."

"It'll be wonderful to see him," Aunt Mariah agreed. "Oh, and Thomas, while the Grants are out of town next week, I've given Emma and Harlan a standing invitation for dinner."

"Excellent idea," Uncle Thomas said, turning to wink at Finley and Oliver. "I'm sure the kids won't mind, either."

Oliver put an arm around Emma and said something to his mom, but all Finley could think about was Oliver and Emma having even more time together. Then a second thought came to her mind: What humiliations would Harlan Crawford have in store for her? She forced both thoughts from her mind. Liam was coming home. Nothing else mattered.

* * *

~O~

The next morning, Oliver was heading down the stairs for a late breakfast/early lunch in his pajamas. He'd been sleeping in for the last few days, but when he bumped into Finley coming down from her room, he saw she hadn't been. At least not today. She was already dressed for the day and wearing a new . . . everything. He didn't recognize a single thing, except her flip-flops, with the small Brazilian flag on each strap.

He stopped and waited for her to catch up. "You look nice."

"Thanks. You're . . . really working those pajamas."

He chuckled and dropped his voice low, like he was trying—and failing—to sound sexy. "Yeah, girl. You know I am . . ." He paused. "That was awkward, right? It felt awkward."

"Super awkward." She laughed. "So, uh, how are things going with Emma?"

"Good."

Good? he thought. *That's weak. You gotta say more than that.*

"Really good. She's awesome."

Fin nodded. "I'm glad. I think you're going to be really good for her."

"What do you mean?"

"Just that she's had a pretty skewed upbringing because of her parents. It'll be nice for her to see the good in people, I think."

Oliver smiled as they entered the breakfast nook. "I think she'll see that more from being your friend than she will from being my, um, girlfriend." He stuffed a piece of bacon in his mouth. "Anyway, what are you up to today?"

"First day of—"

The doorbell interrupted her. Fin got up to get the door and returned a minute later looking as if someone had peed on her toast. When Harlan appeared behind her with Emma, Oliver understood why.

"Hey, buddy. What are you doing back early?" Oliver asked, gesturing for Harlan to sit down and giving Emma a side hug when she sat beside him. The stripe in her hair was back to a bold green, which matched her oversized pajama shirt.

"Misdirection at its finest," Harlan said, snagging a waffle from a plate. He offered the plate to Finley, but she refused. "I finished my interviews yesterday and talked all about my vacation plans. Then I sent my double to Florida for a few weeks, along with a couple of bodyguards. TMZ and E! should be too busy trying to catch pictures of my double doing something stupid to know I'm here."

Oliver laughed. "Nice."

"Anyway, it's good to see you guys." Then he turned to Fin. "Miss Price, you look lovely this morning."

Fin hid behind her hair.

"Excuse me," Oliver said, feigning offense. "Am I chopped liver?"

"Shh," Harlan said. "Don't spoil the moment. There's still a chance that she'll respond."

"Harley, you're going about this all wrong. Our dear Finley hates being noticed as much as most other girls hate being ignored," Emma said, popping a grape in her mouth. "Anyway, Fin, why are you already dressed for the day? I know why Harley is, and, P.S., it's right up your alley, but why you? Please don't tell me you got another job."

Finley grabbed a waffle. "No, I didn't get another job. I have a production meeting. The past few summers, I've volunteered doing sets and stuff for an amateur theater company. My drama teacher at school is the director of the company, and he reserves the summer play for high school and college students to give us experience. Anyway, he told me he has something big in store for me this summer, and if I don't take it, he's sticking me on a run crew. So," she spread her arms, "Clark Street Community Theater, here I come."

"President Price," Oliver bowed. Fin threw a crumpled napkin at his face. "But I thought it started next week. Why are you going in today?"

"I actually don't know. Mr. Weston sent a handful of us an email and asked us to come in this week."

"Well, have fun," he said before looking at the others. Emma and Harlan were grinning at each other. "What are you guys smiling about?"

"This is too perfect!" Emma said to Finley.

"What is?"

"You and Harlan are doing the same thing! It's all part of his ongoing effort to give back to the community. Very noble, isn't it?"

She squeezed her brother's cheeks. "And to think, he came up with the idea all on his own."

Fin's doe eyes were caught in headlights. "Wait, he's volunteering with *Clark Street Community Theater?* No. No! Of course he's not." She turned to Harlan. "Tell her. Of course you're not."

"I wouldn't dream of contradicting my sister. Especially when she's right."

"That's it." Emma clapped. "Ollie, honey, get dressed. We're walking the kids to school."

* * *

Harlan and Emma donned their full disguises for the quarter-mile walk to the community center. Harlan was telling his sister about his interviews while, next to Oliver, Finley was seething.

"Stop grinding your teeth," he muttered to her. "You chucked your night guard, remember?"

"This isn't funny," she said. "Why is he doing this? Is he getting back at me or something?"

"For what, Fin? Come on. He's trying to avoid becoming like his dad. Giving back to the community is hardly a bad thing."

She frowned. The sun reflected off her sunglasses and blinded him for a moment. "Do you really think he didn't know I'd be involved?"

"How would he have known? Did you mention it to anyone? I know I didn't."

After a pause, she shook her head. "I just don't trust him."

Oliver looked at Harlan, so animated and happy talking to his sister. Over the past couple of months, they'd become friends. He liked Harley. But he didn't want him dating Fin—

Stop it. You don't get to decide this for either of them. Now be supportive.

"I'm not saying you should trust him, just that it's okay to play nice. He's going to be around a lot this summer, and it'll be easier if you guys can at least get along, won't it?"

"I make no promises."

Emma laughed loudly at something Harlan said, then pushed him away. "Okay, now you're just being ridiculous. Go. I need less brother, more boyfriend." She grabbed Oliver's arm and pulled him ahead next to her.

"I didn't mean to put you on the spot earlier when I said you looked pretty," Harlan said to Finley a moment later. Oliver tuned out the conversation behind him.

"So, Emma, any chance I can get you to volunteer with us this weekend?"

Her laughter rang like chimes. "You're really set on this, aren't you? It's not that I'm against volunteerism and helping the downtrodden, etc., but I prefer to volunteer in my own way. Like, I donated over a foot of hair a couple years ago."

"That's true," Harlan said from behind them. "When you were going through that pixie-cut phase, right?"

A pink tinge coming to her cheeks, Emma turned and smacked her brother's shoulder. They stopped at the light across from the community center.

"*And* I donate all my old clothes and electronics, *and* I visited two different children's hospitals in Manhattan earlier this year." The light changed, and she marched across the street.

Oliver squeezed her hand. "You don't have to defend yourself. I just want to spend more time with you."

She peeked at him from the corner of her eye. "Nice save."

At the community center, Emma stopped the group and put her hands on Finley's shoulders. "Okay, sweetie. Remember, you are strong and smart and beautiful. You can do anything you set your mind to. Never drink anything someone else gives you. And don't run with scissors."

Finley rolled her eyes but couldn't keep from smiling. "Bye, guys," she said, walking inside. Harlan followed.

"Bye, Fin," Oliver whispered.

CHAPTER FOURTEEN

~ℱ~

The director of the summer theater, Isaiah Weston, smiled at Finley when she entered the room. He was a long-retired actor whose portrayal of Othello on Broadway had made him famous in the eighties. He was also one of the few people who knew about Finley's application to the Mansfield Theater Youth Program; he'd written one of her letters of recommendation. She sat next to his granddaughter, Anaya, whom she also knew from school.

Anaya was fiddling with a dreadlock. She dropped it when Harlan sat on Finley's other side.

"Is that—?"

Finley groaned. "Don't ask."

Mr. Weston came over and smiled at Finley and Anaya before shaking Harlan's hand. "We were so happy to get your call. Thank you for donating your immense talent."

"It's my pleasure, sir. Thanks for letting me be here."

Mr. Weston looked at Finley over his glasses. "Are you ready to stretch yourself?"

Her foot bounced. "I guess we'll see."

Mr. Weston returned to the front of the room and greeted the last member of the production crew. Harlan leaned over to Finley.

"So you don't know what you'll be doing?" he asked. "What are you hoping for?"

"I don't know. Stage manager."

"Stage manager? It's a waste of your talent."

"Are you kidding? It's a huge responsibility."

"Which you've already shown you can do. No, you're going to be AD. Just watch."

She let out a sharp laugh. "Assistant director? That sounds likely."

When he didn't answer right away, she glanced over to see his eyes roaming her face a bit too carefully. "You really can't see how valuable you are, can you?"

"Right, and you can?"

"At least as well as Rosa and your theater buddies from school. Why *wouldn't* he ask you?" Harlan shook his head. "You're just too scared to believe in yourself."

It was everything she could do not to scream at him. Instead, she asked, "Who do you think you are? You don't speak for me."

Thankfully that shut him up.

After Mr. Weston's opening remarks about the importance of theater in the community, he made introductions. Finley recognized a few of the production crew and designers from last year. When Mr. Weston introduced Anaya as the costume designer, Finley's insides bubbled like a can of shaken soda. The moment of truth . . .

"And now, I'd like to introduce my prize pupil. Sorry, Anaya," Mr. Weston said. Anaya and the others all laughed. "Most of you already know Finley Price, but this year, you'll know her as my assistant director," Mr. Weston said, emphasizing the words in a rich baritone that dared her to refuse. "Won't they, Finley?"

Her smile wasn't fooling anyone, but at least she wasn't throwing up. "You're the boss," she said.

He chuckled and began introducing Harlan. She was already too worried about letting Mr. Weston down to listen to what Harlan would be doing—shadowing, maybe? Pestering her, certainly.

"Told you," Harlan whispered after Mr. Weston moved on.

Too bad all eyes were still on Harlan and, by extension, her. "Shut. Up."

From the corner of her eye, she saw him smile.

Mr. Weston finished introductions and passed around agendas before taking a seat. "You're probably wondering why I asked you to come in this week, so I'll refer you to the question at the top of your agenda: What play should we perform?"

Finley's wasn't the only confused face. Plays were typically selected before the beginning of the season. This particular play—an original—had been announced months earlier. "Our esteemed playwright is currently facing some . . . embarrassing legal issues. The board and I feel it's best to distance ourselves from the scandal."

The nods from the designers told Finley they already knew this.

"I have included a list of plays that the designers and I feel are feasible with our budget and timeframe. Because you all want to make theater a career, I brought you in early this week to show you what goes into the decision-making process, like the budget, design, and build schedules. But rehearsals still start next week, so we are on a tight schedule. By tomorrow, if the group has not selected a play together, Finley and I will decide."

Finley thrust her nose into the agenda, already scribbling notes.

"And with that," Mr. Weston said, "I'll turn the time over to you. Talk amongst yourselves until break. We'll come back together afterward to narrow down the list."

Soon, the room was buzzing with conversation. None of the plays were new to Finley or, judging by his running commentary, to Harlan.

"Overdone, overdone, overrated, boring, overdone, classic—"

"You just called *The Little Mermaid* boring, *Newsies* overdone, yet *Our Town* is the classic? It's one of the most performed plays of all time. Let me guess; if it were up to you, we'd put on *Romeo and Juliet* for the sheer novelty."

He leaned over to see her notes. "Says the girl who circled *West*

Side Story. Or do you think a derivative work managed to improve on Shakespeare?"

"On the story, no, but on the tragedy, absolutely."

He turned so his whole body seemed fixed on her. "Are you out of your mind? You think a *musical* is more tragic than one of the most tragic works in literature?"

His tone made her want to breathe fire. "All both couples want is to be together—now and forever. Romeo and Juliet both die. Both families are devastated, naturally, but neither lover has to live without the other. Meanwhile, Tony is killed, but Maria lives. They don't get to be together in life or in death. Instead, Maria has to live out the rest of her life with this heavy weight on her. Who knows if she'll ever get over it, and what her hatred could do to future generations? She was such a light, beautiful person who becomes a damaged, bitter shell of her former self."

Harlan huffed. "Romeo and Juliet are kids who commit suicide rather than live without each other. A huge part of their tragedy is that they live in a world that drives them to do something so desperate."

"Tony was shot in a world of gang violence where your accent or the color of your skin signs your death warrant. Is that really better?" she asked.

"Tony didn't have to get shot. He was *looking* to get killed because he thought Maria was dead!"

Finley laughed. "And Romeo wasn't? Romeo couldn't stand a world without Juliet so he killed himself rather than pause for ten seconds to think things through—or, you know, see if she was breathing! And then Juliet wakes up to find him dead and refuses to live without him? Would it kill these two to brave a world with actual heartbreak?"

"Oh, come on," he said. "Like Maria's so brave and thoughtful? As if she isn't a coward for not just standing up to her family before everything spiraled out of control—"

"Uh, do you hear yourself, Harlan?"

His face darkened. "You don't know what you're talking about."

"You just said that cowards don't stand up to their families, or were you not talking about—"

He jumped up. "Don't—"

"Okay, okay," Mr. Weston's voice cut over their argument.

Harlan dropped heavily to his seat, running his hands through his hair. Finley looked around the room, but the others were too busy with their own arguments to notice. "I'm so sorry, Mr. Weston."

"No apologies necessary. What is theater without passion?" He smiled. "That said, your objections to both plays are noted."

Emotions were running high all around the room, so Mr. Weston called the break early. Finley walked over to one of the community center's kitchens, where she shoved quarters into a vending machine. When her Mountain Dew didn't come out, she smacked the side of the machine. Nothing. She smacked it again. Again. And again.

"Are you imagining that's me?"

She whipped around to see Harlan looking almost sheepish. A strange mixture of emotions swarmed her. She felt annoyed at seeing him, upset by how her emotions had overcome her, and . . . and . . .

Exhilarated.

She'd never argued with someone like that before. But she cared so little for his opinion that she didn't have to filter herself as she did with everyone else. It was freeing, if scary. So much anger was buried inside of her. Something about Harlan made her want to let it all out.

"Still deluding yourself that I think about you, huh? No, I just really wanted that Mountain Dew."

With a nod, Harlan walked across the linoleum and put his own quarters into the machine. He pressed the button for Dr. Pepper and—of course—two sodas came out. He held one out to her with a rueful laugh. "I don't suppose you'd—"

"Yeah, thanks." She took the soda. "And, um, I'm sorry for earlier. I shouldn't have said that about you and your family."

"I got mad because you're right. It was a hypocritical thing to say." He faced her. "I know you don't like me—you've made that abundantly clear. But you of all people should know that what the tabloids say about someone is hardly true."

"The tabloids have nothing to do with my opinion of you," she said, although a part of her realized it wasn't true. All of the times she'd seen him drunk and disorderly had certainly made a mark. If that was all just a ruse . . . well, it didn't matter. She'd still seen him with Juliette. And he was still an insufferable, cocky jerk.

He looked genuinely upset. "You don't think I know what a jackass I've been? I'm trying here."

She studied him. Every inch of his face was famous, but she hadn't seen him look like this before. Styled hair messy, full mouth tight, piercing eyes a bit too wide. "Trying what, exactly?"

He seemed to be taking in just as much of her. "I honestly don't know."

Anaya ducked her head into the kitchen. "Hey, guys. Sorry to interrupt, but break is over."

Harlan took one long drink of his soda, then threw the rest in the trash and walked out. Biting her lip, Finley followed.

* * *

The next day, Finley got a text from Harlan asking if she wanted to walk with him to the theater. She didn't respond. She even snuck out of the house early to avoid the possibility of running into him.

She shouldn't have bothered. He was sitting on her stoop, waiting for her. At least he had an extra Mountain Dew with him.

He hopped up. "Miss Price."

"Why are you smiling?" she asked, taking the soda and walking down the stairs.

He kept up. "You have a problem with me smiling now?"

"When it's like that, I do."

"And how am I smiling, exactly?"

She squinted, annoyed she forgot her sunglasses. "Puckishly."

Their walk over wasn't as hostile as she'd expected it to be. He mostly asked her questions, and the only way to get him to stop asking was to answer. They were all theater and film related, fortunately, so they were hardly topics outside of either of their comfort zones.

Halfway through a discussion about a recent "Greatest Comedies of All Time" list, they reached the community center.

Harlan opened the door for her. "You can say *Fargo* is the better film—"

"But to include it and leave out *O Brother, Where Art Thou?*—" she said.

He nodded. "It's absurd."

"Exactly," she said. "And did you notice the same director kept coming up?"

"I know," he said. "Didn't he have something like eight films on the list?"

"Which is at least six too many."

"It's just another example of how the industry is run by old, rich, white men. There's no explanation for the lack of diversity."

His words surprised her. "What would you have included?"

"Offhand, *The Legend of Drunken Master. Friday. I'm Gonna Git You Sucka. Pitch Perfect.*"

She nodded. It was a good list.

Anaya arrived a few minutes later, and Harlan invited her into the discussion. He was nice and funny with her, even though her knowledge of movies was lacking. Harlan invited a few more people to join the discussion as they walked in, and he was equally polite and interested. When two pretty college girls joined the group, Harlan didn't pay them any more attention than he did the others. He schmoozed and charmed everyone equally, smiled and laughed with everyone individually. Yet these people had nothing to offer him. What was he doing?

The meeting started right on time, and Finley leaned over to Harlan just as Mr. Weston welcomed everyone. "What was all that back there with the crew?"

He kept his eyes on Mr. Weston. "Just something I learned from your dad."

The previous meeting had ended with the group having narrowed the list down to three plays. Today, Mr. Weston reminded them that the play needed to be chosen by the first break, and he asked everyone to keep an open mind as the discussion began. Quickly, people were arguing for one play over another. One of the college girls, Sasha, kept eyeing Harlan. He didn't seem to notice.

The subject of putting on a family-friendly play or an edgy production came up, and Sasha grew more and more adamant. "People go to their kids' middle school plays for family fun. I just think we should branch out," she said, gesturing to Harlan. "And with all due respect, Shakespeare is really overdone."

Beside Finley, Harlan snickered softly. He covered his mouth with his agenda and whispered to Finley, "I think you and Sasha might agree on *Romeo and Juliet.*"

"I said it wasn't novel, not that it was overdone. It's freaking Shakespeare," Finley muttered.

"Uh-huh, sure," he said.

"We need to be bold and push the envelope," Sasha was saying. "Do something like *Equus* or *The Full Monty.*"

"Those plays aren't even on the list," Finley groaned to Anaya. The girl didn't hear her. But Harlan did.

"Didn't you get the memo?" Harlan whispered. "Sasha's just here to see a dude's wang."

Finley bit back a laugh. "You know she thinks *you're* starring in our production, right?"

"Are you serious?"

"Why else would she look so *excited?*"

Harlan held the paper higher, hiding his laughter.

Someone disagreed with Sasha, and the girl bristled. "I want to be true to our theatrical roots! The purpose of theater is to challenge the human experience, to elicit growth—"

Harlan's snort was too loud to hide; he jumped up and ran for the drinking fountain, pretending to cough.

Finley wanted to run laughing right beside him. Instead, she wiped her expression as Mr. Weston turned to her. "Finley, I'd be interested to hear your thoughts."

She clutched her folder. "I know what you're trying to say, Sasha, but I think Shakespeare is done so often for exactly the reasons you're mentioning. He examines the spectrum of human emotions, and personally I think every one of his plays touches something deep inside of people."

The girl's friend asked, "So you think we should do Shakespeare?"

Finley barely noticed Harlan sneak into his seat. "I'm saying that we don't need to pave new ground to be bold or meaningful. We've already narrowed it down to some great plays. I think if we focus on the audience experience, we'll find the right one."

The discussion moved on, and Harlan leaned over. "I'd have gone with 'keep it in your pants, ladies,' but that was well said, Miss Price."

She side-eyed him. "Thanks, Mr. Crawford."

CHAPTER FIFTEEN

~*F*~

Mr. Weston held Finley back after the meeting to discuss some technical matters. So when she was about to leave, she was surprised to see Harlan and the sound designer putting chairs away. When she heard her name, she ducked back around the corner before they could see her.

"So is there something going on between you and that Finley chick?" the guy asked.

She was pretty sure his name was Dylan. She was equally sure Harlan was about to laugh in his face.

He didn't. "Why do you ask?"

"She's kinda hot. I'd get with that—"

"Dude, you don't even know her."

"I'm just sayin'."

"Well, don't." Harlan stacked a chair against the wall with a loud clang.

This needed to end. She made some unnecessary noise before walking around the corner. "Oh, hey, guys."

"Hey, Finley." Dylan's smile made her skin itch. She gave him an awkward wave, clutching her bag tighter.

Harlan's gaze darted from Dylan to her. "Hey, you mind if I walk out with you?" Before she could answer, he was ushering her outside into the soft rain.

She shook off his hand from her back. "What are you doing?"

"Trying to get you away from that creep. Why are you mad at me?"

"Because the only reason that creep even noticed me is because you've made me noticeable."

"How did I make you noticeable?" Thunder cracked through the air, competing with the noisy streets.

"You're paying attention to me. I've gone almost seventeen years without guys like that knowing I exist, yet all of a sudden, I have one leering at me in the only place in the world where I feel comfortable. Do you know how badly that sucks?"

"Have you considered that he noticed you *because* you're comfortable? You let yourself be seen in that room in a way you don't anywhere else. And news flash, Miss Price," he said sarcastically, the rain misting his face, "you're beautiful. People notice you." She didn't know what to say to that, but Harlan wasn't finished. "Also, actors are pigs, so you'd better get used to getting hit on by guys a lot worse than him. You have to learn to shut them down because they're not going to learn to stop sucking."

He was fuming when they crossed the street. "Why are *you* mad now?" she asked.

"Because I should have stopped that douche back there, and I didn't, and now you're uncomfortable." His hands were jammed in his pockets, probably to keep his ten-thousand-dollar watch out of the sprinkling rain.

"I don't need you to shut anyone down."

Two minutes away from Mansfield Square, another clap of thunder shook the sky. Instantly, a downpour drenched them.

"You have to be kidding," Harlan yelled at the sky.

"It's just a little rain, dude. Calm down."

"Dude?" Interest replaced frustration on his face "Did you just call me 'dude'?"

Water dripped off her lashes. "Yeah. Why?"

"You don't hate me anymore."

"I wouldn't go that far."

Harlan stepped around a puddle near their houses, but Finley went through it. One of her flip-flops struck the water at an angle, causing her to skid forward. She slipped, squealing. Harlan turned just in time for Finley to knock into him and grab his shirt, trying to catch herself. He toppled backward. She fell with him, landing directly on top of him. For a moment, their faces were almost touching. Then she recoiled.

Harlan winced. "Oh, that's gonna leave a mark."

"I'm so sorry!" Finley rolled off of him and fell butt-first directly into the puddle. She jumped up, feeling the back pocket of her jeans. Her phone. "You have to be kidding!" she screamed.

He eased himself up, dripping wet. "It's just a little rain, *dude*," he teased.

She pulled the phone out and pressed the home button. An image flickered to life, then faded. She jammed the button over and over, but nothing happened. "I've ruined it. After wasting Uncle Thomas's money . . . he'll be so upset."

Harlan grabbed Finley's elbow and guided her beneath an awning where they were sheltered from the rain. "It's not a big deal. I have an old phone—"

"No, absolutely not," she said.

He rolled his eyes. "Fine. Then do the rice thing."

"The rice thing?"

"Yeah, where you stick it in a bag of rice and let the rice absorb the water for a few days?"

She looked at him blankly.

He tugged on her sleeve. "Come on, I'll show you. But let's get out of the rain."

They continued to her house. At the steps, Finley hesitated. "Um, I'm just going to change. Do you want to—"

"I'll change and be over in a minute, okay?"

She paused. This was the type of thing Oliver would normally help with. But she couldn't ask Oliver. He had moved on. "Okay. Thanks." She darted inside and closed the door.

Twenty minutes later, Finley had changed, and her wet clothes and the contents of her backpack were laid out, drying. Nothing had gotten damaged, thankfully. Just the phone. She cursed herself for not stowing it in her bag. Having to accept Harlan's help rubbed her the wrong way. Especially when she could have just looked up how to do this online the second she got to her room. Stupid Finley.

Her teeth chattered, even though it wasn't cold. She combed her fingers through her wet hair. She should dry it. She didn't need to be any more uncomfortable around Harlan than she already was. When her hair was mostly dry, she grabbed an elastic hair band, slipped back into her Havaianas, and left her room. Styling her hair into a loose side braid, she walked downstairs.

At the second floor landing, she heard laughter coming from the great room. She frowned. Oliver and Emma couldn't make that much noise. Her sandals flapped against the hardwood as she turned the corner to the great room. Oliver and Emma were sitting in the plush loveseat, their smiling profiles to her. Harlan was in a leather armchair, facing Finley and talking to someone sitting on the couch. The mystery man's back was to Finley. She could see only chestnut brown hair. Harlan's eyes landed on hers, and he grinned.

"We've just been getting to know your—"

The head on the couch popped up, and Finley squealed. "LIAM!" She ran around the end table, almost tripping over his suitcase. She threw her arms around her brother, laughing. "You're early!"

"I know! I wanted to surprise you!" Liam laughed, squeezing her tight before letting her go. Her eyes pored over him. He was darker than she was, thanks to soccer practice. He had more freckles, too.

His big light brown eyes crinkled, reflecting the joy beaming from her face. She hugged him again. "You nerd! When did you get here?"

Liam laughed and pulled her braid. "Three minutes ago. I literally just got here."

"Well, I hope you packed your A game in that enormous suitcase."

"Whatever. I'll eat you for breakfast."

She shoved him. "No way. I almost beat you last year!"

"Yeah, *almost,* Finny Fin Fin." Liam looked at Oliver, slinging his arm over Finley's shoulders. "Have you been letting her win or something? She's gotten way too sassy."

Oliver held up his hands. "Don't look at me, man. I beat her once when she was down with the flu and doped up on NyQuil. She's gotten better. Watch out."

Emma spoke up. "What are you guys talking about?" She looked at the three of them, and her eyes landed on Finley's.

"It's a game my dad made up. We watch the worst movies we can find, and every time you hear something cliché or see a rip-off of something else, you yell out the name of the movie it came from," Finley said.

"You gotta watch Liam with the tiebreakers. Dude has a photographic memory for obscure movie trivia," Oliver said. "But Finley's the quick draw."

Finley caught Emma and Harlan looking at each other. "We have to play," they said in unison.

"I don't mind," Liam told Finley and Oliver. "I can beat four people just as easily as two."

Finley narrowed her eyes. Since her dad died, the game had only ever been the three of them—Liam, Oliver, and Finley. Since the Crawfords' arrival, her few comforts kept being torn from her. She looked at Harlan. His mouth was tight again, as if he was biting the inside of his lip.

Adapt or die, Finley.

Brad Pitt, Moneyball, *2011.*

She turned on her brother. "I can humiliate you just as easily in front of three people as one."

"Game on, sis."

* * *

~*O*~

Emma pulled Oliver onto one of the overstuffed beanbags in the theater room. She snuggled under his arm, while Finley and Liam fell onto the couch and kicked their legs up on the ottoman in unison. After a moment's pause, Harlan dropped down on Finley's other side. For a moment, Oliver envied him in that position—*his* position—but Emma snagged his attention with a kiss to his neck.

Boxes of Milk Duds and Hot Tamales littered the floor. The aroma of buttery, salted popcorn filled the air.

"You're up, Ollie," Liam said.

Oliver stood and held out a movie to the group.

"*Make It or Break It,*" he said. "The story of a teenage boy determined to take his mad break-dancing skills to the 'World Dance Classic' in New York City. The only problem? He'll be competing against the girl of his dreams, and winning it all may mean losing the only person he's ever cared about." Finley and Liam groaned. "For those of you just tuning in, points in dance movies come from knowing the music as well as clichés."

Liam made a farting noise and held out his hands, thumbs down. "Weak." Then he jumped up. "I present to you all *Bride of the Leprechaun.*"

"Is it a sequel to those cheesy *Leprechaun* horror movies?" Emma asked.

"I'm glad you asked," Liam said, pointing at Emma. "No. It's the story of a teenage girl who's captured by trolls in the woods when her family goes camping in Wyoming. The troll king plans to use her to create a breed of troll-humans that will take over the world. If she can't escape, her virtue, freedom, and the human race will all be lost."

"The title mentioned a leprechaun," Harlan said.

"It did."

"But there aren't leprechauns in the movie?" Harlan asked.

"There sure aren't."

"Awesome."

"And keep in mind," Liam told the group, "points in horror movies also come from ripping off things like plot, imagery, and monsters."

"Okay, okay," Oliver said, waving Liam back down. "Stop grandstanding. Fin, what do you have?"

Finley stood and took a stately walk to the front of the room. She cleared her throat and held out a movie. Liam's presence made her more comfortable than anything else could—the fact that she was hamming it up in front of Harlan was proof of that. "Ladies and gentlemen, for your viewing pleasure this evening, I present *Quake Gators*."

"What?" everyone asked.

"That's right, *Quake Gators*. When a crew of gator poachers in Florida uses two hundred pounds of C4 to blow up a swamp, they unwittingly send thousands of alligators through the earth's tectonic plates, causing the creatures to mutate. And when mutant-alligator-spewing earthquakes start devastating the eastern seaboard, the hot, young military geologist Nick Bunbee must embrace the gator-poaching past—and girl—he left behind if he wants to stop the quake gators from destroying his new life."

"Yes," Harlan blurted. "I've never wanted to see something more in my life."

"That's not how it works," Finley said. She handed pencils and slips of paper to everyone. Emma winked when she took her paper and pencil, about Harlan's flirting, no doubt. Fin narrowed her eyes at her friend and continued talking. "Everyone writes their first, second, and third choice in order, and we pick based on most votes."

The votes were quickly in, and *Quake Gators* narrowly beat out *Bride of the Leprechaun.*

"Wow," Liam said, looking at the pieces of paper Finley had spread out over the ottoman. "An all-time low with no first place votes for your movie, Ollie. That's harsh. Looks like Fin isn't giving you pity points anymore, huh?"

Oliver blushed. It didn't matter that Fin didn't vote for him. He looked at Emma. "You didn't vote for me?"

"You're not *that* cute."

He fell back on the beanbag, holding his heart. "Ouch."

Emma leaned over him. "I'll kiss it better, okay?"

Harlan threw popcorn at them just as the movie started.

* * *

In the end, Liam and Finley destroyed them all, with Liam narrowly beating Finley by a single point. Harlan made a fine showing, particularly for a noob. It wasn't surprising, but the fact that Finley had actually gotten along with him was. A ripped-off quote from *Romeo and Juliet* had them both jump up and shout at each other, but when Harlan couldn't come up with one of the answers, he yelled out "Wang!" and Finley had shaken with laughter.

With anyone else, Oliver would have shrugged it off. But she hated Harlan. Didn't she?

Liam and Fin teased each other on the couch until she yawned and Liam gave her a one-armed hug. "Get to bed, sis. I'm expecting a call from a recruiter in Spain at 2:00 a.m. anyway, so I'll be up for a while still."

"I'll stay up with you," Finley said.

Liam smiled. "I have a couple of weeks before practice starts back up. We'll have plenty of time to catch up. Get some sleep."

"Or at least come downstairs with me, Fin," Emma said, yawning and slinging an arm over Fin's shoulder. "Mama needs another cookie before bed."

"Let's go, Mama," Fin said, leaving the room with Emma.

While the guys straightened up the room, Harlan asked Liam about his soccer prospects. Liam had wanted to play internationally since he was a kid, and his coach at Notre Dame had all but promised he could make that happen. Yet the better Liam got, the more his coach balked, probably to keep his star player on the team. Earlier in the semester, Liam had sent a handful of international teams his stats and video of him playing. Last week, he finally got a phone call from a recruiter.

"Well, it sounds like you have a real shot," Harlan said. "Good luck with the call tonight."

"Thanks, man," Liam said, then looked at Oliver. "Hey, I was meaning to ask you earlier what the plan is for Fin's birthday on Saturday."

The bowl in Harlan's hands clattered to the floor. "It's her birthday? This Saturday? How has no one mentioned this?" he asked.

Oliver coughed. "Well, she and I usually do our Old Town tour—"

"No, it needs to be something big," Harlan said, as if he knew anything about what Finley would want. He hadn't even known it was her birthday.

But Liam was nodding. "Yeah, it does. Do you remember those parties my dad used to throw, Ollie?" Then to Harlan: "She likes to pretend she doesn't care about her birthday, but my Dad threw her a surprise party every year before he died. Even though we did it every year, she was always so shocked about it. She loved them." He smiled. "She makes a huge deal out of everyone's birthday, but she never expects anyone to even remember hers. I'll talk to Uncle Thomas and see if we can get something going."

Harlan was smiling, too. "Let me know when you're gonna talk to him. I want to help."

"Sure thing," Liam said. As if they needed Harlan's help.

When they'd finished straightening up, Oliver and Harlan went downstairs and ran into the girls coming from the kitchen.

Emma gave Oliver a tired hug, folding herself around him. "Mmm."

Near them, Harlan was speaking quietly to Finley. "You know, I could have sworn you were about to name that last movie before Liam did. Funny how you missed it and he managed to win because of it."

Fin had given Liam the last point? That was so like her. And so unlike Harlan to notice it.

"He got lucky," Finley said quietly. "I didn't give him the point."

Oliver heard the smile in Harlan's voice. "Of course. My mistake."

Finley looked half-amused, half-weary when Harlan held out a hand to her. After a hesitation, she took it. "Good game, Miss Price." Harlan shook her hand gently, holding on to it a moment longer than he should have. And then one moment more.

Finley broke the contact just before Oliver broke it for them. He watched Harlan's eyes follow Finley toward the stairs. "Good night," she said.

Emma yawned in Oliver's arms, almost making him jump. How had he forgotten he was holding this beautiful girl? He shook his head.

Maybe Emma was right. Harlan would be good for Fin. And that would be good for Oliver.

CHAPTER SIXTEEN

~O~

The following evening, Oliver and Emma were walking by his dad's office after a lazy day in the Grants' pool. They stopped when they noticed Liam and Harlan in there, too. Oliver's dad said something, and both boys' heads snapped around to Oliver and Emma. Harlan waved them in.

"Come in quick, and close the door," Harlan said.

Oliver looked at Emma, but they did what he asked.

"Was Fin anywhere out there?" Liam asked.

"No, she's up with my mom. What's going on?" Oliver asked. He and Emma walked toward the desk.

"We're talking about Finley's birthday," Oliver's dad said. "Harlan has offered the use of the Grants' house to throw a surprise party, and I already confirmed it with them."

"Ollie, we need you to act like you forgot so you and Emma can help decorate," Liam said. "I'm going to say I'm meeting with a scout, too."

"Then she's going to think we all forgot her birthday?" Oliver's hand tightened around Emma's unconsciously. She flexed.

"Ow," she muttered.

"Harlan is going to take her out for the day," Oliver's dad said. "So you need to be sure to tell her that you and Emma have plans tomorrow so she doesn't try to make an excuse."

They finalized the plans, and Oliver tried to swallow the sick lump in his throat. To make things worse, Emma kept casting him sideways glances. When they finally left the study for the kitchen, she squeezed his hand.

"What gives?"

Oliver grabbed snacks from the pantry. "I feel bad about letting Fin think I forgot her birthday."

Emma crunched down on a chip. "It's a surprise party, Ollie. That's kind of how it works."

"Yeah, I know. You're right, it's silly." He kissed Emma's cheek. "The party will be perfect."

The flapping of sandals against the hardwood alerted them to Finley's presence before they saw her.

"Hey, guys," she said, entering the kitchen. "What are you doing?"

Emma straightened up. "Just talking about our plans for tomorrow."

Finley's body seemed to pause in midstride. "Oh. What are you doing?"

"A walking tour of Old Town," Emma said. "Ollie was telling me how cool it is, so I'm making him play tour guide."

Oliver felt as if he'd been dipped in hot candle wax. Emma could have made up anything. Why did she have to say that? Fin's shoulders pulled up at Emma's words, making her look far too much like the Fin of two years ago.

When he'd taken her on that first Old Town tour, she'd seemed so small and scared. They'd been friends most of their lives, but since moving in with them a couple of months earlier, she'd had the look of a cornered animal, always looking for an escape. Oliver had convinced her the tour would be fun, but his nervous prattle about the neighborhood's history managed to highlight only the most boring things. When he'd started talking about the theater movement that had helped revive the area, Finley had perked up. He'd told her a theater joke that was actually pretty funny, and the corners of her mouth had lifted. He'd made her smile. It had almost knocked him over, it felt so good.

He ached remembering it.

Emma was chatting as Finley rummaged through the fridge. "Ollie's a great tour guide. I'm sure you'll have fun," Fin said, her back to them as she sliced an apple.

"Yeah, I'm looking forward to it." Emma's stool screeched as she pushed it out from the counter. "Anyway, we're just on our way to see a movie. See you later, girl."

"Later, Fin," Oliver said, his voice sounding fake in his ears.

As they left the kitchen, he thought he heard a sniff. He put an arm around Emma and kept walking.

* * *

~*F*~

When their footsteps retreated, Finley put the knife down on the counter and closed her eyes. She felt so pathetic. How could she think her birthday would matter to Oliver now that he had a girl-friend? Had it even mattered to him before, or had she just been someone to kill time with?

Don't, she told herself. *Ollie cares about you. He probably thinks that because Liam's in town, you're going to spend time with him instead.*

She nodded. That made sense. She picked the knife back up and finished cutting her apple, unable to keep her thoughts from straying back to Oliver. Did he have to take Emma to Old Town? That was *their* thing.

Not anymore.

"Enough," she told herself out loud.

"What's enough?" Liam said, coming into the kitchen with Harlan. He reached around her and grabbed an apple slice, throwing it into his mouth before she could stop him.

"You stealing my food, that's what," she said, putting a hand over the slices.

"Nice try." He knocked her hand up and snaked another one before rounding the island and sitting next to Harlan.

"So how was the call with the scout last night?" Harlan asked Liam.

"They want me to come out this summer to try out for the reserves," he said.

"So why do you look upset?"

"It's a small club, and they're pretty underfunded. The chances of them taking me are good, but the development would be iffy. It could be a waste of some valuable years on my part if I sign with them." Liam snapped his fingers and looked at Finley. "Speaking of scouts, someone from the Chicago Fire wants to meet with me tomorrow, so I'll probably check out the facilities and stuff most of the day."

Finley choked down her disappointment. "I thought you didn't want to play locally."

"I don't, but if everything else falls through, I need to have options in the US. It's just their developmental league, but it's better than staying with my tool of a coach for another year."

"And with Liam gone and Ollie and Ems going out," Harlan said, "I wondered if you wanted to hang out with me Saturday?"

Finley's heart went into panic mode. They'd just started being nice to each other. What was he doing? "Sorry?"

Harlan smiled. "I asked if you'd hang out with me."

"No, we can't."

"We can't?"

"I . . . I mean, I can't ask you to do that. You have a busy life, interviews and stuff to do."

There was no mistaking the offense on Harlan's face. "I'm *asking* you to hang out with me. This is hardly a charity case."

Liam looked disappointed, too. Harlan may have won over her brother, but not her. She couldn't stand Harlan Crawford.

Okay, that wasn't totally true. In the last week, she'd been surprised to see a moderately likable side to him. And he'd known about their dad this whole time and had never treated her differently because of it. But then, there was everything with Juliette. He'd kissed her, knowing she had a boyfriend. Sure, Juliette wasn't blameless there, and if she hadn't chased Harlan so hard, it probably never would have—

Was she seriously making excuses for the guy? No. No way.

"I'm sorry, Harlan. I just don't think it's going to happen."

Harlan's face crumpled. He looked at Liam. "That's fine. I'll call the owner of Piper's Theater and tell him to cancel it. I just thought—"

"Cancel what?" she asked before she could help herself. Piper's Theater was one of the oldest movie houses in Chicago.

"It's nothing. I was able to get the owner to rent out the main theater to me for the day. I thought it would be cool to watch a marathon of *Supernova*'s best episodes on the big screen, but you obviously—"

Finley blinked through misty eyes. "You did that? On your own? For me?" He met her eyes, and he looked so . . . exposed. "Harlan, I . . . I'm sorry. I didn't know."

"Don't worry about it. The deposit is refundable if I call—"

"No, don't. Please don't cancel." She smiled. "I'd love to hang out with you tomorrow."

Liam and Harlan exchanged looks. "Cool," Harlan said, his eyes bright. "I'll pick you up around ten?"

Finley nodded. Liam and Harlan talked for a bit longer before Harlan headed out.

Liam got up and rounded the counter. He put an arm around

Finley. "Sorry about missing a day with you," he said, "but I'm glad you'll be with Harley. He's a good guy."

Finley snorted.

"What's that about?" Liam asked.

"Harlan Crawford may be a lot of things, but 'good' isn't one of them."

"You know I love you, Finny, so remember that when I tell you you're too black-and-white. You fit everyone into categories of being a good or a bad person. Life's not that simple. Dad wasn't all good. Mom isn't all bad. Okay, that's not the best example. But Harlan isn't all bad. Put yourself in his shoes. Two super dysfunctional parents who can't see past their hatred of each other to remember their kids? We had a really hard few years after Dad died, you more than me, but before that, at least we had Dad." Finley started trembling, and Liam wrapped his arm tighter around her. "Try to remember that when you're with Harley tomorrow, will you? Give the guy at least half a chance."

She squinted at her brother. "Why, though? Why is he doing this?"

Liam studied her. "You're kidding, right?"

"No. What am I missing?"

He just smiled. "Nuh-uh. I'm not ruining the surprise." His arm still around her, he led them out of the kitchen. "Come on, let's go upstairs and do crappy translations of a telenovela."

* * *

~ℱ~

At 9:55 the next morning, Finley was pacing in the foyer. She kept looking at herself in the reflection of the French doors to Uncle Thomas's study. Was a skirt the right thing to wear? It was new. It fit her well. Maybe too well.

Uncle Thomas came down the stairs and smiled when he saw her. "You look nice. Are you looking forward to your date?"

"Date?" She paced faster. "Do you think he thinks this is a date?"

He put a hand on her shoulder, and the pressure calmed her. "I'm glad you're going out, Finley. You deserve to have someone treat you like you're as special as you are." He kissed her forehead. "Try to have a nice time, won't you? Harlan is a nice young man." The doorbell rang, and Finley flexed and released her hands. "Allow me."

Uncle Thomas opened the large front door, but it wasn't Harlan standing there. It was Nora. She stormed in.

"Nora, I didn't expect you till later. Is everything all right?"

"No, Thomas. We have a huge problem—" she stopped and looked at Finley. Her gaze went over the outfit, her curled hair, and ended on her lip gloss. "Finley. You look all done up. I see your uncle has bought you some new clothes. How nice for you."

Finley frowned.

"Isn't it, Nora? She looks beautiful, and I'd gladly spend ten times more on her, if I thought she'd accept it." He opened his study doors for Nora, then patted Finley's shoulder. "Enjoy your date with Harlan."

Nora popped back out. "Harlan? And you?"

"*Nora,*" Uncle Thomas snapped. He gave Finley an apologetic look and closed the French doors on Nora's face.

Finley's cheeks burned and her eyes stung. She didn't even want to be going. She wanted to turn around, run upstairs, and just shut everyone and everything out.

Or maybe storm into that study and rage at Nora.

The doorbell rang. Her eyes jumped to the grandfather clock that read ten o'clock, right on the nose. With a deep breath, she opened the front door and stepped outside before she'd even said hello.

Harlan's brow creased beneath his sunglasses and Kangol hat. "Uh, good morning, Miss Price." He held out a simple bouquet of tulips. "I'm thrilled you're so eager to get going, but you may want to put these in water first."

Finley stood motionless. He'd gotten her flowers. *Beautiful* flowers. But putting them in water meant passing the study where Nora would surely see her.

"What's going on?" Harlan asked.

"I don't want to go back inside," she blurted, hating how hot her cheeks felt.

"The Bertrams all know I'm taking you out. What's the big deal?"

"Nora is in there. I don't—"

"Ah. Right," Harlan said. He took a step down the stairs and stopped. "Right."

He thrust the flowers into her hand, walked back up to the door, and dragged her in with him. Finley's face was on fire. Grabbing her elbow, Harlan waved at Uncle Thomas and Nora, popping his head into the study. "Just putting these in some water. I promise to take good care of her, sir."

Uncle Thomas grinned. Nora didn't.

Harlan pulled Finley into the kitchen, asked Aunt Mariah's nurse for a vase, and handed her the flowers. They were back through the hallway, waving to Uncle Thomas, outside, and walking to the L station before Finley knew what was happening.

Had Harlan just paraded himself in front of Nora? For her?

She looked at him from the corner of her eye; he was standing a bit closer than she'd like. She stepped around a crack in the sidewalk and stayed a more comfortable distance away from him. "So, um, that was really cool of you."

"What?"

"You know, with the flowers and Nora?"

Harlan shook his head. "That woman is a huge bi—"

"Don't."

"You disagree?"

"No." She smiled. "But just because it's true, doesn't mean you need to say it."

Harlan laughed. "You're a lot like your dad, you know that? He was so nice to everyone. The people in wardrobe, the production assistants. If someone made a mistake, he never got mad at them. He was always telling people whatever they needed to hear to do their best. I never understood how he did that." He held the door to the L station open for her and followed her in. They swiped their cards and walked up to the buzzing platform. "You're just like that. So nice, I almost don't know how to talk to you."

Finley shook her head, wishing he'd stop comparing her to her father, especially when Harlan was the one who'd done that same thing with the production crew just the other day. Harlan, not her.

"I'm not that nice," she said under her breath.

"What?"

"Nothing." She looked around the platform.

The train was pulling up. Harlan put his hands on her shoulders and guided her into their car. Among the locals, tourists stood out, comparing guidebooks and apps on their phones. A handful of kids around their age stood across from them in the car. One of them nudged the others, and they all turned to look at Harlan, whose hat and sunglasses couldn't hide his identity. Finley turned away from the group so she was looking right at Harlan. In the reflection of the door, she saw a pretty redhead purse her lips and look Harlan over. She sighed inwardly. Watching him flirt was hardly what she'd wanted for her birthday.

Harlan caught her eye. "Work with me, okay?" he whispered. He lifted a hand and softly played with a strand of her hair, grazing her cheek. She barely managed not to flinch. A slow smile spread across his face, and he leaned in close to her. She was about to back up when she noticed the redhead in the reflection; the girl's mouth fell open and an eyebrow arched angrily. Harlan's face was only inches from Finley's. He brought his lips close to her ear. "Red sure looks pissed."

A laugh burst from Finley. "Yeah, she does." Red whipped around to her friends, who started laughing at her. A couple of them stood on tiptoes over each other, straining to see the girl with Harlan Crawford.

When they grabbed their cameras, Harlan ducked and angled just enough so they couldn't catch his face. His smiling eyes were directly across from Finley's. "It's weird. I don't remember inviting them on our little outing. Did you invite them?"

"Naturally."

He peeked over her head and slipped back down before they could react. "Well, they seem pretty intent on joining us. Are you sure they aren't closet *Supernova* fans?" She almost managed not to smile. "I'm serious! Do you see the girl with the tattoo on her wrist? The one with the blue jacket? Look at her eyebrows and tell me she isn't a *Kerothan*."

She glanced at the girl's reflection and another laugh escaped her. She pushed Harlan's shoulder. "Stop it."

"*You* stop it."

The train slowed and a recorded voice announced their stop. Instead of exiting through the doors nearest them, the group of teenagers walked over to the door by Finley and Harlan. Harlan grabbed Finley's shoulders and turned them so their faces shielded each other from the group. She caught them in the reflection of the windows now. They were trying to get a good look, but Harlan's angles were too exact. He'd done this before.

"Quick, check the guy in the track pants," Harlan said. Finley's eyes found him in the reflection. "That's a *Twobuttian* if I've ever seen one."

The train doors closed and Finley and Harlan returned to more normal positions. She looked away but couldn't keep from chuckling. "There's no such thing as *Twobuttians*. And don't fat-shame."

"I'm not fat-shaming; I'm fashion shaming. If the dude wore pants that fit, he wouldn't have to jam-pack his butt cheeks into them."

"You're awful."

"And you like it," he said, still with a grin. He hadn't stopped smiling since they'd left.

Why?

Her eyes narrowed; his grin faltered. The train reached their stop and Harlan ushered her out of the car, along the platform, and onto the street. The theater was a block from the station. They walked in silence till Harlan directed her attention to the marquee above the theater. The last line read, "A Tribute to Gabriel Price."

Finley put a hand to her heart, then looked at Harlan.

She smiled, took his arm, and they entered the theater.

CHAPTER SEVENTEEN

~$\mathcal{F}$~

Some eight hours and eleven of *Supernova*'s best episodes later, Finley and Harlan were exiting the train to their street. Mingled among the comments about her dad's performance as Captain Souza and arguments about whether episode sixteen was really better than episode twenty-three, Finley couldn't stop thanking him. Today shouldn't have gone so well. She'd been forgotten by everyone who mattered most to her. The sting hadn't faded—not by any means—yet somehow Harlan had managed to make the day memorable. Special, even.

Harlan Crawford.

"Honestly, I just can't believe that you got the director's cut of his last episode. Liam and I wrote the director letters after . . . you know . . . and he never responded. I can't thank you enough."

"You don't have to thank me."

"But you must have gone to so much trouble. Seriously, thank—"

Harlan held up a hand. "Please, you have to stop thanking me. You're acting like I orchestrated all of this to make you grateful. I didn't, okay?"

They were getting closer to their homes. "Why did you do it all?"

"Because I loved that show. Because I loved your dad like he was my own father," he said, and something on his face looked almost wild. "Because watching those episodes with you today was the closest thing I can imagine to seeing him again."

He was looking at her so closely—her eyes, her mouth, even her few freckles—but the scrutiny didn't leave her feeling self-conscious so much as curious. If anything, she'd say *he* seemed self-conscious. What was going on in his head?

They stopped in front of their houses, where the porch lights were on but the lights were off inside both. No one was home. The sadness of the day's end struck her. She didn't want to go into the house to find it empty and alone. She didn't want to wallow in the abandonment that had plagued her for years. Not right now.

As if sensing her despair, Harlan grabbed her hand.

"Do you really want to know why I did it? Why I arranged the movie theater and got the director's cut of that final episode?"

She bit her lip. He was biting his, too. She gave him a small nod.

"You. Okay? I did it for you. I like you, Finley Price. A lot. More than I've ever liked anyone, and it's freaking me out. A lot. So please stop thanking me. Making you happy today was the most selfish thing I've ever done in my life."

A thousand thoughts crossed her mind. Her chest was burning, expanding. She felt her eyebrows raise and furrow. Her mouth didn't know whether to frown or smile. But one thing was certain.

"That's probably the nicest thing anyone has ever said to me."

Harlan exhaled noisily. "I'm glad you didn't say I'm the most selfish jerk you've ever met."

"I didn't *not* say that."

He laughed. "Why don't we grab some ice cream from my aunt's freezer before heading over to your casa."

He was still holding her hand.

Wait. He was holding her hand?

She broke their grasp gently. "Harlan, that was really nice—"

"Please stop thanking me."

"—of you to say that to me," she continued with a smile she

should have contained. "And today was really fun. But I don't like you like that. I don't want to lead you on."

She saw a foreign look of pain on his face. Not the pang of pride, but actual hurt. She didn't want him to hurt, she realized, but that wasn't a reason to commit to something she didn't feel. Not that she didn't feel *anything*. She . . . liked him. Liked hanging out with him. But she didn't reciprocate. Of course she didn't.

The ache she'd seen on his face faded, and he leveled her with his gaze. "Miss Price, I'm talking about ice cream, not my undying love. I went to the trouble of finding out your favorite flavor. Bubble gum? You *have* to eat it, because, believe me, no one at my house is going to eat that crap."

She gasped. "What do you mean, crap? Bubble gum is the best flavor!"

"When you're six, maybe. Get with the program, Price. And come get your crappy kid ice cream out of my freezer."

She shook her head dramatically, tsking all the way up the stairs with him. She stopped him just before he put his key in the door. "So it's just Price, huh?"

"Huh?"

"You usually call me Miss Price, but you called me Finley Price earlier. Then you just used my last name. Which is it?"

He peered into her eyes and threw the door open. "Just get inside, Price."

She stepped inside the dark house.

The lights flew on.

"SURPRISE!"

Shock, excitement, gratitude, and more shock flooded Finley's mind. Through the cheers and shouts of the few dozen people there, she searched for Liam. Her face broke out into a grin when she saw him. He bowed.

She whipped around to Harlan, and her smile wavered. "You

were in on this?" He nodded. "So today . . . " The thought that it was all for show, for a surprise, it *hurt*.

Emma ran over and threw her arms around Finley.

"Yes, but I meant everything today," Harlan said over his sister, holding Finley's gaze. "All of it."

She blinked, and the warmth in her chest spread up to the corners of her mouth until she was grinning. Soon, friends from her clubs and school and the theater were there, hugging her and wishing her a happy birthday. Then Oliver and his parents approached.

"Do you hate me?" Oliver asked, hugging her. "I had to pretend I didn't know. It was killing me all day that you thought I forgot."

Finley's eyes were wet, and she was looking at everyone, smiling. And in the background was Harlan, watching her as if he couldn't stop.

He really liked her?

Wait, Oliver had asked her something, hadn't he? She looked at him and smiled. "I couldn't hate you."

"But you know I'd never forget, right?" Oliver grabbed Finley's chin and lifted it so she was looking him in the eye. "Never."

She swallowed. She didn't want these emotions right now, didn't need to revisit her heartache. Fortunately, her aunt and uncle moved Oliver to the side. "All right, stop hogging the birthday girl."

They wrapped their arms around her, and she let her happy tears fall.

* * *

A half hour later, she'd greeted everyone at the party, perhaps thirty people in all. Oliver must have been in charge of the guest list, as they were mostly friends from drama and the humanitarian club. Yet she spotted a couple of people from the community theater whom Harlan must have invited. The thought that he'd cared enough made her smile.

She went into the Grants' kitchen to wash off the cake Liam had smashed into her face. He followed behind her, teasing her about her date.

"Hush your face," she said. Harlan and Emma were coming into the kitchen.

"Why, Finny? Because you don't want Harley knowing you had a good day?"

Emma heard. "Um, of course she had a good day. Harley is the best." She patted her brother's cheek before planting her elbows on the island across from where Finley was washing her hands. "But Fin, we have to talk about this guest list. Thirty people? Why do you hate fun?"

She sprinkled water on Emma's face. "You guys invited everyone, you nerd."

"I know, but your boys—Harley, Liam, and Ollie—all insisted that you'd want an 'intimate party.' But just so you know, intimate parties are boring, and I'm embarrassed for you."

Harlan put a hand over Emma's mouth. "Don't mind her, Price. She's probably just mad there's no paparazzi here." Emma scoffed, pushing his hand away. "For someone taking a break from acting, my sister sure loves an audience."

"Well, Fin doesn't," Liam said. He grabbed a large, wrapped box from the counter. "Which makes now as good a time as any to give you this."

Finley squealed and started ripping off wrapping paper and opened the box. Inside was a smaller wrapped gift. And a smaller one inside of that. She chuckled as she unwrapped five nested boxes. When she opened the smallest, she covered her mouth. It was an iPhone case with a picture of her, Liam, and their dad on it.

Her eyes found Harlan's. Her phone . . . the rice trick hadn't worked.

Somehow, Harlan read the panic in her gaze. "That's awesome," he said, grabbing the case. "Too bad your sister left her phone at home today. I guess she didn't want anyone interrupting us on our hot date."

"Keep telling yourself that," Finley said with a smile. Then she side-hugged her brother. "Thank you, Liam. It's perfect."

He hugged her tight, then kissed her head. "I love you, sis."

She watched Harlan pull Emma out of the room. She was grateful he'd covered for her, but Liam would be around for another two weeks. He'd soon know something was up.

She had to get a new phone.

* * *

She didn't see Harlan again for an hour, maybe more. She promised herself she'd have fun, despite the phone fiasco. She danced with Anaya and Rosa, heckled Liam when he sang karaoke, chatted with people, and ate way too much. The party was in full swing when Harlan asked if he could steal her from Oliver and Liam.

He was smiling as he led her from the room. She was, too. "Are you having a good time?" she asked.

He laughed. "It's your party. Are *you* having a good time?"

"Yeah, I really am. Thanks for all of this, Harlan. I . . . I don't know what to say."

"For starters, you can do me a favor and stop saying thank you."

She chuckled. "Yeah, sorry."

"And stop apologizing."

"I know, sorry."

"Price!"

"Okay, I'm . . . I'm *not* sorry, okay?" She laughed. Then she sighed. "I don't know what to do about my phone. Is that ridiculous? I don't have the heart to tell Liam, and I can't stand the thought of asking Uncle Thomas for another one."

"That's actually why I grabbed you." They reached the stairs, and Harlan pointed upward. "I have a plan. Come with me."

She followed him upstairs to Emma's room, where the girl was waiting with four old phones laid out on her bed in colors Finley didn't even know were options.

"Before you object," Emma said, "I'm bored with you not accepting anything from anyone. I'm not doing this because I feel bad for you. I'm doing it because it's easy, and it'll mean one less phone I donate, because, as you know, I wouldn't be caught dead with something old. So do me a favor and take one of these relics off my bed." She picked up one of the phones—a simple white one—and handed it to Finley.

As much as she wanted to, Finley couldn't argue. She knew Emma pretty well by now, and everything the girl had just said was true. So she swallowed her pride. "I'm accepting this under protest," she said, taking the phone and snapping Liam's case on it. "But thank you."

Emma gaped. "You mean that actually worked?"

Finley shrugged. "You're a hard person to argue with."

"See, I *knew* I was rubbing off on you," Emma said. "I make it a point to accept everything nice that anyone does for me."

"And to only believe the nice things people say about you," Harlan added.

"Obviously."

Finley smiled at them both, not letting herself get too emotional, no matter how much her heart swelled in gratitude. She even kept her voice steady when she spoke. "Thank you both. It means a lot to me that you guys care. Now I'm going to go show Liam." After giving Emma a quick hug, she almost bounced from the room, with Harlan and Emma following.

Downstairs, they ran into a handful of party crashers Finley didn't recognize, and one she did: Dylan.

She nearly bumped into him. "Oh," she said, backing up into Harlan.

"Hey there. I just came to wish you a very happy birthday," he said, eyeing her. Then he nodded behind her. "So Crawford, what's up, man? I expected more people."

Harlan put a hand on Finley's shoulder. "And we expected only the people who were invited."

Dylan looked Emma over. "It's cool. We're all friends here."

"Ugh, are you kidding?" Emma said, shuddering dramatically. "Go home."

Emma took Finley's arm and pulled her from the foyer. But Finley could still hear Harlan talking.

"What are you doing?" Harlan asked. "Why are you guys here?"

"What's got your panties in a bunch? She still not putting out?" Dylan laughed. "The way I hear it, you've already gone through half of your neighbors—"

"You don't know what you're talking about. Go home, Dylan."

She was glad she missed the rest of the argument. A few minutes later, when she was hanging out with Liam, Harlan came over, looking upset.

He put a hand on her arm. "Can we talk for a minute?"

She hesitated, but after everything he'd done for her tonight, she could spare a few minutes to talk. "Sure."

He took her to a small library and closed the door. "I don't know what you heard Dylan say—"

Heat crept up her cheeks. "It doesn't matter, Harlan."

"Yes, it does. It's not like that, okay?" He ran a hand through his hair. "What he said—that I'm 'going through the neighbors,' that's not what's happening."

"Why should I believe that?" She wasn't accusing him; she genuinely wondered. "After everything with Juliette—"

"I didn't care about Juliette."

"I know. That's the problem. You hurt her and you didn't even care about her."

"And it would have been better if I'd cared?"

"Yes, actually. At least it would have been real."

"Do you want me to apologize to Juliette? Because I will. Please, Price." He looked as if he wanted to grab her, to hold her. "Don't shut me out."

She sighed and sat on the arm of a chair. "I'm not shutting you out, Harlan. I'm just remembering that a single good week can't make up for a lifetime of you being you."

He flinched. "Maybe I don't want to be me. Have you thought of that? Have you considered that the reason I like you is because you make me want to be better?"

"I'm not your personal savior, Harlan. But I can be your friend. Can you accept that?"

"I don't know." His back hunched ever so slightly. After a pause, he handed her a thin package from his back pocket. "But happy birthday."

She opened it to find a copy of the director's cut of her dad's last episode. Emotion swirled through her chest like butterflies. "Oh, Harlan."

"You're welcome."

She met his eyes. He looked tortured. *Tortured.* Over her.

"I'm going out of town for a few days. I hope you'll see me when I get back."

"Of course," she said softly. "I'll see you when you get back."

He walked to the door, and something about his stance and mussed hair gave her heart a twinge. "Wait," she said. She crossed the room and threw her arms around him. He breathed into her hair. "Thank you," she whispered.

"Yeah, yeah." He exhaled a laugh, holding her tightly.

"See you when you get back, okay?" she asked.

"Okay."

CHAPTER EIGHTEEN

~ℱ~

Two nights later, Finley and Liam were watching *Kung Fu* reruns when Oliver walked into the room. "Hey, Emma just texted me. Turn it to *The Tonight Show*."

Finley changed the channel. The host was doing a desk piece on unintentionally obscene headlines. "Where is Emma, anyway? I haven't seen her all day."

"She left for New York this morning. She'll be back in a couple days."

Liam slapped Finley's leg. "Isn't that where Harlan is?"

Finley slapped him back. "How should I know?"

Oliver grabbed the popcorn bowl from her and dropped onto the couch on her other side. "Because he's five seconds away from being your boyfriend. Isn't he?"

She wished her face didn't feel so hot. "No. I am not planning to date Harlan."

"'The lady doth protest too much, methinks,'" Liam said. "Why don't you like him, Fin? He's a nice guy."

"He's not that nice." She turned to Oliver. "Right? I mean, you wouldn't want me dating him . . . would you?" Her heart beat a frantic, desperate beat.

Oliver looked down at the popcorn bowl, scooping up a handful. "Why not? I like Harlan."

The popcorn turned to lead in her stomach. "Maybe. I don't know."

Liam slapped her leg again. "Check it! There he is!"

On the screen, Harlan walked out to cheers and screams from adoring fans. He waved at the audience. In jeans and a black leather coat, he looked every bit the teen heartthrob. He flashed his dimples, and the audience swooned. Finley chuckled.

The host started asking him about Chicago and his wild success with the play. "So you're performing Shakespeare, which is like the most pressure an actor can feel, and suddenly you fall. You have to be thinking, 'My life is over.' But then you jump up and, in character, deliver this line that is the talk of Hollywood and Broadway and Way, Way Off Broadway. What was the line, again?"

Harlan laughed and delivered the line. The host clapped, along with the audience. "Incredible. How did you come up with that?"

"I can't take all the credit," he said.

"You mean someone gave you the line?"

Harlan waved his hands. "No, nothing like that. But I was given advice from someone whose opinion means a lot to me. She told me to think of everything that could happen in character and know how my character would respond. Is my character the type to get mad? To overreact? To brush things off? So, I took her advice, and it paid off."

"Yeah, it sure did," the host said. "So this 'her' means a lot to you, does she? Ladies, you can't be too thrilled about that." Half of the crowd cheered, the other half booed. "Does 'her' have a name?"

Harlan laughed. "She knows who she is."

"Are you dating, then?"

"I'm hoping to."

"*Hoping* to. But you're Harlan Crawford. Have you told her this? Does she know this?"

Finley felt two sets of eyes on her. She pulled her knees up and hugged her legs.

Harlan laughed again. "Believe me, she knows. That's part of the problem."

"The problem? How is that a problem? Should we call her right now and tell her that's not a real problem?"

"No, hopefully I'll get the chance to convince her of that when I get back to Chicago."

"How are you going to do that?"

"All in good time, man." Harlan shifted on the couch. "But I hope I can at least convince the audience of something." The crowd erupted into cheers again.

"I think you could convince them to get tattoos of you on their faces," the host said to laughter.

"Well, I'm hoping to convince them to take an active role in something else that's important to me. I volunteer with Make a Difference Chicago, and we're in desperate need of supplies for underfunded schools. So please, next time you're out shopping, grab extra notebooks, pens, rulers, anything, and donate them. And, please, talk to your local M.A.D. representative about how you can get involved in the cause."

Finley's mouth fell open. She and Oliver looked at each other. He was wearing the exact same expression.

"You're really serious about volunteering?" the host asked. "I didn't realize you were such an activist."

Finley stared at the screen. "Is this really happening? Are we dreaming this?"

Liam bumped her. "Told you he was a good guy."

The rest of Harlan's interview was about future projects. Finley was surprised to hear that he was planning to stay in Chicago indefinitely. When the host asked him about his reaction to his parents' public dysfunction and divorce, he sat up straighter.

"My parents don't define me. I have a sister, Emma, here with me tonight who's my best friend in the world." The camera cut to a radiant Emma, who waved from backstage. "I have an aunt and uncle who are great supports to me. And I have the memory and example of my mentor, the legendary Gabriel Price. I'm doing okay in the family department." The audience clapped at this, too.

The host wrapped up the interview. Finley replayed Harlan's responses over and over in her head.

Had this really all been for her?

"That dude has it bad, Finny," Liam said, yawning. "I'm gonna hit the sack. See you tomorrow."

She stared at the TV screen for some time before realizing Oliver was still sitting beside her. She felt embarrassed, as if he'd caught her swooning over pictures of Harlan in a teen magazine or something.

"You know, it's been a while since we went up to the roof and looked at the city. Want to go up?" he asked.

Her thoughts flew from the interview. "Yeah, let's go."

Up on the roof-deck, it was raining. Oliver grabbed an umbrella from a stand and popped it over them while they looked out at their neighborhood. Through the slivers between buildings, she caught glimpses of downtown. The night air was warm and muggy, and the pattering of rain joined the chorus of engines and horns and screeching tires that filled the night. Bright city lights blotted out the stars.

"Man, I love this city," Oliver said.

"Me too."

She heard rustling, and the next thing she knew, Oliver was handing her a small, plainly wrapped package.

"What's this?" she asked.

"Your birthday present. I didn't have a chance to give it to you at your party."

She beamed and opened it. Her eyes jumped to his. "You got me a phone?"

"Yeah, I heard yours got wet."

"Ollie!" She pulled the phone from her back pocket and snapped it out of its case.

"What's that?"

"Oh, nothing. Emma gave me one of her old ones when she heard."

"She did?" A smile stole across Oliver's face. "She likes to hide it, but she has a really good heart."

Finley cursed herself. How had she turned this moment into an opportunity to remind him about his fabulous freaking girlfriend? She tried to snap the case onto Oliver's phone, but he stopped her.

"No, no, you can't." He grabbed the phone he'd given her and handed her Emma's. "Emma gave you that! She'd feel awful if she knew you got rid of her phone as soon as a new one came along."

"I really don't think she would. She told me she wouldn't be caught dead with an old phone."

"Obviously she just said that so you'd actually take it."

"What do you mean?"

"Just that you're not the easiest person to give a present to. You tend to assume people are nice to you out of pity, when nothing could be further from the truth," he said, nudging her with his shoulder. "I'm glad Emma was clever enough to find a way around that. There's a lot more to her than you'd think."

She clenched her jaw. *Stupid Finley,* she thought. She took the white phone of Emma's and was about to snap the case back on when an engraving on the back caught her eye:

With love, Harlan.

Finley's eyes popped. "That sneaky little—"

"What?" Oliver grabbed the phone, then chuckled. "Wow. Well played, Harlan."

"Well played, nothing! She held this one out to me specifically, so naturally I took it. Does this mean she regifted something Harlan gave her? Or was it his way of sneaking me a gift?"

He was still laughing. "I think it's safe to say the gift was from both of them."

"I should give it back."

"Or you could just accept that people care about you and keep it. Let mine be your backup for the next time you fall in a puddle." He smiled.

Reluctantly, she nodded and turned back to look over the city, telling herself to let it go. Let it all go. She felt a splash of rain and moved closer to the center of the umbrella when she noticed Oliver was only halfway under.

"Ollie, you're soaking. Get under the umbrella, already."

Was it her imagination, or did he hesitate? "When did you get so pushy?" he asked, getting under the umbrella. Their arms had to touch for him to be out of the rain. Not that she minded. At all.

"I'm not pushy. Why does everyone keep acting like I'm so different all of a sudden?"

She felt Oliver's gaze on her. "Because you are different. Over the last few weeks, you've been . . . more open. Bolder."

"Ha. I've been bold?"

"Not compared to Emma, maybe," he teased. "But compared to you, yeah. And I'm really proud of you." He looked down at the cars on their street. "Harlan brings out a different side of you. And you obviously bring out the best in him."

She frowned. "I propose we go the rest of the conversation without talking about the Crawfords."

"Hmm, I don't know. What will we talk about?"

"Good question. We were hardly friends before they got here. I mean, we barely even spoke."

"Gee, you're right," Oliver teased, then exhaled slowly, resting his head against hers. "It's so peaceful, isn't it? I've missed this."

"Me, too," she whispered, willing her heart to keep beating.

They stayed like that for a few minutes. A few glorious minutes.

"So my dad told me about your Mansfield application," Oliver said, his voice a bit lower than normal. "Good for you."

"Well, I heard that you're building a school in Guatemala next month."

"Yep."

"And that you still haven't told your dad you don't want to be a lawyer."

He picked at a cuticle. "So, about those Crawfords."

She bumped him with her hip. "You're always telling me to stand up for myself, to have a voice. Am I the only one who values your advice?"

"You value my advice?"

"Always." Her breath quickened. "Not *that* much has changed, has it?"

Oliver turned his head toward her. With their arms touching, their faces were agonizingly close.

"I don't know. Sometimes it feels like everything has changed," he said. The streetlights glistened in his eyes. He licked his lips, and Finley couldn't take her eyes off of them. "And then at other times . . . right now . . . I think maybe nothing has."

She bit her bottom lip, right where the ridiculously tempting freckle on Oliver's own lip was. The feelings she'd been tamping down for weeks pushed forcefully to the surface. She needed to bury them again, needed to beat them into submission until they could stay down where they belonged. And she needed to bury them soon, or she was going to do something stupid. Like keep looking at his mouth. Like lean closer and watch him lean closer, too, and close her eyes and . . .

And . . .

Nothing.

She opened her eyes to see that Oliver had backed away and was looking over the city again. He wore a sad smile on his face. Did he know what she'd just about done?

"Emma thinks I'm ridiculous for not wanting to be a lawyer," he said. "She thinks I should declare political science and give it a couple of years to take all my electives. See if I don't change my mind. Maybe she's right. Maybe I'll want it more after seeing more of how the world works."

Finley gritted her teeth. "Maybe. You can always change majors. But is that what you want?"

"It doesn't hurt anybody to try."

"Doesn't it? Every phone call and email with your dad will be about what you're learning. Every weekend and holiday at home, there'll be talk of nothing but how great it'll be when the Bertrams take over the firm. Won't that hurt you? And won't it hurt your dad if you tell him then that you've changed your mind rather than telling him now that your mind is already made up?"

Oliver let out a slow, ragged breath. "But what if my mind isn't made up anymore? What if I'm torn between what I've always wanted and what I *should* want? What I *could* want?"

"You can't base your entire life on a sense of obligation," she said. Oliver's eyebrows arched at her. "This isn't about me," she added.

"I hear what you're saying, Fin, and I promise I'll think about it." He squeezed her shoulder, but let go quickly. "I'm going to chat with Emma and then go to bed." He handed her the umbrella. "You coming down?"

"No, I'm going to stay out a bit longer. See you tomorrow."

When Oliver went downstairs, Finley put down the umbrella. The rain had eased into a light mist. She closed her eyes and wrapped her arms around her chest, a familiar ache settling into her bones.

Oliver was changing himself to be with Emma. Finley loved the girl, but she wasn't good enough for Oliver. Granted, Finley had hardly proved good enough for him, trying to kiss him when he had a girlfriend. How could she have done that to him? To Emma? It didn't matter how Finley felt, that she was in love with him. He was

with someone else. *That's* what mattered. She squeezed her temples.
She was no better than Harlan. She'd let her feelings become more
important than the feelings of two people she cared deeply about.

Everything was upside down.

She stayed there in her thoughts, watching a neighbor walk his
dog from one side of the street to the other until she felt a vibration
from her back pocket. On her phone was a message from Harlan.

Did u watch? What'd u think?

She texted back:

Who was that and what did he do with Harlan Crawford?

A response flashed almost instantly.

My stunt double. I send him in for all the dangerous stuff.

She smiled and typed.

He was very convincing. He almost fooled me.

Really?? Did u like what I said?

What you said about volunteering was amazing.

And the rest?

She scratched her nose, thinking. She replied honestly.

I don't know...

I meant every word.

You mean your stunt double did.

☺☺☺ He says whatever I tell him to say. My dad wasn't happy.

Oh no! Why?

A movie he's pushing on me. Assassin in training. Not exactly
the vibe he's trying to promote.

I thought you got excellent practice for the movie tonight.

☺☺☺

You killed it. ☺ I was really proud of you.

He didn't respond right away. Had she upset him somehow?
Was he in a lot of trouble with his dad? Was she not taking this
seriously enough?

I texted Juliette to tell her I'm sorry.

A grin spread across Finley's face. She texted him back immediately.

And now I'm even prouder.

Another pause, and then he wrote:

Don't string me along, Price.

She sighed.

Not trying to. Just trying to be a good friend.

You'd be a better friend if u weren't so damn cute.

She laughed.

I'll see what I can do. When do you get back?

Tomorrow at noon. See u then, Price.

* * *

The following morning, Uncle Thomas joined Finley and Liam in the breakfast nook. "How are you kids?" he asked, patting Liam's back and squeezing Finley's shoulder as he sat next to her.

"Good, Uncle Thomas," Liam said. "Did you see Harlan's interview last night?"

"No, how was it?" he asked, pulling out the paper and taking a bite of toast.

"He's become a humanitarian," Finley said.

"Has he?" He flipped through to the entertainment section. "Why, yes he has." He skimmed the article, then set the paper down and looked at Finley. "You seem to be a very good influence on that young man."

Finley poked at her blueberries, blushing. "It's not like that."

Uncle Thomas and Liam both chuckled.

Partway through breakfast, Liam's phone chimed. "That's odd," he mumbled.

"What?" Finley asked.

"I just got an urgent email with a flight itinerary for this afternoon to Madrid. Is this spam?"

"What? Who's it from?"

"Hold on, Harlan's texting . . ." Liam's eyes flew over the screen. "Holy crap. Holy crap! He got me tryouts with Real Madrid! And Arsenal! And West Ham!" He jumped up and kissed Finley's head. "I don't know what you've done to that dude, but don't you dare stop. I have to pack!"

The rest of the morning, Finley and Oliver helped Liam get ready for his flight. His cab was due to arrive just after noon to take him to the airport, while Harlan and Emma were due home shortly before then. A few minutes before twelve, the three were waiting on the Bertrams' stoop when a town car pulled in front of the house. The door opened, and Harlan and Emma hopped out. Emma ran to Oliver, kissing him hard when she reached him. Finley swallowed and looked away . . . to Harlan, sauntering from the car. She shook her head but smiled to see him beaming at Liam.

Liam jumped up and gave Harlan a big hug, slapping his back. "You are the best, man. How'd you do this?"

"My dad reps some athletes. It wasn't that hard to get him to make a few phone calls for a friend. It helps that your stats are as good as you said."

"I don't know how I can repay you."

"Don't think about it. Just do your thing, man. You're gonna be great."

A few minutes later, Liam's cab arrived, and he grabbed Finley's shoulders. "I love you, sis. Give Harley a break, will you?"

Finley smiled. "Enough. Go kick some butt, Liam." She hugged him tightly. "Love you."

She waited to cry until her brother was pulling away from them, waving feverishly.

Oliver grabbed Emma's bags and took them into her place, leaving Harlan and Finley standing on the curb.

"That was so, so amazing of you," she told him, wiping her eyes. "How can I thank you?"

"Go out with me."

"Harlan." She pushed him and he grabbed her hand.

"Please. Say you'll go out with me, just for dinner. We can go anywhere you want. Just let me prove to you that I'm not the guy you think I am."

She bit her lip. "How did Juliette respond to your text?"

Harlan winced. "She said, and I quote, 'Whatever.' Then she sent me a picture of her and Raleigh kissing on the beach."

"That sounds about right."

He held her hand to his chest. It was firm, and his heart was beating frantically. "Dinner tonight. Say yes, Price."

She narrowed her eyes. "Just dinner."

His grin nearly split his face apart. "I'll pick you up at six, and wear . . . anything. Nothing." She blushed but laughed. "I don't care what you wear. I'll see you at six."

CHAPTER NINETEEN

~O~

At six o'clock that night, the doorbell rang. Oliver, his parents, and Finley were all in the study, but no one was in the mood to move. His dad looked at him, and Oliver reluctantly slipped out of the room to answer the door while Finley clutched his mom tightly and wept.

It took a moment—a long one—for Oliver to compose himself. He took a deep breath and opened the door to see Harlan. What was he doing here? Had he heard?

Harlan gave him an odd look. "Are you going to invite me in? I'm here to pick up Finley."

Pick up Finley? "For what?"

Harlan narrowed his eyes. "Our date. Didn't she tell you?"

Resentment and surprise clashed inside him like fire and ice. "Finley's not going to make it tonight."

Harlan pushed past him into the house, looking around. "What's—" He spotted Finley in the study, still sobbing against Oliver's mom, and his face paled. "Is she okay? What's going on?"

"I don't know if I should say," Oliver answered, itching to push Harlan back out the door so he could return to Finley. She was hunched over, crumpling up the letter that had caused all of this. He heard her whimper, and the sound pierced him like a rusty knife. She *needed* him.

"Don't leave me hanging right now. What's going on?" Harlan said, looking pained. As if he had any idea what this pain felt like.

Finley released Oliver's mom and threw the letter on the ground, stomping on it. Oliver felt like his heart was being stomped on just watching her. He felt so helpless, especially now, out here getting rid of Harlan when he should have been comforting her. The need to help somehow, anyhow, was overpowering.

Oliver's dad's voice was soft and soothing, but a single phrase reached them: "... don't have to go ..."

Oliver swallowed hard, tamping down the urge to run to Finley and hold her.

"Ollie, please," Harlan said, begging. "You have to tell me what's going on."

"Fine." With a glance at Finley's shaking form, Oliver led Harlan to the piano room, closing the door behind them. Disgust and fury tinged his words. "Fin's mom was diagnosed with throat cancer and is scheduled for emergency surgery on Friday. She asked to see Liam and Fin before she goes in for surgery, but with him being gone, she still wants to see Finley." Oliver gnawed at a cuticle to keep from punching the wall. He knew if he started, he wouldn't stop till he was bleeding. "She had the nerve to write Fin a letter, so my dad called the prison and they actually talked about 'compassionate' medical release. As if she doesn't deserve to rot in prison."

Shock covered Harlan's face.

"You know about Fin's mom, don't you? Deirdre Ryan Price? Well, Google it. I can't even talk about it." He didn't know how to feel about Harlan's ignorance on the subject. He just wanted the guy to leave.

"Talk about what, dammit? What is going on?"

The words exploded from his mouth. "She beat Finley, okay?" Oliver cursed and ran an unsteady hand over his face. "After Gabriel died, the woman became a freaking alcoholic. A prescription drug addict. One night, she came home with some dude she'd picked up in a bar to find Finley watching one of her dad's old movies. She freaked out. Beat the crap out of Finley and broke her jaw."

Just saying the words made Oliver's blood boil and his eyes water. He wanted to put Fin in a bubble and never let anyone hurt her again. He wanted to go to the prison and make Deirdre pay. Violently.

Nice thought from the guy who'd always pushed Finley to get closure. He was such a hypocrite. And he had no intention of changing that, because if he ever got his hands on that woman . . .

"*How?*" Harlan asked through gritted teeth. "How could anyone do this to her? To Finley?" Harlan's voice hitched on Finley's name, and the sound made Oliver wince. That feeling Harlan was just learning—that combination of powerlessness and shock, protectiveness and savage, brutal rage—was something Oliver had lived with for years.

Oliver's voice trembled with emotion. "I don't know. The guy with her was an off-duty cop. He caught her before she could do any more damage, but it was . . . it was *bad*. The first few weeks Fin lived with us, her whole face was one giant bruise, and her jaw was wired shut. She wouldn't talk to anyone but Liam and my mom. She was always flinching and hiding. Liam slept in her room most of the time, because she was so terrified. She'd wake up with these awful nightmares—" He shook his head, but he couldn't stop picturing her broken face and haunted eyes, couldn't stop hearing her screams. Angry tears blurred his vision. He blinked them away, wishing the memories would go with them.

"Emma always teases me about being overprotective of Fin, but sometimes when I see her, I can't stop picturing her like that. I can't stop remembering her face and the way she'd *cower* when anyone got too close to her, and I just—" Oliver rubbed his eyes. "I want her to be strong, but the idea of something else bad happening to her . . . it *terrifies* me. I have nightmares about it, man. Seeing her hurt—"

"I get it." Harlan clapped a hand to his shoulder. "I've only known her for a few months, but the idea of someone hurting her makes me . . . murderous."

Oliver sniffed. "You don't know the half of it. For the first couple of months Fin lived with us, I used to go upstairs and turn on her dad's movies and fall asleep in the theater room, just so she'd have a place to go when she woke up screaming. She came every night. Liam came most nights, too."

Harlan's voice cracked, and his eyes were wet. "How did she ever get past that?"

"She didn't." *That's why I have to make her see her mom,* Oliver thought. A hard resolve formed in his gut. *If I'm there, she'll be okay. I can help her get through it.* Finley needed this, and she needed him there. He could put his own anger aside if it helped Finley confront hers. He had to.

They stood, seething, for several moments before Harlan spoke again. "Is there any chance she'll get this early release?"

"My dad doesn't know. I guess with her celebrity status, it was a huge surprise that she went to prison in the first place. But she assaulted the arresting officer and showed up high to court—"

"She didn't."

"My dad says it's a good thing for Finley she did, or she probably just would've gotten probation and Fin would still be with her . . ." Oliver slammed his eyes shut, the thought like a physical blow.

He was wrong. He couldn't let Finley go to the prison. What kind of a monster would ask her to see that woman again?

Stop it! It's not about you! She has *to do this.*

Harlan cursed, and scattered thoughts poured out of him. "I need something to do. I have to help. I should . . . I should call and cancel the reservation for tonight. And, um, I'll let Mr. Weston know she'll miss auditions this week. Will you tell her I . . . I . . . what do you say for something like this? Aagh! This is so messed up."

Oliver nodded, pulling his own thoughts together. "I'll tell her you're sorry and that you're thinking of her."

"Thanks, man."

Oliver took Harlan—*finally*—back through the hallway. He opened the front door, and Finley's head whipped up. Her face was blotchy and her eyes were puffy from crying. But instead of looking at Oliver, she looked at Harlan—*Harlan*.

It didn't matter. Knowing Fin, even now, she was just being nice. Besides, Harlan was just passing through, while Oliver would always be there for her. Always.

Harlan gave Fin a sad smile and wave before leaving. She returned it.

And Oliver returned to the study, where he belonged.

* * *

~*F*~

What can I do?

Finley stared at Harlan's text for what felt like ages. It was nice of him to be thinking of her, but she felt lost. Uncle Thomas had sent Ollie out of the house, thankfully. He was too upset to be of any use to her, bouncing back and forth between opinions like a ping-pong ball. Go to the prison. Don't go. Go, but only if he was with her. Or maybe he should go in first and talk to her mom before Fin did.

She was sick of it.

Another time, she may have felt guilty thinking that, but she didn't have the emotion to spare. She couldn't be around Ollie when he was trying to put her in Bubble Wrap and pop it at the same time. And she'd already cried on Aunt Mariah's shoulder for the last two nights. The woman needed a break.

But Harlan . . .

What do you know? she texted.

As much as u want me to know. Nothing more.

Does your dad rep the warden at Rockford Women's Detention Center? ☹

No. ☹ But Mr. Bertram has connections, right?

Yeah. He's already called Raleigh's dad, too. He said he's calling in every favor owed him to make sure she's denied medical release.

I can call my dad, too. He knows a lot of powerful people.

I don't want you to have to contact your dad again. I know you're going through crap of your own with him. Uncle Thomas will take care of everything. I just feel sick

Sick. That didn't begin to describe how she felt. She felt like blowing up the world and drowning in the ashes. But she also hated how much this was affecting her. So she added to her text.

and stupid

Then another:

and embarrassed

Harlan's response came quickly.

Don't feel stupid or embarrassed. Let me come over & bring u something. Are u hungry? Thirsty? Need distraction?

She paused. What did she want? She looked around her bed, tissues scattered everywhere, angry scrawling on a pad of paper of things she wished she could say to her mom. She didn't want this.

Distraction would be nice.

I'm on my way.

Relief washed over her.

Thanks.

* * *

Finley was curled up on the couch in the darkened theater room watching Magic Bullet infomercials when she heard a voice.

"Did someone order a distraction?"

She lifted herself from the couch, aware of how swollen her face was from crying. But Harlan didn't seem to mind. He just plopped down next to her and pulled two spoons and a gallon of bubble gum ice cream from a bag. She laughed and wiped her nose.

"You didn't have to do this."

"Have you seen yourself? Believe me. I had to do this."

She smiled, rubbing her eyes. "What else is in that bag?"

"Movie selections. What do you want to watch?"

"I honestly don't care."

"What was that? You're dying to watch something with me in it? Excellent choice," he said, pulling out the talking dog movie he'd done several years ago.

A laugh burst from her lips. "Your finest work."

"Just eat your ice cream. Liam told me that another one of your favorite hobbies is to make fun of terrible movies. I thought I'd oblige." He put the movie in the DVD player and returned to the couch.

"Y . . . you talked to Liam?"

He sat beside her and popped the lid off the ice cream. "I was worried about you."

Finley grabbed the remote and pressed play. Then she moved closer to Harlan. He held up his arm. "Come here." She paused. "I won't try anything, Price. Just come here."

Maybe her judgment was compromised. Maybe she couldn't handle being alone right now with her demons. Or maybe Harlan was just exactly what she needed. She slid under his arm, put her back against his side, and curled her legs up on the opposite side of him. When Harlan rested his head against hers, she felt him sigh. She handed him a spoon, and they started the movie.

* * *

~*O*~

Just after midnight, Oliver and Emma returned from the date Oliver's dad had forced on him. He'd been livid with his dad for kicking him out of the house, but he made a point of keeping his cool with Emma. She didn't need to see him at DEFCON 1.

"Do you mind if I just check on Finley before going home?" Emma asked. "I can't stop worrying about . . . what?"

Oliver looked at her, at the concern on her face, and some of his own concern melted. He lifted her chin and kissed her. She put her hands to his cheeks and kissed him softly back.

"Mmm. What was that for?" she asked.

"For being so sweet." He kissed her nose. "I'm sure Finley will appreciate it." Hand in hand, they walked up to the fourth floor. A low hum from the theater room guided them in. The credits were rolling on a movie. Rounding the couch, they found Finley nestled under Harlan's arm, her head lying on his chest.

"What—" Oliver began, but Harlan waved at him with his free hand.

"Shh!" he said in a hushed voice. "She's finally asleep."

"How is she?" Oliver whispered back, suppressing the urge to yank her out from under Harlan's arm.

"Not great. She's nervous about what to say to her mom tomorrow."

"So she's going, then?"

Harlan made a face. "I tried to talk her out of it, but yeah, she's going."

Oliver blew out a slow breath. As much as he hated the thought of Fin in more pain, it was the right thing. And with him there to help her, she could finally move forward. "Good. She needs to see her mom if she wants to move on."

"All due respect, man, but you're dead wrong. Seeing her mom is the last thing she needs."

Oliver wanted to slap Harlan's smug confidence from his face. The guy had known Fin for a few months. Like he had any idea what she needed. "And all due respect back, but you don't know what you're talking about. The fear of seeing her mom has been eating at her for years. She needs to face this. I'll help her through it."

Harlan's smirk was ugly. "Too bad you won't be there."

"What are you talking about?"

"I'm taking her."

"No. No chance in—"

"Shut up," Emma whispered, getting between them. "Shut your stupid machismo mouths right now, or I will stab you both in the eye. Let the girl sleep."

Oliver was still staring daggers at Harlan when Emma pushed his chest. "Ollie, come on. Let's leave them alone." She grabbed his hand and started pulling. "Harlan, you take care of her, or I will end you."

Harlan held up his hand. "Of course. She'll be fine."

Emma pushed Oliver out of the room, stopping when they reached the hall. "What was that, huh? You think you're the only person in the world who cares about her?"

"I know I'm not—"

"Then let us help her! Let Harley help her. You've said it yourself, he's good for her. She's been more vocal since she met him, right?" He gave the smallest, most begrudging of nods. "He likes her, Ollie. I know you're protective of her, but so is he. I've never seen him care about someone like he does her. Let him fight her battles for a change."

"That's just it," Oliver cried. "I don't want anyone fighting her battles for her. I want *her* fighting them! She can do this; we just have to let her."

"Says the guy who wants to go with her! What were you planning to do, stay in the car? You know she shouldn't have to do this alone. No one should."

He ran his hands across his face. "Maybe you're right. I can't exactly see straight when it comes to her."

She put her arms around him. "I know. You care about your family. It's one of the things I love about you."

Oliver's head snapped up, and his chest grew warm for an entirely different reason. "Love?"

Emma arched an eyebrow. "Don't get ahead of yourself there, buddy." She kissed him. "Now, come on and walk me home."

CHAPTER TWENTY

~$\mathcal{F}$~

Late the following morning, Finley, Oliver, and the Crawfords sat at the breakfast table with Uncle Thomas, who had taken the morning off.

"Are you sure you don't want me to come with you?" Uncle Thomas asked.

Finley nodded. "I'm sure, thanks." Harlan squeezed her hand under the table. She squeezed back.

"If it's still all right with you, sir, I'll drive her there and back," Harlan said. Oliver's eyes narrowed, but he didn't say anything.

"It's fine with me, as long as it's what Finley wants," Mr. Bertram said with a softness she'd rarely seen from him. "Is it what you want?"

Oliver, normally so mild and composed, seemed to loom over her. Disapproval rolled off of him in waves. She avoided his eyes. "It's what I want."

"Then we'll see you at dinner."

Twenty minutes later, Harlan and Finley were driving his Range Rover out of town on I-90.

"Do you know what you're going to say?"

She sighed. "Not a clue. What do you say to a woman like that?"

"How about 'You suck, I hate you, and I never want to see you again'?"

Finley tapped her lip. "Too vague."

Harlan laughed. "Okay, how about 'I never want to see you again. Good luck with the cancer'?"

"Too nice."

"'I'm sorry, have we met?'"

"Perfect." Her smile faded as quickly as it had appeared.

"You don't have to do this, you know."

"Yeah, I do. She asked me to come. I don't want to look back on this and have regrets."

"Screw regrets, Price. She doesn't deserve your regrets. She doesn't deserve your time or your kindness or—or a second of your thoughts. Think about what she did! Think about the fact that she hasn't contacted you in over two years! She doesn't deserve you."

She frowned, but her eyes hardened. "You know, you're right."

"Then blow this off! Show her she doesn't mean anything to you."

"No," she said, her will becoming steel. "If I'm going to show her what she means to me, she needs to see it."

An hour later, Finley and Harlan were being escorted into the visitor's area of Rockford Women's Detention Center. The floors and halls were a dull gray, but the booths and stools were eggshell blue with flowers painted around the sides. The dash of color did nothing to brighten Finley's mood. She tapped the table with her thumb, burning nervous energy as she glanced at visitors in other booths. Despite a few brave smiles, the place was rotten with disappointment.

She made eye contact with a little girl whose eyes were as wide as they were blue. The girl sucked on a strawberry blonde curl. Her mother came to the glass, and the girl's father held her up to the phone. When she saw her mother, the little girl screamed and flailed. Her pink dress caught around her legs, and she kicked to be free of it. The father's voice caught and he put the little girl back down. She sobbed and hugged her father's leg as he spoke to his wife.

"I can't do this," Finley whispered. "I can't be here. I can't face her."

"That's fine; let's go," Harlan said.

He grabbed her hand when a buzzer sounded, pulling Finley's eyes back. A thin woman with limp brown hair was being escorted through a door. A long-sleeved white shirt and baggy black pants sagged around her. Her once bright brown eyes looked dead, despite the makeshift eyeliner she had expertly applied. The wrinkles on her gaunt face were a sign of hard living more than age. She pursed her lips and sat down on her side of the glass, gesturing to the phone.

Finley's heart hammered as she picked it up. Her breath came in short bursts. She had to brace herself before she could bring the phone to her ear. Harlan's hand rested on her shoulder.

"Finley," the voice on the other end of the phone rasped, sounding nothing like the sharp voice that occupied her nightmares. The woman's lifeless eyes watered. "My Finley."

Tears sprang to Finley's eyes. "Don't," she whispered. "Don't act like you've missed me after what you did. You haven't even written to me until now."

"I didn't know what to say." She held a bony hand to the glass. "I started a hundred letters to you, but the words always fell flat. I want you to know I've been sober for sixteen months." Finley noticed a bronze sobriety chip on the table. "I wanted to give this to you so you can know how sorry I am." She clutched the chip. "I've tried to make it up to you by cleaning myself up." The tears in her mother's eyes rolled down her cheeks, dripping onto the booth. "I've tried so hard."

The woman on the other side of the glass looked nothing like the coarse, cruel woman she remembered, or the vibrant, larger-than-life figure she remembered from before that. Nothing like the

Ms. Illinois who married her college sweetheart. Her face was lined with grief and sickness. Her eyes pleaded with every tear. Finley felt her resolve waver.

Harlan's hand tightened on her shoulder. His face was only inches above hers, close enough to the phone to catch what was being said. "Convenient that she missed the step about 'making amends' in her twelve-step program," Harlan growled. "Don't tell me you're falling for this, Price."

Finley's throat constricted, and her spine stiffened. He was right. "How could you have that chip, Mom?" Her voice grew stronger. "Isn't one of the steps to make amends with the people you wronged? How did you make amends with me?"

The hand on the glass slipped. "It's like . . . it's like I said. I've tried to make amends by cleaning myself up. I've been going to therapy—"

Harlan snorted.

"And nowhere in this therapy or in your 'cleaning up' did you think, 'Hmm, maybe the daughter I *beat* could use an apology'?" Finley snapped. Her mother's eyes went wide, and she started weeping. "You never thought to tell me that you were sorry for breaking my jaw? Or for screaming and throwing dishes at me whenever I talked about Dad?"

She threw down the phone and yanked up her sleeve, revealing three hideous scars. Flashes of the old apartment seared themselves into the backs of her eyes, but she knew she wasn't there. She was here.

And she was pissed.

She pressed her arm against the glass. "Are you even sorry for this, Mom? For burning me with cigarettes *on the day of Dad's funeral*?" She grabbed the phone again, crying furious tears. "I had to treat these at home so Liam wouldn't freak out and call the cops and ruin the funeral! We lied to everyone that you were too grief-stricken to leave your bed! But you weren't even upset about

Dad! *You were high!* How did you make amends for this, Mom?" She screamed and slapped the glass. "HOW?"

A guard caught Finley's eye. "Keep it down, miss," he told her, pointing to the little girl. Her eyes were glued on Finley.

Finley's mother crumpled in the booth, gripping the phone at her ear, sobbing. Finley jerked her sleeve down, not wiping her tear-stained cheeks. She picked up the phone and heard her mother whispering, "I'm so sorry. I'm so sorry."

"I don't accept your apology," she spat. "Do you know I still hyperventilate at the smell of alcohol? That I flinch when someone reaches for me? Do you know how long it took me to even let Uncle Thomas hug me, or that for the first two months I lived with them, I slept under the bed, because I was so afraid of someone coming in to hurt me? Do you have any idea what that was like? I probably wouldn't have a friend in the world if not for Oliver—" Her throat stuck. Thinking of Oliver filled her with a host of emotions she didn't want to think about right now.

"I'm so sorry, Finley. I'm so sorry," her mother kept whispering. "I don't deserve your forgiveness."

"No, you don't," she hissed, unable to stop the flow of tears. "Good luck in surgery, Mom." She slammed down the phone, and her mother's face flew upward, contorted with grief.

Finley watched her mother being escorted from the visitor's area. With eyes fixed on her daughter, she kept mouthing, "I'm so sorry."

When her mother was out of sight, Finley ran from the room, out into the hall, and slammed into the doors, waiting for the guard to let her out. She pushed and pushed the panic bar until the door buzzed. Then she stumbled into the sunlight and fell to her knees on the grass.

Harlan was a breath behind her. He crouched down and put his arms around her shaking shoulders. "You were incredible," he whispered into her hair. "Incredible."

"Then why do I feel so wretched right now?" she asked between sobs.

Harlan wiped hair from her face and put his hands on her cheeks. "You just faced up to your nightmares, Finley. How else could you expect to feel?"

"I don't know. Empowered?" She hiccupped. "Free?"

"Don't let Oliver's after-school special B.S. get into your head. Your mom was trying to manipulate you, probably so you won't have Mr. Bertram fight the medical release."

"She looked so sad. But maybe you're right."

"You know I'm right." He smoothed her hair and kissed her head. "You're the best person I've ever known."

"I'm not. I'm the angriest person you've ever known."

"No, you're the best person I've ever known," he repeated, "and you just stood up for yourself for a change. You let her know she doesn't own you." He kissed her head again. She nodded. "You were incredible, Price," he whispered, kissing the tip of her nose. "Incredible." He kissed the tears from her cheeks. "Incredible." He kissed her closed eyes.

The warmth from his lips trailed across her face. She lifted her head, waiting for another kiss. It didn't come. Disappointment opened her eyes. Harlan was looking at her, stroking her face with his thumbs. He caught her eyes and kept them, bringing his face closer. "You were incredible."

His lips met hers. The kiss started slow and light. But tentative lips gave way to a burning need. Finley grabbed his shirt and pulled him closer, pressing his lips against hers. The heat from his body seemed to fuel her onward. Her hands found his hair while his found her waist, grazing her exposed skin. She hadn't even realized he'd pulled her to a stand. His lips still on hers, he picked her up and carried her to the SUV, all the while making out like their mouths were made for this and nothing else. When they reached the SUV, he put her down at the passenger door. He broke away for a moment to unlock the door, but Finley grabbed him and pulled him back in.

Muggy air swirled around them, but the only thing she could think of was his mouth. Time lost all meaning. She was adrift in space, and his lips were her only anchor. She lost all sense of herself, existing only in him. In his mouth. His taste. It was wonderful.

Why had she waited so long to kiss someone? An answer bounced around in the back of her head. A single word—a name—pushed itself forward so forcefully, she broke apart from Harlan. When his face moved away from hers, he looked as dazed as she felt. His mouth was red from the pressure, and he seemed to be having a hard time focusing. They were both panting.

"Believe me, I'm not complaining, but where did that come from?"

She tried to cover her face with her hands, but he grabbed them and pulled her in for a hug. His arms were strong, but gentle. "I don't know. I'm sorry—"

"You don't get to apologize for kissing me like that. You should teach classes in making out." He brought his face down and kissed her softly, tenderly, until she was lost in him again.

"Are you okay?" he asked when they broke apart.

She leaned her head on his chest. "I don't know. But thank you for being here."

"Always."

He opened the door for her and she climbed in. Her phone, which she'd left in the cup holder, was blinking with a missed text. She pulled it out to see a message from Oliver sent right after they'd arrived at the prison.

I know you're stressed about seeing your mom. I should have said this before you left. I can't imagine how hard today must be. I know you're angry & hurt. You have every right to be. What she did to you is unthinkable. I won't tell you how to act with her or what to say because only you can know that. Just remember that you've worked really hard to forge your own path & to become the amazing person you are. Stay true to that path & you'll do yourself proud. That's all that matters. Love you Fin.

Harlan climbed into the seat beside her and was just buckling up when he noticed the phone. "Someone text you?"

"Yeah, but it's nothing," she said. She dropped the phone back in the cup holder, wishing she could erase the bitter taste Oliver's message left in her mouth.

While they waited for the gate to open so they could leave, Harlan leaned over and erased the taste for her.

***

The trip to the prison had taken ninety minutes. The trip back took nearly twice that. Only partially to distract herself from the guilt, she found herself kissing Harlan at every stop sign and every stoplight.

"Stupid. Green. Lights," he muttered between kisses when a horn behind them began honking. He faced the road. "Price, I'm going to get into a wreck if you don't cut this out."

She pulled her feet up to sit cross-legged. "Unfortunately, this won't be a problem once you get on the freeway."

"You know, freeway driving is responsible for a lot of accidents every year," he said, changing the route on his GPS. "Maybe we should take country roads."

"Country roads, huh?"

He looked behind him, abruptly changing lanes. "Yes. Slower pace. Far, far more stops." He pulled up to a light.

"Stops are good," she said, leaning toward him.

"Very good."

They made it back home just in time for dinner. Finley pulled down the passenger side mirror to see bright red lips, the skin around them pink and chafed.

"How am I going to hide this?" she moaned.

"Most girls would consider that a badge of honor." Harlan opened the door and stepped into the Grants' garage.

She hit his arm. "I'm serious. I look like I've been burned or something."

"No, you look like you've been having a really good time." He held the door into the house for her and kissed her cheek as she passed him. "Just put some makeup on it. Isn't that what girls usually do?"

"How would I know? I've never made out before! And Juliette said the makeup I have is 'for little girls.' I don't even know what that means."

When Harlan didn't respond, she looked at him. "You are unlike any girl I've ever dated. No, known. I mean that in a good way," he reassured her. "Now wait here. I'm sure Emma has something you can use."

Even with her lips and face back to a normal color, thanks to Emma's many concealers, Finley couldn't quell her nerves. Harlan guided her toward the dining room where the Bertrams and Emma were waiting. She should have felt lighter, freer than when she'd left that morning. But shaking off the weight of that conversation, the weight of her mother's regret, would take a lifetime of its own.

So she felt a perverse sense of karma that Nora was at the table when they entered the room. Aunt Mariah gave her a long, steadying hug before Emma jumped in to hug her. "Was it just so awful?"

Oliver hugged her next. She locked her eyes on Emma rather than risk looking at him. "Kind of."

"Don't let her fool you, though," Harlan said as they sat. "It may have been awful, but Price was brilliant."

"What do you mean?" Uncle Thomas asked. Blood rushed to her cheeks, but she was spared answering.

"She stood up for herself. Her mom was spinning some crap about AA and being sober and seeing therapists, all for the medical release, no doubt. And Price just let her have it." Thankfully, Harlan left out a few details, such as Finley showing her mother the burns on her shoulder, but he gave a faithful representation otherwise. Hearing him relay her words was hard enough, but her mother's grief-stricken eyes haunted her and drove her lower and lower into her chair.

At one point, she looked up to see the reactions of the others in the room as they hung on Harlan's every word. Uncle Thomas looked satisfied, Emma thrilled, Nora . . . appraising.

Oliver was looking right at her, sadness covering his every feature. Shame crawled its way up her throat, almost choking her. She grabbed Harlan's leg, and he trailed off. "I'm not doing the situation justice, but I was really proud of her." He looked at Finley. His pride buoyed her spirits.

"Good for you," Emma told her. Uncle Thomas agreed, telling her how happy he was that she could get closure. Even Nora nodded to this.

Nearly everyone agreed that she'd done the right thing. Why couldn't Oliver just agree, already?

Why couldn't she?

After dinner, Finley excused herself to go to the bathroom. She lingered for several minutes longer than necessary, staring at her reflection, trying to ground herself. Her eyes were still bloodshot from crying, and her lips still puffy from kissing. She almost didn't recognize the face staring back at her. When she finally came out, Oliver was waiting for her.

"How are you feeling?" he asked.

"Fine," she lied. "I'm just glad it's over."

"You got closure, then?"

She dropped her eyes, shaking her head. "I knew you were going to be like this."

His voice sounded heavy. "Like what?"

"Disapproving. I did what I did, okay? I deserve to have my voice heard. Isn't that what you're always telling me?"

"Was it *your* voice that was heard?"

"What are you trying to say?"

"Nothing, Fin. I'm just asking questions. If you're happy, if you feel like you have your well-deserved resolution, I promise you, there's no one in the world who's happier for you than I am."

"But you don't think I did."

"It doesn't matter what I think. Do *you* think you did?" he asked, looking almost desperate.

Her eyes stung. "So I was just supposed to sit there and let her take advantage of me? After everything she's done," she rubbed one of the round scars on her shoulder. "I was just supposed to forgive her because she's in AA?"

"Not if you didn't want to." His eyes grew wet. "Are you relieved, Fin? Please, just tell me you're happy with how you dealt with everything, and I'll never bring this up again. *Please*," he begged.

She rubbed her nose. "I don't know, okay? I feel sick about it! And I don't know if it's because of everything she did to me or because she looked like she's actually trying to change or if it's because this isn't the kind of thing you ever really get over. I don't know! Maybe I made a mistake—I sure feel like hell—but if I did, it was *my* mistake to make, not yours. The least you could do is stop judging me for it."

He dropped his head. "I'm sorry, Fin. I'm so sorry."

"I can't do this right now." She stepped around him and into the dining room, where she went to Harlan's side. He was talking to Uncle Thomas and Aunt Mariah, but when he saw her face, a V formed between his brows. He put his arm around her and pulled her close.

"I'm here now," he whispered in her ear. "You don't have to worry anymore."

CHAPTER TWENTY-ONE

~O~

At 10:30 Saturday morning, Oliver saw Emma step out of a silver BMW. A moment later, she turned up her nose and lifted up her boot to look at whatever she'd just stepped in. He laughed to himself. He watched her grab her bag from her car and mutter to herself as she walked through the parking lot of the run-down elementary school where M.A.D. was volunteering.

She passed through a break in a chain-link fence and looked up, catching his eye on her. She gave him a playful glare. "Ollie, it's a good thing you're so cute." She looked around at the school's faded orange walls and rusted playground equipment. "I wouldn't be caught murdered here."

He laughed again and set down his clipboard on a splintered picnic table. Then he crossed the distance to her and put his hands on the sides of her cheeks. "It is so," he said, kissing her, "so good to see you. What made you decide to come?"

"I thought I'd cheer you on. Paint! Hammer! Yay! Besides, you know how sexy that shirt makes you look."

"Yes, I'm devilishly handsome, aren't I?"

She dropped her bag and hugged him, running her hands over his back in a way that turned his legs to jelly. "Mmm," she said when they broke apart. "So, you having fun?"

Oliver pulled her over to a more secluded spot. "The volunteer coordinator with the school here kinda sucks. Nothing we've done has been good enough for her all morning. She's probably watching me right now, judging how I tilt my head when I kiss you."

Emma looked around, but the coordinator wasn't in sight. Thank heavens. She ran a finger down his arm and played with his palm. "Well, if you're looking for pointers," she teased. He smiled, tucking her under his arm and kissing the side of her head.

"Gee, thanks."

She laughed wickedly. "So what're Harley and Fin up to?"

Oliver pointed their clasped hands across the schoolyard to where the two stood with paintbrushes next to a wall covered in graffiti. Harlan painted a long yellow stripe up Finley's arm. The tiny girl bumped him with her hip and kept painting. Emma took a picture of them and showed it to Oliver. The distance made it blurry, but Oliver could see Harlan smiling and Finley's hair covering her laughing face.

Emma took the phone back and posted the picture to all her social media sites. Oliver watched over her shoulder, glad that Finley's face was indistinguishable.

Little bro @HarlanCrawford in love? #Priceless #Volunteering-Rocks #MADChicago

Oliver studied the tweet a moment longer than necessary. Then he shook his head as Emma rifled through her bag.

"I almost forgot," she said, pulling out a Mountain Dew.

He yanked it from her hand. "Ah, I love you, Emma Crawford."

He was already guzzling the soda, so she couldn't see his face flush the deepest red of all time. Love? What was he thinking? He liked her, yeah. He was kind of wild about her and the way she could make him laugh one second and want to tear his hair out the next, all while making his pulse race.

But love?

When he dropped his head back down, wiping his mouth,

Emma's eyes were all sorts of seductive. "You wanna get out of here before the Volunteer Dictator shows back up?"

He groaned. "I'd love to." He kissed her again, a long, slow kiss that left them both a little breathless. "But I'm supposed to be watching for 'outstanding participation' today so I can finalize the people who should be invited to Guatemala with me to build that school in July." She pushed off of him, not hiding her annoyance. "Ems, don't be like that."

She folded her arms and looked over the volunteers. "Why only three weeks? Why not the rest of the summer?"

He guided her face back around to his, hating how much this bothered her. "Emma, you know I'm not leaving *you*, right? This is something I've wanted to do since I was a freshman. It's not like I'm going down there to party. I'm going to help people."

"Right, with Sally Sexypants over there." She gestured to a girl in zebra print leggings who was working with a paintbrush. "Or were you thinking more Betty Bouncy—"

"Do you want me to pick you? Say the word, and I'll put your name down right now." The offer was out there before he even knew what he was saying. Nearly a month in another country with Emma? Was he ready for this?

"Safe move, Loverboy," she said. "I'm not even part of your club."

His heart jackhammered inside of him. He couldn't take it back. But as he looked into her eyes, so firm yet vulnerable, he didn't want to. He liked her. He really liked her.

"Then sign up," he said. "If you think I'm going to a Third World country to hook up with some chick I've been avoiding for years, you've lost your gorgeous mind. On the other hand, if there was a chance that my ridiculously hot girlfriend would actually agree to come with me, then I'd be a fool not to let her." His chest felt warm as he stroked her hair. Good warm. And only a little scary.

She peered into his eyes, so full of emotion. "Are you serious? You'd want me to come with you?"

"Yeah. Come with me." He kissed her neck.

"Really?" she whispered.

His heart stopped. *Really?* "Yes."

She leaned back and grinned. "Nah."

"What?" He backed away feeling . . . everything. Confused. Annoyed. Betrayed. Relieved. He shook his head, annoyance winning out. "You were just playing me?"

She kissed the tip of his nose. "No, but I did wonder if you'd care enough to try to convince me." She grabbed his hand and pulled him along with her. "Now get that clipboard and come observe Harley and Fin's outstanding participation, all right?"

He fumed but went along with her.

Across the school grounds, the other couple had finished painting and were now assembling bike racks. With instructions in one hand, Finley was gesturing to a wrench-wielding Harlan, who was shaking his head. He jumped up and stood behind her, reading the instructions and occasionally tickling her.

"Is it just me, or are they maybe the second cutest couple of all time?" Emma asked, grinning up at Oliver.

Oliver swallowed a lump in his throat that wasn't as big as it used to be. He nodded. Because as much as it still pained a part of him deep, deep inside, Emma was right. They were cute together. And most important, Finley looked happy.

Harlan's head dipped lower and lower behind Finley, and soon, he was nibbling Finley's shoulder. She tried to redirect him, but he dropped the wrench, held her arms in one hand, and started tickling her. She squealed.

"No! Crawford!"

"Price, you're asking for this!" he said over her giggles. "No one is supposed to scowl that much when her boyfriend is putting together a friggin' bike rack."

Emma smiled, then pulled out the sodas she'd brought for them. "Don't worry, Fin, the cavalry is here."

Still holding Finley, Harlan turned them to face Emma and Oliver. He reached a hand through Fin's pinned arms to grab the Dr. Pepper Emma was opening for him.

"Why, thank you, Emma," Harlan said with a falsetto voice, pretending to be Finley. He brought the bottle up to Finley's lips. Laughing, she tried to dodge the drink. He poured it anyway, and it spilled down her chin and shirt. "Mmm, this is delicious, Emma," he said, still as Finley. "You're as kind as your brother is super, painfully hot. I do love you Crawfords so very dearly."

"Enough," Finley giggled and wriggled free. Harlan spun her to face him and kissed the Dr. Pepper from her chin. Right in front of Oliver. "Why don't you take a break?" Finley asked. She wasn't blushing or self-conscious or anything. She just looked . . . happy. "Then maybe I'll finally be able to figure out these instructions."

"Too bad they're not in Spanish for you," Harlan joked.

"Ha-ha." She kissed him quickly and snatched the drink from his hands.

Harlan tried to grab her, but she hopped out of his reach, grinning. Then Harlan and Emma walked over to a ratty picnic table hidden under an overgrown ash tree while Oliver stood there, torn between sitting with Emma and talking to Finley. He looked at Emma inspecting the table before putting her elbows on it, then at Finley, whose brow was furrowed as she looked at the bike rack instructions.

She'd kissed Harlan in front of Oliver. Oliver kissed Emma in front of her. This was his world now.

The realization was bittersweet. He was glad they were both happy. He was. And it was easier to see her with Harlan knowing the guy cared so much about her.

So why the bitter? Why wasn't it all sweet?

Maybe you just never completely got over your first love, no matter how one-sided it was.

He shook himself. This wasn't even a real problem anymore. He liked Emma. *Real* like, not just because she was famous or beautiful . . . he liked her irrespective of that stuff. What he felt for Emma had nothing to do with Finley. Why couldn't he just let it go?

He looked over at Emma, smiling at her brother, laughing and glowing with a vibrancy that belonged only to her, and made his choice. He started walking to their table in time to catch part of her conversation with Harlan. But her words stopped him. Oliver pulled out his phone, glad for the massive tree separating them, and pretended to read something in case they spotted him. He should walk away now. He really should.

He dropped his head and listened.

"You have it so bad," Emma was saying to Harlan.

"You have no idea," he said. "Ems, I'm so into her. I just want to protect her from everything. Everyone."

In the reflection of his phone, Oliver could see Emma grinning. "OMG, you're in love with her, aren't you?"

His face matched hers. "Maybe I am."

"This is perfect, Harley! When you said you wanted to see if you could make her fall for you, I was furious. But now look at you! What started as a pathetic attempt at a conquest has turned out to be your saving grace."

What was she saying? Harlan had started all of this to see if Fin would fall for him? Oliver wanted to smash his fist into the tree. Or into Harlan.

He listened as Harlan joked. "Excuse me? I didn't need a saving grace."

"Yes, you did," Emma said. "You needed to be saved from Dad's scummy cynicism and from a lifetime of dating and cheating on ho-bags."

He scoffed, but he didn't deny it. "I'm glad everyone's going to see her the way they should now. Juliette, Nora, everyone at her school."

Emma arched an eyebrow. "And how's that?"

"As the type of girl who deserves to be noticed." He rapped the table. "Everyone's going to finally see how funny and talented and hot she is. They're going to appreciate her the way they should have this whole time. And when they do, they'll feel stupid for overlooking her. They'll kick themselves for not seeing her before."

Emma pointed a finger at him. "Not everyone. Oliver saw her. And *I* saw her before you did."

He smiled. "And there was no hidden agenda there, huh? You didn't do it for Oliver?"

"Oh, at first, sure," she said. "But as soon as I got to know her, I adored her for her and no one else."

"Well, you're smarter than the average bear."

"I still can't believe you're volunteering for her."

"Hey, I signed up before we were dating."

"Yeah. To convince her to date you."

"I actually don't mind it," Harlan said. "And if it pisses Dad off in the meantime, all the better. You know how he feels about volunteering. 'It's for résumés and radicals.' He was so mad after my *Tonight Show* appearance. Said I'm going to regret changing my image." He scowled. "Yeah, 'cause I want to be seen as a teen idol until I'm too much of a joke for a reputable director to even look at me? No thanks."

She swore. "He sucks. I'm glad you found a girl like Finley to keep your head on straight for a bit longer."

Harlan's voice changed. "I don't know if it's staying on straight, or not. Man, the things I want to—"

"Ew, okay, I'm still your sister," Emma said.

Harlan teased her about something, and their conversation shifted, letting Oliver's thoughts wander. He wanted to beat Harlan's face for making Finley into some kind of game. And he was mad at Emma, too. She'd known, and she hadn't done anything to stop him.

He was debating his next move when he heard Harlan.

"What the hell does she think she's doing?" he asked.

Oliver followed Harlan's eyes to where the awful volunteer co-ordinator was approaching Finley. A moment after Harlan started running, Oliver did, too.

Volunteers were coming over to witness the scene when they got there. Harlan looked as enraged as Oliver felt and sidled up to Finley.

"Guys," Oliver said to the nearby volunteers, "why don't you get back to work, okay? I've got this." When they left, it was just Finley, Harlan, Oliver, and the coordinator. Even Emma was standing a bit away from them.

The coordinator was fuming. "You should have completed three bike racks, and instead, I'm looking at the same scraps of metal we gave you when you showed up hours ago," she was saying.

Finley looked like a caged rabbit. Her eyes flitted around, landing on Oliver's. He smiled at her, nodding. She could do this. She took a deep breath. "Unfortunately, we've had a hard time with the instructions—"

But Harlan cut her off. "No. Price, you don't have to explain yourself." Harlan glared at the woman, but Oliver couldn't help but notice Finley's face. She looked relieved, but . . . what else? Disappointed? Frustrated? He used to be able to read her so well.

"You know we're volunteers, right?" Harlan said. "We're giving up *our* time to fix this run-down hellhole. You think you can just yell at us for not getting enough of *your* job done?"

The woman's face turned beet red. "Excuse me, was I talking to you? This girl committed to completing three bike racks." She looked away from Harlan to Oliver. "Is this how you run your orga-nization? No accountability? I turned down other volunteer groups because I was assured you could get the job done."

Oliver clenched his hands, but he kept his tone as calm as he could, as if this was a perfectly reasonable conversation. "And I'm sure we still can. Why don't we talk away from—"

"I don't want diplomacy, young man, I want results. I want you to take Little Miss Flirt off this project immediately and put someone on it who will actually work."

Finley's eyebrows shot up, but it didn't compare to the outrage on Harley's face.

Nostrils flared, Oliver spoke again. "Thank you for the suggestion, but I've found her to be an exceptional volunteer in the past." He looked at Finley. "Fin, do you want to keep working on the bike racks? Your call." Harlan turned to Finley, and her brows knit tightly together. "Fin?" Oliver repeated more quietly.

Harlan grew more and more incredulous. "No! No, she's not going to keep working on these stupid bike racks if she's going to be treated like this! We're giving up our day to help." He spun on the woman. "If that's not enough for you, then we're out of here." The woman huffed at him. He put his hand on Finley's back. "Come on, Price. Let's go."

Finley locked eyes with Oliver and mouthed, *"I'm sorry."* He just shook his head and watched Harlan usher Finley through the schoolyard to the parking lot, where they climbed into Harlan's SUV and peeled out.

How had this day gone so totally to crap? And why did Finley have to choose the one guy who inspired her to fight for her own opinion yet squelched it before she could say a word? He hated this. He hated that Harlan was his friend yet was nowhere near good enough for Finley.

He hated that the same was true of him. He'd never silenced her, but hadn't he pushed his voice on her under the guise of "empowerment"? Who was he to resent Harlan?

The coordinator's shrill voice cut into his thoughts. Oliver ignored her and strode over to Emma. She put a hand on his arm, and her face showed her concern. "You okay? You wanna take off now?"

"More than you can know." He kissed her hard, heedless of the coordinator breathing down his neck. "I'll call you later."

He kissed Emma again, then turned around to the seething woman.

"I'll build your bike racks, but we need to talk."

CHAPTER TWENTY-TWO

~ℱ~

Finley rested with her back against the headboard of her bed, running a finger absently over her lips as she read a text from Harlan. He sent a picture of himself looking dejected. She smiled at it, though she understood the feeling. Their bubble was about to burst. Juliette would be getting home at any minute.

As if on cue, a knock sounded at Finley's door. Her stomach churned as she called, "Come in."

A long, tanned arm pushed open her door, revealing a spectacularly bronzed Juliette. She was sporting cutoff shorts and an expensive t-shirt designed to look as if it had cost two bucks instead of ninety. "Daddy told me I'd find you here," Juliette said, a little too brightly.

Finley fumbled with her phone, dropping it on the bed. "Oh, did he? H . . . how was your trip?"

Juliette crossed the room and sat at the foot of Finley's bed. "A. Mazing. Amazing!" Her smile was huge. Too huge. "Raleigh's parents were seriously lovely. And their place in Costa Rica was . . ." she sighed and closed her eyes, "breathtaking."

Finley picked up her phone, rotating it rapidly. "I'm so glad," she said. "And Raleigh?"

Juliette combed a hand through her hair and dropped a long, sun-kissed blonde strand on Finley's floor. "OMG, he's so good.

The draft is this week, and his agent is sure he's going to go in at least the second round."

"Wow! Congratulations to him. And to you!" Finley gushed, stumbling over her feigned happiness. When she met Juliette's eyes, they were seeing right through her.

"Fin, oh my gosh, you are too funny." She rolled her eyes. "I know about you and Harley. Emma's been tweeting it like all week. She even posted a picture of you two."

"Sh . . . she did? I'm so sorry, Juliette, I wanted to be the one to tell you."

She moved on to another section of hair, pulling out and dropping more loose strands. "It's so fine. I love Raleigh. Just because Harlan was trying to break us up doesn't mean I can't be happy for you guys now that he's moved on. And honestly, it was kind of inevitable."

"Oh, yeah. Sure." She spun the phone around again. "Why do you think that?"

"Because you're exactly what Harlan needs, of course. That boy is torn between wanting to be the jerk who gets everything he wants and wanting to be the knight in shining armor to a damsel in distress. It's lucky for him that he found you."

Her eyebrows creased. "You think I'm his damsel in distress?"

Juliette stood up, shaking out her hair before patting Finley's shoulder. "No, sweetie, I think he's his own damsel. You're his armor. If he keeps you close enough, he can wear your problems instead of facing his own."

Finley's crease only deepened as Juliette swung the door closed after her. It was several minutes before she could text Harlan with the all clear.

Seriously?? How'd she take it?

Well, I think? She said she thought it was inevitable and that she's happy you've moved on and that she loves Raleigh.

I believed u until that last part.

I'm serious! That's what she said.

She's trying a bit too hard to convince u, doncha think? How could someone so smart be in love with such a clown?

Finley hesitated.

Don't talk about me like I'm not here.

His response was instantaneous.

WHAT????? What r u trying to tell me, Price????????

She tapped a fingernail on her teeth, smiling.

That you should meet me outside.

Fifteen seconds later, his reply came.

Where r u?

She smiled, slipped on her flip-flops, and ran downstairs.

* * *

The Grants' roof-deck was an oasis, with hedges bordering their pool and hot tub, and with a cushy sectional where Finley was sitting in her swimsuit and wrap. Her production notes were placed carefully around her. Rehearsals were in full swing, and Mr. Weston was letting her provide a lot more feedback than she'd expected. Meanwhile, Harlan paced poolside, growing angrier and angrier.

"Dad, this is my career, my life. If Ben Affleck wants to pay me in peanuts, I'm taking it." He grabbed the back of his head and squatted down. "I know it's more money, but . . ." a long pause followed. "I know, but . . ." Harlan pulled the phone away from his ear and swore loudly. He brought the phone back up. "Dad, I'm not working with that no-talent tool, Blaise Kane. He is everything that sucks in Hollywood. I'm either getting a new agent, or you're calling Ben back right now." Another pause. His eyes burned. "What do you mean, 'you need the commission'? Divorce mom on your dime, not mine!" A long, ugly string of obscenities followed before Harlan hung up. He threw his phone against a chair.

Finley stood and picked up the phone where it had fallen. Harlan looked on the verge of tears. "I'm sorry," she whispered, putting her arms around him. "Do you want to talk about it?"

"No, it's fine." He kissed her, then rested his head on hers. "While we're on the subject of my career, I've had about a dozen different magazines contact me and ask for an exclusive whenever we're ready to go public. Apparently, no one's content with pictures of me with the back of your head."

"Hey, sometimes you can see my hands—"

"Covering your face, yes. If the paparazzi don't beat me to the punch, one of these times, I'm gonna catch you head-on smiling, or even better, kissing me. And it's on, Price."

She smiled halfheartedly. "How about this: once you're in that movie of Ben Affleck's, I'll be on the red carpet with you, okay? But if you do Blaise Kane's ridiculous *Robo-Lords* movie, you're on your own."

His smile didn't reach his eyes. He shook off a distant look. "So, any word on your mom's medical release request?"

Finley frowned. Was he changing the subject or just that curious? "No, the warden said he'd have a decision within thirty days of her request, so he has two weeks to decide still."

He pulled her over to the couch and draped her feet over his lap, playing with her hair. "Mr. Bertram told me the surgery went well, so it doesn't sound very likely that she'll be released."

"When did you talk to Uncle Thomas?"

"Every time I run into him at your place." He put his arm around her and pulled her in close.

"So . . . what are you going to do about your dad?" she asked.

"Nothing. He'll come around. He thinks he's trying to help me." He paused. "You know he was a big producer until about ten years ago, when he had a couple of flops. When he decided to become our agent, he told Emma and me his philosophy up front."

"Which was?"

"That we should make as much money as we can now, invest,

and then do all the movies we actually care about once we're set for life. Of course, Emma couldn't stand it or working with my dad, hence her break to focus on college. But I've played ball until recently, because it was working."

"Right. The talking dog movie worked really well," she teased.

"Easy, Price." He pinched her knees, causing her to squeal.

She settled back into the crook of his arm. "So, what changed?" She felt his chest rise and fall. Rise and fall.

"Me, I guess." She didn't say anything. She just listened to him breathe. "There I was, just off of a huge box office success, on the cover of every magazine, and all my parents cared about was using the publicity to drive more nails into the coffin that is their marriage. So Emma and I left."

"What are you going to do now?"

Harlan ran a finger down her cheek and neck, lingering on her collarbone. Her skin tingled where he touched her. "I'm going to make out with you until everything else stops existing."

Her whole body grew hot. Her eyes closed almost against her will; she fought to keep from giving in, from letting him off the hook. She didn't want to be his armor. "I'm serious, Crawford. I'm worried about you being stuck in the middle of all this and getting hurt."

"My career will be just fine."

She backed away. "I'm not worried about your career. I'm worried about you."

"You really care that much?"

"Of course I do."

His eyes gleamed with emotion. "You're too good for me, Price."

"Then I'm glad you don't mind having what's too good for you."

He laughed. "Oh, I don't mind in the slightest." Harlan guided her face toward his and kissed her until the rest of the world faded into nothingness.

* * *

By late June, the regular cast at the Bertram family dinners had grown. In addition to Nora's occasional visits, Harlan and Emma were now permanent fixtures. Juliette, on the other hand, had practically moved in with Raleigh's family. Between her time with the Rushworths and her elite summer academic program at Northwestern, Finley almost never saw the girl.

Nora aside, Finley hadn't been happier in years. She sat across the ornately set table from Oliver and Emma and thought wistfully of a time when she'd hoped for something different. She never could have imagined that she'd be so happy for it to be Harlan's knee pressed against hers rather than Oliver's. For it to be Harlan squeezing her leg under the table when someone said something ridiculous that they'd laugh about later.

She watched Oliver lean over to Emma and whisper something, followed by Emma's tinkling laugh. Oliver looked enchanted by her. As if he couldn't believe his luck. Finley glanced at Emma, picking at her potatoes and calling the table's attention to something amusing. Did Emma realize that *she* was the lucky one in their relationship? Whatever fate awaited the daughter of two such damaged people as Mr. and Mrs. Crawford, Oliver would save her from it.

Just as Harlan would save the daughter of Deirdre Price, convicted child abuser and cancer survivor. Her mother's surgery was a success: the tumor had been removed and follow-up tests looked good. She'd been denied compassionate release earlier that day.

"What are you thinking about, Price?" Harlan murmured in her ear, pulling her from her reverie.

"What happiness looks like."

"Me, obviously," he said.

The corner of her mouth twitched up.

"Finley," Uncle Thomas said from the head of the table, "I forgot to mention that there's a letter for you on the hall table."

"For me? Who would write to me?" She squirmed, her mouth going dry. *Please, don't let it be from my mom.*

Uncle Thomas smiled. "You really can't think of anyone? Or any theater, perhaps?"

"What? Seriously?" She ran from the table and into the hallway. Uncle Thomas's low chuckle followed her all the way down the hall. She ripped open the letter bearing the "Mansfield Theater" logo and skimmed past the infuriating thanks and pleasantries—*Get to the point!*—until her eyes caught words like "interested" and "very impressed" and "would like to."

But nowhere was there a "yes."

A vexed sound escaped her throat. She leaned over the hall table, poring over the letter. After a couple of minutes, she felt breath blowing against her hair. Harlan was standing over her shoulder. She flipped the letter over.

"You applied for a youth theater program?" he asked. She nodded, suddenly self-conscious. "Why didn't you tell me?"

She gripped the paper. "I didn't want to tell you till I knew if I got it or not."

He looked hurt. "Why? Why wouldn't you tell me about something like this?"

"I submitted it before we were . . . us. And it's embarrassing. They didn't even say yes."

He tugged the letter from her hand. "Not yet, but they want to interview you mid-July. See?" He pointed to a line on the letter. "They're interviewing all their final candidates."

"They're just trying to soften the blow—"

Harlan scoffed. "Trust me. When you know this business like I do, you know they're never softening the blow. This is a huge compliment, Price. That's a really prestigious program."

She tried to keep the annoyance off her face. Yeah, he knew the business better than she did, but she wasn't exactly a novice here. "My dad was a big star there, okay? I guess I hoped they'd see in me what they saw in him and . . . I don't know."

"Hire you without an interview? That *would be* impressive." Harlan pulled out his phone, glancing at a number on the bottom of the letter. "I'm calling the program director."

"No!" Finley tried to pull the phone from his hands, but Harlan held it tightly. "Crawford, don't. I don't want a pity yes, okay? I want to do this on my own."

His eyebrows flew sky-high. "'Pity yes?' Price, I'm just going to give you a recommendation. What they do with that is on them."

"How can you give me a recommendation?"

His nostrils flared. "You remember that we're working on a production together right now, don't you? And let's not forget that without you, I'd have been booed off the stage after I fell on my glorious face while performing, who was it again? Oh, right. Shakespeare. Instead, I pulled out a showstopping line and garnered rave reviews, all because of your direction. I think that qualifies as me seeing your work."

She pulled the collar of her shirt over her mouth. She hated how condescending he sounded. "Please, listen to me. I want to earn this, Harlan."

"You have earned this. Why can't you get that?" He tugged her collar down from her mouth and kissed her. "Everything I just said is proof that you deserve to be seen. Hell, they already know that, or you wouldn't be so far along in the process. Just think of this as an added reference. The interview is still on you, and the call is still theirs. Okay?"

Resignation was settling in, but still, she protested. "Why won't you listen to me?"

"Trust me, it's for your own good." He was already dialing. "Why don't you go back in and tell everyone the good news? They're all eager to hear."

She wanted to grab his phone and throw it across the room,

but instead she shuffled back into the dining room. She slapped a fake smile on her face before she walked through the doorway.

"So?" Oliver asked, catching sight of her before the others did.

"I've made it down to the final cut, and now they just want to interview me to see if I have the 'excellent communication and organizational skills necessary to be a Mansfield Theater director.'" She grabbed a roll and tore off a hunk of it. "Isn't that great?"

Her tone must have tipped Oliver off. He frowned.

"That's great, Fin!" Emma said. "They'll love you. Do you want help interviewing? I don't mean to brag, but I can nail those suckers in my sleep."

The roll felt dry in her mouth. She choked it down. "Yeah, sure, that'd be great."

"You'll do wonderfully, Finley. Congratulations on reaching this step," Uncle Thomas said. "But where's your young Mr. Crawford? I can imagine how proud he is of you."

She waved toward the hallway. "Oh, he's just making a call."

After more niceties, none of which were from Nora, Harlan returned to the dining room grinning. "It's as good as done."

"What is?" Oliver asked.

"The Mansfield spot. I just talked to the program director, and she assured me that they're 'very, very eager' to meet Miss Price, and that if she has half the ability I described, they would be thrilled to have her join this summer."

Finley felt as if she'd been thrown into a fire.

"Excellent," Uncle Thomas said. "You can never have too many people vouching for you. With Mr. Crawford's recommendation and Ms. Crawford's interviewing help, I'd say you're set, Finley."

She smiled and nodded without conviction.

After dinner was cleared, she escaped to the kitchen, under the pretense of needing something for a headache that was threatening to become real. She ran into Nora as she was leaving.

"Congratulations, Finley," Nora said.

Blood rushed to her cheeks. "Thanks, Nora."

Nora laughed darkly. "You know, I'd actually started thinking that you and your mother may be different people. I should have known better."

"Excuse me?"

"You found a boy who'll take care of all of your problems for you, didn't you? How terribly lucky for you. When something isn't going your way, you can just call on your little boyfriend and he'll make everything right." She looked angry enough to spit. "You can't understand the value of work, because you've been handed everything. Just like this theater program. Did you even bother to submit an application, or did you just have your uncle and Harlan Crawford arrange the whole thing for you?"

Finley's body burned at the awful, hateful words. She wanted to open her mouth and scream. She wanted to tell Nora that she was wrong, that she'd worked hard for the things that she'd gotten. But right now, it felt like a lie.

"Nora," Emma said, coming into view from the dining room. Oliver was a step behind her, and he looked angry. He'd heard Nora, then. She didn't know whether to feel ashamed or relieved. "Mr. Bertram was just telling us that you're planning to run for state attorney general. What a surprise, when everyone thought he would run. And to have Senator Rushworth backing your nomination? Wow. Now, didn't you actually set up Juliette and Raleigh in the first place?" Emma smiled and batted her eyes, as if amazed by how things just work out sometimes. "I don't know if she'd have stayed with him so long without all your pep talks. What a funny coincidence."

Instead of responding to Emma, Nora gave Finley a look that said, "*See? Even she's fighting your battles for you.*"

Another voice entered the mix before Finley could even think about responding. "Price, you ready for some intense—" Harlan's eyes landed on the rest of the group, "—drama preparation?" He looked at Nora, unconcerned by the fact that, with her heels, she was three inches taller than he was. "What's going on here?"

"Just congratulating Finley on her interview," Nora said, looking down at Harlan. "Things certainly seem to fall into place for her, don't they?"

Harlan screwed his face up. "Hmm, let's do the math here. Her dad died. Her mom beat her. Oh, and then she gets the pleasure of being consistently tormented by the coldest douche-chill in the greater Chicago area—"

"Crawford!" Finley gasped.

He continued, moving his finger in the air as if doing equations on a blackboard. "So if we carry the one . . ." He looked at Nora flatly. "Not so much."

The temperature in the room went arctic. Nora arched her eyebrows and stepped around Harlan as if he were a bug. Then, glancing back at Finley, she smiled and returned to the dining room.

"Oh, I hate her so hard," Harlan growled. "Is she always like that?"

Finley said, "Yes," as Oliver said, "No."

Oliver looked at her then, his face growing a deep, angry red. "I know she's been rude to you, but . . . but you're not saying she's always like *that,* are you?"

"Did you really think otherwise?"

"Obviously! Why haven't you said anything to me? Or my parents?"

She rubbed her shoulder. Harlan held an arm out, and she tucked herself under it. "What's there to say? Nora puts up a front if anyone is around, just making the passive-aggressive little comments you've caught over the years. But when it's just the two of us, well, you saw."

Oliver breathed out a curse. "I should have done something."

Emma kissed his cheek. "Good thing it's Harley's problem now, huh?"

He scowled, but Emma was right: this wasn't Oliver's problem. It never had been.

Harlan squeezed her. "Come on, let's finish going over notes for the play."

She nodded. "You wanna go up to the deck and I'll meet you there in a second?"

When Harlan and Emma left the kitchen, Finley grabbed a bottled water while Oliver took a soda from the fridge.

"I didn't ask him to call the director," she told him.

"And I didn't know Nora was that bad. But it wouldn't matter to me if you did ask Harley."

"It wouldn't?"

His smile was small, but kind. "Fin, does he make you happy?"

"I want to punch him sometimes, but yeah. He does."

"Then isn't that all that matters? He loves you. He wants to help you. So what if it's different than how I'd do things?" His face looked red. Why did that cause a pang in her chest? "Maybe Emma's right and it's okay to let someone else do the fighting for you sometimes."

Her grip tightened on her glass. "Do you really think that?"

"Does it matter?"

She set her glass down on the counter and walked over to him. He was taller than Harlan; she'd forgotten that. She put a hand on his arm and looked up at him, her head just reaching his chin. Before Harlan, the hint of question in his blue eyes would have made her heart go haywire. Now, her heart just felt warm. "Yes, it does."

"Then I think you should tell the rest of us to shut up and trust yourself. What do *you* want to do, Fin?"

His words made her stand taller. "I want to forget the reference and go nail that interview so hard, they don't even remember who Harlan is."

His eyes crinkled. "They won't know what hit them."

They left the kitchen together, and Oliver stopped at the dining room, where Emma was talking to Aunt Mariah.

"I think this is your stop," she said.

"Yeah. Hey, I'm really sorry about Nora. She's no match for you, though. I hope you know that."

She smiled. "You're right. Thanks, Ollie." Without thinking, she stood on her tiptoes and kissed his cheek.

CHAPTER TWENTY-THREE

~*F*~

Finley turned from Oliver, speeding through the hallway and up the stairs before he saw how red her cheeks were.

What was that? she asked herself.

The kiss or the running? You have a boyfriend now. It's only natural that you'd feel weird kissing another guy's cheek.

Even if it's just Oliver? We're practically family.

Whatever you have to tell yourself.

She tried to shake off her embarrassment before she reached the deck. When she stepped out of the stairwell, she stopped and stared. Juliette and Raleigh were sitting on the couch across from Harlan. They were . . . laughing.

If he were with anyone else, she would smile and marvel at how Harlan's easy charisma could defuse even the most awkward situations. Maybe she *should* see it that way.

Juliette spotted her before Harlan. "Fin! Come cuddle with your boyfriend and chat with us!"

Finley warily crossed the deck to sit by Harlan. He put his arm around her. Across from them, Juliette and Raleigh were similarly snuggled up. With the muggy summer heat, it was already too warm. Cuddling made it sweltering.

"Fin, we were just picking Harley's brain about publicity." Juliette looked at Raleigh with doting eyes. He smiled dopily back. "Now that

Raleigh's been drafted, he's been approached by Calvin Klein to be the face of their performance line because he's the hottest . . ." Juliette trailed off so she could kiss Raleigh with an intensity that Finley felt should be reserved for, frankly, any time she wasn't watching.

Finley put her mouth up to Harlan's ear. "Is it just me, or is this weird?"

"Really weird," he whispered back. "They've been taking make-out breaks every two minutes since I got up here." He paused. "Interesting technique, though. You should try that thing with—OOF." He rubbed his ribs where she elbowed him. Then he leaned back in to nibble her ear, causing shivers to run through her body. "They don't look like they're going to end anytime soon. Want to go to your room?" He kissed her neck, and her whole body turned to jelly. "To hang out?"

She kissed him. "Nice try," she said with less conviction than she felt. His mouth was that warm and sweet. "We can hang out in the theater."

Harlan grumbled, but stood up.

"Wait," Juliette said, easing up on Raleigh long enough to wipe her mouth. "We don't mean to drive you out." She smiled guiltily. "I just can't keep my hands off this boy."

Raleigh gave Juliette an intense look, and for a moment, with his intense eyes, strong jawline, and wavy blond hair, Finley could see the appeal. Until he gave a painfully hokey shrug. "What can I say? She can't keep her hands off me."

Harlan groaned and Finley stifled a laugh. "Seriously guys," Juliette said, "Raleigh and I were just leaving." Raleigh jumped up and pulled Juliette to her feet, bringing her in for a lingering kiss. When they broke apart, Juliette smiled at them. "Man, it feels like we haven't seen you two in years! But at least we'll see you in Manhattan next week, right Harley?"

Harlan nodded. "Yep, see you guys then."

When Juliette and Raleigh had tickled and giggled their way to the stairs, Finley glanced up at Harlan. "Manhattan?"

He grabbed her legs and twisted her so she was facing him on the couch. He immediately started kissing her neck and cheeks, turning her into goo. "Yeah, it's funny timing. Juliette is going for her summer smarty-pants program, and Raleigh is going to Connecticut for an interview with ESPN."

She tried to stay focused. "And you?"

He grinned. "I'm meeting with Ben Affleck about his next movie. Just found out while you were downstairs."

"Crawford, that's amazing! So your dad relented?"

His smile fell. "No, actually. I texted the casting director and told him that I'm in for any role he wants. It could be 'Dead Hooker #2' for all I care. He arranged the meeting for me."

"What does that mean about your dad, then?"

He glanced down and tickled her palms. "Don't I have to fire him?"

"That's your call."

"But you think I'm right, don't you?"

Of course I do. "I think you know what you need to do better than anyone."

"In other words, you agree, but you don't want to come between us. Well, you won't have to worry about that. I'm going to set up meetings with a couple of other agents in New York. When I find one, Dad's out." He shrugged, as if it wasn't monumental. "He's never going to forgive me."

"Can I do anything?"

He let out a bitter chuckle. "Yeah, come with me."

"Okay."

"Really? You would come and watch me fire the man who destroyed my family?"

"You met the woman who destroyed mine. I'm there, if you want me."

His eyes locked into hers. "I do. I want you there. I want you here. I want *you*, Price."

Her heart was a runaway train, ready to burst from her chest. It wasn't just the emotion in his eyes or the fire in his words, it was the vulnerability. He was baring himself to her in a way that Juliette had thought impossible. He was taking off his armor, letting her be something more to him. She felt almost dizzy.

A million thoughts flew through her mind, scattering over the streets of Chicago. She was so proud of him. She wished she could tell him how sorry she was that his relationship with his father had reached this point. She could only imagine how scared and alone Harlan must feel. But he wasn't alone. She needed him to know she was there, no matter what.

"I love you, Crawford." She curled against him. "I'm proud of you and I love you."

With her head against his chest, she felt his pulse double, matching hers. She heard the excitement, the joy in his short bursts of breath, breath that blew against her hair, causing strands to tickle her face. Harlan deliberately, slowly cradled her in his arms and put his head on hers. They sat like that for a long time, clinging to each other. When his pulse had returned to normal, he whispered, "I love you, too."

She smiled and closed her eyes.

* * *

The next thing she knew, someone was shaking her awake. Her eyes flew open. Behind her, Harlan was stirring. "What's going on?" he asked.

She rubbed her sandy eyes and saw a pajama-clad Oliver looking down at them. She and Harlan had fallen asleep. When had that happened? She shook her head, trying to clear it. "Ollie, what time is it? Is everything okay?"

Oliver shook his head and folded an arm across his chest. He looked haggard. "I don't know. Midnight, maybe?" He rubbed his forehead. "Fin, it's Tate."

She jumped up and grabbed his shoulders. "What do you mean? What's wrong?"

"We just got a call from the hospital. Tate was stabbed."

Shock numbed her. "*Stabbed?* Why? How? What happened?"

"I don't know," his voice cracked. "Dad and Mom are going to the hospital and asked me to stay here."

His sobs ripped through her. She pulled him into a tight embrace, letting him cry on her shoulder. She couldn't think. She didn't know how to process Tate being hurt.

She looked over Oliver's shoulder to a pacing Harlan. "Can I help?" he mouthed.

She gave a little shake of her head. "I'll call you tomorrow," she mouthed back.

Harlan quietly gathered his things and squeezed her hand before slipping downstairs.

Finley held on to Oliver and watched him leave.

* * *

The reports from the hospital came in all night. Aunt Mariah updated Finley almost compulsively. Her first text explained that she didn't want to upset Juliette or Oliver, but she had to tell someone what was happening. Finley was the natural choice.

Sifting through Aunt Mariah's texts, she was able to piece together what had happened. Tate's gambling had gotten out of control, and he owed some bad men a lot of money. When they came to Tate's apartment to collect, Tate jumped off the second story fire escape into the dumpster below, but he landed on a metal curtain rod. One of Tate's roommates found him ten minutes later and called 911. The rod had pierced through his side and nicked his intestines. The wound was already infected when the ambulance arrived. Tate had lost a dangerous amount of blood.

"What's Mom saying?" Juliette asked from the breakfast table. She'd been unbraiding and rebraiding her hair for the last twenty minutes. Her eyes were red from the late night, but she had yet to cry. Finley stared at the new message on her phone.

"They're still monitoring him. He shouldn't need another blood transfusion. He's out of surgery . . ." Another message came in. "And she thinks he's fine!" Finley put a hand to her chest and exhaled. She opened her eyes to see Juliette nodding and Oliver's head resting on clasped hands in what looked like prayer.

Oliver's phone chimed, and he dropped his hands to look at it. Hope drained from his face. "It's from Dad. The surgery stopped the internal bleeding and he's on antibiotics to prevent infection, but the surgeon is worried he's not rebounding fast enough."

Finley shuddered, closing her eyes. "He must be too afraid of upsetting your mom to tell her the truth."

Oliver cursed and read from his screen. "He's going to send Mom home soon and wants us to watch her and make sure she's okay. He doesn't want the media finding out, so he asked Mom's nurse not to come in for a few days. He wants us to help her, instead."

Finley nodded. "Of course."

A few moments later, Juliette stood up. "If you're both staying home, I'm going to go," she said, pulling out her braid again. "Mom doesn't need all of us. Besides, I have a million things to do before my trip next week. I already missed half my morning courses when I'm not supposed to miss any for this program, and I have to study and prep and pack and Raleigh's playing in a tournament this week and . . . I have to finish getting ready. Just text me the second anything changes."

Oliver watched his sister head upstairs, the shock plain on his face. "How can she do this? How can she be so selfish?"

Finley ached to look at him. Still in his pajamas, with hair sticking up all over, Oliver looked as if he hadn't slept a wink, though she knew for a fact that he had.

It had been a long night, remembering the passion in Harlan's eyes when he asked her to come to New York with him. And the night was only made longer when Oliver laid his head on her lap, exhausted and spent. She'd run her hands through his hair and hummed an old lullaby of her father's until Oliver was finally able to sleep.

Once he was out, she'd tried to move out from under him. He'd moaned and said her name. Her heart had ached then as it did now to see him so crushed.

"He's going to be okay," she told him.

"How do you know that?"

"Because this is Tate, and he lives for the drama of a story like this. He's going to get better, and then he's going to milk that scar for everything it's worth. He'll never wear a shirt again; he'll be so busy showing off the way the scar turned his six-pack into a seven-pack."

He snorted, then sniffed.

A knock interrupted them. She got up and walked to the door to find Harlan and Emma standing there, dressed for the day. Emma pushed past her.

"In the kitchen," Finley called after her.

"You look great," Harlan said, putting an arm around her. "Not tired at all. And have I seen that outfit on you before?"

"Ha-ha."

"So what's the latest?"

She told him as they walked slowly toward the breakfast nook. They found Emma talking to Oliver.

"But why didn't you at least respond to my texts? I had to get updates from Fin through my brother. I was so worried about you."

Oliver rubbed his temples. "I know, I'm sorry. I've just been really worried and I didn't want to worry you, too."

"But that's what I'm here for, isn't it? If your brother's dying—"

Oliver drew back. "He's not *dying*."

"You know what I mean. He's in a bad way, and I want to be there for you."

"I know, I'm sorry." He grabbed her hand. "Thanks for coming."

Harlan and Finley retreated to the other end of the kitchen. "You don't look like you've slept at all. Why don't you go take a nap?" Harlan asked.

"I can't. Uncle Thomas is sending Aunt Mariah home. She's not handling things very well, so Oliver and I are going to try to keep her distracted."

Harlan made a face. "They expect too much of you."

"Crawford, come on. What am I supposed to do?"

"So you stayed up all night taking care of Oliver, then you're going to take care of Mrs. Bertram all day, and then what? You're going to the hospital to watch over Tate so everyone else can rest before heading to the theater?" He cursed. "When will you get a break, Price? Who's going to take care of you?"

"It's not like that. Tate's family. He's like a brother to me. I wouldn't be able to sleep if I tried, anyway. Please." She grabbed his hand. "You understand, right?"

He huffed. "Yeah, sure. I just wish I could take you from all this for longer than a week."

"I know. And when Tate gets better, I will fly the plane myself."

He pulled her in for a quick kiss, then looked at the clock. "Ems," he called, "we gotta go." To Finley, he said, "We're meeting a producer for lunch. He's kind of a douche, but, well, he knows people. I'll come over when we're done."

Finley nodded and gave him one last hug.

Heels sounded from the hallway, and Juliette appeared, looking as if she'd just stepped out of a magazine. "Hey, guys," she said to Harlan and Emma. "You heading out? I'll walk with you."

In a few short moments, they said their good-byes and Finley and Oliver were back at the table. They sighed.

"What do we do now?" he asked.

"Wait."

CHAPTER TWENTY-FOUR

~ℱ~

Two days later, Tate was due home from the hospital. He'd stabilized since his surgery, which meant the Bertrams and Finley were breathing a little easier. Finley was getting the guest suite ready when she heard a knock at the door, followed by the sound of the door opening.

"Hello?" Harlan called, closing the door behind him. "Price? Oliver?"

She set down the clean towels and sheets and met him in the hallway, where Harlan was holding balloons and flowers. She hugged him tightly, breathing in his scent. "I'm so glad it's you."

When she let go of him, she saw him studying her with wide eyes. "You look exhausted. When was the last time you ate? Or slept?"

She waved him off, but his tone stung. She tucked a loose strand of hair into the messy bun atop her head. "I don't know. It's been a little hectic getting things ready. I forgot how huge this house is."

She led him into the guest suite across from Uncle Thomas's study. A hospital bed had been moved into the spacious room, and medical supplies and vitamin drinks littered the coffee table and dressers.

She'd spent all day cleaning and doing laundry to prevent any chance of Tate's wound getting infected again. But she didn't want to tell Harlan that.

"Is Tate home yet?" he asked.

"No, but he should be any minute. I'm just finishing making his bed, but Aunt Mariah is in a lot of pain and—"

"Don't you guys use a cleaning service? Where's Mrs. Bertram's nurse? Where's Oliver?" Harlan demanded. "Why are you doing all of this yourself?"

She grabbed the sheets and started making the bed, stopping occasionally to make air quotes. "Nora 'strongly advised' Uncle Thomas to keep this 'in the family.' She said it'll be 'bad for the firm's image' if people find out what happened to Tate. She insisted that the cleaners and cook and nurse have the week off."

Harlan laughed, an incredulous, angry bark. "So that means all of this is getting dumped on you, doesn't it?"

"Not just me. Oliver's helping at least as much as I am. He's up with his mom right now."

"And Juliette?"

Finley tucked the corners of the sheet around the bed. "Getting ready for the summit next week."

"She's the only smart one in this house."

Ouch. "What do you mean?"

"I mean this isn't your problem! Why are you acting like you owe these people your life? Your *health?* Have you seen yourself today? I'm worried about you. You look like you've been through hell."

Her face flushed a deep red. "I'm not exactly the top priority in the house right now, okay? I don't *want* to be."

"That's exactly the problem, Price! You're never the priority, not even to yourself!"

"That's not true! This family has done a lot for me, especially over the last few months. My uncle and aunt support me—"

"Yeah, they support you just enough so that when they treat you like a doormat, you're too grateful to argue."

The desire to scream at him was overwhelming. She forced

herself to breathe, to stay totally, painfully calm. "What would you like me to do, Crawford?"

"Let them dig themselves out of their own mess. Don't let them use you like this."

She spoke in a cool voice. "And what about what *I* want? Does that matter?"

"Not when you've been taken advantage of for too long to know what's good for you."

"So how am I supposed to know what I should want?"

He looked her over, and she could imagine what he was seeing: her small, fragile body, dark circles under her eyes, a sloppy bun, and yesterday's clothes. "You've had so many people pulling you different ways for so long, I don't think what *you* want could possibly be what's best for you. You have to trust that no one in this house cares about you as much as I do and *just listen to me!*"

"So what does that mean? Just leave right now? Leave Tate when he's gravely injured? Leave Uncle Thomas when he's at his wit's end and hasn't left the hospital except to shower and change clothes? Leave Oliver to help his mom when she's suffering? When *he* is?"

"Leave the nurse to take care of your aunt and Mr. Bertram and Oliver to take care of their family! This isn't your problem, Price! Why can't you get that?"

"Then what is *my* problem?" She pounded her chest over her heart. "My mom? My Mansfield interview? You helped me because you love me, right? Well, I'm trying to do the same thing. I'm trying to help the people I love!"

"Oh, yeah? What about me?" His features twisted. "While you're busy taking care of everyone else you love, I'm going to New York next week to face my dad *alone*." He gave a sharp, ugly laugh. "At least I know where I fit in with your priorities: right below the Bertrams. Surprise, surprise."

She felt like a balloon deflating. "Oh, Harlan, I'm sorry." She sat heavily at the edge of the freshly made bed, her eyes watering.

She felt so tired. "Under any other circumstances, I would be right there with you. But we can work something out. You were planning to meet with the other agents alone, right?" He gave a reluctant nod. "What if you go to New York and find your agent, and then I join you at the end of the week when you talk to your dad? We can still make it work."

Harlan sighed, joining her at the foot of the bed. "I think you need a break," he said just above a whisper. He put his lips to her ear and kissed along the side of her face to her jaw until she swayed.

His lips met hers with a spark that burned. As they kissed, he seemed to grow more urgent, as if he wasn't just trying to kiss her but to dissolve her will. She'd wanted to turn her head off for a minute, but his frustration and disappointment were too obvious. The more they kissed, the worse she felt.

At the sound of the garage door, she pulled away. He let out a string of curses.

She held out a hand to help him up. Instead, he pulled her down to him and kissed her hard, injecting every breath and movement with a furious passion. His lips seemed to demand everything of her. She felt as if she was being consumed. As voices made their way through the halls, she broke off. "Enough, Crawford. Help me finish?"

He clenched his jaw but didn't help, instead watching her straighten the bed and put Gatorade on the nightstand. She felt a flash of resentment for how he was spinning everything, followed by a flash of guilt for not being more understanding. When the door swung open to reveal Mr. Bertram and Oliver wheeling Tate in, she was actually relieved.

Finley ran to hug Tate. He reached up, then winced. "I'm so glad to see you," she said in his ear.

He groaned. "Now this makes almost dying worth it. Hot damn, you look good, girl."

She laughed, knowing too well that she looked like crap. But why was Tate the one making her feel good when Harlan should have?

Stop it, she told herself. She released Tate and looked at the men surrounding her. She saw exhaustion in Mr. Bertram's eyes, the strain in Oliver's smile, the judgment in Harlan's folded arms, and the fear behind Tate's forced laughter.

They needed her. And she wanted to help.

She felt a second wind as she finished setting up the room. Every time she laughed at one of Tate's jokes and gave Oliver a supportive smile or squeeze, she felt happier. She couldn't fix everything, but this was a start.

After Tate was settled in, Finley climbed up beside him on the bed and turned on the TV. Then she noticed that Mr. Bertram and Harlan were talking, and they looked serious. When both sets of eyes turned on her, she glanced away.

A few minutes later, they finished their conversation. Harlan came over to the bed and kissed her for a bit longer than was appropriate, given their audience. She backed up.

"I'll drop by later before my flight," he said.

She put a hand on his face. "Okay. I love you."

"You, too."

CHAPTER TWENTY-FIVE

~*O*~

The next night, Tate was settled in the guest suite with enough pain medication to sedate a baby elephant. As Oliver and Finley crept from Tate's room, his dad met them in the hallway and pulled them aside.

"How is he?"

"Fine," Oliver said, stretching his arms. "He's milking the wound for all it's worth, that's for sure. He made us watch three hours of *Cops* reruns before he finally fell asleep."

His dad smiled. "Good. And your mom is fine, too. In fact, Nora's coming over to spend time with her. How about the three of us take a break and walk down to Thai Lily?"

Finley grabbed her stomach. "That sounds heavenly."

Oliver nodded. "Must . . . have . . . pad . . . thai."

"Good. Let's go."

They left the house, and Oliver noticed Finley glance up at Harlan's darkened room at the Grants'. He and Emma had left the night before. Part of Oliver felt relieved that they were gone. The other part of him felt guilty for feeling relieved. He pushed both thoughts from his mind.

When they reached the restaurant at the end of their street, the owner, Lily, waved to them. Despite the Saturday night crowd, she gestured to a table and sent a server to meet them.

The server led them to their usual table and pulled Finley's chair out for her before taking their orders. Soon, veggie rolls and hot and sour soup were brought out, and they each dove in.

"I want to thank you both for everything you've done to help Tate and the family over these past few days," Oliver's dad said when he finished his soup. "You've both picked up a lot of slack, and it has meant a great deal to your mother and me."

"I don't think either of us minds, Dad. That's what family does," Oliver said, looking at a nodding Finley.

"Yes, well, that's very generous of you. And, Oliver, I'm sorry to do this, but I have to ask still more of you."

"Of course."

"Tate's . . . accident has caused a bit of a ripple at work. Nora and your mother and I have discussed the situation and think it would be better if Tate takes a break from his internship and focuses on taking care of himself."

"You mean getting clean," Oliver said.

His dad cleared his throat. "I'm afraid your brother's gambling debts are . . . considerable." Oliver's pad thai was set in front of him, but his appetite had vanished. Next to him, Finley rubbed her chopsticks together nervously.

Oliver nodded. "I thought as much. Are you thinking about an intervention? Rehab? There's a really good facility in Iowa that specializes in gambling and behavioral addiction. It's a luxury facility, and it's far enough away that he wouldn't have constant reminders or access to his addiction. They have a few different programs, but given the extent of Tate's addiction, I think the three-month program is probably his best option."

His dad's face clouded. "I don't think he needs to go so far as to enter rehab. We were thinking of sending him to someone local that Nora suggested. She's a very respected therapist here in Chicago. It'll allow us to keep things quiet."

"I don't think that's the right move, Dad. I've been researching gambling addiction since Tate was taken to the hospital. All the experts agree that it's really important that we not try to cover this up, for Tate and for ourselves."

"I don't think that's fair to the rest of the family to air our dirty laundry."

"And I don't think it's fair to Tate to hide it," Oliver argued. "If we cover for him now, he won't get the message that we think he has a problem. We'll basically become accomplices for him to keep doing worse and worse stuff. But if we can show him that we think he has a serious problem and admit it to the people around us, it'll help everyone come to terms. Most important, Tate. There's no shame in admitting he has a problem, only in refusing to act on it."

"All right. I'll talk to your mother about it," he said, but his words lacked conviction. Disappointment settled deep in Oliver's stomach. "That actually brings me to my next point, son. With Tate's . . ."

"Addiction," Oliver said.

"Right. I need your help."

"Help?"

"Call it an internship," he said. Oliver's mouth went dry. "We'll shuffle Tate's duties amongst the other interns, but I'd still like your help with the more routine tasks. The pay will be generous, I promise." He smiled.

Oliver stared at his plate. Finley's small hand slipped into his and held it tightly. Her touch made his chest grow warm. "Dad, you know I'm planning to go to Guatemala in a few weeks."

"Oliver, don't you think there are more important things than playing around this summer?"

"*Playing?* Dad, I'm building a school for orphans."

His dad leaned in, his voice lowering. "I thought you would be thrilled at this opportunity. Any of a hundred other kids would gladly take your place there. Do you know how many candidates applied for this position? Do you realize how this will look on your law school application in a few years?"

"What does that matter, Dad? My future's already set. Poli-sci major, then law school, both at your alma mater. Then it's on to working at the firm, right?"

His dad sat upright in his chair. His nostrils flared, but he looked tired. "Oliver, I'm not some puppet master controlling your future. Your brother is sick and I'm asking for your help. That's all. If that isn't enough for you, think about your girlfriend. Do you really want to spend weeks away from her when you have so little time together before college?"

Oliver let go of Finley's hand. It was the same argument Emma had been making over and over again since they'd started dating. The fight drained out of him. "I'll think about it, Dad."

"Good." His dad picked up his chopsticks. "That's all I can ask."

Oliver returned to his food, but it may as well have been cardboard for all he could taste. It was several moments before he even realized his dad was talking again.

"Harlan told me you've been making plans to go to New York with him and Emma next week."

Oliver's head snapped to Finley. A strange sense of betrayal filled him. How could she leave now, of all times? Color rose on her cheeks. "He did?"

"Yes, and he also reminded me that Juliette will be in New York next week as well, so saying no to you wouldn't exactly be fair." His dad gave a wry smile.

Finley's expression darkened. "He shouldn't have done that. I told him I'd talk to you."

"He's trying to look out for you," his dad said. "He already sent me the number and address to the hotel, along with the room number you'll be sharing with Emma. After giving it some thought, I think he's right. It's hypocritical of me to allow Juliette to go in the middle of our family's drama and not to allow you. So I've taken the liberty of buying your tickets." He smiled. "You leave tomorrow."

"Tomorrow? No, you mean Thursday, don't you?"

"Thursday? Why would I mean Thursday? Harlan said it would be a week."

Finley grew cold in a way Oliver had never seen. Her fists were balled on her knees. When she spoke, there was an unsteady quality to her voice, as if she was trying badly to stay in control. She stared at her plate. "He wanted a week. I told him I wouldn't feel right abandoning Tate or any of the family for that long—"

His dad interrupted, wearing a knowing smile. "Harlan said you would try to convince me of that. He said you wouldn't think it was right."

"And I told Harlan that it wasn't about a sense of obligation; it's what I *want*," she said, looking his dad in the eye now. "I want to support the people I love, whether they need me or not. Doesn't that matter to anyone?"

His dad looked shocked. Finley had never spoken so boldly to him before. And yet, in the wideness of his dad's eyes, he thought he saw something like pride. The same pride bursting in Oliver's chest. His dad reached across the table and put a hand on her shoulder. "Of course it does, Finley. I'm sorry I didn't ask you first. Why don't you tell me what you'd like to do?"

A smile found its way to her face.

An hour later, Oliver's dad had to take a call, leaving Oliver and Finley to walk home alone. Although she'd seemed content after working out her plan for New York, the look in her eyes told him she was still angry.

"I can't believe he did that," she said as they left the restaurant. "How could he talk to your dad behind my back like I'm some child?" Oliver didn't answer. "I explicitly told him I wanted to stay here to help. We worked out that I'd go up at the end of the week after he'd settled on another agent so I could support him when he fires his dad—"

Oliver grabbed her arm. "Hold up. He's firing his dad?"

"Yes. I know. It's a huge deal. But he was planning to fire him before we'd ever talked about me going up, which, by the way, was about two hours before we found out about Tate." They resumed their walk. "He kept trying to convince me that I shouldn't stay. It was like he thought that because he *told* me I shouldn't want to, that I wouldn't want to."

He liked Harlan, but this was hardly a surprise. "Have you considered that this is how he shows you that he cares about you? That he thinks he knows you better than you know yourself?" The words struck an uncomfortable chord in his own chest.

Finley's dark eyes reflected the streetlight with a fiery spark. "Why can't he just believe that I know what I want?"

"He's probably scared. Giving up control can be hard when you care so much about someone." He cleared his throat. He was talking about Harlan, not himself. Obviously.

Finley tapped a fingernail against her teeth. "Juliette thinks he's using me as his armor."

"Armor?"

"Yeah, like he uses my problems to protect him from dealing with his own."

"Huh." He nodded slowly. "Man, she devotes so much time to worthless crap that it's easy to forget how brilliant she actually is."

"No kidding. Maybe she's the future therapist in the family, huh?" she said. Oliver winced. "Shoot, I'm sorry. I didn't mean it that way."

He shook his head. They had reached the house, but neither of them seemed ready to go inside. He sat on the stoop, and she dropped down beside him.

"I know," he said. "It just sucks."

"You don't have to work for your dad, Ollie. You're almost eighteen. You're starting college in a couple of months. Help your dad understand what you want."

"But what if I don't know what that is anymore?"

She knocked his leg with hers. "I don't believe that for a second.

I heard how passionate you were when you told your dad about the rehab center. You live for helping people."

"Like my dad does."

"Yup." She smiled. "Neat how some things run in the family, isn't it? But just because you share a trait doesn't mean you have to go about it in the same way. Be honest with him, Oliver. And if you really want to help him, why can't you just do it before you leave and when you get back?"

"Well, look who's all about solving problems lately."

"A director worth her salt has to have excellent communication and organizational skills."

"Oh, does she?"

"Mmm-hmm."

"Then you're set, Finley Price."

She smiled, staring at her clasped hands. Their legs bumped again. Out of nowhere, Oliver's heart thudded at the touch. No. He couldn't handle this. He couldn't handle his relief at his missing girlfriend, his happiness at being with Finley, how wild his insides went just being near her. He jumped up. "I'm going inside. You coming in?"

"No." She clutched her phone. "I have some 'communication and organization' to do."

"Poor Harlan."

"Poor Finley," she said. "He's not going to be happy."

"But you will be. Right?"

She half-smiled. "I'll let you know how it goes."

* * *

~*F*~

It did not go well.

"So you mean to tell me that your uncle bought you a ticket, and you still refuse to spend the week with me?"

How did he turn this around on her? How was she the bad guy?

"I mean to tell you," she said, staring at Harlan on her phone's screen, "that it bothers me that you went behind my back on this. I told you I want to stay and help out. This is my family—"

"No, it's *Juliette's* family. You don't see her skipping out on her gifted summit to take care of anyone."

She looked away from his glare, wishing she hadn't video-called him. "I don't want to go over this again. I told you what I wanted, and you went behind my back like I'm some little kid incapable of making my own decisions."

His handsome features contorted. "Maybe you are! If it weren't for me, you would have folded with your mom like you do with Nora and Thomas and everyone in your life. You *need* me to make decisions for you! So I made this one. Just agree, already!"

Her heart felt heavy, and the words almost stuck in her throat. But she couldn't let them. "No, Harlan. I love you, but I can't just sit here while you make choices for me that I don't agree with. I *want* to stay and help Tate and everyone get settled, and then I *want* to come out next week and be there for you when you need me."

He turned from the screen and swore loudly. She flinched. When he glanced back, he looked wounded. He closed his eyes. "I can't believe you'd do this to me. After everything I've done for you." Her whole body registered the pain of his words. "After what I did for Liam—I went out on a serious limb with my dad for him because he's your brother. He's been holding that over my head for a month." His voice was so bitter, she almost didn't recognize it.

"I'm sorry, Harlan," she whispered. "You know how much it means to me that you care—"

"Yeah. I only wish *you* cared as much."

Her mouth fell open. "That isn't fair. You know I care about you. Can't you see how hard this is for me? My family needs me—"

He scoffed. "I know you don't think they're my family, but they are! I love them and I love you and I don't know what else to do but try my best to help both of you! Why is this so hard for you to understand?" she cried.

He still wasn't looking at the screen. "I'm pissed off, okay? And I'm disappointed. You should be here. You should be with me. I . . . I miss you." He shook his head, and she saw his anger crack just like her heart. She hated seeing him in pain. He looked back at the screen. "Besides, I have like a hundred things lined up with my publicist, and I wanted to do all of that stuff with you. But instead, I have to show up at everything with my sister and trust that everyone believes that the chick with the black hair all over my Instagram feed actually has a face. And a hot one, at that. It's getting ridiculous that I can't show you off."

She let out a shaky laugh. If he was angry about not showing her off, he wasn't *that* angry. "I know. Your girlfriend is super hot, okay? And when I get there on Thursday, I'll have Emma doll me up and you can take a thousand pictures of us, and I'll show my face in every one, okay?" Her voice faltered. "That is, if you still want me to come?"

He rolled his eyes. "Of course I want you to come. But you can't know how many people are asking me if you're real. Get your cute butt out here, already. We're going public, Price."

"Okay," she said, breathing deeply. It didn't matter if people dug into who she was; everyone she cared about already knew they were dating. So if she finally had to step into the spotlight, she could do it for him. She *would* do it for him. "I didn't realize how much pressure this has caused you."

A trace of annoyance remained on his face. "My publicist is making a huge deal over it. After my *Tonight Show* appearance, she thinks it would look really good to have some exposure about the girl whose heart I won through my charity and activism and all that crap."

"Crap?"

"You know what I mean. Magazines are beating down my door."

She shook it off. "Yeah, I know what you mean. So . . . are we good?"

His eyes softened. "We're good, Price. But you'd better be here Thursday, or I'm kidnapping you." She smiled. "Listen, I gotta go. Emma and I are meeting some old friends for dinner."

"No hot chicks, all right? I know where you live."

He held up a hand. "Whoa, easy there, Price. Talk tomorrow?"

"Tomorrow. Love you." She hoped he didn't catch the hint of a question in her tone.

"Love you, too."

She ended the call and sighed. He still wanted her there. He loved her. All wasn't lost. But something told her that all wasn't right, either. She rose from the stoop and brushed off the back of her shorts.

Time to check on Tate.

CHAPTER TWENTY-SIX

~ℱ~

The following evening, Finley was talking to Harlan before he and Emma headed off to a club. "Man, I've forgotten how much I missed New York. Why haven't we been doing more stuff like this around Chicago?"

"I don't know, because we're seventeen and can't get into most clubs?"

"I'm Harlan Crawford. You don't think they're going to let me and my plus one in?"

"Ooh, so I'm a 'plus one' now, am I?"

He grinned. "You know it. Oh, and you will be this Friday, too. We're going to a house party in Manhattan—"

A door opened in the background of Harlan's hotel room, and soon Emma walked into view, wearing a gold sequin dress and more makeup than she'd ever seen the girl wear before. Emma was on her phone.

"Ollie, I just think it's selfish of you to still want to go to Guatemala when your brother is in such a bad place." She paused. "Fine. We'll talk about it later." Another pause. "Okay. Kisses. I'm going to crash Fin and Harley's phone date." She ended the call with an eye roll and tossed her phone onto a nearby couch in Harlan's gold-and-cream suite. "Fin!" She crowded Harlan out of the picture. "How are you, darling? How's Tate? Is he mobile? And is

Ollie serious about trying to have Mr. Bertram send him to rehab? That would suck for the family, wouldn't it?"

Finley blinked in rapid succession. Was Emma waiting for a response to any of her questions? When she paused, Finley spoke up. "Yeah, but it's not about us, right?"

Emma shrugged. "I just don't see why Tate's screw-up has to impact everyone else. Everyone messes up sometimes. Just keep it in the family, you know?" Emma's phone chimed. "And Juliette agrees. She said so at lunch, didn't she, Harley?" Harlan mumbled something. "Ooh, sorry, I need to get this. Heart you. See you soon!" Emma backed away and was quickly on her phone walking to another room in the suite. "Misha, you big slut! How are you?"

Harlan returned the phone to his face. "Ah, Emma. Sparkling as always, isn't she?"

"As always," Finley agreed, trying to forget her irritation at Harlan and Juliette having lunch together. And at Emma—her *friend*—for just watching it all happen. "Anyway, how did your meeting with that first agent go today? Weren't you supposed to have lunch—"

"Oh, I rescheduled it for tomorrow." He scratched his nose. "There was this big charity auction at the Guggenheim that my publicist and I thought would make great press for my new image. We ran into Juliette's summit crowd there, actually."

"Great," she said, feigning enthusiasm.

"Yeah, it really was. It was the new Simon Cowell charity, and he asked me to be a celebrity judge next season. Isn't that killer?"

"Yeah. Totally. Killer."

Emma came back into the room. "Time to go, Loverboy," she yelled, waving at Finley. "Keep Ollie out of trouble for me, and try to convince him to stay back this summer and help your uncle, okay?"

Finley was spared answering.

"Okay, gotta run," Harlan said, standing up. The phone rustled as he grabbed his keys.

"Love you," she said.

"Love you, too, babe."

His face was frozen on the screen for a few seconds before the call ended. He was smiling at her, the background a blur.

She sat for several minutes, thinking about the difference a couple of days had already made in Emma. She seemed so . . . phony.

No, that wasn't fair. She was catching up with friends and cramming several months' worth of fun into a single week. If Emma was nothing more than a streak of sequin across Harlan's screen until Finley saw her in person, who was she to judge?

She slipped on her flip-flops and left her room, heading downstairs to see Tate. Downstairs, she cracked open the door to his room. Oliver was sitting on the chair next to Tate's bed, Connect Four on a tray between them.

"Dude, you can't slip two discs in at the same time and think I'm not going to notice." Oliver lifted a red disc out and tossed it at Tate, who instantly grabbed the coin, fidgeting with it. "You suck."

Tate laughed, then grabbed his abdomen. "Have some mercy, bro."

"Looking for pity wins now, huh, Tate?" she teased, walking in.

He flashed a grin. "I'll take whatever pity you'll give me, Fin." He looked at Oliver. "What happened to our girl, here? Every time she misses me, she has to go and get hotter just to hurt me? That's cold, Fin."

She rolled her eyes and climbed onto the foot of his bed. "You don't need to cheat to beat Oliver at Connect Four."

"Hush it!" Oliver ordered.

"I don't, huh?" Tate asked, suddenly interested.

She arched her eyebrows. "No. He always follows—hey!" She ducked as M&M's pelted her.

Oliver pointed at her. "Let that be a lesson, Fin. Snitches get stitches."

"Dude, too soon," Tate said.

Laughing, she picked up an M&M from the bed and popped it in her mouth. "All right, all right. Your secrets die with me, Ollie."

"Don't you forget it."

Oliver put away the games, despite Tate's protests, instead turning on the TV. Finley lay down beside Tate and he rested his head on her shoulder. She thought she saw Oliver frowning, but a moment later, the look was gone. Over the next hour, they flipped through the channels with running commentary about everything they saw.

When Tate started to nod off, Oliver caught her eye and jerked his head toward the door. They crept out, turning off the light and closing the door quietly behind them.

"Did you notice how twitchy he was while we were playing?" Oliver asked. "It's like he was compelled to find a way to win a friggin' game of Connect Four. He needs serious help. I have to convince my dad to get him into rehab."

"Maybe you're right."

"I know I am." He rubbed his forehead. "Anyway, on the phone, I heard Emma interrupt you and Harlan. How's he doing?"

She held out a hand and teetered it from side to side. "Fine, I think." She filled him in on the charity auction and Harlan rescheduling his first agent meeting. Oliver looked disappointed.

"That's too bad. Hopefully it will help him cement his image with his new agent, right?"

"Yeah, that's a good way of looking at it—"

Her phone vibrated, derailing her thoughts. Then it vibrated again. And again. Oliver's did the same. They frowned at each other and pulled out their phones, scanning their messages

"Um . . . why are all my friends asking if you and Harlan broke up?"

She groaned and showed him the texts coming in from Harlan. "Because he ran into Juliette at a club," she explained, summarizing his text. A picture came through of Harlan and Juliette hugging.

Raleigh was even in the background. "It's on like six different websites already."

"That's ridiculous."

Her throat caught. "He warned me that he's being hounded for info on who I am. I guess he wasn't kidding." Another text came in with a screenshot of a website asking, "Harlan's True Love Revealed?" She squeezed her eyes closed. "This is a nightmare."

"No, it's not. This kind of thing happens all the time. People will wonder for five days, then the pictures of you two will start pouring in, and no one will remember that Harlan was seen with a trashy blonde anywhere."

She laughed at the description of his own sister. He put an arm around her shoulders and she leaned into him. His presence reassured her in a way nothing else had since Harlan left. "It's going to be fine, Fin. You'll see."

She inhaled slowly, letting her cheek rest against his chest. "Yeah. I'm sure you're right."

Another text came in to Oliver's phone. "It's from Emma. She said she's with him right now and they're both livid about the crappy journalism." Another text. "She just sent a link to her comment. Looks like it's on most of the sites. Okay . . . she told the journalist that the girl Harlan saw tonight was just a close friend. She said, 'Harley's very much in love with his girlfriend, and he's excited to introduce her to the world soon.' See? So everything's fine."

She nodded, relieved. "Am I ready to be introduced to the world?"

He gave her a crooked smile. "Ready or not, here you come."

$$* * *$$

$$\sim O \sim$$

Over the next couple of days, Tate grew more and more anxious. His wound was healing well, but his addiction was becoming increasingly clear. At least to Oliver. But it wasn't until their dad caught Tate playing online poker on his work laptop with several thousand dollars on the line that he was ready to admit that Tate needed real help.

Oliver found his dad at the grand piano in the music room, still wearing his suit from the few hours he'd managed to squeeze in at the office earlier. Oliver opened the French doors and listened to him play Chopin's "Raindrop" prelude. It had been months, maybe longer, since he'd heard his dad at the piano. When he was little and couldn't sleep at night, he would sneak downstairs whenever he heard his dad play. He'd sit outside the doors of the music room and just listen, letting the music lull him to sleep. More often than not, he'd wake up to find his dad carrying him upstairs to his bedroom. He always pretended he was still asleep.

Oliver got lost in the melody and the memories, his dad's fingers falling on the keys with as much passion as precision. As the music went from major to minor chords, hope gave way to regret. The relentless chords spoke sorrow and longing to his heart more directly than any words could.

His dad hit a wrong note, and the discord pulled Oliver from his reverie. His dad stopped and hunched over the piano, a sob escaping him. He put his elbow on the piano, a jumble of dissonance striking the air.

Oliver stepped lightly across the Persian rug, sitting next to his dad on the bench. His dad didn't react. Oliver picked up where his dad had left off, though with far less skill. He fumbled over the notes, confidence building the longer he played. Slowly the yearning in the song faded, leaving a solace that filled the room. When his fingers left the last key, his dad patted his back. He was nodding.

"You were right," he said.

"I wish I weren't, Dad."

"I know." He wiped his eyes. "I know. Email me the link to that rehab facility, will you? It's time I give them a call."

"Yeah, right away," Oliver said. His pulse quickened. "Dad, there's something I need to tell you."

"Anything, son," his dad said, his fingers returning to the piano. He started to play "Clair de Lune."

His breathing hitched as he mustered up all the courage he could find inside of him. "I don't want to be a lawyer; I want to be a therapist." His dad paused for only a moment, but then he resumed playing. He pressed the keys delicately, invitingly, as if willing Oliver on. "I want to help you out this summer, but I also want to go to Guatemala. So I'd like to do both. Help out until I leave, then keep it up when I get back. I'll even help full-time while I'm here so everything you need gets done."

His dad's fingers stiffened, but he gave no other sign that he had even heard Oliver. His fingers danced over the keys, playing arpeggio after arpeggio. The notes felt light and airy and filled the room. When he hit the last few measures and the song reached its final, peaceful cadence, Oliver felt his dad's acceptance. His agreement.

The song ended and his dad smiled at him. "I'm proud of you, son."

Oliver smiled back.

After they left the room, Oliver emailed his dad the link and then left the house to grab takeout from a Greek restaurant in their neighborhood. He opened the front door and was met by a gust of wind that almost pushed him back inside. A voice called to him, and he stopped, uncertain where it was coming from.

"Ollie!" the voice yelled again, carried on the wind. He closed the door, whirling around to see Finley leaving the Grants' house. They both walked down the steps, meeting on the sidewalk. She was wearing a pageboy hat that, moments later, flew off of her head and landed squarely in Oliver's face. He laughed and pulled the hat off of him. Her hair whipped around her face, making her look like a raven-haired lion.

Without thinking, he grabbed her and hugged her tightly. "I did it! I told my dad that I want to be a therapist and that I want to help at his office but still go to Guatemala, and he agreed!" He didn't care that he was holding her in the way that he held his girlfriend. He didn't care that he was smelling her hair or that he hadn't let go yet. He wanted to share this moment with her and only her.

"I'm so happy for you!" she cried in his ear, still holding him, too. When they released each other—far too soon for his liking—she grabbed the hat from his hand and pulled it tightly over her head to contain her hair.

"This is new!" he yelled into the wind, flapping the bill of the hat.

"I'm trying it out. Anaya and I went shopping last night after rehearsals."

"I like it. A lot," he said, suddenly grateful for the wind-chapped look that would mask his flushed cheeks.

"Thanks. Where are you going?"

"Grabbing takeout for dinner." He gestured the way, and she started walking with him. He noticed a small bag in her hand. "What's that?"

"Oh, Emma asked me to bring her one of her lipsticks when I fly out in a couple of days. She said it's from France and she feels naked without it."

My girlfriend, ladies and gentlemen, he thought.

They darted across the empty street and stepped up onto the sidewalk. "How are they doing today?"

"Busy, from what I can tell. I've only had a handful of texts from him all day. I guess Juliette's summit group is going to a Yankees game tonight, and Emma and Crawford are going with them."

"How did his agent meetings go today?"

A dark cloud rolled across the sun, matching Finley's look. "He's having a hard time fitting the meetings in. I badgered him last night about it, so he talked with one of them on the phone today, at least, and said he really liked her. But he's worried that word is going to reach his dad, so now he thinks he should meet his dad for lunch tomorrow."

"To fire him, or . . ."

"That's the question."

"But wasn't that the whole point of you going to New York? So you could be with him when he fires his dad? Why do it early?"

"Exactly," she said.

Harlan and Emma had both told Oliver enough about Mr. Crawford to be sure this lunch would backfire, no matter what they talked about. Which, Oliver realized, was probably what Harlan was looking for: a response from his dad.

"What about Emma?" he asked. "How's she?"

"You haven't talked to her today?"

He shrugged. "She's busy with all her old friends. I'll see her when she gets back."

Finley gave him a suspicious look. In truth, he hadn't even tried to reach her today. And since talking to his dad about Guatemala, he was reluctant to tell her before he had to. She would be angry, and an angry Emma was a nearly impossible Emma. He didn't feel like spoiling his good mood.

They reached the restaurant and were soon in and out. In the few minutes that they were waiting, though, the clouds had become darker and the wind more menacing. They could barely talk to each other over the shrieking wind on the way home; they got back as quickly as they could.

* * *

By Thursday morning—the day Finley was supposed to leave for New York— the rain hit, hard and furious with reports of flooding in several parts of the city. The forecast only promised more storms. In fact, Oliver heard a roll of thunder as he finished filing some paperwork at his dad's office. He got a text from one of his buddies while he was going to the car.

did fin and harlan break up?

He texted back, No. Why?

heard a rumor. if it's true i was gonna ask her out before someone else did

"Are you kidding me?" he shouted at his phone. A woman in the parking garage gave him a wide berth as she walked past him to get to her car.

Well it's not true. So back off.

A moment later, his friend responded.

i was just asking dude, no need to freak out

Was he freaking out? Probably. It was one thing for her to be dating Harlan. She'd asked him and he'd basically convinced her to do it. The way he'd convinced himself to date Emma.

But this? His friends hoping that she was available so they could ask her out?

No. No way. If she and Harlan broke up, he'd be first in that line.

Stop it. You like Emma, and Fin loves Harlan. If they split up, she'd be heartbroken. Do you really want to see her in that much pain?

Still, when he got to his car, Oliver texted her to see if he could pick her up from the community center after rehearsal. He was already zooming along the roads when he got her answer.

Yes.

He reached the community center in record time to find a handful of stragglers putting up chairs. Finley was a little way beyond them, laughing with Anaya and a couple of kids who looked like actors. Boys, of course.

Oliver walked toward her casually. Confidently.

When she saw him, she gave him a funny smile. "What's with you?"

"What do you mean?"

"You're walking weirdly. Did you hurt your foot, or something?"

"No," he said, mentally shaking himself and his stupid walk. "Did you hurt your . . . face, or something?"

She pushed his shoulder. "I'll hurt *your* face, you sass me again. Now give me a minute to talk to Isaiah. I mean, Mr. Weston."

Mr. Weston was speaking with someone else. While they waited, Oliver saw a familiar-looking guy approach. He had bleached blond tips and a face that looked like it needed a good punch.

"You were great today. And you looked good doing it," the guy said.

Finley glanced at Oliver, arching her eyebrows so only he could see. "Hey, Dylan," she said.

"I saw Crawford all over the tabloids with that girl—your cousin, right? Have you dumped the loser yet?"

She smiled as if this was the sweetest thing anyone had ever said to her. "Not yet. But you'll be the first person I call when I do."

"I'd better be."

"I'm joking, Dylan. But you should know that even if Harley and I broke up, you and I would still be better as colleagues," she said, kind and firm.

Nonplussed, Dylan walked backward to the door. "All right. I can take a hint."

"Obviously not," she muttered to Oliver.

Mr. Weston finished his other conversation, and he and Finley talked quickly. When they finished, Fin and Oliver made a run for the car.

He was glad he'd driven the SUV, because the water in the streets was reaching a dangerous level. His wipers were on the highest setting and were barely keeping up.

"So, that guy back there sucked," he said over a clap of thunder. "Does that happen a lot?"

"I'm a girl, so . . ." she chuckled darkly. "But yeah, since Crawford and I started dating, it's picked up. But he's a littler overeager with shutting people down. Last time a guy smiled at me, Harley practically barked at him."

"Well, you handled that really well."

Her smile was bemused. "Thanks, I guess. I've always wanted to be complimented on my ability to reject guys."

"Good one," he said, his laugh beyond awkward. What was wrong with him?

"Okay, weirdo." She pushed his shoulder again, and his pulse raced at her touch, her nearness. This was bad. He shifted farther in his seat from her, though not as far as he should have. Fortunately, her flight for New York left in a few hours, and when she got back, Emma would be back, too. Dating Emma was like a carnival ride—fun, bright, flashy, and the bottom could fall out at any moment. She was the perfect distraction.

And as Finley laughingly told him about something ridiculous that had happened during rehearsals, he needed distraction. Because he had a girlfriend and she had a boyfriend and nothing else had changed.

Except her.

Once they reached the house, she dropped her flip-flops in the garage. When she looked up, she caught him watching her. He blushed.

"Hey, what's the deal with you today? Are you okay?" she asked. He kicked off his waterlogged checkerboard Vans. "Ollie, you know you can tell me anything, right?"

"Yeah, I know. I'm like a brother to you."

She blew a raspberry with her tongue and they walked into the house. "Hardly. If you were like my brother, there'd be a lot more noogies and biting." In the kitchen, she turned and put a hand on his shoulder. "But you are my best friend. Are you worried about Tate? Or is this about you and Emma?"

Her eyes were so big and earnest and her hand on his arm so soft. He couldn't handle this. She needed to get on a plane and go to Harlan now. Yet even as he thought it, every nerve in his body revolted. No. He couldn't take the thought of Harlan holding her. Of his lips on hers. She couldn't get on a plane to see him.

A crack of thunder shook the house, followed almost instantly by a flash of lightning through the windows. The storm was almost on top of them.

Finley's phone vibrated, and she went pale as she read the incoming text. Then defeat settled over her.

"What's wrong?"

"Crawford is going to kill me."

"Why?"

"I just got a text from my airline. The mayor has declared a state of emergency. O'Hare and Midway airports have canceled over a thousand flights . . . including mine. No word yet on if it'll be rescheduled."

He schooled his features, but his insides were throwing a party, piñata and all. "What are you going to do?"

"Call him. I don't know what else to do." She looked so forlorn, the party inside of him almost—but not quite—broke up. "Will you, I don't know, stay nearby when I talk to him? He's going to be so mad."

His heart soared. "Of course. But Fin, do you feel like he has any right to be mad at you?"

"No. Disappointed, sure, but not mad. I haven't done anything wrong."

He couldn't resist. He grabbed her hands, telling himself she was his best friend. He was allowed to hold her hand without creating any awkwardness, without worrying about any tension, any incredible, building tension that was bound to culminate any second in him grabbing her and kissing her so good and hard, they'd melt into the floor. "Good. Remember that, okay?"

"Okay." They sat at the bar, where she pulled up her speed dial and selected the third name on her list. Liam's was first. His was second.

Oliver smiled.

Harlan's face appeared on the screen moments later. Oliver moved out of view of the camera.

"Babe!" He sounded abnormally happy, even for a Crawford. He was outside, wearing sunglasses and walking down a busy street. "Great news! I'm going to meet that producer my dad's been hounding me to meet tonight after you get in, and when I told him about you, he said he was dying to meet Gabriel Price's daughter. So you're coming along! Awesome, right?"

Finley looked—there was no other word for it—disgusted. "You mean the *Robo-Lords* guy? Blaise Kane?"

"Yeah, he's actually not that bad. He's willing to change the script however I want if I'll do the movie. They'll even work around the Ben Affleck schedule so I can do both. Isn't that great?"

She scrunched her nose. "But Crawford, you said he stands for everything that's wrong about Hollywood, except with like forty f-bombs. You hate that guy. *I* hate that guy."

"Listen, my dad thinks it would be rude of me to just turn down the part without at least a meeting."

Her head shook. "But you're firing—"

"Can we just debate this tonight after you meet him?"

Her hand gripped the phone more tightly. "That's actually why I called you." Harlan pulled off his sunglasses and stared hard. "The rainstorms are out of control and Chicago's in a state of emergency and . . . my flight was cancelled."

Oliver could hardly believe the range of expressions that flickered over Harlan's face.

"I'm so sorry, Harley. But I'm going to look into taking the train. It takes almost a full day, but I could be there by tomorrow night, assuming they're leaving—"

Harlan shook his head, steadying his emotions. "No, don't worry about it, Price. I'm a big boy and this isn't my first rodeo. I'll see you when I get back Monday."

"No, Crawford, I want to come—"

"You have enough going on at home, Price. Stay." He smiled. "I love you and I'll see you Monday. Okay?"

"Are you sure about this?"

"Positive."

Finley's brow smoothed and a smile lit up her face. "I love you. Thank you for being so understanding. But don't let Blaise Kane or your dad or anyone else talk you into doing a crap-fest of a movie, okay? You're so, so much better than that. Call me later?"

"Later," he promised.

Finley set down the phone, her whole body looser. "I could kiss that boy."

And I could kick myself, Oliver said to himself. *Did I honestly hope they'd get into a big fight and break up? What is my problem?*

Finley said something about going upstairs. He watched her walk down the hall, a spring in her step. She was happier than he'd seen her in years. More confident. Stronger. How could he want to take that from her? It was one thing to be jealous of Harlan, but that wasn't even the extent of it. He resented him. He resented the fact that Harlan had helped Finley find herself more surely than he ever could have.

Oliver had helped her at one point. He knew he had. After Liam had left for college and she was too afraid to open her mouth, he'd helped her find the strength to do so. But his pushing and prodding had lasted far longer than it should have, and because he couldn't let go, he'd lost her.

Hopefully not forever.

CHAPTER TWENTY-SEVEN

~F~

On Saturday morning, Finley closed her eyes and let her feet pound on the treadmill. The whirr of the belt calmed her mind, something she badly needed. Tate's intervention had happened the previous night at dinner. After two hours and a lot of heartfelt words and tears from all parties, Tate had finally agreed to go to rehab. Uncle Thomas and Aunt Mariah immediately packed him into the car and drove him to the center in Iowa.

She and Oliver stayed up to wait for the phone call from his parents telling them they'd arrived and that Tate was checked in. The call didn't come till nearly three in the morning. So they'd held a Hitchcock marathon until then. And because it was a Hitchcock marathon, Oliver was just scared enough not to want to be alone, though he would never admit it in the light of day. They slept on the enormous sectional in the theater room, feet on opposite sides of the couch and their heads less than a foot from each other.

When she awoke, their faces were even closer together. He'd looked so peaceful and . . . cute. There was no denying it. She'd had to move lightly to leave without disturbing him.

It felt good to run. She felt grounded, connected to her body through the steady stream of blood coursing through her veins. She felt in complete control of herself, with rushes of adrenaline and endorphins intensifying the feeling of being totally alive.

Things were finally going her way.

Well, mostly. Things with her mom were no better than before the visit. The memory of her mother looking so sorry and so pathetic gnawed at her like an ulcer. But at least things with Crawford felt okay again. They hadn't talked much since Thursday night, but she knew how busy he was. And Liam was only weeks away from moving to England to play with West Ham's developmental squad. Oliver had settled everything with his dad, though the way he stared off, picking at his nails, told her he was hiding something.

So everything wasn't perfect, but she was happy. She liked being happy.

When she hit seven miles, she stopped the treadmill and went to the roof to stretch. The morning air felt good after her hard run. She dropped to the ground and checked her phone while she stretched. She had a message from Emma from two hours earlier. Someone had an early morning . . . or a late night, knowing Emma. She scanned the brief paragraph. Her heart dropped.

Fin—A vicious, awful rumor was picked up by some tabloids. DO NOT BELIEVE A WORD OF IT. Count on it, in a few days, some responsible journalists will show that this is complete and utter B.S. Harley obsesses about you all day and loves and misses you so much, he took an early flight back to Chicago this morning to be with you. This will all blow over. But still, why couldn't you have just come with us? UGH!!!!!!!!!!! XOXO

She frowned at the phone. What could be so awful that Emma would send her a warning? Had Harlan signed on to that awful movie? He obviously hadn't fired his dad yet—was never going to fire his dad. But why all the stuff about Harley obsessing over her? Because she'd be disappointed in him?

She ground her teeth. Ever since he'd returned to New York, he'd been making worse and worse decisions. He always told her that she made him want to be better, but she'd thought it was just flattery. Maybe he needed her more than she thought.

A text appeared on her phone.

u ok sexy? I'm here if u need me. Dylan

Everyone in the play had swapped numbers weeks ago, but as dogged as Dylan's attention was, he'd never texted her before. She wanted to roll her eyes, to tell the goose bumps crawling over her body that this was nothing. A coincidence.

She didn't believe it.

Her chest felt hot, her throat tight, her mouth dry. A feeling of sick, ugly certainty settled over her as she pulled up the Internet and searched Harlan's name.

She doubled over with a sob.

But one site wasn't enough. She felt like torturing herself. Like tearing out her heart. And she had to be sure. She went to another site and another and another. The story was the same; the evidence was overwhelming. The pictures ranged from Harlan at a party to Harlan with his arm around some girl. But when she saw a picture of his crumpled navy shirt on the limo floor and the back of a half-dressed skeezy head, she dropped the phone.

Harlan had cheated on her.

She collapsed on the ground in agony. The memory of Emma's text taunted her in big, cruel font. Emma was right. Finley should have been there. If only she'd been there.

WHY HADN'T SHE BEEN THERE?

She hugged her legs tightly. Sweat evaporated from her body, and she began to shiver despite the muggy July heat. She didn't have energy enough to move. And she was having trouble swallowing. Was she choking? Was she even breathing anymore? What was the matter with her?

The door to the roof opened, and Oliver stood there in his pajamas, shock all over his face.

"Fin—"

She covered her face with her hands. "I can't—I can't—this can't be real," she cried, breaking down again.

A moment later, Oliver was at her side, his hand on her back. She leaned into him, and he wrapped his arms around her, letting her cry and cry against him.

Maybe ten minutes—or ten years—later, the roof door opened again.

Harlan stood there, wearing the same jeans and fitted black t-shirt from the pictures the night before.

Oliver jumped up. "What the hell are you doing here? Haven't you done enough?"

Harlan looked tortured. "Please, Oliver, just let me explain."

"Explain what, you lying sack of—"

"Ollie, don't," Finley said, pulling herself up. She couldn't even look at Harlan. Every part of her hurt too much. "He's not worth it."

"Yes, I am! Just let me explain," Harlan said, running past Oliver to her. He reached for her hands.

"Don't you dare touch me," she snarled.

"Finley, *please*," he begged. He looked desperate, exhausted. His hair was standing on end, and his eyes were bloodshot. And as he leaned in again, she realized something else.

"You're drunk!"

"No, I'm not! I'm . . . I'm—"

"Hungover," she said, stepping farther away from him and the stench. She wrapped her arms around her shivering body, wishing she had a thousand more layers and a million more miles between them. "You said you *never* drank! You lying snake."

"Just let me explain!"

She forced the words from her chest, cursing the tears spilling down her face. "Explain what? All the ways you've lied to me?"

"No, it's not what you think, Price! Nothing happened!"

"Define 'nothing.'"

"We went to a party and what I thought was punch obviously wasn't and the next thing I knew, I was waking up in my limo with Juliette—"

"Juliette? You took Juliette?" She backed up, bumping against the wall. The back of that trashy, blonde head . . . How could this have gotten worse?

"Yes, but I swear, neither of us meant for anything to happen. I don't know if anything even *did* happen!"

He kept talking, but Finley pulled out her phone, not caring that he was begging her to stop, to look at him, to listen to him. She pulled up the tabloids, twisting the knife harder and deeper. She clicked on the headline "Harlan Crawford Caught with Sexy Blonde" and looked closely at the pictures.

It was Harlan and Juliette, all right, looking wasted and all over each other in his limo. She swiped through the pictures. Harlan, Emma, and Juliette holding Solo cups at a house party. Harlan and Juliette dancing in a club. Juliette, Emma, and Harlan back at the party. And then, Juliette wrapped around him in the limo.

Her eyes landed on Harlan's miserable face. "You know how mad I was that you didn't come last week. And then you missed your flight and weren't with me when I needed you! You know how much this week meant to me! That must have been in my subconscious when I drank whatever that was, or something. You have to know I would never hurt you! Not knowingly!"

Her muscles tightened. He looked awful. Wrecked. But there was no way he was telling the truth. "Do you expect me to believe that you thought you were drinking punch? Come on, Harley."

"I'm serious! This wasn't some rager! Please, please believe me!"

He sounded so earnest, looked so distraught. And she wanted so, so badly for this to all be a misunderstanding. "So are you trying to tell me . . . you think you were roofied?" She hated the desperation in her voice even more than the hope.

"I don't know. Maybe. Everything's like a haze. If you'd just been there . . ." Behind Harlan, Oliver's eyes became enormous; he looked as if he could shoot missiles from them. She appreciated the concern, but she wished he'd just go, already. This was between them. "This—whatever happened—it never would have happened if you'd just been there. You know I love you, right?"

She dropped to the ground and tossed her phone to the side, not wanting to see more pictures. She already knew more than she wanted to. But he was right: she also knew he loved her. He loved her and he took care of her in a way nobody had since her dad. She didn't have to worry about what someone would say or do to her anymore because she had him. Even when she didn't need him, she had him. That's what mattered.

She could see his side: after everything he'd done for her, she'd bailed when he needed her most. If he hurt her, it was only because she'd hurt him first.

Stupid Finley.

Harlan sat beside her, wrapping an arm around her. She closed her eyes, but the sound of the roof door popped them open again. Oliver was nowhere in sight.

She leaned into Harlan's warmth, hating herself for loving it.

"We can get past this," he whispered. "We're gonna be okay."

She hiccupped and nodded, thinking of what Emma always said: people messed up. If Harlan really wanted to be with her, wanted to make amends, she could forgive him. She *had* to. The weight pushing against her chest would crush her if she didn't.

"I know you must blame yourself for not being there, but don't. Promise me, okay? It's my fault, too, babe."

The words were like a record scratching.

"Babe?"

Something clicked in her mind and oxygen flooded her lungs. She leaned away from him. "You know, judging by those pictures, you guys must have been driving around a lot last night."

Harlan grabbed her hand. She fought back a shudder. "What do you mean?"

"I mean that you went to a house party and *then* to a club

together. Or was it to a club, and *then* to the house party? Of course, if you were roofied, you probably wouldn't remember."

"Yeah, you're right." He swore, drawing it out as if in an epiphany. "Man, we must have been really out of it. I only remember being at that party. You believe me, right? I can't live with myself if you don't believe me."

She let him put a hand to her face, wanting desperately to slap it off. To scratch his eyes out. "I'm confused, though. Did you guys pack a change of clothes, too? I mean, Juliette was wearing a white sheer shirt with a shimmery tank top at the club, and then she's just wearing a tank top at the house party, so it's hard to tell. But I could have sworn you were wearing a navy t-shirt in the club pictures . . . and the limo. Yet the black one you're wearing now was in the others—"

His head dropped. He looked broken. Dejected.

Busted.

And with every crack in his armor, she felt herself grow stronger.

"I don't know anymore, Finley. What do you want me to say?"

She was steel now. She jumped to her feet. "I want you to admit that you're a worthless, cheating bastard who tried to manipulate me into thinking that what you did is somehow my fault!"

"This *is* your fault!" he yelled, standing. "You know how much I need you! If you'd have just come with me, this never would have happened!"

"No, this never would have happened if you *hadn't cheated on me.*" A sob tried to escape her, but she choked it back. "Why did you do it? Why would you do this?"

He sounded desperate, reaching for her despite her backing away. "I didn't mean for it to happen! I swear. I was so angry when you said you wouldn't come, and that first night when we ran into Juliette and Raleigh, she made such a big deal about how she couldn't handle being away from him when he'd be in Connecticut. So Emma invited her to hang out with us. I was pissed that she did, because I knew you wouldn't like it. But you know Emma. Then the next night, Juliette was so awful and cold, she wouldn't even look at me. I kept trying to get her to just talk to me. I asked her if she'd ever gotten my apology, if she was really okay with everything."

Finley's tears dried up, but the memory of them burned a stream down her face. She wrapped her arms around her chest.

"Then finally, I got her to crack. She said she forgave me. So we went to the game with her while Raleigh was doing interviews. By the next night, I didn't even realize she thought I'd been leading her on until she made a move. The media was everywhere, and all I could think about was you seeing her kiss me and what you would believe. I had to keep her from making a scene! So I had security sneak us out to the limo." He sounded so distressed.

"You are unbelievable."

"It's true! When we were in the limo, I had to convince her not to run out and make a huge scene. We agreed that this had to stay a secret, that it was a 'what happens in New York, stays in New York' thing for you and Raleigh. She didn't want to jeopardize things with Raleigh when he's about to make it big, and she knew I didn't want to hurt you. Our first thought was keeping you from being hurt."

Her stomach churned as she did the math. "This was before my flight was even canceled, wasn't it? You were going to let me come anyway and just lie to my face every second. How could you do that to me?"

"It wasn't like that!"

"Were you going to tell me?" He didn't answer. She spit. "Your concern for me is overwhelming. Too bad the paparazzi had to destroy all your good intentions, huh?"

Harlan leaned against the wall, holding his head. "No. It was Emma who found us. She took the picture as blackmail so that if either of us was ever this stupid again, she'd ruin us. She's so mad at me, she can't even look at me."

"Emma?" Her lip trembled, a new feeling of betrayal overcoming her. "She leaked the pictures? She knew it was true when she texted me?"

"She didn't leak the pictures. Her phone was hacked." He pushed himself off the wall. "You have to forgive me. I was just trying to keep you from being hurt! I didn't know how else to keep Juliette—"

"Save it," she said. "We're over."

"NO!" he cried, grabbing her shoulders. She couldn't shake him off. "Just listen to me. We can work through this, okay? We can get past this. People get past this sort of thing all the time."

"I can't."

His face turned hard, his voice authoritative. "Yes, you can. Finley Price, you *will* forgive me. You have to. Think of everything I've done for you: everything with your mom, getting your brother a spot with his dream team, standing up to Nora, and . . . and Mansfield! *You need me!*"

"I loved you," she said, aware of how sad she sounded. "But I don't need you."

"Price, no! Don't do this!"

"Good-bye, Harlan." She pointed toward the door. He didn't move. "GO!" She stood strong, watching his face fall, his shoulders slump, and his feet drag him from the roof. When the door closed, she fell to the ground and wept.

* * *

The sun was high overhead when the roof door flew open, tearing her from her darkest thoughts. She shielded the sun from her puffy eyes and saw Emma rushing to her. She blinked as Emma threw her arms around her.

"I'm so sorry, Fin. I'm so, so sorry," Emma said, and Finley sank into the hug, against her better judgment. "Harley was a fool. A scared, selfish fool."

Finley nodded, tears threatening again.

"I'm furious with him," Emma said, holding her at arm's length. "So, so pissed. But you have to know, he really thought he was protecting you. He was horrified when I found him. He couldn't believe it."

Finley shook Emma off, angry. "He was horrified that he *got caught!* Emma, why can't you guys understand that this isn't okay? I would have forgiven him for getting caught with Juliette hanging all over him at a club! But he took her into his limo and *hooked up with her* so that he wouldn't have to admit he was wrong for spending time with her in the first place!" She threw her arms in the air and screamed at the sky. "How is this happening?"

Emma grabbed her arms. "Don't throw everything you have away because he was a jackass! He felt like you rejected him, and he made a mistake. People make mistakes, Fin! If you'd have just been there—"

Finley broke her grasp. "He shouldn't require constant supervision to not cheat, Emma!"

"Of course not, but he was so hurt, and he defaulted to the life our dad has shown him, and . . . Mr. Bertram bought you a ticket, Fin! You *chose* these people over him. How was that supposed to make him feel?"

She shook her head. "You're right, Emma. I tried to have it both ways, and I couldn't."

"No, you couldn't." Emma rubbed her face. "Don't you see how badly you're hurting him? Do you even care that Harley is crying for the first time *in his life* because of you?"

"Not because of me." Her words sliced the air. "If he's upset, he has no one but himself to blame."

Emma looked as if she was about to protest, but she stopped. "He's my baby brother, Fin."

"I know." Her voice cracked. "And he broke my heart."

Another voice cut over theirs. "What is going on here?" Oliver said, appearing from the stairwell. "Emma?"

Emma ran to Oliver and threw her arms around him. "Where have you been? I don't know what to do, Ollie. They're done, and I don't know what to do."

Oliver caught Finley's eye. "You didn't take him back?"

"Of course not."

A shadow of a smile formed on Oliver's mouth. "Fin, why don't you go downstairs? I need to talk to Emma."

She nodded, walking toward them while Emma started to cry. As Finley passed, Oliver grabbed her hand and squeezed it for just a moment. Trembling, she opened the roof door, stepped into the stairwell, and waited for it to close.

She sat down on the top step. The heavy door dampened their voices, but she could hear just fine.

"I can't believe any of this happened," Emma said, her voice filled with regret. "I can't believe Harlan could be so stupid. I never should have taken that picture of them . . ."

Oliver interrupted. "Emma, the picture *showed* what happened. It didn't make Harlan cheat."

"I know, and I'm sick about it, Ollie! All I've ever wanted is for him to turn out better than our dad, and with Finley, that finally seemed possible. But he screwed up! I know she's mad, but it happened! Why can't she forgive him?"

"You can't say, 'it happened,' and expect everyone to just agree and move on. That's not how people work!"

"That's how *I* work! You have to forgive and forget, or you'll lose everyone you love!"

"There are limits to how much people can forgive, Emma! You have them with your dad, or you wouldn't be taking a break from acting just to spite him."

"That's different! *My dad doesn't care about me,*" Emma yelled, her words raw and throbbing. "But Harlan loves Fin! He'd never want to hurt her. Can't you see the difference?"

Everything was quiet, and Fin knew she was missing something—an embrace, probably. Then Oliver said, "I know you think he made a mistake, but he chose this."

Emma sniffed. "No, Fin did. She's the one breaking up with him. She can change her mind. She *has* to."

Oliver's voice was almost too quiet to hear. "He chose to sleep with Juliette, so he has to accept the consequence, and you can't change that. You have to let Finley do this."

"I don't want to, Ollie," she cried. "I just want everything back the way it was before we left for New York."

"I know. I'm sorry. For you and for Fin."

The sound of Emma's sobs reached her, adding to her pain. Her friend's voice shook. "This has been the best few months of my life, and just like that, it's over."

"It's not just *over*," Oliver said.

"Ollie, come on. We've known this was coming. I'm moving to France in the fall. Harley can't stay in Chicago now, and I'd never stay without him. We're all we have."

"Emma, that's not—"

"Besides," she said over him, her voice heavy with regret, "you're going on your trip in a couple of weeks, and I'm not the person you'll be thinking about while you're gone. She is."

What? Finley thought.

"What?" Oliver asked.

"You're in love with Finley," Emma said. Finley could practically hear the girl's heart splitting in two. "You have been since the day we met, and this is the chance you've been waiting for. She's broken, and now you can pick up the pieces and make her whole."

"Emma—"

"Am I right?"

"You're . . . you're right," he said with a sigh. Finley's heart stopped. What was he saying? "I care about you so much, Emma, and I've loved dating you. But I love her. I tried to convince myself that I didn't, and that wasn't fair to you. I'm so sorry."

Tears sprang to Finley's eyes for a different reason than they had all day. She heard Emma sniff again.

"But I don't want to save her," he continued, "and I'm not picking up any pieces. In fact, I'm not going anywhere near her until she's whole, all on her own. I'd like to be here for you, though. If you want a friend."

Emma said something Finley couldn't hear, but she'd already heard enough. She ran down to her room and threw herself onto her bed.

Oliver loved her.

She missed Harlan.

Oliver loved her.

She ached with betrayal and longing and sorrow.

Oliver loved her.

CHAPTER TWENTY-EIGHT

~F~

"So, Miss Price—"

She winced. "Again, please call me Finley." It was the second time she'd asked them during the last twenty minutes.

"Okay, Finley. Why don't you tell us why you're the best director candidate for the Mansfield Theater Youth Program?"

Their questions so far had been technical, and therefore easy. And this one should have been a gimme, too. But they were asking more than they thought. What they were asking struck to the core of who she was. She looked past the stage, out to the four interviewers sitting in the mezzanine, with their serious faces and glasses and even a scarf or two. They looked as if they could have played theater directors in a movie. The thought made her smile.

"I was made for this—"

"You mean because of who your father is? Forgive the impertinence, but you look remarkably like him."

She coughed. "No. It has nothing to do with my genes, at least not more than an inclination and spark of talent. I should say instead that I've made myself for this."

The program director narrowed her eyes behind her glasses. "Please explain."

Her pulse picked up. "Since I was a child, theater—and film, unsurprisingly—has been a near obsession for me. I have seen hundreds of plays and studied every element of theater, especially directing. I've worked tirelessly to understand the minutiae that make the difference between a stellar production and a good one. In every way possible, I am a student of this craft."

Her words were met with nods. The stage lights struck her as though they were purposely beating down on her to intimidate her. But it didn't work. If anything, this was finally her time to shine.

"But until recently, I couldn't execute because I was too afraid to be heard. I gave away my voice rather than risk heartache or rejection or pain. I used to view theater as a way to experience the spectrum of human emotion without actually having to live it. I even said so in my application. But I was wrong." She looked down at the scuffed stage floor. Her eyes didn't linger, though; they returned to her interviewers. "That girl didn't deserve this spot. But that's not me anymore.

"I have been brave enough to live, inside and outside of a theater. I have fallen in love. I've had my heart broken and have mended it myself. I've run from my personal demons, just to turn around and scream at them. I've even convinced my horny youth theater group that putting on *The Full Monty* isn't the only way to be bold," she said to chuckles. "I have it in me to put on the best performance anyone has ever seen . . . with some expert mentoring, of course." She smiled. "I've worked hard to make myself ready for this." Her breath quickened with courage. "So as I see it, the question isn't why am I the best candidate, but rather why are you interviewing anyone else?"

The directors glanced at each other with surprise and—there was no mistaking it—respect.

"Miss Pr—I mean, Finley," the program director said with a smile, "we aren't interviewing anyone else. Not anymore." Finley stopped breathing. All of the energy in her body was turned to producing a megawatt smile. "In truth, we wanted to meet you to see if you could live up to your application. Your essays were poignant and compelling. And your recommendations were glowing, to say the least."

Finley's smile faltered. "If you're giving me this spot because of what Harlan Crawford said, I'm afraid I have to decline." It had been two weeks since they'd broken up, but just saying his name felt like ripping out stitches in a wound.

Four sets of eyebrows jumped. Another interviewer pulled a microphone down to his mouth. "No. We aren't. Although it was interesting to hear his perspective, you piqued our interest in your application. You had so much knowledge and enthusiasm, but your spirit felt . . . buried. We wondered why you were holding yourself back. Yet your references spoke with a passion and enthusiasm about your love of theater that one rarely sees these days. One of your references, Isaiah Weston, said how indispensable you have been in past productions, both at school and in the community. He said that you're the type of person everyone listens to, even when you don't say anything at all, but you're even better when you say something." The interviewer smiled. "It's high praise, but still, we couldn't quite get a sense for you. We couldn't quite hear you."

He looked at the other interviewers. "I think I speak for all of us when I say that we hear you loud and clear now, Finley Price." They all nodded vigorously.

"Welcome to Mansfield Theater."

* * *

Five minutes later, Finley burst through the thick doors into the lobby. Sun streamed through the glass entrance, blinding her momentarily. Then she saw two very nervous boys.

"I got it!" she squealed, galloping up to them. She threw an arm each around Liam and Oliver, and their heads bumped hers. They jumped up and down, heedless of the anxious, envious applicants scattered throughout the hallway.

"We're going to celebrate!" Liam said. "My treat." She let them go, but he left an arm around her shoulders, and Oliver left an arm around her waist. When Liam released her to grab the door, Oliver squeezed her close.

"I'm so proud of you, Fin," he whispered in her ear before letting go. Her waist felt cold where his hand had been.

Liam led them down streets crowded with locals and tourists alike, guiding them to a hot dog stand with a line halfway down the street. "What?" he asked in response to their level looks. "This may be my last chance for a real Chicago dog till Christmas."

As they waited, they peppered her with questions about the interview, grinning as they heard her answers. The line moved slowly, and soon they were on to other topics.

"So, are you and Emma okay now?" Liam asked.

"Kind of," Finley said. "She's finally stopped asking me to give Harlan another chance. And her last text was a picture of a handbag that she said was tata punch-worthy." A ghost of a smile crossed her face. "I'm hopeful."

"I'm glad, sis," Liam said, before asking Oliver about the breakup. Finley didn't pay much attention to his answer. He was leaving out the most important part, anyway. The part she still didn't know what to do with.

Oliver loved her.

The thought hadn't spurred her to action. It hadn't transformed her pain into joy or miraculously healed her heart. It had simply softened the blow, the way a parka would a sledgehammer.

Oliver loved her.

It was there, in the back of her mind, when she'd confronted a spiteful Juliette a few short days after the breakup.

The girl hadn't even looked Finley in the eye when her dad marched her into his office and ordered her to "make this right."

"Sorry, Finley," Juliette had whimpered, slumping into a chair across from her. Her hair looked as if it hadn't been done in days, the truest possible sign of her distress.

Finley had no tears for Juliette. "Did you even like him? Or did you just do it to hurt me?"

"Yes."

"To which question?"

"To both," she said. "You stole him from me."

Finley tsked. "You had a boyfriend at the time, Juliette. *Both* times."

"Don't you think I know that? I'm not proud of what I did, but let's be honest: we both know I never cared about Raleigh."

"Or about me, obviously."

Juliette brought a chunk of hair in front of her eyes and picked off the split ends. "It should have been me dating him, not you. It wasn't personal."

Finley couldn't believe what she was hearing. "You two deserve each other. But don't wait by the phone, Juliette. You have to know he never cared about you." To her surprise, she took little joy in the words. Seeing Juliette, curled up in a chair in day-old jeans with her hair looking like a rat's nest was more pitiable than satisfying. It was as if she was seeing into the girl's soul, and it wasn't pretty.

"Like I'm going to listen to you about Harlan. You couldn't even keep him."

"I didn't *want* to—" She put her hand on the back of her chair, struggling for composure. "Your dad told me that your punishment is mine to deliver." The girl blanched, which, if she was being honest, was a little satisfying. "I thought about it, and I've considered every possible punishment, including being the bigger person and letting you off the hook. But that's not fair to anyone, especially you. You don't care about people, Juliette. You use them and chew them up and spit them out. But that's not my problem anymore. I'm going to let your dad decide what to do with you."

She left Juliette stewing in the office and ran into Uncle Thomas, pacing in the hallway. She gave him a rundown of the conversation, leaving nothing out, for Juliette's sake. He looked sad.

"What do you think about her punishment?" he asked.

"I'd say she needs a few months to think of anyone but herself. But I think it should be your call."

He put his arms around her in a big, fatherly hug. "These last few weeks have shown me my failings as a father more harshly than anything could." His voice trembled. "But if . . . if I've had any small part in the incredible young woman you've become—"

"You have," she said, tears springing to her eyes. "You have."

"Then at least there's hope for me, eh?" With a final squeeze, he let go of her and smiled. His eyes were wet. "I'm so proud of you, Finley. I couldn't love you more if you were my own blood. In fact, I probably love you more because of it."

She laughed. "I love you, too."

He put a hand on her cheek and smiled, a small, sad smile. "I still remember your first few months here, how scared you were. I wanted so badly to wrap you in my arms and keep you safe from your demons." His voice caught, and tears spilled from his eyes. "But I couldn't. I felt like such a failure for not knowing how to help you. Your dad was my closest friend, and I should have done more. I should have kept trying to let you know how sorry I was for everything that happened, yet how happy I was to have you here. How thrilled I was to watch you grow. It sounds so selfish—"

"No." She had shaken her head when he said that and smiled through tears. "It sounds perfect."

Finley's phone vibrated, pulling her back to the present. She shook off her daze and saw that they were almost to the food truck. The smell of Vienna beef dogs and tangy pickles made Finley's stomach growl.

While Liam debated his toppings aloud, Oliver leaned down to her. Ever since his conversation with his dad about his future, he'd seemed taller, somehow, as if he'd shrugged off the heavy load of his dad's expectations and could finally stand straight. "Is that Harlan? Is he still texting you?"

She felt a stab of panic at the thought of yet another text from Harlan. Since their breakup, she'd had five, sometimes ten texts from him a day, up and down, from pitiful to heart-wrenching. Apologies, assumptions that she'd take him back, angry texts blaming her for the breakup, him telling her that he was doing the Robo-Lords movie because he really felt that the producer had changed, but he wished he could talk to her and get her opinion. That text had been the hardest to ignore.

They're changing the movie so that it's more than your typical action/disaster movie. They really want me involved with this. Please, Price, as an expert, tell me what I should do.

She'd struggled for hours, days, wondering if she should respond. He was a brilliant actor, no matter what had happened between them, and if she became as successful as she planned to be, they'd run into each other in the future. Besides, her father had cared about Harlan. He would want him to get good advice from someone. So in the end, she decided to text him. As an expert. Just this once.

If Guillermo del Toro is directing, do it. If it's anyone else, though, the movie's going to end up being a cheap imitation of an already crappy franchise. But it's your call. Always has been.

When he responded moments later, asking if she'd forgiven him, she wasn't surprised. She'd anticipated another dozen texts before he realized it was a courtesy, not an invitation. So when he sent more and more messages about the movie, the script, the director—who wasn't Guillermo del Toro, but who was still awesome—she didn't reply again.

He'd stopped sending messages a few days later—only a few days ago, in fact. She hoped she didn't have one now.

She checked her phone, then smiled at Oliver. "No, it's from your mom. She wanted to congratulate me on my interview."

He nodded with his whole body. "Good. He shouldn't be bothering you still."

"He's not," she said. "Mostly."

Liam was only two people from his last-Chicago-dog-till-Christmas, and he was bouncing on the balls of his feet. "I should just go all in, right? Get everything? It doesn't matter that I hate tomatoes. I should get tomatoes."

They didn't have to respond. He was back to looking over people's heads at what they were ordering.

"So . . . are you . . . how are you?" Oliver stammered.

She leaned into him, putting her head briefly on his shoulder. "I'm good, Ollie. But I'm still sad, if that's what you're asking."

He rested his head on hers. "Yeah, that's what I'm asking."

"It's better knowing that I have people who love me who would never treat me the way Harlan did." She almost winced at the use of "love," but it was the truth.

"I'm glad you know that." He lifted his head and pushed her in front of him and Liam so she could order first.

"One jumbo dog, loaded, chili cheese fries, and a large Mountain Dew," she said. Liam gaped. "Man up, big bro."

"Uh, yeah, I'll have what the lady's having," Ollie called into the truck.

"Make that three," Liam said, pulling out money and handing it to the cashier. They walked over to the park across the street and dropped down on the grass beneath an enormous ash tree. "Where are you even going to put all that food, Finny? I don't know if you've gotten the memo, but you represent the Lollipop Guild."

"*Wizard of Oz,*" she said, before taking a huge bite. Mustard and relish, pickles and tomatoes, onions and peppers all fell from the corners of her grinning mouth.

"That's disgusting."

"Unh-unh," she groaned, shoving a fry into her overstuffed

mouth and chewing slowly. "Ollie, are you still planning to come with me to visit my mom this weekend?"

"Yeah, for sure."

She nodded, taking another bite. Visiting her mom had been the hardest thing she'd done since the breakup, and it had taken her a week to work up the courage to do so. She'd taken the bus out to the detention center alone, replaying her first trip there with Harlan the whole time. It had been excruciating to remember his touch, his kisses, and his support, misguided as it was. She kept recalling her mom's shattered, broken face when the guards dragged her from the visiting area.

Sitting in the cramped booth waiting for her mom to be brought out, she wasn't ready for the swell of emotions inside of her—remorse, fear, shame, and the tiniest hint of hope. The conversation went well enough. She told her mom that she was sorry for the way she'd blown up, but that she still didn't forgive her. They had a brutally frank talk about her mom's addiction, how she'd hurt Finley, and the counseling she'd received since being in prison. Her mom seemed truly sorry, but that didn't mean Finley was ready to put herself in a position to be hurt again, just that she didn't feel consumed by fear and anger anymore.

Things between them were a long, long way from being good. They didn't eat at her the way they had, though. The freedom she longed for finally felt possible.

All because Harlan had cheated on her.

No, she corrected herself. *All because I decided to pick up the pieces of my wreck of a life.*

She wasn't putting the picture back together the way it had been before her dad died or before the Crawfords moved in next door. She was splicing the images and creating a collage out of her joy and grief, her pain and pleasure, like a healing montage in a movie. She didn't know what the end result would look like yet, but for the first time in years, she was sure it would be epic.

"This is so good, it hurts," Liam was saying, halfway through his hot dog.

"Lightweight," Oliver said, tucking into his fries.

"Dude, some of us are in training, okay?" Liam said. "We can't all eat gut bombs seven days a week like you can. But I guess you have to pack on the pounds while you can, right? I mean, a few weeks in Central America, and the food is going to be sliding right through you. Montezuma's revenge, bro. Get ready."

"Gross." Finley tossed a fry at her brother and he caught it in his mouth. She took another bite of her hot dog and looked at the two boys on either side of her, clutching their bulging stomachs. In only a few days, Oliver would be in Guatemala, Liam would be in England, and she'd be here without them. For once, that was okay.

"All right, boys," she said, licking the last of her hot dog from her fingers and turning to her fries. "I don't run seven miles a day for my health. Let me show you how this is done."

CHAPTER TWENTY-NINE

~O~

Oliver glanced at the review of "Clark Street Community Theater's production of *West Side Story*" as he ran on the treadmill. He'd already read it ten times, but he'd missed the play's entire run, so this was the closest he could get to experiencing it. Besides, the review quoted Finley twice and had a picture of the cast and crew. Finley hadn't stood in the back for the photo, but in the front. Where she belonged.

When his legs were officially jelly and his lungs officially on fire, he stepped off the treadmill. He stripped off his sweat-drenched shirt and wiped his face with it as he lay back on the weight bench. Had someone set the thermostat at ninety degrees, or something? Or was he just that out of shape after Guatemala?

No, the real problem was that he'd been running for seventy-three minutes in the hope that he'd bump into Finley.

He'd gotten home last night, and his excitement at seeing her again had been overwhelming to the point of awkward. A good night's sleep had his head on straight again, though. Mostly.

Why didn't I just ask her if she was going to run this morning? He strained beneath the weight of the barbell, barely returning it to the bench. *She's not even here. Why am I pretending I can lift a small horse?*

He sat up and grabbed his water bottle, chugging it. He poured the rest on his head, then squealed from the cold.

Which is precisely when Fin walked in. She stood in the doorway, wearing her little shorts and a fitted blue t-shirt that was definitely not a hand-me-down. Self-conscious, he looked at her eyes and found that hers were on his shirtless body. She walked over to him and put a hand on his stomach. It was dripping wet.

"Ollie," she said, sounding as though she'd already been running. "You have abs. When did you get abs?"

He grinned. He liked the feel of her hand on his bare skin. "What, these old things?" She was still staring. "Hey, Fin, my eyes are up here."

He didn't even try to hide his smile as she stumbled onto the treadmill.

"Are you already done?" she asked with a hint of regret.

"No, I always look like this," he said, gesturing to his bright red, completely damp face and body.

She shook her head. "Oh, right. Sorry. I'm, uh. Dang, I should have gotten up earlier."

He moved to the side of her treadmill. "Why?"

"You've been gone forever, and you're starting college in a couple of weeks. I don't have enough time left with you, Ollie." She punched the incline up so high his hamstrings ached just thinking about it.

"I could hang out while you're running."

"What, and you just watch me get grosser and grosser as I sweat? No," she moaned.

His grin returned. "Why, Finley Price, are you embarrassed because you don't have luscious abs like mine?"

She laughed. "Hush, you." She was already panting. "Do you . . . maybe want to see a movie tonight? The new—"

"Yes."

"Oh." She stared at her progress on the screen. "Good."

He was hyperaware of his shirtless state, and the fact that he suddenly had goose bumps. It may be just a movie to her, but to him, it was a date. Or at least a tryout for the million future dates he wanted with her. He needed to get her away from the house and all the drama these four walls had seen of late. He wanted a chance for her to see him differently. As a possible boyfriend. As the only boyfriend she'd have for the rest of her life. He folded his arms over his torso, then unfolded them just as quickly. "Okay then. So, pick me up at six?"

She rubbed her nose. "How about five? I thought we could try this new sushi place your dad was talking about. If that's okay?"

"Yes, that sounds perfect." He dropped his burning face. "I'm gonna go downstairs." He scooped up his shirt from the floor and held it in front of his stomach. Then he turned back around, bumping the door open with his butt. "Have a good workout."

Her smile almost stopped his heart.

Waiting until five was awful. It was torture. It was the worst, most ridiculously pointless thing he could imagine. So by midmorning, he poked around the house, looking for her. He wandered in on his mom sitting in the library. "Mom, have you seen Finley?"

"Not since breakfast, no." She swiped at the tablet on her lap. "What are you doing?"

She put the tablet down and stretched out onto the leather couch. In jeans and a tunic, she looked comfortable. If she wasn't in pain, it was a good day. "I'm looking at dogs, sweetie."

He sat beside her, picking up the tablet. "A pug, huh? What brought this on?"

His mom reached her arms around him and gave him a hug. "It's getting awfully lonely here without all of you."

"Mom, not that much is changing. I'm going to be six train stops away. Heck, I'll probably stay here as often as I stay at the dorms."

"I know, sweetie. But this summer has been like a preview of things to come. With your trip and Tate gone and all of Juliette's mission trips this summer—"

He smirked. "I still can't believe you guys sent her on mission trips. What church was it?"

She waved a hand in the air. "Oh, all of them. She's on a new trip with a new church every week until school starts back up."

"And it's all in Canada?" he asked, delighted.

"Yes, in Manitoba and . . . Saskatchewan? Saskawoon? Some odd place. I think your dad just has her going back and forth to those two provinces all summer."

"With complimentary chastity belts, I hope?"

His mom attempted a stern look, which Oliver saw through. "They're all-girl groups, actually. And they might only speak French." She laughed, then sighed and rubbed his hand. "We got lucky with you and Finley."

"You guys didn't do too badly by any of us, Mom."

A voice called from the hallway. "Aunt Mariah?"

"In the library, dear," she called back.

"Oh, good," Fin was saying as she strode into the library in a t-shirt and pajama pants. She'd curled her hair and . . . was that lipstick? His stomach flipped when he saw her with an armful of clothes. "Can you help me pick out—Ollie!" She almost dropped the clothes. "Wh . . . what are you doing here?"

He smiled, wondering if she could hear his pulse. "I'll leave you two alone."

"Actually," his mom said, "why don't you get Oliver's opinion, Finley? Isn't he the one you're dressing for, anyway?" She patted Oliver's cheek, then winked at them and left the room.

"Uh," Finley said, looking at the door.

"Um," he agreed. "Were you coming in here to ask my mom what to wear tonight?"

"No. Maybe."

He smiled. "I think you should wear exactly what you have on and we should go. Right now."

"This?" She laughed, a blush blooming on her cheeks. "I can't."

"Okay." He walked over to her. With barely controlled breathing and eyes locked on hers, he took her armful of clothes, set them down, and pulled the first thing he touched from the pile. "Then wear this."

She was biting her lip. Her eyes flitted to what he held in his hand. "That's a scarf."

He wanted to punch the scarf in the face for not being jeans. He looked at the stack of clothes and grabbed a pair of white shorts and a plaid shirt, placing them in her hands. "Here. Be downstairs in ten." He was still holding her hand, and her smile was getting bigger.

"*Sabrina,* huh?"

"Sorry?"

"The outfit. It's like the one Audrey Hepburn wears when she goes sailing—"

"Fin?"

"Yeah?"

"Zip it."

"Okay. Meet me downstairs in ten."

She squeezed his hand, kissed the side of his face, and ran from the room, leaving him with hope and a lonely cheek.

* * *

~*F*~

Eight and a half minutes later, she flew down the steps, fully dressed. When she reached the bottom floor, Uncle Thomas was walking in circles around the foyer, talking on his phone. Oliver ran in from the kitchen, skidding to a stop right in front of her when he saw his dad. He caught Finley's eye. They grinned at each other.

"Uh-huh. Yes. I'll call you the moment the decision is handed down." He stowed his phone. "That was Juana. The Illinois Supreme Court is reading her decision at ten." He adjusted his cuffs and swiped at imaginary dirt on his sleeves.

"That's less than two minutes from now!" Finley darted into her uncle's office and turned on the wall-mounted TV, flipping it to C-SPAN. A picture of the state supreme court building in Springfield was on the screen, with a journalist explaining details about Juana's case.

Oliver stood next to Finley, so close that their arms were touching. The cells in her arm buzzed where their skin touched. With a minute to spare, Uncle Thomas brought Aunt Mariah into the office, and they all crowded around the television. Thirty seconds to go, and the front door flew open. Nora darted into the house. She spotted everyone in the office and came in, not meeting Finley's eyes.

She'd been avoiding Finley for more than a month now, not talking to her in the halls even when they were otherwise alone. It was a welcome change. Finley didn't know if her aunt or uncle had spoken to Nora or if Harlan's words all those weeks ago had simply left their mark, as Finley suspected they had. Maybe it was both.

Either way, she was grateful.

"You're just in time," Uncle Thomas told her.

A voice came on the TV, and pictures of Juana and her baby covered the image of the state supreme court building. A justice read a bunch of legalese that may as well have been Greek. She and Oliver just looked at each other. Nora and Aunt Mariah clutched hands, and Aunt Mariah put her other arm around Uncle Thomas, who couldn't leave his cuffs alone.

The very room was ripe with anticipation as an image of the Illinois Supreme Court came on the screen and the chief justice began to speak, stating the decision under review. Finley struggled to listen for the pertinent information until Uncle Thomas took in a sharp breath.

The chief justice's words were firm and precise, punctuating the moment. "We hold, based upon the foregoing, that the trial court and appellate court did err, and their judgment has been reversed."

Uncle Thomas shouted for joy! He and Nora both threw their arms up into the air. Uncle Thomas kissed his wife, then pulled out his phone to call Juana. Tears streamed down his face as he told her that the court had found in her favor. The amount she would receive in damages would take care of her and her son for ten lifetimes.

It was beautiful. Finley couldn't have scripted a more perfect scene: tears, hugs, and love, all tenderly delivered. She felt a tug on her shorts and saw Oliver gesturing to the door. She slid her hand into his and they crept out together.

She kept his hand as he opened the door and they walked outside. She felt safe, holding onto him. Strong, too. She wondered if he felt just as safe and strong as she did.

"So what are we going to do?" she asked as they crossed the street.

"Tour of Old Town? We were robbed of our chance this year, if you remember."

"Oh, were we?" she joked. "But at least it turned out well for both of us."

They walked past a newsstand, where Harlan and his new Robo-Lords leading lady, Viola Butler, were on the cover of a magazine, kissing.

He looked at the magazine, then at Finley, clearly wondering if she was being sarcastic. She wondered the same. "Did it?" he asked. "Are we better off because of it?"

She glanced at the magazine, at the tightness in Harlan's eyes, and wondered if it was a marketing ploy or if he had genuine feelings for the girl. He was better than Viola Butler, but it didn't concern Finley anymore. Despite how their relationship had ended, she didn't regret a single moment with Harlan.

It had led her here.

She nodded at Oliver. "I know I am. You?"

He held her gaze with an intensity that told her exactly what he thought. It was everything she could do to keep walking.

Soon, they were walking beneath the wrought iron Old Town gate that marked the beginning of their tour. The first time Oliver had taken her on the tour was her fifteenth birthday. She'd been so quiet and nervous while he'd talked so confidently about the area's German population in the early 1900s, about the hippie movement and recent gentrification. It wasn't until he'd made a terrible theater joke that she'd been able to relax even a little.

When they'd gone for his birthday a few months later, he'd insisted that she give the tour, fumbling and awkward as she was. By her next birthday, they were taking turns. And by his next birthday, they'd conducted an "alternate history" tour, where they'd made up fake historical events, complete with the paranormal and the undead.

This year, neither of them seemed much up to talking. Oliver made a halfhearted attempt to point out the Chicago History Museum, but Finley couldn't peel her eyes from his lips as he spoke. She had no idea when he finished talking. All she could think about was the kissable little freckle on his bottom lip she'd noticed only a few months ago.

She wanted that freckle.

"Fin?" His voice was low and gritty. He cleared it, and with a Herculean effort, she moved her eyes to his. He ran a hand lightly down her arm, and she threatened to dissolve into a puddle. "Should we keep moving?"

She looked around and realized they were in the middle of the sidewalk in front of the museum. People were giving them looks as they sidestepped them. She caught their reflection in the glass between passersby. They looked flushed. Wild.

"Come with me," he said, his voice still gruff.

He pulled her across LaSalle Avenue and up Wells Street, where an art festival had brought out even more people. The crowd meandered lazily. Oliver growled, his body coiled with tension as he tried to weave them through the throngs. It could almost be funny, if she weren't just as eager as he was.

Finally, they reached a stone column that read, "Crilly Court / Private." They ran into the secluded, historic neighborhood of stone row homes and private apartments.

Every part of her was on high alert, specially attuned to him. Halfway down the street, she stopped him with a tug on his arm. They stood under a tree, but if they'd been in the middle of the road, she wouldn't have cared. She couldn't handle waiting for another instant. Her skin was aflame where their hands and arms touched. His gaze sent shivers down her spine.

"Ollie," she whispered, letting go of his hand and putting hers on his face. His skin was smooth over his strong jaw. She put her other hand on the back of his neck, fiddling with his hair. His breath caught. There was so much she wanted to say. So much she needed him to know.

But she wanted to do this first.

She stood on her tiptoes and pulled his face closer. His eyes searched hers until the last possible moment as they breathed one another in. Then he put his arms around her. She closed her eyes and their lips met.

And they were finally kissing. Deliciously, wonderfully kissing. Kissing with a slow, burning heat. But she wasn't being consumed by the fire, she was being forged by it. Refined. She felt stronger than she'd ever felt in her life. Kissing Oliver was like a journey into finding herself. His kisses were nothing like Harlan's. She didn't feel lost or formless or as if she could scatter apart at any second. She had never been more certain of where she was or who she was. She was cemented in place. She was growing roots that would dig so deep she could weather any storm. Yet her body seemed to swell until she was surely touching the sky. They were overtaking the earth and heavens. Filling them.

Oliver's lips demanded nothing. They offered her his spirit, his heart, his love. And she poured the same back into him. Every part of her soul was his for the taking.

When their kisses slowed, she moved her face from his and held him. He lifted her off the ground, kissing her tear-stained cheek. She hadn't even realized she'd been crying.

He put her back down on the ground, and she sniffed while Oliver wiped tears from her face. She looked up at him and saw hers weren't the only wet eyes. They laughed.

"So, um, I guess now is as good a time as any to tell you that I love you," he said.

She laughed again, burying her face in his chest. He held her in a way that told her he wouldn't let go—would never let go—until she wanted. "Yeah. I may have heard you and Emma up on the rooftop."

"What? You did? You've known this whole time?"

"Yup."

"Why didn't you say anything?"

She squeezed him. "I didn't want a shadow between us when I told you I loved you back."

She felt his heartbeat against her cheek, the pulse strong and fast and a little bit nervous, but beating just for her. "So there's no shadow between us anymore?"

She chuckled. "I don't think there's room for anything between us anymore." She felt him laugh. "Because I love you, too. And I don't want you to think that I expect anything in return. I don't want you living at the house when you want to live in dorms. I don't want you changing your major or doing anything you don't want to do. I just want you to take me along for the ride sometimes, okay?"

He kissed her cheek. "I will if you will, President Price."

She ducked her face in his arm, laughing. "Why didn't you ever tell me you liked me?"

"Are you kidding? I was giving you signs, left and right. You brutally rebuffed me."

"What? No."

"Yes! I tried to kiss you the first night we watched the Crawfords rehearse! You were in that scene, and you were so raw and . . . fierce."

She peeked up at him. "Fierce?"

"Fierce. Beautiful. Unstoppable. And I tried to kiss you, even though I felt like I was taking advantage of you. Even though I knew you didn't like me."

"I did like you!"

"No, you didn't."

"I did! I just didn't realize it until that moment."

"*That* moment? That's when you realized you liked me?" he asked. She nodded. "Were you ready?"

"Honestly? I don't know. But I am now."

He put a hand in her hair and kissed her again.

When they broke apart, she laughed. She had to be floating. That was the only explanation for how light, how happy she felt. "You know, I almost asked Uncle Thomas about flying down to Guatemala halfway through your trip when the play was done. But I didn't want to be a distraction—"

"You would have been a huge distraction." He kissed her again. "A tiny." Another kiss. "Enormous." Kiss. "Distraction." And then he didn't say anything for a long time.

A long, long time.

Eventually, they wandered back to the main streets, through the art fair, where they flirted and kissed and pretended to look at the contents of the booths. They ambled through Old Town and over to the L station.

"What are we doing?" Oliver asked, pulling out his pass and scanning it after her. She gestured them toward the platform that would get them to Michigan Avenue.

"I'm taking my boyfriend to the movies. If you still want to, of course."

He grinned. A train pulled into the station, and they got on together. "I want to. What are we going to see?"

They sat down and she promptly nestled under his arm. "That depends. What do you want to see least?" she asked.

"Are we going to make fun of it or something?"

She gave him a wicked look. "Or something."

"I'm good with that," he said, his nose touching hers. "I'm very, very good with that."

They kissed through stop after stop until their destination was announced. Then they walked hand in hand from the platform, through packed streets, and into the theater.

It was the best movie of their lives.

ACKNOWLEDGMENTS

I've read the acknowledgments of virtually every book I've ever picked up, and to write my own now is positively dreamlike. I'm overcome with gratitude for my extraordinary agent Bree Ogden, who took a chance on me and saw so much potential in this book. In my best Simon Pegg voice: Thanks, babe.

Thank you to everyone at North Star Editions, including Megan Naidl, Shelley Jones, and Chris Loke, as well as all those behind the scenes. You are the most dedicated team I could imagine. McKelle George, thank you for falling in love with this book. Kelsy Thompson, thank you for helping me fall more in love with it. With every comment and suggestion, you've made me feel like a better writer until I think I've actually become so.

Huge thanks to the amazing writers who critiqued this book: Gina Denny, Lissa Gilliland, Kaylee Baldwin, Elizabeth Staple, Jennifer Park, and Lisa Davis. Thanks to Danielle Mages Amato for her theater expertise. And squishy, sparkly hugs to my beta readers: my YA soulmate, Amanda Domino, and my soulbestie, Aubrie Baird. To my Midwest peeps for supporting my dream of becoming a writer when I was supposed to be paying attention in meetings, Alt 3 (also, sorry!). Sissy Poos: my heart bursts with love for you. I am who I am because of you.

I grew up in a huge, ridiculously awesome family that is not easily impressed. To the BCL Universe—the center of *my* universe—thanks for being impressed by me. I am eternally grateful for your love and support. Special thanks to Joel Bikman, whose constant encouragement and unfailing belief in me have always made me feel that I can do anything, including writing. To Molly Tagge, for reading every word I've ever written and for helping me bring every character to life: may the Soda Gods grant you an endless, kidney-stone-free supply of delicious Diet Coke. To my in-laws, thank you for putting your lives on hold to support me with every conference and writing retreat. And thank you to my parents for instilling in me a love of reading and for buying my first book all those years ago. I love you.

Most important, thank you to my beautiful, spectacular little family, Jeff, Elsie, and Hugo. There aren't enough words to express my love and gratitude. Jeff, you drop value like the Beastie Boys drop science (or bring value like Public Enemy brings the noise, if you prefer). You are my rock. I couldn't do any of this without you. Elsie and Hugo, you make my world the most joyful, beautiful place imaginable. The three of you are my heart. I love you more than everything.

And last, massive thanks to YOU, dear reader. You friggin' rock.

Kate Watson is a young adult writer, wife, and mother of two, and the tenth of thirteen children. Originally from Canada, she attended college in the States and holds a BA in philosophy. A lover of travel, speaking in accents, and experiencing new cultures, she has also lived in Israel, Brazil, Utah, and the American South and now calls Arizona home.

Seeking Mansfield is her first novel.

QUESTIONS WITH KATE WATSON
How *Mansfield Park* inspired *Seeking Mansfield*

1. Are you a Jane Austen fan? Why did you decide to use Mansfield Park as your inspiration for this book?

I am a huge Jane Austen fan, or a Janeite, as we call ourselves. I first read *Mansfield Park* as a teen, and the plight of Fanny Price resonated with me. I fell in love with her story, and I ached for her situation, and ever since, *Mansfield Park* has held a special place in my heart. At the same time, I recognize that it's generally people's least favorite Austen book, with its antiquated storylines and meek heroine.

A few years ago on a reread of *Mansfield Park*, I was struck with an image of Finley with cigarette burns on her arms. It was too powerful an image to ignore, and I kept wondering how that would fit into a modern retelling. Almost every passage I read inspired some new idea that I jotted down on a notepad. As soon as I finished the reread, I put my notes aside and started outlining Finley's story. I hope it's a worthy update of one of my favorite classic novels.

2. You made some changes to the Fanny character from *Mansfield Park*. Beyond changing the character's name from Fanny to Finley, how did you update the character?

Fanny is a tough character for modern readers to appreciate. Unlike most of Austen's heroines, Fanny isn't witty, lively, or adventurous. But she is observant, principled, and strong in a way none of the other heroines needed to be. While I changed much of Fanny's personality in Finley, I wanted to keep those core characteristics. Finley is a child of abuse, and that has shaped her. She is completely at the mercy of the Bertrams and naturally feels a profound debt to them. She may come off as weak-willed or even as a doormat to readers, but in my eyes, she's doing exactly what she has to in order to survive, and she's doing it with PTSD and a history of trauma. Her strength in the early chapters manifests in her allowing herself to dream. In later chapters, she finds her voice and learns that using it not only doesn't drive the people she loves away, as she feared, but rather, it has allowed her to become closer to everyone she loves. While there are some corollaries with Fanny's situation, I think Finley's motivations are a driving force that Fanny never had.

3. Why did you decide to set the story in Chicago?

I've always loved visiting Chicago. The city is like a steel sculpture—a beautiful mix of grit and culture. Setting *Seeking Mansfield* in such a big, bustling city was a significant departure from *Mansfield Park*. In the original, when the Crawfords come to the country, they bring an urban worldliness, if you will, that the Bertrams and Prices haven't experienced in their rural setting. Yet, I knew I wanted theater to play a large role in the story, and Chicago has an impressive and important theater scene. Having the Crawfords represent Hollywood helped me give them a seductive aura that they otherwise couldn't have had while keeping the story in a city I love.

4. Landing a suitable husband is a huge factor in *Mansfield Park*, how did you update that conflict for *Seeking Mansfield?*

In the Regency era in general, finding a suitable husband was essential to future happiness, and love wasn't considered necessary for that happiness. Jane Austen's heroines had the distinction of marrying for love, but that wasn't the prevailing marriage philosophy in her day. Austen's secondary characters often married for practical reasons; a quest for a good match was a quest for the best status. That quest for status dominates much of Juliette's thinking in *Seeking Mansfield*. I imagine that in her mind she has reached the highest levels of popularity that she could attain on her own, and so she feels that the only way to elevate herself into the highest possible level of high school royalty is to be part of a power couple. Unfortunately, the other half of said power couple is the oafish Raleigh Rushworth. He's not her equal in wit or cunning (although he's a far better person than she is), but his wealth and status more than make up for it. At least until she meets Harlan.

5. You included Oliver's point of view in the story. Why was that important to add?

I've never liked the way that Edmund Bertram tried to control and shape Fanny Price and how she fell for him in spite of it (or because of it, even). In *Seeking Mansfield*, unlike in *Mansfield Park*, Oliver falls for Finley before she falls for him. With Finley's history of abuse, it was important to me that she not be saved by a man, but, rather, that she learn to save herself. Oliver presents an interesting problem on that front, because he views himself as someone who encourages, challenges, and empowers her. At one point in their history, he certainly did all of those things, and his friendship played a key role in her comfort and development when she first moved in with the Bertrams. But by the time *Seeking Mansfield* starts, she has outgrown his "challenging" and "empowering." It isn't until Oliver sees Harlan with Finley that he recognizes his own hypocrisy and realizes that his efforts have an undercurrent of control to them. I needed Oliver to have this epiphany and work to improve before I could allow him and Finley to be a couple, because they could never work together otherwise.

6. What other elements work to give the story a more modern twist?

When I began outlining *Seeking Mansfield*, I had to consciously ignore the source material, because I needed the story to stay true to my characters' arcs above anything else. I also made some changes that mattered to me, like Mr. Bertram advocating for immigrant rights. Including theater was a fun way for me to play with an outdated subplot in the original—a scandalous home play!—and I enjoyed adding allusions to the original without being tied to following the plot.

One of my favorite changes is having Finley and Harlan fall in love, something Jane Austen allowed as a possibility if Henry Crawford could have remained steadfast in pursuing Fanny. Finley's own growth aligned so well with Harlan's (arguably selfish) attempts at self-improvement that it just felt inevitable for them to get together. At the end, when Finley and Oliver are asking if they're better off because of their relationships with the Crawfords, the only possible answer is yes, at least in my mind. First love isn't always forever. Not every breakup is for the worst, even when it hurts. I like that both Finley and Oliver learned so much about themselves by being with someone else before getting together.

7. Which character was your favorite to adapt and write about? Why?

I adored writing Harlan and Emma. I've always had a soft side for Henry Crawford. I prefer unapologetic rakes to bad boys, so it was fun to bring him into modern day (although I think Henry Crawford would have adjusted just fine on his own). I enjoyed the interplay between him and Finley, and I loved their relationship, even with the way it ended.

As much as I love Harlan, though, Emma was probably my favorite character to adapt, simply because she lives in this complex, delightful gray world, rather than the black and white world that Finley sees. While Emma can be a little shallow, she's hilarious, deeply loyal, and fiercely loving. I made her a little more Emma Woodhouse than strictly Mary Crawford, and I have an entire head canon of what happens to her after *Seeking Mansfield*. Her moral compass doesn't always point north, but her friendship with Finley changes both girls, and I imagine that they'll remain friends for a long time.

8. Beyond *Mansfield Park*, where did you find inspiration for this book?

One of my favorite YA novels is *Ella Enchanted* by the brilliant Gail Carson Levine. It was the first YA novel I ever read, and I loved the clever, imaginative adaptation of *Cinderella*. I appreciated how she made the story feel fresh and new, while still honoring the classic fairytale. Beyond that, little touches throughout the book are pulled from things I know. For instance, my husband and I do, in fact, make a game out of watching the worst movies we can find (*Troll 2* is our hands-down favorite). And Finley's habit of wearing Havaianas flip-flops at weather-inappropriate times is a trait she and I share (as is our refusal to wear any other brand of flip-flops).